Maril~~ Todd & Claudia

'A fast-moving mystery with an engaging heroine who could make Madonna blush.' *Coventry Evening Telegraph*

'A thoroughly entertaining mystery. This heroine will run and run.' *Richmond and Twickenham Informer*

Virgin Territory

Marilyn Todd was born in Harrow, Middlesex, but now lives in West Sussex with her husband, one hare-brained dog and two cats.

Virgin Territory is the second in her series of Roman mysteries, following *I, Claudia*. Marilyn's third novel, *Man Eater*, is published in hardback by Macmillan, priced £16.99.

Also by Marilyn Todd in Pan Books

I, Claudia

Marilyn Todd

Virgin Territory

A Roman Mystery

First published 1996 by Macmillan

This edition published 1997 by Pan Books
an imprint of Macmillan Publishers Ltd
25 Eccleston Place, London SW1W 9NF
and Basingstoke

Associated companies throughout the world

ISBN 0 330 34477 3

1 3 5 7 9 8 6 4 2

A CIP catalogue record for this book is available from
the British Library.

Phototypeset by Intype London Ltd
Printed and bound in Great Britain by
Mackays of Chatham PLC, Chatham, Kent

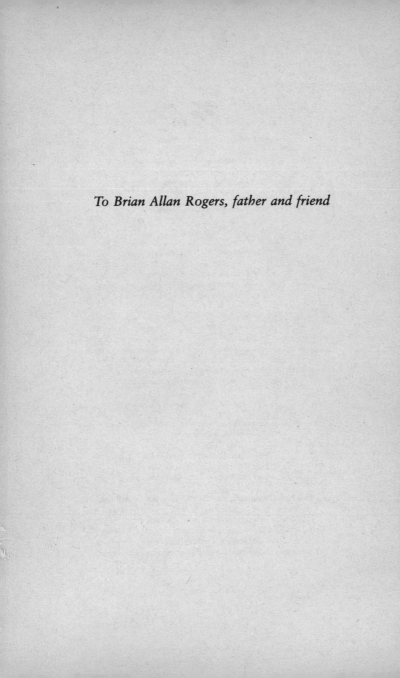

To Brian Allan Rogers, father and friend

I

It wasn't his fault. Captain Herrenius hardly knew her. How could he possibly predict that, despite keening winds and raging seas, no amount of persuasion would winkle this beautiful young creature from her niche in the prow?

'It's for your own safety,' he urged, and the lack of response threw him. He was sure his voice had carried above the clamour of his crew, the crash of the waves. 'You'll be more comfortable in your cabin.'

He couldn't mean that dingy mop-hole where she slept? Bilge rats had better bunks. 'Don't be ridiculous.'

When there were problems to be faced, there was only one way Claudia Seferius tackled them. Head on. Besides, storm or no storm, she had no intention of being bundled out of the way like a redundant artifact.

But her words had been carried into the churning Ionian, and all Herrenius could make out was a quivering mass of dark curls as she drew her cloak even tighter. Scared, was she?

'Don't worry, m'dear, I'll look after you,' he said – only this time he found himself on the receiving end of a glare capable of cracking walnuts at fifty paces. Checking that the water cask was secure, he wondered whether, given time, he would ever understand women.

As the ship rolled to starboard, Claudia's cloak went

skimming down her back to form a black heap on the boards. For one ghastly heart-stopping moment, she could see nothing but the liquid marble of the water, then the ship righted itself. She snatched up her wayward garment. It was made of goat's hair, favoured for its resistance to salt water, and as she shook the dirt off this old work-horse, she had a feeling it was about to be put through its paces. Spume was being whipped up like egg white.

Noting the set of her chin and never one to admit defeat, the *Furrina*'s captain inched closer. Young girl alone on the seas, needed looking after, what? He cleared his throat. Charming filly and no mistake. Needed a man, though. A strong, capable man to help her weather the storm. A man with – what was the word? – experience, that was it.

Inching closer, he caught the heavy scent of her perfume and felt a stirring in his loins as he remembered her at the stern rail yesterday, the breeze ruffling her hair and flattening her tunic against the outline of her body. Fully aroused at the memory of those taut, high breasts, the points of her nipples, the curve of her belly, the sweep of her thighs, Herrenius nevertheless waited until the ship gave another violent lurch before making his move.

'Take your paws off me, you odious little greaseball!'

To his credit, the captain's expression didn't alter as his fingers unlaced themselves from her waist. Stuck-up bitch, he thought, but it was with immense care that his hands remained firmly clasped behind his back as he made his way aft as nonchalantly as he was able.

'Come by the boat!' he snapped, and the bosun looked up sharply. The jolly had been hoisted aboard this half-hour past. But he knew that mood, and to avoid being gouged deep into the woodwork. They stood no chance! They were going to hit it! They were really going to hit it!

Then, with a sudden merciful lurch, Neptune relented and the ship, spinning in the current, missed that rock by the smallest whisker on earth. Claudia didn't hear the cheers. She was too busy promising white bulls. To Jupiter the Storm Maker. To Neptune, lord of the sea. To the Tempestates, whose shrine stood just outside the Capena Gate. Anything they wanted was theirs. She was rich now. She could afford to be generous.

In fact the very first thing she'd determined was that Gaius had left in his moneybox a float of 23 gold pieces, 1 silver denarius, 835 sesterces, 6 asses and 12 quadrans. Hardly a fortune, but ample funds to finance the odd flutter. Her mouth twisted down at the corners. She ought to stop. Hadn't she been taught a lesson once already? Except the old excitement had taken hold, more and more with each wager – which in turn became heavier and heavier, wilder and wilder. The addiction was back. With a vengeance.

'Boredom,' she told herself.

And so rather than face up to the fact that the weight of her inheritance was too great and she simply couldn't cope, Claudia immersed herself in the thrill of the chariot race, the combat of the gladiators. Here it was easy to ignore pressing commercial problems and decisions up at the farm. Here you could escape in-laws clamouring for a decent settlement. With breathtaking alacrity that liquid float turned itself into a paper deficit of over 700 sesterces, the equivalent of a labourer's annual wage. Claudia sighed. It was true, the old saying. The best way to make a small fortune is to start with a large one . . .

Therefore that letter from Sicily, coming out of the blue, had been nothing short of a godsend. One Eugenius Collatinus, an old friend of her husband, sends condolences to the grieving widow and invites her to stay with him and his family for as long as she needs. If, however, she does decide to visit, would she mind chaperoning his granddaughter, Sabina, returning home after thirty years' service as a Vestal Virgin?

He lived just outside Sullium, he said, not far from Agrigentum. Claudia, who barely knew where Sicily was, much less Sullium, rooted out an ageing map etched on ox hide, blew the dust off and unrolled it. Triangular in shape and large enough to be a continent in itself, Sicily was plonked right in the middle of the Mediterranean and it wasn't so much a bridge between warring nations as a breakwater. It was easy, now, to see how the province had become Rome's first conquest. Where are we? Ah yes, there's Agrigentum, on the south coast. So where's, what's it called, Sullium? Claudia's finger trailed along the cracked surface of the hide until she found it. West of Agrigentum. Oh good. Right by the sea.

After that, the hard work had begun in earnest, but a thorough – and she meant thorough – search of Gaius's business papers for transactions involving this Collatinus chappie came up empty-handed. There was nothing in his personal correspondence either.

But she did find something else.

Something very, very important.

Something which put her whole future in jeopardy . . .

Claudia lost no time winging off a reply along the lines of how she desperately needed to get away from Rome. Each street, each sound, each sight reminded her of poor, dear Gaius, taken before his time, she could not bear to stay here any longer.

As to chaperoning Sabina, she'd be delighted – and that, at least, was partly the truth. It was a damned prestigious role, Vesta's priestess. Conspicuous in bridal dress, celibate and serene, these six women took prominent roles in many festivals and, like everyone else, Claudia was aware of the system. Every five years, after a thirty-year stint, the senior Vestal retires and the next oldest steps up to take her place. At the same time, a little novice, a specially invited initiate aged between six and ten, slips in at the bottom and the rota continues. Representing the daughters of an ancient king, they tend the hearth of Rome itself – and legend says should the sacred fire ever go out, the city will be destroyed for ever. Was it surprising they were held in such reverence?

Or, to put it bluntly, Eugenius Collatinus needed considerable clout to have got a granddaughter ordained and Claudia, for one, had no intention of letting a chance like that pass by.

Thus she did everything that was necessary. She'd avoided her in-laws, evaded her debt collectors and commissioned a special cage for Drusilla, and finally the whole kit and caboodle had arrived at Ostia's wharf last Tuesday – by which time Herrenius's ulcer was twitching badly. Another hour and the wind wouldn't have been strong enough, he'd have had to set sail without her. After a smile that did more to neutralize his ulcer than half the limeflower infusions he guzzled down, she was ushered towards Sabina's cabin with the respect and veneration associated everywhere with the Vestals.

'How do you do?' Sabina, smiling coyly, rose to meet

her chaperone as the ship weighed anchor and began to bob gently on the waves.

Claudia stared hard. Tall, willowy and dressed in an elegant dove-grey tunic, the woman was a picture to behold. Her eyes seemed a little distant, as though she was staring *through* Claudia rather than at her, and she was clutching what appeared to be an empty blue flagon to her bosom – but apart from those two anomalies, this was one of the most handsome specimens Claudia had ever seen.

Pity the woman was a total stranger. Because whatever else this creature might have done with her thirty-six years, she hadn't spent the last three decades serving Vesta.

In fact, two weeks hadn't passed since she came face to face with the Holy Sister at the Feast of Jupiter – and unless that girl had taken extensively to drink in the meantime, this was not the same woman.

As the ship cleaved its way through the seething white water, rain bouncing off the heavy goat's-hair cloak, Claudia groaned.

What am I doing here?

In debt. In a storm. With an imposter. In a little wooden bucket. Bound for a place I've never heard of. To stay with someone I don't know. While my whole future hangs in the balance and the crew want to chuck my cat overboard . . .

Hell, on top of that – look, I've broken my bloody nail.

II

Ask yourself this. If you'd just spent the past three days being tossed around boiling seas with salt water chapping your cheeks and bilge water slapping your ankles, would your first thought on stepping ashore be for a fortune teller?

Claudia barged past.

'I see the image of a ram,' a Sicilian voice called after her, 'and arrangements for a wedding.'

Claudia rolled her eyes. Every man, woman and child in Syracuse could see the image of a ram, that was the shape of the *Furrina*'s red, carved sternpost.

'I see a funeral—'

'You'll see your own bloody funeral if you don't get out of my way, now clear off!'

Where was her bodyguard, for gods' sake? Surely Junius had got his sea-legs back by now?

'—and I see love blossoming for you. A tall—'

Don't tell me. A tall, dark, handsome stranger. Claudia pulled up short and heard a satisfying thump as the fortune teller tripped over a rope. What was it about these people, hustling you all the time? Respected astrologers she could understand, theirs was a science, an art – but these frauds? Weddings, funerals, tall, dark, handsome strangers. Originality was hardly her strong point.

To her credit, the fortune teller, with her mass of red hair and generous bosom (neither of which was her own), might have many things to learn, but tenacity wasn't one of them. She'd already picked herself up and was limping up the wharf after her quarry.

'For just two sesterces, I can whisper the name of your future husband in your ear.'

'For just two sesterces, I can have any one of these big, burly porters throw you in the harbour.'

'You wouldn't . . .?'

But the look on Claudia's face told the fortune teller that she just might, and the subsequent arrival of a muscular, Gaulish-looking slave at her elbow tended to confirm the issue. The redhead vanished.

To Claudia's surprise, Sabina had not been at all perturbed by the storm, though neither had she been eager to stretch her legs. She'd wait till the last minute before disembarking, she said. Well, that was her loss, because Syracuse was fun. It was big and bustly, noisy and colourful. Fortune tellers apart, it thrust its wine shops and whores, food stalls and physicians upon you the instant you set foot on solid land and after a long sea voyage, Claudia decided, as she marched back to supervise her luggage, the men would probably need them all. It was merely a question of priorities.

On every step, round every pillar, under every towering statue along the harbourside, clerks and merchants, watermen and wharfies went about their business through the constantly changing tide of humanity, waving, gesticulating, holding up fingers – *five, I said five* – as bales and crates and sacks changed hands to the clank of the tally pieces. Donkeys brayed under the noonday sun, bright pennants and banners flapped in the breeze.

Despite an abundance of temples, theatres and other public buildings to testify that, regardless of two hundred years of Roman occupation, this was still the gem in a once-Greek crown, the city had a curiously cosmopolitan feel, with its assortment of brightly coloured tunics and dark coloured slaves. Great tusks of ivory lay piled on the quay alongside Lebanese cedars and Carthaginian camels honking in protest. A tigress, bound for the arena, snarled inside her cage. A Syrian aristocrat in floppy hat and pantaloons gathered together his brood of little Syrian aristocratlets. Yet for all that, Syracuse had contrived to remain Greek.

Yes, there were togas in evidence, but it seemed the good men of Sicily weren't perhaps so status-conscious as their counterparts in Rome, for here far more of them took advantage of the Greek pallium. It was lighter and smaller and draped in such a way as to leave the right arm and shoulder bare, making it a much more attractive garment for the climate, as well as considerably less restrictive than the conventional toga. However, one man who had not adopted this cool and casual form of dress stood out in the crowd. Not necessarily because of his height, which was above average, or because of his looks, which were compelling rather than handsome, but because at this very moment Claudia was being pointed out to him by one of the men off the ship. His bearing proclaimed a military background, which was confirmed when he marched straight up, stopped abruptly and all but saluted.

'Mistress Seferius, my name is Fabius Collatinus. Follow me, please.' He strode off down the wharf.

So much for the army. It teaches a man how to build roads, bridges, aqueducts and fortresses. It teaches a man how to fight, build siege engines and guard frontiers. It does not, unfortunately, seem to teach a man manners. Claudia resumed supervision of her baggage.

It was a rather less confident Fabius who returned. 'Excuse me, you *are* Claudia Seferius?'

'I am.'

This time she didn't even bother to look up. Amongst legionaries he might be a giant among men; among the Claudias of this world he was a mere babe in arms. She turned to the porters, who appeared to be handling Drusilla's cage with some trepidation.

'That crate's to travel with me.'

'It's my duty to escort you onwards to Sullium. There's a passage booked on board the *Isis*, she sails within the hour.'

'Then she'll have to sail without us.' She turned towards him and smiled prettily. 'I can't leave Syracuse until their eyes open.'

He cocked his head to one side. 'I beg your pardon?'

Claudia indicated the crate at her feet. 'The kittens. I've promised Drusilla we won't embark on the next leg of the journey until their eyes open.'

'Drusilla?'

'My cat,' she explained cheerfully, beckoning over a food-seller and selecting a venison pie. 'Now, Fabius, I don't suppose you know of a decent tavern, do you?'

He shook his head, and it was difficult to tell whether Fabius meant no, he didn't know of a tavern or whether he shook it out of pure bewilderment.

'Where do *you* recommend?' she asked the pie-seller. 'The island here or the mainland?'

For a moment the poor man was speechless. Not once in his life had the nobility canvassed his opinion on any subject under the sun, let alone asked him to recommend accommodation. But he had a shrewd eye for business (how many pie-sellers bothered to meet incoming ships?) and therefore suggested an establishment he knew to be frequented by visiting dignitaries.

'Oh, the island, m'lady. Without a doubt!' The fact that the place belonged to his brother was, he felt, neither here nor there. 'I'll lead the way.'

That was worth three asses, he reckoned. Add on a cut from his brother and with any luck he'd be pissed before twilight. To his dismay, the man in the toga sought directions then dismissed him with the princely sum of two copper quadrans, which just happened to be the price of the pie.

'Which reminds me, Fabius.'

The soldier spun on his heel. 'Yes?'

'Would you be so kind as to arrange a couple of sacrifices for me? Two white bulls – that's one for Neptune, one for Jupiter – and something nice for the Tempestates while you're at it.'

'*White* bulls? They cost a fortune!'

'Then it's as well you're only shelling out for two, isn't it?'

He didn't look particularly happy as he set off down the sidestreet indicated by the vendor.

Munching on her pie and careless of where the gravy dribbled, Claudia gestured over a litter. If that marblehead thought she was accustomed to walking up and down wharfs, he was very much mistaken. Where she came from, ladies travelled in vehicles which reflected their station in life!

Heaving Drusilla and her family into the litter and wiping her greasy hands on a cushion, she began to have serious misgivings about this whole wretched enterprise. What sort of family were the Collatinuses, for heaven's sake, expecting their womenfolk to *walk*? Before instructing the bearers to move on, she prayed to whatever spurious gods they worshipped in this isolated land that it was simply Fabius who was unused to a civilian lifestyle. The last thing she wanted was to be stuck with a family of misers!

'One other thing, Fabius.' She poked her head through the curtains as the litter came alongside.

'Oh?' There was more than a hint of concern in his voice.

'Mmm. The woman at your elbow. That's your sister, Sabina. Since you forgot to ask . . .'

III

Despite the innkeeper having only one eye, Claudia could not really fault the establishment. It was neither verminous nor damp, which was more than you could say for most city taverns, and was far less of a fire hazard than it appeared from the outside.

Within seconds of Claudia returning from dinner, feeling a whole new woman now the incrustations of salt had been scraped away, there was a knock on her door. The wine—

'Hi! Remember me?'

The fuzz of red hair and Sicilian burr were unmistakable. Claudia slammed the door, wondering whether the fortune teller's eager face would pull back before woodwork actually connected with nose, but a hand shot out of the blackness and the door bounced off it. Well, not a hand, really. More a paw. And a damned big one at that.

Claudia's eyes followed it up the arm to the gorilla on the other end. Really, she thought. If she hadn't seen it for herself, she'd never have believed life could be that cruel.

'That's Utti,' the redhead explained. 'He's my brother.'

'How lovely for you.' Claudia found the door wouldn't budge. She pointed to the ham propping it open. 'Would you mind?'

'Huh?'

It speaks, it speaks.

'The door, Utti. Would you please remove your grubby fist.'

'Uh...' It glanced down at the redhead, who was dwarfed by its presence.

'No, wait!' It was more of a plea. 'You're in danger, great danger—'

'So are you. There are four tough guys standing right behind you.'

The redhead smiled cheerfully. 'No problem,' she said. 'Utti's a wrestler.'

Claudia's bodyguard, no slouches themselves, would be no match for a good professional. 'Come to the point,' she snapped.

The girl's face took on a pained expression, about as genuine as her hair and her bosom. 'There's no point to come to. You're in danger, and we're here to help. Oh, I'm Tanaquil, by the way.'

'And I'm very sorry. Now run along, there's a good girl.'

Utti had been forced to remove his hand when he turned to face out the bodyguard, so Claudia smartly shut the door. Almost immediately there was a second knock.

'What?' She flung it open.

A struggle was in progress, in which three men had been pinned to the ground – and Utti wasn't one of them. Tanaquil seemed totally oblivious to the clouds of dust and flying furniture, to the shouts and the grunts and the blood.

'You're going to Sullium, aren't you? Well, I told you

I saw a ram's head. Eugenius Collatinus is in wool, isn't he?'

Is he? Since Sicily was one of the four great granaries of Rome, Claudia had blithely assumed he was in wheat.

'Fabius said so,' Tanaquil continued happily. 'And he also says his grandfather is planning a wedding for Sabina, so you *must* believe me now!'

Claudia wrenched her eyes off Utti, who was kneeling on Junius's stomach and punching one of the Nubians while he kicked at the other. Idly she wondered whether he'd noticed the Cilician, Kleon, clinging to his back.

'Tanaquil,' she said calmly, 'I don't care whether you spend your leisure hours staring into the future or staring into the bottom of an empty wine glass. I neither want nor need the services of a fortune teller.'

The redhead wagged a playful finger. 'That's what you think,' she said, 'but don't worry, you'll hardly know I'm about.'

Claudia winced as Kleon dug his fingers into Utti's eyes, then winced harder as Utti casually shook him off like an old cloak and the boy went bouncing down the staircase.

'Even Utti will be on his best behaviour.'

'He's not behaving very nicely with my bodyguard.'

Tanaquil turned round. 'Oh, is that who they are? Sorry.' She put two fingers in her mouth and whistled. 'Utti, they're friends,' she said. 'Friends. Yes. Put them down.'

The gorilla's mouth formed a wide O and he clambered to his feet, pulling Junius up with one hand and one of the Nubians with the other. The second Nubian was still unconscious. All five were covered with blood.

'Horry.'

Claudia mouthed, 'Cleft palate?'

'Broken nose, but don't worry, he's used to it.'

'Obviously. Well, goodbye, dear. Goodbye, Utti. Pleasure to have met you both.'

The big ugly lump smiled so broadly you could see both his teeth. 'Bye!'

'Not goodbye, silly, good*night!*'

Irrepressible little thing, wasn't she?

Tanaquil leaned towards Claudia. 'He's ever so excited about meeting the family. We've never stayed with posh people before.'

'Then he's in for a big disappointment. I don't want you. I don't need you. You're not coming with me.'

This was not open to discussion. Claudia slammed the door shut and leaned her weight against it until all went quiet on the landing, then she threw herself down on the couch.

Straight away there was a rat-a-tat-tat.

Heaven help us. 'Go away.'

A second, louder rap followed.

'Can't you get it through your thick skull you're not wanted. Now GO AWAY!'

After half an hour she decided she'd waited long enough. 'Landlord, where's the wine I ordered?'

He shrugged. 'I sent it up.'

'Lie to me once again, you thieving vermin, and I'll poke your other eye out.'

He had an odd sense of humour, finding that funny. 'Gods' honour,' he said. 'Dodger took it.'

'I did.' A small, swarthy, bandy-legged Sicilian came

20

stumping up. 'You sent me away,' he said accusingly. 'Twice.'

'Don't try to wriggle out of it!' Claudia fixed him with a scowl. Small wonder they called him Dodger. 'Just fetch the wine.'

Across the room, Drusilla extricated herself from the heaving mass of kittenhood and stretched every joint to its limit before making her way over to Claudia. She'd spent the last leg of the voyage sprawled on her side in a haze of pure bliss as four minuscule bundles of fur sucked and squeaked and snuggled and dozed – but now, like all good mothers, she recognized you could take only so much of a good thing.

'I saved you a lump of boiled calf, poppet.' Claudia broke the cold meat into pieces and fed them to her one at a time. 'Tougher than we're used to, but for a busy tavern it's not too bad.'

When Drusilla had eaten her fill, Claudia began stroking the cat's dark brown, glossy coat. 'You heard the outcome, I suppose?'

'Prrr.'

'Exactly. Talk about lumbered!'

Tanaquil had lost no time in ingratiating herself with Sabina and had now wormed her way into going to Sullium.

'I can't imagine what she hopes to gain from it.'

Fabius wasn't going to part with his brass (just look at the fuss he'd made about reimbursing the landlord for damages!) and Sabina didn't look as though she knew what money was.

'Perhaps that's the idea?'

Squinty eyes closed in pleasure as the rhythmic mass-age smoothed away loose strands of fur.

'Perhaps she's hoping Sabina will cough up without question?'

Enlightenment would come swiftly enough. Vesta's little playmate was so far out of touch, she'd have to seek advice from her brother. All that Claudia could see happening was for Tanaquil to be stranded along the south coast, along with that galloping great oaf Utti.

Her fingers moved up to tickle Drusilla's ears and in response paws began to knead soft dough on Claudia's lap.

'What do you make of Fabius, then?'

My, how he'd squirmed when Claudia introduced him to his long-lost sister! On the run-up to forty and newly released from two decades in the army, he found women every inch as baffling as the civilian life he was thrust back into. His mission had been to escort Claudia Seferius to Sullium and this he had undertaken with organized zeal. No doubt had his orders been to escort Sabina back to Sullium, Claudia would have been equally excluded, but even so—

'Rrrrrr.'

'No, poppet, hardly a touching reunion.'

'Sabina?' he'd said, his jaw dropping. 'Holy Mars, you're nothing like the chubby kid who left home.'

The woman's reply transcended belief. 'I thought you'd be older,' she said.

Give me strength!

Claudia leaned back in her chair and up-ended the jug of wine as Drusilla curled into a ball on her left breast, secure in the support of her mistress's arm. What to make of Sabina, that was the question. Quiet was an understatement. Excruciatingly polite, Sabina rarely spoke unless spoken to, and then it was only to utter spooky statements in that toneless voice of hers. For instance, at their initial introduction, before the *Furrina* had a chance to unfurl her sails, she had said, without preamble and certainly without irony:

'I have seen you many times.'

Oh, really?

But before Claudia could frame the other question hovering on her lips, Sabina continued, 'You are a cat and I know your ways. The chase, the play, the pounce. You see in the dark.'

Terrible thing, nerves. Especially before a long and arduous journey. Sends you reaching for all manner of drugs.

Unfortunately, after a day or two, Claudia began to have a dragging feeling in her stomach and an overriding wish that if only it were that simple! She tried. Honestly, could anyone have tried harder? But trying to converse with Sabina was like drawing teeth: impossible without the right tool; and whatever might be required to open the woman up, Claudia didn't possess it. Instead, Sabina would creep up on her and that strange monotone would swing into action.

'I have witnessed mountains split asunder,' she would say, 'spilling rivers of blood and drowning the land. I have witnessed fingers turn to claws and skin turn to feathers as men and women took the form of vultures and tore each other to pieces.'

That wasn't all. Her favourite theme was invisibility,

how she could make herself disappear at will and no one was any the wiser . . .

Drusilla shifted her position and began to snore softly against her mistress's ear, cheerfully blocking out the neighing and the shouts and the clatter of hooves from the yard outside as a runaway horse was cornered.

'It's difficult to say whether she's mad or not.'

Her movements were careful, yet not too precise; elegant, without appearing rehearsed. At first Claudia blamed the contents of the little blue flagon. Drink or drugs, it had to be the answer. However, when Sabina fell asleep one afternoon she examined it and found it completely empty. Not so much as one tiny droplet inside. No smell, nothing. It was exactly as it appeared to be – an empty blue bottle.

Where did that leave her?

Had Sabina been born insane, she'd have been smothered or put to the sword because, like it or not, this was the norm. Rome needed to breed healthy, strong and perfect citizens or the empire would be weakened, and any disabilities – mental or physical – were eliminated at birth. With someone like Sabina, the signs might not have been so easy to detect, but there was little compunction in snuffing out a sickly life, even at the age of five or six.

What was going on here?

That Claudia was involved in an elaborate hoax was obvious, but who was the perpetrator? Surely not this strange, ethereal creature? Odd by any standards, yet as far as Claudia could determine, Sabina seemed totally without guile and for a woman practically old enough to be her mother, she behaved more like a small child, she thought. Or no. Rather a docile, domesticated pet . . .

Carefully, so as not to disturb Drusilla, Claudia positioned her glass on the floor, but the cat woke on the first movement, instantly alert for the safety of her brood. Satisfied they were still sleeping soundly and could manage a little longer without her, she began to wash, her purring vibrating all the way down Claudia's breastbone.

'What do you think, poppet? Have the holy sisters been secreting the Strange One within their enclave?'

Drusilla's head began to butt Claudia's chin.

'That's what I thought. Since there can only be six at any one time, the Vestals are hardly likely to break their sacred vows, are they? And in any case the woman's perfectly capable of performing basic rites and rituals.'

Point her in the right direction and she'd obey smartly enough. Silently, yes, but instantly.

She certainly had the unlined face of a celibate, and put it down if you like to the vacant eyes, but Sabina could easily pass for five years younger, a boast few Roman matrons could make. If Claudia had as few grey hairs in twelve years' time, she'd count herself very lucky indeed.

'But the most telling thing, Drusilla, is the Vestals lead an indoor life.'

'Mmmmrr.'

'Precisely. Their days are either spent tending the Eternal Flame inside that tiny circular temple, or else they're tucked away in their living quarters next door.'

They appear in public only for certain festivals, so their skins aren't tanned the way Sabina's is, nor are their hands rough from work. Their nails would not be short and dirty, their fingers would be as soft as any noblewoman's.

25

Which raised another question. Where had Sabina been for thirty years?

'Suppose Eugenius is the hoaxer?' she asked a stretching Drusilla, as she turned down the lamp.

The cat jumped soundlessly on to the tiles. 'Mmmr.'

'You're right. Completely out of the question.'

How could he possibly foresee Claudia would only just catch the boat and not denounce the imposter much earlier? Ah, but suppose she isn't Collatinus's real granddaughter? Suppose the retiring senior Vestal was the real Sabina? What had happened to *her*?

Drusilla could be heard finishing off the veal in the darkness, and Claudia cupped her chin in her hands. The warm winds of Africa were redolent with a pungent mix of salt air, spices, wine and meat roasting in the tavern kitchens. The punch line of a joke filtered up above the babble and chatter below, followed by a chorus of such raucous male laughter that the listener was left in little doubt as to the nature of the jest. The atmosphere was heady, intoxicating.

'Broop-broop.'

'Of course I don't miss Rome, why should I?' She punched her fist into her bolster. 'It's not as though there's anyone waiting for us.'

Drusilla arched her back and began to rub round Claudia's ankles.

'All right, there was that investigator chappie. Whatsisname.'

'Mrrap.'

'Maybe I *do* remember his name, so what?' Claudia sniffed loudly as she threw back her bedcovers. She thought she'd built up something of a rapport with that

Orbilio fellow, but she'd neither seen nor heard from him since those grisly murders a few weeks back. 'He can boil his head in porridge for all I care.'

Two sandals ricocheted off the wall to prove the point.

She had jettisoned all ties with the past in order to wangle herself a wealthy, ageing husband and the new Claudia had emerged like a bright and splendid butterfly, every trace of those dark days kicked over so many times the trail was impossible to follow.

Unless, of course, you were a particularly tenacious member of the Security Police.

Her thoughts were interrupted by a knock on the door. 'Madam, it's me. Cypassis.'

What was it with this woodwork that made it so damned attractive to knuckles?

'Well?'

Her big-boned maidservant slipped furtively into the room, carrying the most foul-smelling tallow candle ever to have been moulded. 'It's about—'

'For gods' sake, girl, put that out.' Claudia jumped out of bed, flung open the door and fanned new, if not fresh, air into the room. She lit an oil lamp before asking, 'So?'

The customary dimpled smile had disappeared, and the girl's eyes were as wide as sieves.

'It's Mistress Sabina, madam,' Cypassis said. 'She's disappeared.'

IV

Claudia's eyes narrowed to slits. 'Define *disappeared*.'

They breed them tough in Thessaly, but not tough enough. Cypassis's lower lip trembled when she spoke. 'Just that. One minute she was in her room, the next . . .'

Claudia picked up a large, bronze mirror by its lotus handle and waved it menacingly. 'You've been at it again, haven't you?'

'I—'

'Dammit, girl, we've only been here five minutes.' Lamplight glinted on bronze. 'Whose bed was it?'

The mirror was now so close Cypassis could see her own reflection. She knew better than to try a denial. 'Dodger's,' she said weakly.

What? That bow-legged little runt? Claudia shook her head in despair. This was typical of Cypassis. She was neither a marriage-breaker nor a heart-breaker, she simply left a trail of warm memories and hot mattresses wherever she went. Commendable sentiments, which didn't excuse her behaviour tonight.

'Give me one good reason why I don't turn you into cash this instant.'

Tears welled up in the slave girl's eyes. 'I was only gone a half-hour. She was sleeping when I left, I thought . . .'

Claudia waved her hand in a dismissive gesture. 'Never mind what you thought, have you asked around?'

Cypassis's thick plait bounced as she nodded. 'The tavern, the stable yard, the street – everywhere. No one's seen her.'

Or admits to having seen her. It was that sort of town. Claudia yanked aside the window hangings and peered up and down the street. 'Fabius?'

'He's out visiting army vets, he hasn't come back yet.'

Ah. 'So apart from us, no one knows Sabina is missing, is that right?'

The plait bounced up and down again.

'Quick. Round up Junius and Kleon and the others,' Claudia said. Assuming they can walk.

'I'll make up for this, madam, I promise.'

Claudia slipped out of her shift and kicked it across the room. 'Damn right you will. In the meantime, you make bloody sure the boys are mustered by the back stairs in ten minutes flat.' She plucked the first stola from the top of the box.

'Let me—'

'You've done enough damage. Now hop to it before I change my mind about selling you.'

Frankly she couldn't give a toss what happened to that silly cow Sabina, and the only reason Cypassis was involved was because Fabius hadn't thought to bring female servants for his sister. Honestly, that man! Two decades of army life had developed his muscles to such an extent they completely filled the space in his cranium. Without the constant discipline and routine he'd grown used to, Fabius could no more think for himself than fly backwards.

However, Claudia urgently needed to find Sabina. The whole idea was to travel to Sicily under the Collatinus umbrella – she certainly didn't want her own name bandied about. Word travels fast in the Empire. Especially if you go around losing Vestal Virgins left, right and centre.

The party headed straight for the Temple of Minerva, because if Syracuse was the island's capital, its hub and its nerve centre, then this was the kernel of Syracuse. Minerva, patron of Sicily. Minerva, patron of October. And since yesterday was the first of the month, the sacred Kalends, the temple would have been a magnet for worshippers. It was the obvious place to start – this splendid monument built by the Doric people who once ruled here – but not on account of its gold and marble and ivory. Minerva, like Vesta, was a virgin.

Inside, the group split up with Claudia choosing the gallery. Not that she suspected Sabina to be up here, but the portraits were exquisite. Let the others search the nooks and crannies. She was halfway along when Junius beckoned.

'Look,' he whispered reverentially. In his open palm was a garnet ring. Sabina's sole adornment.

'Where did you find it?' Unlike his, Claudia's voice echoed to the vaulted rafters.

'At the foot of the statue, with the other offerings.'

Claudia's breath came out in a rush. It meant Sabina had simply gone walkabout. No kidnap, nothing sinister.

Just as I'd hoped, she thought. Sabina came to give thanks for safe-conduct . . . which means she won't be far away.

'Cypassis, you go back to the tavern in case she's returned, and Kleon, you go with her.' This was not the time of night for a girl to be wandering alone. 'Oh, and if Fabius gets nosy, say she's taking a late bath or something. You two,' she addressed the Nubians, 'try the Temple of Apollo, and while you're up there, check the bridge to the mainland. See whether the sentry's let her pass, or whether he's noticed anything unusual tonight.'

You could never be too careful. There was a definite smell of fish in the air.

'Junius, follow me.'

The young Gaul brightened visibly as Claudia made her way towards another temple with bronze doors and a richly cladded pediment. No sign.

'She kept telling me she could make herself invisible,' she said irritably. 'I'm beginning to believe her.'

She stopped to ask a whore, fat as a hippo and black as a banker's mood, her tunic flung wide in invitation, but she laughed in their faces.

'I only watch the men, dearie.' She waggled huge breasts at Junius. 'Fancy your luck, laddie?'

Cheeks aflame, he followed Claudia deep into the bustle and banter of what was known, quite rightly, as the best natural harbour in Sicily. A myriad of tiny yellow lights flickered on the ships moored in the bay. The dockside swarmed with humanity from all walks of life and Junius kept close to his mistress. Syracuse might be the island's arsenal and by day her air might reek with the smell of her foundries and ring with the sound of her hammers, but when the sun went down, no matter how hard-working and earnest, men were men the world over.

They were now entering that part of the city where apprentices spent money they didn't earn on women who gave them more than they bargained for, and where pick-purses and cut-throats gorged on drunks and greenhorns.

'There's no way she's down here,' she said, but as they turned to head home, a familiar face stood out in the crowd. Claudia shouldered her way through the drunken throng.

'Sabina!' The face had disappeared. '*Sabina*!'

Jumping up to look over the human sea, she saw Sabina turn left. What the devil . . .? Didn't she know that was the docks? Sharp elbows cleaved a fast path through the crowd. In the narrow street, two wagons rumbled towards each other on a collision course and Claudia dashed between them. Vaguely she was aware that Junius was trapped on the far side, shouting and gesticulating for her to wait. He'd catch up.

'Sabina, what on earth are you doing down here this time of night?'

The fake Vestal Virgin smiled a dazzling smile at Claudia's right ear. 'The sky is a deep, dark treacherous pool,' she said, stroking the little blue flagon. 'It sucks you in and drowns you.'

Oh, well. Long as I know.

'Come on.' She took Sabina's arm and pulled her roughly along the street. Laughter and light spilled on to the cobbles from taverns and food shops, the smell of frying fish and charcoal hung thick in the air.

Damn. Was it left here? Or right? She couldn't remember. Left. Definitely. Suddenly she realized the alley ahead was blocked by four reeling, drunken sailors.

'Need some company, darling?' one of them roared.

'Or d'you need something else?' another said.

'Yeah. Something stronger.'

'Or harder?'

As though these men were of no consequence, Claudia steered her docile charge in the opposite direction. Their footsteps echoed on the cobbles behind her, but the advance was slow and no threat. Why, then, should she be shaking?

'Shit!'

She was in a dead end. And the footsteps and the catcalls came closer and closer. The high sides of the storehouses magnified the sounds.

Claudia looked round, her eyes quickly growing accustomed to the darkness of the alley. She did not feel out of place. She'd spent a large chunk of her childhood in alleys such as this, whenever her drunken mother threw her out. Somewhere in the distance, two tomcats were squaring up.

'The one on the left looks the softest,' she hissed under her breath. He reeled more than the others, could barely keep upright. 'When they come close, hit him with this.'

She held out a piece of broken timber.

Sabina's hand hung limp at her side.

'Take it, dammit!'

The alley was musty, stale. Smoke from a stoke pit drifted over, grey like a sea fret. Grey like a grave.

She could see them clearly. Frames solid from outdoor work. Frames which would not damage easily. Sailors, definitely. Wharfies didn't have these excesses. Wharfies didn't have the rolling gait. Sailors, their first night ashore after how long? Too long. What started off as a game had turned ugly, but they were drunk. And drunk meant slow . . .

Ratface was the leader. She knew the type. 'Waiting for us?' Snigger. 'That's nice, innit, boys?'

The yowl of the tomcats sent a shiver down her spine. 'Go to hell.'

'I likes a bit of red meat.' More sniggers.

'Then eat this!' She bounced a piece of fallen masonry off Ratface's forehead. He reeled, blood streaming down his face to blind him.

Laughing and whooping, the other three tumbled forward. Claudia screamed 'Hit him!' but the silly cow just stood there. She'd dropped the makeshift club and was stroking that bloody blue flagon, even when one of the sailors made a grab at her tunic. Ratface was mopping blood with his kerchief. Funny how the face bleeds so copiously! Claudia swore under her breath. Kicking one assailant's legs from under him, she flung herself at the piece of timber and whacked Sabina's attacker hard on the kneecap. He buckled, screaming. She used the reverse swing to hit the fourth man in the stomach. She was right – he *was* the softest. He was spewing his guts up.

Before she could run, Ratface threw one arm round her waist and his hand clamped over her mouth.

'Want to play dirty, do yer?'

Kicking and fighting and squirming and squealing, she caught Sabina's eye.

Run! Run, you silly bitch, and get help!

Sabina stood stock-still in the middle of the alleyway. Claudia thought she could hear humming.

Shit!

Ratface's companion was back in the fray and together they dragged her face-flat against the warehouse wall. She could feel her stola being pulled up round her waist, felt Ratface's blood dribble down her neck.

'Me first, darlin'.'

His breath smelled of stale wine and bad teeth. The hands pummelling her flesh were calloused and rough. His laugh came from Hades.

The bones in Claudia's legs had turned traitor. All that was left in their place was jelly. Plaster and dust filled her nostrils.

'Hold her, Squint, while I ditch me loin cloth.'

Ratface's hand fell from her mouth and Claudia gulped in the stale night air. Screaming was pointless and Squint's grip was like iron. Across the alley, two men were retching and groaning. Soon they would recover. She prayed Sabina had run for help. Only somehow she doubted it.

Claudia forced herself to go limp. She pretended to whimper and Squint, befuddled by drink, relaxed. She counted. One, two, *three*! Spinning round, she jabbed her fingers in his eyes. He fell into the blackness, roaring like a wounded bull. Ratface, caught half-in and half-out of his loin cloth, seemed undecided. Claudia made up his mind for him and rammed her head straight into his genitals. His breath came out in a long, low moan and he fell to his knees, writhing in agony.

'Quick!'

Grabbing Sabina, she raced down the alley, heading for the first lighted street they came to. Outside a tavern, she paused to pin the woman's torn tunic with her brooch then ran as fast as she could in the direction of civilization. Finally, she fell puffing and panting over a balustrade.

Below lay a bed of wild papyrus, their feathery heads nodding gently in the breeze.

Sabina smiled serenely. 'Isn't it lovely here?'

Claudia looked up sharply. 'Don't you have any conception of the danger we were in?'

'Don't be silly,' she replied. 'I made myself invisible.'

You did not, Claudia wanted to scream. You did not make yourself invisible, you stupid, selfish bitch. You stood there while I saved you from those animals and you'd have watched them rape me, you callous, egotistical cow.

She couldn't trust herself to speak, and when Junius came running up, his face pinched and white and anxious, she had to stop herself from falling on his shoulder.

'What happened?'

'Just boys wanting for free what they can't afford to pay for,' she said flippantly, but he couldn't make out the words because her teeth were chattering.

'I'll summon a litter to take you back,' he said, but Claudia shook her head.

Not yet. She needed to calm down, recover her senses.

Minutes passed. Within the tall stems, a duck honked out two rapid notes then the deep pool fell silent once more. A couple of bats (or were there three?) flitted over the surface of the purple waters. Strange to think that here you are, only twenty paces from where the salt sea laps the rocks and you're dipping your fingers in a spring of fresh water. Claudia splashed her face, washing away the dust and the blood and the memory of Ratface. She lifted her head. It was a fine night. The storm had moved on and was nothing more than a distant memory, as a million and one stars twinkled in the blackness above.

'There's fresh water out there.' Wouldn't you just know Sabina would spoil it?

'It's here.' Claudia pointed with her toe, too tired, too weary to be angry any more. If skies are pools which drown you and rape makes you invisible, why should fresh water in the sea be a surprise? 'Poets say the nymph Arethusa was pursued by a lecherous river god, and it was only when she was turned into a spring herself that she could dive underground and escape him.' She spoke because she needed to get her vocal chords operating normally. 'Pity Artemis didn't turn us into water back in that damned alley, eh?'

She could have saved her breath.

'No, *there*.' Sabina waved a languid arm across the bay. 'That's fresh water. You can drink it, but it turns you white.'

It would be easy, of course, to forget all about Collatinus and the holiday. To leave flaky Sabina with her brother, take the next ship home (poor Junius!) and ... and what? More schedules, more meetings, more talk about vines and vintages and heaven knows what. Not to mention earache from the moneylenders.

Claudia gazed up at the fattening moon, lighting the way for the watermen and showing clear the sacks and barrels stacked along the quayside. With a gentle sucking sound, a trireme shipped its oars and the bark of her bosun's orders carried high over the babble of foreign tongues clamouring to make themselves understood on the wharf.

Easy, but not viable. She needed to travel under the Collatinus party's name for a bit longer, which meant she needed to stay with Sabina for a bit longer.

At least until she'd eliminated the threat which hung over her future. After that, Sabina could go to hell, and good riddance.

It was only much later, in the comparative comfort of her own room, lying wide-eyed on her back counting the stars through the open window, that Claudia wondered whether the night had been quite what it seemed.

The carts blocking the road. The men who, actually, did no harm. And the escape, which – when you took a step back and thought about it – wasn't really that difficult.

V

Marcus Cornelius Orbilio stared up at the self-same stars twinkling high above Rome and decided he was glad to be home. Bloody glad, in fact. He was dog tired, he needed a bath and a shave and he had blisters on his bum, but every ache, every pain, every stiffened muscle was worth it. He called for a bowl of hot water and began to whistle as he threw off his dusty clothes.

He could have taken his time had he wished, travelling in style and comfort instead of sitting astride one cantankerous bag of bones after another, except he chose to hurry.

'You'd best bring me up to date, Tingi.'

That was the thing about having a good steward, one you could truly rely on. He'd separate the important from the dross, the urgent from the trivial, and after several weeks away from home the last thing a man needed was a pile of rubbish to wade through. Tingi, whose face gave the impression he was pining for his Libyan homelands whereas in reality he was like a lamb in clover, read from the list he had prepared while his master splashed water over his face and a slave helped him into fresh clothes.

'Splendid!'

With nothing more pressing than an instruction to report first thing in the morning to Callisunus, his boss and head of the Security Police, on the outcome of the case he'd been investigating in Ostia plus a note to write to his sister, congratulating her on the birth of her second child, Orbilio felt life was rather less of a lemon now he was home.

'I'll have my supper, Tingi, then I'm off for a good, long soak at the baths. That'll stop the old joints creaking.'

'Very good, sir. I've asked the cook to prepare your favourite, the chicken in pepper sauce. It won't be too rich, will it, after your ride?'

'Rich? Never! After the pigswill I've been living on these past weeks, I never want to see plain food again.' Orbilio ran a comb through his tangled mop and winced. 'Take my advice, Tingi, never take a job as an undercover agent.'

The Libyan smiled. 'I think I might have difficulty passing the physical, sir.'

Orbilio laughed aloud at the prospect of this African mingling unobtrusively among the Roman aristocracy . . . Yes, indeed; it was good to be home. It had been a damned nuisance, to say the very least, being posted to Ostia straight after that murder business. Callisunus, as he'd half expected, came away with all the credit for solving it, while he, Orbilio, had been lumbered with finding out who was fiddling a few measly sesterces in taxes. He'd spent six weeks, six rotten, godawful weeks, acting the part of tutor to two rotten, godawful boys before he got to the root of the problem.

There *was* no thieving. Thanks to bureaucratic incompetence, five hundred citizens had been missed off the bloody register.

'And the other matter, Tingi? That er, rather delicate issue I left with you?' The smell of the chicken began to gnaw at his stomach. He hadn't realized he was so hungry. Damn those wretched nags!

'Ah!'

He didn't like the way his manservant said that. Come to think of it, he didn't much care for the expression on the fellow's face, either. A whole host of wild scenarios rushed into his mind. He'd been gone only a few weeks and . . . she'd married someone else, that was it. Would he be old and in the grip of terminal halitosis like her last husband, or would she have opted for a younger, more athletic model? How young? He was only twenty-four himself, the same age as she was. No, no, it was too soon, she couldn't be married. Sick, then! That was it, she was ill. Nothing too serious or Tingi's tone would have given the game away, so what was it? Pleurisy? Pneumonia? Jaundice? All three? He couldn't stand the suspense.

'Ah *what*, Tingi?'

The Libyan, noting the slave had pretty well finished adjusting his master's clothing, dismissed him with a nod of the head. Orbilio was not reassured by the gesture.

'She has left the country, sir.'

'She's *what*? Did you say, left the country?' Orbilio rubbed his forehead. 'Where's she gone?'

'Sicily.'

Orbilio puffed out his cheeks and stared up at the ceiling. This was just his luck. Callisunus had made bloody sure he was out of the way (and fast!) after those murders, there was no time to call on her, and he hadn't been able to word a letter correctly. Say too much and it's open to ridicule. Say too little and you're misunderstood.

Empty stomach or not, he poured himself a large glass of wine and waited until he felt it warm him inside before pressing for details. And then he wished he hadn't waited, because there were no details.

'How do you mean, no one's letting on?'

Tingi spread his hands. 'Not to me, any rate. I tried bribing that Macedonian steward of hers, but he threw me out on my ear.'

Not strictly true. He got two of his burlier servants to do the job for him.

'Shit.' You could hear the resignation in Orbilio's voice in the next street. 'Help me on with my toga, would you.'

It might be late, but dammit, he had to know where she was. Every night he was tortured by the memory of Claudia Seferius, her thick hair escaping from its moorings, the sun bouncing back blazing tints of gold and copper and bronze. Every night he dreamed he was running his hands through those luscious locks, watching the curls tumble over her shoulders, down, down, down to cover her breasts. And what breasts! He had seen them once, firm and arrogant, a sight never to be forgotten. He longed to kiss her, hold her in his arms, feel his manhood against her. Inside her. Love or lust he wasn't certain, but he'd give either a go tomorrow, given half a chance.

'Stay with you through thick and thin, Orbilio? Till you're thick round the middle and thin on top, you mean. No fear!'

Those words had never actually been spoken, but it was only a question of time, he felt. Unless he could win her over – and he was unlikely to do that while she was swanning around Sicily!

The smell of chicken in pepper sauce tormented him

as he passed through the atrium, clutching nothing more interesting than a poppyseed loaf to chew on the way. Who was she with, he wondered, elbowing his way through the throng of late night revellers. What made her take off for Sicily, of all places? He prayed to Venus it wasn't with a man – the mere thought brought a sharp pain to his gut. As if to drive salt into a wound, he practically collided with a young couple, panting and intertwined, against a street corner. The sight of the boy, one hand on the girl's buttocks, the other fondling her exposed and naked breast, stirred his loins. How long since he'd taken a woman himself? He'd been tempted in Ostia, but always at the back of his mind was a picture of one woman whose beauty made others wilt in comparison. The flounce in her walk, the toss of her head – who could come close to matching her? Orbilio felt his desire rising as the boy tugged at the girl's tunic to expose her soft white parted thighs and he forced himself to walk on. The sages had it wrong, he thought. It was *abstinence* which made the heart grow fonder.

The admittance of wheeled traffic into the city from sunset onwards meant he had to avoid the main thoroughfares in order to make any kind of progress, but the sidestreets presented hazards of their own. Once, as he passed the tenements, he only just managed to dodge a torrent of filth which came flying through an upstairs window and in the Forum, at the foot of the steps to Venus's temple, an ugly brawl was in progress and Orbilio counted himself lucky not to be sucked into it. Almost everywhere beggars huddled in doorways, waiting for daybreak when they would clamour for position at the city gates, with their fake sores and sham bandages, to cry for alms.

It was late when he arrived at those all-too-familiar double doors, rapping so hard, tiny slivers of cedarwood lodged in his knuckles.

'Fetch Leonides!'

He pushed his way past the porter who, knowing authority when he saw it, obeyed instantly.

The beanpole of a Macedonian appeared almost by magic, still hastily belting his tunic. When he recognized the officer responsible for investigating that series of gruesome murders six weeks ago, the colour drained from his face.

'Master Orbilio! Has something happened?'

'I was rather hoping you'd tell me. Mistress Seferius has gone to Sicily, I understand.'

'She's escorting the retiring Vestal Virgin home, yes.'

As the steward filled in the details concerning Sabina, Orbilio began to feel foolish. Here he was, dragging Leonides out of bed in the middle of the night, simply because he'd overreacted. He suddenly felt very conscious of his beard growth, of the smell of horse which still clung to him. Come on, Marcus, she's a woman who drives a man to overreact, he thought, in an attempt to justify his actions, but found the explanation wanting in every department. He scratched irritably at his stubble.

Inexplicably he found himself asking, 'Whereabouts in Sicily?' and wasn't entirely surprised to hear the steward reply that he was very sorry, he wasn't privy to the address. It was that sort of a day. When lemons piled up by the bucketload.

Orbilio was on the point of saying, 'No matter,' when

he remembered something. Part of Tingi's report. Croesus, what was it? At the time, when every bone in his body was still jarring from the ride and his eyes had joggled up and down so often he still couldn't focus, his brain discarded everything that wasn't a priority.

He tapped his finger against his lips in the age-old gesture of recollection, his mind racing over the list his manservant had called out to him and, click! He remembered. *The recent retirement ceremony of the senior Vestal.* As a member of the Security Police, the Vestal Virgins came under his jurisdiction, he was briefed on their movements as a matter of course.

' . . . after which,' Tingi had read, 'Fulvia Papinianus returns to her family in Graviscae, where marriage to Senator Lucius Livius Cocidius will take place.'

Fulvia Papinianus. He remembered her now. Came from a good patrician family, had tight round cheeks and one of the most winsome smiles this side of the Alps. The last time he saw her was the day he left for Ostia. It was up on the Capitol, he had just made a sacrifice to Jupiter, she was leading her little troupe of sisters and a po-faced priest up the steps of the Temple of Plenty.

Fulvia Papinianus. Not Sabina Collatinus. And Graviscae was north of Rome, on the coast.

Orbilio looked round the house. *Her* house. Burning braziers lit the walls, the friezes and frescoes dancing to life under the flickering flames. He was by no means surprised Claudia had gone off without doing her homework properly. An impressive network of spies kept him abreast of her gambling activities, which might explain her desire to let Rome cool down somewhat before tackling her mounting debts. And Orbilio's own experiences

45

told him how prone she was to jumping in feet first without thought of testing the waters beforehand.

'Leonides, my friend,' he said slowly, crooking his finger to beckon the steward across. 'I think you and I ought to have a little chat.'

There could be a whole host of reasons why a wealthy young widow might be lured away to distant Sicily, but at the moment Orbilio could think of only one.

One which put the life of Claudia Seferius in considerable danger.

VI

Perched on the bluff, high above the bay, Claudia conceded this had to be one of the loveliest views she had ever seen. To her left, Pharos Point stretched out to sea, crowned by the stubby lighthouse from which it took its name. On the far side of the headland, where the terrain changed dramatically to dry scrub and sparse vegetation, lay the shacks and shanties that comprised the poor and insignificant fishing village of Fintium where she'd landed, demonstrating clearly how the island's geography contributed to its fluctuating fortunes.

Now when was it she'd put ashore? So much travel, so much change of scenery, it was confusing. She totted it up on her fingers. Today is Monday, which makes it, let me see, the ninth day of October. That's right, because we arrived in Syracuse last Monday, which was the second, had that run-in down by the docks, sailed on Tuesday and put ashore in shabby Fintium three days ago, on Friday.

Had nothing gone according to plan on this trip? Claudia gazed at the tableau laid out in front of her.

The tightly packed pines below, into which the blue flash of a jay disappeared.

The sweep of white sand, deserted as always, which

would take every bit of an hour to cover, headland to headland, on foot.

The flat white rock a half-mile westwards upon which Eugenius Collatinus had chosen to site his villa.

Further on, where the outcrop dropped away and therefore out of sight, ran the river from which, at exorbitant cost, Eugenius had his water pumped up.

Behind her, barren hills rose almost vertical except for a plateau to the west. A mile north the grey, hilltop town of Sullium nestled between two peaks.

Claudia let her eyes rest on the gentle bob of the African Sea.

In Rome, travellers talked of how you could see the very walls of Carthage from here. The product of a nimble memory, of course, but to a certain extent that could be forgiven and Claudia had a feeling her own recollections might follow the same route themselves. Africa might not actually be visible, but it was not so very far across these sparkling waters and much of this island's produce – the wine and the olives – ended up in Carthaginian stomachs now that the wars were forgotten. (At least until next time.)

Thanks to an offshore breeze, the heat of the afternoon sun was much mitigated. High in the sky a buzzard mewed and a yellowbird butterfly set a fluttering course for Tunis. Such beauty, she thought. Such tranquillity. Such cleanliness.

So much, it's positively unwholesome!

Where's the graffiti you see at home? She didn't know, until she saw it painted on the wall outside the caulker's, that that stuck-up senator, Longinius, was a bigamist.

And who'd have guessed Vindex the mule doctor was a eunuch?

The hurly-burly of Rome came flooding back, its streets thronging day and night and with entertainment on practically every corner. After just two weeks, Claudia was pining for the gruff shouts of the wagon drivers, the shrill laughs of the whores, the squabbling of the lawyers. It was decidedly odd, not being on guard against a poke in the eye from a porter's pole, not coughing from the dust of the stonemasons' mallets, not sidestepping a sudden swish of dirty water down the gutters. All this scenery – good life in Illyria, she exclaimed to herself, it just wasn't natural.

But what was natural around here? Not the Collatinuses, that was for sure. Barking mad, the lot of them. In fact, the only one who wasn't barking was Cerberus, their soppy, sloppy guard dog, and even Claudia, who knew precious little about canine behaviour, could have told Fabius that a kick in the ribs wasn't the answer.

Nor was theirs a high-spirited madness – good heavens, if only! They were simply unpleasant. There was no other word for it.

Claudia had long forgiven Sabina for her part (or, rather, lack of) in that dockside fiasco last Monday. It was not, she supposed, Sabina's fault she had a cog missing – but her mother ... Holy Mars, Matidia was enough to make a physician break his seal of secrecy! If that woman possessed any brain cells whatsoever, they had to be evenly distributed round her body. Squashed together and concentrated between her ears they might at least have served a useful purpose, but instead Matidia's thoughts were as sparse and as colourless as her hair, which she hid beneath a succession of elaborate – if perfectly hideous – wigs.

Funnily enough, this very airy-fairyness was the strongest evidence yet to corroborate Sabina's claim to Collatinus blood, although even her mother didn't connect the chubby child who left home with the willowy creature who came back.

'I thought your eyes were grey, darling,' Matidia said mournfully on greeting her long-lost daughter and Claudia's ears had pricked up.

Aha! Was the imposter about to be denounced at last?

'Or do I mean blue?'

No wonder her husband, Aulus, dissolved his frustrations in the wine goblet. Since his own father, Eugenius, was something of a tyrant, running both business and household with an iron fist in spite of an accident which left him bedridden, Aulus, at the age of fifty-eight, could perhaps have been forgiven the odd indulgence – had he been less of a bigot and a bully, and uncommonly proud of both qualities. His patronizing air bounced right off Claudia, but probably went a long way towards explaining why the good folk of Sullium rarely accepted his social invitations and dished them out even less.

Of course, in Aulus's case, Claudia thought cheerfully, it was easy to look down one's nose at people. When you've got a hooter that long, what other option is there?

Aulus had sired two other children – sons, both as tall and gaunt as their parents. Portius, a mere eighteen with kohl-rimmed eyes and bejewelled fingers, was probably a mistake in his conception and everything had gone downhill since. He was, Matidia enthused, a genius, a prodigy. He had had the Call, she said. He worshipped his Muse with unstinting devotion, she said. Why, you could catch Portius night and day kneeling to Euterpe, she said, laying offerings at her feet and listening to the notes of her flute that gave him the rhythm to his poetry, notes which we mortals were denied unless we, too, had had the Call. She said.

Then there was Linus. What could you say about Linus? Thirty-one, with his high forehead and receding, gingerish hair, he looked at you the way most people look at cowpats stuck on the sole of their sandals. In true Collatinus tradition he had taken himself a tall, bony wife with a short neck and stooped shoulders and there were, no doubt, many ways of describing Corinna. Mousy, bland and nondescript dashed to the fore. Unfortunately, there were precious few ways of remembering her. She came, and then she went. Finish. No conversation, no animation, no impact.

A far cry from their offspring, four ghastly, unruly brats. Well, let's be charitable and say three, because Vilbia was still toddling. Just give her time.

Add to that a wide range of secretaries, scribes, servants, tutors and slaves. Mix well. Stir in an extra helping of jealousy, vanity, squabbling, back-biting and miserliness, top with a tartar – and a visitor quickly begins to get the picture.

There's Dexippus, Claudia reflected, Eugenius's secretary, with his thick lips and strange, brooding stare. There was Piso the tutor, bald on top apart from a little tuft of wispy dark hair right at the front, with a penchant for the cane. And there was Senbi, their hard-boiled household steward, who, along with his son, Antefa, kept the slaves in line and whose word was law, whose justice was rough.

The guest bedrooms, being at the front of the house and thus well distanced from those of the family which flanked the garden, gave Claudia some degree of protection, but was it enough? Would Rome be far enough from this bunch of callous, self-absorbed individuals?

'And to think I was in a hurry to get away from Syracuse.' Claudia addressed her remark to a pair of swallows describing frantic parabolas overhead.

'Tsee!' Selfish creatures. Totally disinterested in other people's problems. 'Tsee!' They swooped and soared and flew on.

Tuesday, the morning after the alleyway incident, Claudia made the rounds to see who might be sailing west and secured eight passages on the *Pomona*, a merchant galley prepared to drop them off at Fintium. With Syracuse bursting at the seams with army veterans, Fabius had been as happy as a pig in a ditch and she'd had to prize him away in the end.

'I thought you wanted to mark time,' he'd said petulantly, trying to fathom out why his belongings were sitting in a heap at the bottom of a gangplank.

'What on earth for?' The mast was being stepped, it wasn't long now.

'Why didn't you wait for their eyes to open?'

Another good sign, the oarsmen were boarding.

'Fabius, they're animals. One doesn't "mark time" for animals. Do have a care!' A stream of indignant feathers flew from the bars in the crate his toe had stubbed. 'Those are our chickens.'

What *have* I let myself in for? she wondered. Dammit,

they didn't even feed you on these poky little coastal tubs, you had to provide for yourself!

Fabius nursed his injured toe. 'Yesterday you said . . .'

Claudia moved to let a stevedore past, his back bowed with the crate on his shoulder. 'Yesterday I wasn't expecting to be raped behind the storehouses,' she snapped.

'You did say only eight places?' His eyes rested on the red fireball and her pet gorilla haring down the wharf towards them, their progress impeded only slightly by the burden of bedding and provisions. 'What about Tanaquil?'

Claudia stepped daintily into the bow and shrugged, her face a picture of innocence as she asked, was it her fault the *Pomona* was full?

With Sabina having difficulty negotiating the rail, she offered to hold the blue flagon, but the make-believe Vestal declined with her usual infuriating politeness.

'A talisman, is it? Your good-luck charm?'

Distracted momentarily, with one foot on the deckboards and the other on the gangplank, Sabina produced one of her rare frowns. 'Claudia, dear,' she said in the sort of tone you'd use to a backward child, 'I keep my *soul* in it.'

Such was the impact of the statement that Claudia nearly missed the interchange on the quayside. Fabius, clearly untrustworthy, was in the middle of having a quiet word with the captain, man to man, or in this case coin to coin. Within seconds, Sabina's new-found friend and her big, ugly brother were hopping merrily aboard. Which, of course, they would, seeing as how the ship was only half-full. Claudia heard teeth gnashing as the oars began to lap, and wasn't surprised to find they were hers.

Now, across the Sicilian countryside, yellow and parched from the summer heat, Claudia was watching Collatinus's workforce making their weary way to the outhouses for their evening meal. She leaned down and pulled on her own sandals. Why did *nothing* go according to plan?

Contrary to what she told Fabius, her real reason for leaving Syracuse quickly was business in Agrigentum, and once they'd cleared harbour it was her turn to have a quiet word with the captain. It was at this point she discovered Gaius's old ox-hide map was less than accurate. Agrigentum, the captain said apologetically, was not on the coast. He could drop her off at the nearby port of Empedocles? Instant calculations decided there might be mileage to be made from Eugenius Collatinus and so as the merchantman struggled against the prevailing headwind, Claudia squinted into the distance, barely able to make out Agrigentum's honey-coloured walls perched high on the hill.

Damn!

The coaster, manned by oars and therefore less impeded by westerlies than ships relying solely on sail, took barely three days to reach Fintium. More, and Claudia might well have been tempted to jump overboard, what with Tanaquil's incessant chatter and Utti's cauliflower ears all over the place. The only consolation was that Sabina stayed below in her quarters and Fabius was quite spectacularly seasick.

But the upshot was that, after a full twelve days at sea, Claudia did not have the inclination to make the lumpy, bumpy half-day wagon ride back to Agrigentum. Early days, she thought. No hurry. She stood up and straightened a ring on her finger. Tomorrow, she'd see what Sullium had to offer. Because something had to be happening in this tedious little backwater.

Hadn't it?

It was the painted eye which first caught his own. The carved and painted eye which adorned the prow and kept watch for evil spirits. Seemingly alone, it bobbed quietly and unblinkingly on the bright blue swell, gazing up at the cottonball clouds. Then gradually more and more shattered planks hove into sight, and finally Marcus Cornelius Orbilio lent his strong arm to hauling up the bodies. Unlike the eye, these floated face downwards, staring at the sponges and the seaweed, their fingers and arms and necks and ears glistening with jewels which they had hastily crammed on to ensure that whoever found them would have the wherewithal to give them a good funeral.

Two of the men had killed themselves, rather than face death by drowning. They recovered nine bodies in total. And that was just on the first day of his voyage.

Everyone knew about the storm in the Ionian, three tortuous days of it, though the helmsman assured him she'd blown herself out.

He was right, and the knowledge did not make Orbilio feel better.

Faster than a racing chariot, the trireme, sleek and light, cleaved a lovely line through the water. It had set out at first light the morning after he had called at Claudia's house, but by then, as he learned from her Macedonian steward, Claudia had already been gone a week. Except...

The flautist, piping time for the oarsmen, changed his

key, indicating that they would shortly be putting in to harbour. This would be what, Orbilio's seventh night with the navy? He'd really hoped to catch up by now. Unfortunately, as much as the warship made brilliant speed on the water, two hundred men do need to eat and sleep and for that, they put ashore. Swings and roundabouts, he thought. Swings and roundabouts.

Claudia, too, would be held up. Assuming she was safe (praise Jupiter she was, he had no way of knowing), the storm would have added two days to her voyage. Also, he knew the *Furrina* was bound only for Syracuse. Changing ships would add a further day – and suppose she went sightseeing? Or took the overland route?

Gulls wheeled and shrieked as the boat shipped oars. Anchors were heaved over the side. Tired oarsmen, their stiffened, corded muscles glistening with sweat, checked the money in their purses. They were responsible for their own rations, and would have to purchase them ashore.

Orbilio watched the dark waters claim the last segment of the sun. The waning moon was already high. Tomorrow would be the tenth day of October. He might, if the gods were with him, arrive in Fintium before her.

He hoped he was not too late.

VII

Claudia tapped her foot impatiently outside the mercer's shop. Dear Diana, how much longer would that tiresome woman be in there? They were only cushions, for gods' sake! However, Matidia was having unconscionable difficulty. Should one go for all red or should one opt for several different colours? The problem was, once one entered the realms of variety, other decisions were then thrust upon one, such as should one choose blue with green stripes, purple with a red border or gold and green, and really, ought one to co-ordinate the stripes so they ran either all vertically or all horizontally? What did Claudia think?

What Claudia thought was that if Matidia hadn't made up her mind after half an hour, the chances were she wouldn't do it at all, and she was trying to find a way to phrase it politely when Matidia added:

'It's so important one achieves the right effect for dear Eugenius, he has taken so much trouble over his new banqueting hall.' She lowered her voice to an outraged whisper. 'He actually had the temerity to suggest that Actë person should choose the cushions, you know. Can you imagine it? A *slave*?'

Having seen the animated Actë, more companion than nurse to the old man and with more taste in her big toe than the rest of the family put together, Claudia *could* imagine it.

Matidia turned to the mercer. 'Talk me through these cushions again.'

Overhead, a middle-aged matron began shaking a blanket from her balcony and Claudia moved away to dodge the dust and find a place to take the weight off her feet. Not that there was much choice in this town. Talk about small! She began to pace the pavement like a caged leopard. Juno be praised, at least she didn't have potty Sabina to contend with, because Tanaquil seemed to have stepped in and taken the heat off Claudia. You'd have thought that, once reunited with her family, some vestige of the old relationship might have surfaced, wouldn't you? Not necessarily between her and the younger boys, who wouldn't have known her, but what about her mother or Old Beaky or the old man? Instead, they skirted each other like wary jackals . . . which mightn't be altogether surprising should it transpire Sabina wasn't related after all.

What, though, could be her motive as an imposter?

Peering round the street corner and observing a trough, Claudia perched herself on the edge and dabbled her fingers in the water.

She looked neither like nor unlike the family, in so far as she was tall and slim, but then any self-respecting charlatan would be sure to possess such characteristics to stand any chance of succeeding. Succeeding at what, though? And who was behind this charade?

Certainly Sabina had learned her lines well and found no trouble in convincing the family she'd spent thirty years in celibate service. Why should they doubt her?

When Claudia tried to trip her up by inviting her to tell a few amusing anecdotes, she merely smiled her sad, vacant smile and reminded her she was sworn to holy secrecy. The only thing she could say was that it took ten years to learn the rituals, ten to practise and ten to teach.

Which she obviously wouldn't have said had she known it was an old joke among atheists in Rome.

A yellow dog with one raggy ear wandered up to the trough where Claudia was sitting, sniffed all four corners carefully then leaned in and began to lap.

One thing: Tanaquil was spot on about marriage and Sabina was, with great ceremony (by Collatinus standards!), introduced to her prospective husband on Sunday, just two days after her arrival. Gavius Labienus was a respectable, wealthy, widowed oil merchant from Agrigentum, so was that it? Nothing more complicated than a step up the social ladder? The answer was quick in its coming.

'He has violated me,' that grey monotone announced to the startled assembly.

The bridegroom's jowls flapped in denial, but Sabina pressed on.

'Do not doubt my word. I turned myself into a stag, but he turned into a wolf to devour me. I dived into the sea and became a fish, but he followed in the form of a seal to gobble me up.' She began to stroke her little blue flagon. 'Finally I turned into air and became invisible.'

The silence was prolonged – it was difficult to recall exactly how it was broken. Labienus, poor sod, had been shocked to his core at the prospect of being palmed off with a lunatic, Vestal Virgin or no, and even the old man was rendered speechless.

The yellow dog scratched at its good ear with a back paw and chased a flea or two before trotting off to investigate a fishhead in the gutter.

Now there was a wily old cove.

Claudia could not actually recall her husband mentioning Eugenius (which wasn't to say he hadn't done so, since she'd rarely listened to Gaius unless his words happened to impinge on her own activities). However, from receipt of his letter to arrival at the Villa Collatinus, she felt she'd built a good mental image of Eugenius – an image shattered the instant she met him.

Yes, he was old. Old and thin (indeed who in the household, apart from Fabius, wasn't verging on the emaciated?), but wiry rather than weak. Yes, you could see the blue veins stand out on his hands, hands which if you held the light behind them might well show you their bones if you asked nicely, but any concession to age ended there.

'Well?' Black eyes had glittered like obsidian glass.

No greetings, no words of introduction, no platitudes for the grieving widow. There was nothing bland about Eugenius Collatinus.

Claudia had responded in kind, silently scrutinizing walls which were crammed floor to ceiling with life-size figures jostling for shoulder space. Tempted to grin, she forced herself not to, well aware that wasn't the reaction he either wanted or expected. Hers was not the blushing maidenly gasp followed by downcast and averted eyes. Hers was the shrewd eye of the former courtesan who had seen, if not performed, every act on this jam-packed, pornographic frieze. The only difference was in the men. Instead of portraying muscular heroes, these were a ragged collection of hunchbacks and dwarves, lepers and cripples, their ugly faces further distorted by leers. Or maybe contorted by virtue of their gigantic and presumably excruciatingly painful erections.

'Well?' The voice was as sharp as the eyes. 'What do you think?'

Part of a hand, she thought it might be a knuckle, followed the rounded contour of her bottom. Claudia swatted it away.

'What I think,' she said slowly, 'is that Sullium frieze painters are braggarts and liars with a very inflated opinion of themselves.'

The old man chuckled. 'Every other woman who's seen this room has been shocked into silence.'

They were interrupted by the arrival of his thick-lipped secretary, Dexippus, with several letters under his arm, followed by Actë, carrying a steaming bowl of something which resembled cabbage water and smelled worse. Claudia quickly excused herself, but the ice had been broken and she felt an affinity with Eugenius which had not been possible with the rest of the bums and stiffs in his family.

The sun had moved round, throwing the water trough into shade. As Claudia shook the folds in her tunic and adjusted her stola, her attention was caught by a young woman darting furtively along the colonnade across the street. Her hair was dark and wild, her cheeks flushed as she flitted from pillar to pillar in short rapid steps. One-two-three, stop. One-two-three, stop. Not surprising, Claudia thought. The family's barking, why not the locals. And this *was* a local woman, you could tell by her costume, torn and disarrayed as it was. As Claudia headed back towards the mercer's, the woman rushed over to her.

'Have you got kids?'

Claudia rolled her eyes to heaven and moved on, but the woman followed.

'I've got to know!'

Although her eyes were glistening feverishly, underneath there seemed a genuine concern, so much so that for a fleeting moment Claudia thought about mentioning her own fictional brood, invented to hook Gaius. But since they were also fictionally dead, there was no point.

'No.' She brushed the woman's hand off her arm.

The woman darted in front of her, blocking her way outside the harness maker's, and one breast fell out of her torn tunic, staring at Claudia like a malevolent eye.

'You've got to keep a close watch on 'em. My little girl was stole away, no kid's safe.'

Claudia felt a rush of sympathy for the pathetic creature, obviously mad with grief at the death of her child, and pressed two brass sesterces into her hand. To her amazement the woman, poor as she was, refused them.

'You think she's dead, don't you, I can see it in yer eyes.'

'Um—'

'She's not dead. Not my little Kyana. *He* stole her.' She jerked her head to a point over Claudia's left shoulder and against her will yet mesmerized by the woman's desperation, Claudia turned. Harnesses jangled from their hooks, the smell of leather was overpowering. Her gaze turned upwards. A hand's span away, under the eaves of the shop, the most enormous black spider sat in the middle of its web.

'Euch!' Claudia recoiled in horror. She'd seen mice smaller.

'That's right, you be afraid of spiders. He was collecting 'em when he stole my little Kyana.' Her face took on a wistful appearance and tears welled in her eyes. 'You've got to watch 'em so carefully.'

Leaving the local woman sobbing on her knees in the gutter, the sesterces lying forgotten beside her, Claudia turned the corner just as Matidia was emerging, empty-handed, from the mercer's.

'I do hope that awful Hecamede hasn't been bothering you, dear, she's quite deranged you know.'

Claudia bit back the retort about black kettles and pots as Matidia elaborated.

'Went that way after her daughter disappeared.'

'Disappeared? She didn't die, then?'

'Kyana? Oh no. Well, that's to say her body's never been discovered, but the child was five and you know what they're like at that age, forever getting into mischief.'

Somehow Claudia could not imagine Sabina, for instance, getting into mischief, but bit that back as well, concluding that today she had set something of a record for holding her tongue. It didn't come easy. Probably because it was such a teensy-weensy thing, you didn't notice it had run away until it was too late.

'The worst part is,' Matidia was saying, 'three other women have now latched on to the notion of someone stealing their babies. Hysterical nonsense, which one does well to ignore, lest it spread right out of hand. Now tell me honestly, do you think I should have bought the red cushions?'

Claudia glanced at the mercer, wiping his brow with

his handkerchief and shaking his head, and felt little pity for him as she heard herself saying:

'Matidia, dear, why don't you go and have a look at the coloured ones again, just to be on the safe side?'

Watching the shopkeeper's face turn ashen as Matidia disappeared into the back of his shop, she telegraphed him a silent message. It's you or me, chum, and I've had four days of the old windbag.

The one good thing about a small town like this was that you could dispense with the bodyguards and the litter and the conventions, and just be yourself. Claudia paused to pass a critical eye over the work of the bronzesmith (really quite good, she might come back and buy that lantern, it would set off the front entrance). Lingering to watch a Syrian glassblower, her senses were aroused by the commerce around her. The acid tang of rope-making fought for first prize with the sharp smell from the paint seller's before both were knocked out of the ring by the skills of the herbalist. The air was filled with the cries of the fishmonger, his live catch splashing in the tank, together with the agonized squeals of axles begging for grease, the grinding of the millstone and the braying of the donkey that worked it. A doorway draped with greenery signified a tavern, a cracked and smoke-blackened wall stood testimony to the presence of a cookshop. Claudia was passing the stall of the root-cutter, the man who supplied roots and rhizomes to apothecaries and the like, when she spotted the Collatinus family physician.

Blond, athletic and classically handsome, Diomedes could be nothing but Greek. Not a Greek from the north like her own lanky steward, this man hailed from Achaea in the south, and it was tempting to ask whether his income came solely from serving the needs of the sick. A good many matrons in Rome would pay lavishly for his services, women in the rudest of health. With emphasis on the word rude. He wore the pallium, too, revealing a muscular shoulder and tanned chest which bulged in all the right places.

'Claudia!'

His eyes – seducer's eyes if ever she saw them – roved over her and not for the first time did Claudia find herself responding to the frankness of his stare. She hadn't had a satisfactory sexual relationship since . . . since . . . oh for gods' sake, did it matter?

'Going back to the villa?'

No.

'Yes.' To hell with Matidia. 'As a matter of fact, I am.'

'May I walk with you?'

'Walk? Did you say walk?' Claudia cocked her head on one side and grinned. 'Diomedes, if it ever gets back to Rome that Claudia Seferius walked *anywhere*, so help me, I'll sue.'

'Then I'll show you a short-cut.'

She fell into step, conscious of his raw masculinity. Unlike most Greeks, Diomedes was clean shaven and his hair lacked the curls for which his compatriots were famous. As a result, when he shook his head, every hair fell straight back into place as though it had been combed, an action which was having a distinctly hypnotic effect—

His quarters were adjacent to, but completely separate from, the household. No one would see them.

Diomedes was explaining how there was little he could do for Eugenius, but Claudia remembered Matidia gushing about this man's healing powers. Why, he had been here only a week when she was taken ill herself, very ill indeed, and my word, wasn't that man a marvel? Had her cured within a matter of days, she'd have you know, and nothing to show she'd even been poorly.

Claudia, who until now had been of the opinion that the roles of physician and undertaker were more or less interchangeable, had a quick rethink. This was a man worth falling sick for!

'What brings you from Greece?'

He shrugged the sort of shrug that breaks hearts. 'I don't know, Claudia. I wanted to travel, get away from home, the usual things.'

'I heard you trained at Alexandria. Wasn't that exotic enough?'

'Not really.' His accent was thick (deliciously thick!) in contrast to his Latin grammar and vocabulary, which were virtually perfect. 'The more you see, the more you want to see, I just went where the wind blew me. I moved around, selling my services to wealthy families from Smyrna to the Narbonensis until, after four years, I found peace here.'

'Peace?'

They had reached a small plateau and he paused to watch a butterfly, a swallowtail, faded after the long, hot summer, sunning its wings on the stony path.

'It got to the stage where in sunsets, I could see only blood, in the emperor's purple, I could see only the colour of viscera.' He smiled a sad, drop-dead handsome smile. 'Does that make any kind of sense to you?'

Claudia was about to put some conviction into the words 'I suppose so' when she noticed the faraway look in his eyes had changed to something instantly more recognizable. He moved closer, placing the flat of his hand against her cheek. A shiver of anticipation ran through her body, she could smell the sweetness of his breath. His hair, that devastatingly obedient hair, fell tantalizingly into place, but as he leaned forward to kiss her, his eyes dark with passion, the image of another man filled her mind. Tall, with a mop of dark, curly hair and a boyish grin he was forever trying to hide behind his hand.

'Good heavens, is that the time?' She glanced up at the position of the sun. 'I'm late.'

He ran to catch up with her, but the moment had passed. She was cheerfully recounting a story about a senator in Rome and the public meeting between his wife and mistress as the path zigzagged its way down the hill. Stretched out ahead, the African Sea shimmered under a blazing October sun, the pines behind the sand packed as tight as thatch. The white walls of the Collatinus villa were dazzling, the heat haze over the red tiles as thick as steam. As they rounded the bend, Claudia was on to another risqué tale when she noticed Sabina stretched out on the grass, hands at her side, staring up at the sky. Her heart sank. When it came to party-poopers, this woman was in a league of her own.

Diomedes checked his pace. He glanced at her, then began to run. Her heart firmly in her mouth, Claudia raced after him.

Sabina was lying down all right, but she was neither daydreaming nor sunbathing. Her hands and arms anchored her tunic, which had been arranged neatly on top of her naked body. Her eyes stared skywards not in a dream-world, but in death. A pool of blood had seeped into the parched yellow grass, staining it scarlet, but when

Diomedes turned the body over, it was clear Sabina Collatinus had not died from this wound.

Sabina Collatinus had had her spinal cord severed at the base of the neck, which had caused paralysis and ultimately death from asphyxiation.

Worse, from the dark bruises and wheals on her body and the stickiness on the inside of her thighs, it was evident the poor cow had been raped as she lay dying and helpless.

Beside her, smashed into a dozen fragments, lay the tiny blue flagon which Sabina Collatinus believed had contained her soul.

VIII

Damn, damn, and double damn. So much for keeping a low profile! Claudia reached for the jug of wine at her bedside. As breakfasts go, it wasn't ideal, bread or pancakes would have been more sensible, but who on earth wants to be sensible?

'Cypassis, is that you?'

Good grief, where was she? Sleeping late, lazy hussy. Probably with some callow Collatinus slave. How that child has the energy is beyond me, Claudia thought. Work her to the bone and she still finds time to seduce pimply youths. Claudia swallowed half a glass of wine in one gulp. Jealousy, my girl. Just because you can't remember what an orgasm is, no need to deny Cypassis her own pleasures.

Certainly anyone who'd noticed a muscular young Gaul slipping into Claudia's room in the early hours would have jumped to the wrong conclusion. Since the bizarre manner of Sabina's death was likely to generate gossip right across the island, the chances of the name Seferius not cropping up were parchment thin. So much for 'early days' and 'no hurry'. Now she had to eliminate the threat and skedaddle. Fast.

Not that she wasn't shocked and sorry about Sabina, she was. Goddammit, she was. But from the moment she'd realized the woman was an imposter, Claudia had been expecting trouble. In fact, she had covered every contingency . . . bar one.

Life was a bitch and, as irritating as she was, Sabina didn't deserve this. Wherever she went, she had clutched that stupid, empty flagon, slept with it, even, reminding Claudia of a child with her favourite doll.

Yesterday there had been a tang of salt and cypress in the air, pines and wild celery, that made you forget winter was sneaking up on the backroads. The blue of the sea spoke of summer picnics and sleeveless tunics, the suck of waves against sand whispered peace and tranquillity. Neither of them so much as hinted at bloodshed.

Had it been a hot killing, like for instance gladiatorial combats which were bloody in the extreme, that would have put a different complexion on it. Or a crime of passion, where one man drives a knife into another in a fit of jealousy or revenge . . .

And yet passion there was.

Of a sort.

Except the cold brutality of the act was chilling. As was the dangerous and calculating mind behind it.

It was creepy, too, the reaction of the poor woman's family, the callous manner they totally disregarded the violence of the crime yet threw themselves vigorously into the funeral arrangements. In a way it reinforced Claudia's impression that they, too, had believed this strange, ethereal creature could not be one of them and had found a convenient way of covering it up. But why? Why not speak out? Were they all party to the conspiracy? Or was it just one of them, sowing seeds of doubt amongst the others?

Questions, questions, questions. Claudia had barely slept for questions.

A gentle scratching at the door received a peremptory 'Come in,' and a small slave girl, no more than fifteen and with skin as dark as a chestnut, crept into the room. Drusilla stiffened.

'Senbi sent me, madam.'

'Why?'

Drusilla's ears flattened as she let out a low howl from the back of her throat.

'Hrroww.'

The girl blinked rapidly. 'Um—'

'Come on, spit it out. What do you want?'

'Hrrrowwwwww.'

The girl backed up tight against the door frame. 'Your maid's bin taken sick with the fever,' she replied in one frantic breath, her eyes riveted on the snarling cat.

Claudia sat bolt upright. 'Cypassis?'

Dear Diana, she was telling Diomedes only yesterday what a treasure that child was!

She considered the timorous creature flattening herself against the wall. 'Can you dress hair?'

An imperceptible shake of the head.

'Cosmetics?'

A grimace.

Claudia resisted the impulse to scream. 'Is it within your powers, do you think, to help me dress?'

At last, a nod.

'I can try,' she whispered.

Good life in Illyria, what have I got myself into! Claudia threw off the bedcovers and marched over to the window.

'For goodness' sake,' she said, throwing wide the shutter, 'pour some water into that bowl and fetch a towel.'

Drusilla was watching the proceedings very carefully, and only when she was completely happy the intruder wasn't a kitten-skinner in disguise did she ease up on the growling. The girl's sigh of relief was probably audible the other side of the island.

'Bring me that mirror!'

There was no way Claudia intended letting this novice loose on her hair and, without Cypassis's expertise, she wasn't going to spend half the morning fiddling with curls and plaits and ringlets and things. She'd wear her hair in a bun at her neck. Simple, elegant – and well under two minutes to fix.

'Now fetch that misty blue tunic, the one with short sleeves and the flounce along the bottom.'

'And which stola?'

The girl *was* untrained! 'For heaven's sake, you only wear that at formal occasions or when you're going out.' Where on earth had the child been? 'Give me a hand with this belt.'

As the young slave neatened up the overhanging folds, Claudia asked, 'What's your name?'

'Pacquia.'

From the atrium came a clatter, clatter, crash, followed by loud remonstrations met in return with querulous protests that it was not somebody's fault, she'd tripped over Young Master Marius's whipping top. Unlike home, where Leonides would sort the matter out quietly and without fuss, Senbi clearly decided that his presence needed to be felt – and in this case, more than just his presence. Claudia could hear the blow from her room. If that had been Leonides, she'd have his Macedonian ears for breakfast. With garlic on.

'Oi! Pack it in!'

Good old Linus, putting his oar in now the fuss had died down. Typical of the man, a loser if ever there was one. To some extent Claudia could sympathize because he'd given fifteen years to the business and was still, thanks to the law, without an authoritative role.

That was the law which made Linus accountable to his father.

The same law which made Aulus accountable to *his* father, who had no intention of letting go the legal reins.

In other words, the same law which gave Eugenius Collatinus absolute control over every person and every thing that he owned, including his family.

Unfortunately for Linus, Fabius's return after twenty years meant even the weak position he held had now been usurped. It was an unenviable situation by any reckoning, but whatever sympathy he might have earned was blown away thanks to his blatant whoring, his persistent bragging and his bullying. Like father, like son. Nothing Corinna did could please him and as an outsider, Corinna found no allies in this house, not even in Matidia.

Especially not Matidia. The old man wouldn't even delegate the running of the household to his own daughter-in-law, which under normal circumstances was her right as matriarch. Daily, with the others, she had to endure the humiliating morning ritual whereby Dexippus, Eugenius's secretary, passed across to Actë the wax tablet on which he had written the old man's instructions and she would call them out to the slaves. Then, when the slaves had left, Dex would hand over a second tablet and she'd read out the old man's instructions to his family.

Claudia jerked her head towards the hall. 'How are they taking Sabina's death this morning?'

Pacquia twiddled the flounces round Claudia's ankles. 'It's all very sad, madam,' she said without looking up.

'That's not what I asked you,' Claudia replied. 'I want to know how it's affecting them.'

Pacquia's hands trembled slightly, and Claudia relented.

'Look, you don't have to go through the motions with me. I'm well aware they're not playing Happy Families out there, grieving and crying over a much-loved sister. Pass that silver pendant.'

Grief she had not expected. Even assuming the blood line was pure, Sabina had been as much a stranger to them as they were to her, and in four days precious little ground had been gained. Confusing her dream world with reality, Sabina had categorically refused to mix with her relatives and had stuck to Tanaquil like a snail on slime.

'What happened to her prospective bridegroom, Gavius what's his face?'

'Master Labienus? He left on Monday, madam.'

That let him off the hook, then. Sabina was killed yesterday, Tuesday. Not that he could really be considered a suspect. The killer would be a local man.

'Have they caught the culprit?'

'There's a search party out now.'

'I see. And what does the effervescent Tanaquil have to say about the matter?' Some fortune teller she turned out to be.

'Tanaquil, madam?'

'That flame-haired jack-in-a-box who's been dossing in the clipshed.'

Sabina might have attached herself to the girl, but Eugenius wouldn't have what he called the Sicilian trollop in the house. She and the Minotaur had been sleeping rough since they docked.

'Oh, *her*.' Even slaves looked down on these hangers-on, it seemed. 'She's gone.'

There was enough good-riddance in Pacquia's voice for Claudia to save her breath. An admirable decision, she thought, to jump before you're pushed.

The young slave girl's fear seemed to have all but evaporated, and her eyes began to glow.

'You know what they're saying,' she whispered, with all the enthusiasm of a gossip five times her age, 'they're saying she weren't their daughter.'

This was more like it. 'Get away! Who says?'

'Senbi. I heard him talking to Antefa – and guess what Antefa said?'

'Tell me.'

Pacquia glanced at the door. 'He'd heard Aulus, Linus and Portius having a right old barney over how much the master was gonna settle on Miss Sabina.'

'Was that before or after her run-in with Labienus?'

'Mmm . . .' Pacquia closed her eyes in concentration. 'Before.'

Claudia leaned forward conspiratorially. 'And just how much was Eugenius going to settle on Sabina?'

'Eight thousand sesterces.'

Her breath came out in a whistle. No wonder they were aggrieved. Claudia could imagine that, after thirty years, they felt entitled to that money themselves. They wouldn't be happy to see their birthright frittered away on a middle-aged fruitcake whose childbearing days were almost over.

Which was all very interesting, of course, and had Sabina been pushed over a cliff on a dark night, might well explain a few things. But she wasn't. She'd been murdered in a particularly callous and calculating manner.

The timing had to be precise, the wound had to be precise. The man responsible for this bizarre crime knew exactly how much time he had between severing her spinal chord and then, as she lay helpless, stripping her and raping her while she was still fully conscious. Claudia felt a column of insects march up her backbone. Judging by the bites and bruises, this was a vicious and concerted attack; the work of a maniac, sick and depraved. Not the work of a man trying to hang on to eight thousand sesterces.

Pity.

Pacquia selected two lapis lazuli studs from Claudia's hinged jewellery box and began to fasten them on her mistress's earlobes. 'There's a policeman sniffing around, too. Bin here all night.'

Now that *was* a surprise. Claudia's impression was that the family were keen to gloss over the tackier aspects of Sabina's demise. Still, credit where it's due, the woman was brutally murdered and someone somewhere had thought it wise to start an investigation rolling. Perhaps they'd held a council of war? Or was this Eugenius's brainchild?

'He's with Master F. right now.'

More than likely pinned down with a blow-by-blow account of every skirmish Fabius had ever been involved in over the past twenty years. Best of luck to him, Claudia had better things to do. It was another warm day, she'd take herself off to the garden. She could do her thinking and her planning out there.

In the atrium, with the morning sunshine streaming in from the open roof and the water sparkling on the surface of the central pool, the bestiality of the attack seemed far removed and if, in life, the Collatinuses had been proud to have a Vestal in the family, in death they were more so. You couldn't move for cypress. With a torch at each corner, Sabina lay on her bier in full bridal dress, correct right down to her circlet of marjoram and verbena. Even her girdle was tied in that special double loop known as the Knot of Hercules (in itself no mean feat), but not for Sabina ribald jokes about this being the one labour Hercules couldn't manage and wishing the bridegroom better luck. But ceremony she'd had, poor cow.

Claudia adjusted the woollen ribbons running through Sabina's elaborate, conical hairdo which someone had taken great pains to get right.

Since Eugenius was physically incapable of performing the ritual, Aulus had been deputed to clash the two bronze kettles together and spit the black beans from his mouth to speed his daughter's spirit. Afterwards, Eugenius resumed his role as head of the family and led prayers at the family shrine, except he sounded bitter rather than distraught.

You'd have thought that with Sabina's body still cooling in the atrium, some respect would have been shown last night, wouldn't you? Far from it. Aulus and Fabius all but came to blows, Portius drank too much and threw up, Linus openly groped the slave girls. Matidia and Corinna turned their customary blind eye on the pretext of discussing textiles while Eugenius absented himself, as usual. In fact, from what Claudia could gather, this was a run-of-the-mill evening for the Collatinus clan . . . Perhaps they were used to dead bodies littering the establishment?

She was smoothing the bright orange veil round Sabina's face when she heard voices.

'I've composed a lament, Father. I'll read it in full at the funeral, but this is how it starts:

"Twas here that once the tainted air brought forth
A plague that raged with all an autumn's heat.
It slew the herds and every kind of beast,
Infected pools and poisoned pastures sweet.'

Dear me, if they handed out laurels for pretentiousness, you'd mistake Portius for a bay tree.

'Well done, son!' Aulus clapped so loudly the sound echoed round the marbled hall. 'Claudia, my boy here is destined to become one of the great Sicilian poets.' He beamed proudly. 'Wasn't that marvellous?'

'Wasn't that Virgil?' she replied artlessly, without stopping to watch the exchange of expressions.

Passing the dining room she could hear Fabius's strident tones launched into his favourite moan about how the Praetorian Guard are paid three times the salary yet put in only three-quarters of the service. Pity the poor policeman from Sullium, probably fat as a bullfrog and red as a cockerel's wattle, trying to make headway in this house. Serves him right, she thought, about time he earned his keep in that dreary, one-horse town where the only crime was an occasional spot of pilfering.

'Quite so, but if we could just return to the moment you first saw your sister's body . . .'

Claudia stopped in her tracks as though she'd been poleaxed. It couldn't be! Jupiter, Juno and Mars, it bloody couldn't be! She waited until her colour had subsided and her breathing was less ragged before sweeping into the room.

'Well kick me for a cardamom, look what the cat's dragged in!'

IX

'Cat!'

Both men jumped to their feet, anxiously raking the ground with their eyes. Dear, sweet Drusilla! Always made an impression, no matter where she went.

Fabius recovered first. 'Ah, Claudia, let me introduce—'

'Save your breath. I'm fully acquainted with this little tick, thank you very much.'

Fabius looked confused, but the visitor, tall and dark with a mop of curly hair, grinned covertly. 'I think it's her way of saying she's missed me.'

'Yes. Well.' Fabius shot a hopeful glance at the door and the words 'Permission to be dismissed' all but slipped out. He managed to excuse himself on a more sociable note, but the speed with which he reached the doorway spoke volumes.

'Reminiscing about the old days, were we?' She had almost forgotten Orbilio's military background.

'Not exactly.' He motioned Claudia to sit.

Claudia stood. 'What are you doing here?'

'I was going to ask you the same thing.'

'I asked first.'

'Very well.' Marcus Cornelius Orbilio settled himself on one of the red upholstered dining couches, throwing one leg casually over the other. 'Naturally, as a member of the Security Police, I'm extremely disturbed—'

'That's what happens when cousins marry.'

A muscle twitched in his cheek. 'I meant in the worried sense,' he said. 'Since the Vestal Virgins fall under my protection—'

'Sabina will find great consolation in that.'

'She wasn't a Vestal. Claudia, why are you giving me such a hard time?' He swivelled round and caught hold of her wrist. 'You *know* what's between us.'

'My knee in your groin if you don't let go.'

He gave a cockeyed smile as he released her. 'Sooner or later you'll have to admit it. I get under your skin.'

'You get up my nose.'

In three quick strides she was across the room. In the atrium, one slave polished the family shrine, a second, on his knees and singing, mopped at a spillage, while a third topped up the oil lamps. The smell of cypress and incense was cloying.

He blocked her way between pillars. 'Wait. I want to question you.'

Typical. Want, want, want!

'Orbilio, watch my hips.'

The last thing she needed was him sniffing round, rooting up all all manner of things that didn't concern him. She ducked under his outstretched arms. He blocked her way between the next pillars.

'Then let me remind you why I'm here.' Yes? 'This is a murder investigation—'

'You knew she was going to be murdered?'

'Claudia, I'm tired. I've had a long journey and I've been up all night.' Firmly taking her arm, he swung her round 180° and marched her back into the dining room, pressing his weight against the door. He'd forgotten how her eyes flashed like the sun on water when she was angry. 'I want this pervert caught and you could do me a big, big favour by filling in some background information.'

She sliced off a chunk of sheep's cheese. 'You could do yourself a bigger favour by getting a bath.' She wrinkled her nose and flapped her hand. 'Downwind . . . well, I mean to say.'

Alarm flushed his face as he snatched at a handful of tunic and sniffed. It smelled of nothing more offensive than cloves and sandalwood and bay, and he was annoyed with himself for falling for it.

'I'm in no mood to play games.' Orbilio walked across to the table, laid his hands flat and leaned over to face her. 'A woman lies dead and mutilated right outside that door. Tell me about the family.'

She hadn't heard from this man in heaven-knows-how-long and he expected her to do his work for him? Unfortunately, telling a policeman to go knot himself wasn't a particularly clever move. There were laws against that sort of thing. Which was rather a shame, really.

'Eugenius: dirty old man, face like a walnut.' Claudia ticked them off on her fingers. 'Matidia: over fifty, over-dressed, over made-up. Aulus: drunk as a skunk with a nose like a trunk. Fabius:—'

Orbilio wanted to pull her into his arms. He wanted to tell her she looked ravishing in pale blue. He wanted to confess his overwhelming relief that the mutilated corpse wasn't hers. He wanted to bury his face in her thick, wayward curls. He wanted to ask, 'Do you mean an elephant's trunk or a traveller's trunk?' Instead he heard a pompous voice saying:

'Point taken, Claudia. You're not obliged to make an investigating officer's life easy. But you found the body, you are obliged to co-operate on that.'

'Very well.' She folded her arms in a defiant gesture. 'I was proceeding along the footpath in a westerly direction at approximately noon yesterday, when I espied, lying on the grass—'

Orbilio held both hands up, palm outwards, in a gesture of surrender. 'All right, forget it.' He was unable to keep the irritation out of his voice. 'Just remember the key to all successful outcomes, regardless of whether it's solving murders or ... anything else ... is communication.'

That's rich, coming from a man with your liberal attitude towards it.

'I appreciate the advice and now, if you'll excuse me, I have a tan to work on.'

'Wait.' Pushing aside a bowl of grapes, he perched himself on the edge of the serving table, leaving one leg dangling. 'Where's Junius?'

Uh-oh. She made a great show of studying the hunting scene on the floor. 'Junius?' Gracious, that was one ugly stag.

'You know the fellow. Gaul. Aged about twenty-two. Big chap. Muscular.' He paused. 'Heads your bodyguard.'

'Oh, that Junius. Isn't he around?'

'Mother of Tarquin!' She could hear the grate of nails on stubble. 'Must I spell it out? Sabina's been butchered, your bodyguard goes missing. Don't you think that's stretching coincidence?'

Claudia began to count the colours in the mosaic. Excluding black and white, there were five shades of brown, three red—

'Croesus, woman!' His fist came down so hard on the table that the plates, bowls and goblets rattled. 'Don't you care a damn?'

She bit deep into her lower lip. One shade of orange, two greens—

'Sabina was beaten, bitten, stripped and raped while she lay paralysed and dying. Doesn't it prick your conscience just a little, hiding a suspect?'

The look she eventually gave him was as impenetrable as she could make it. His were the only red-rimmed eyes in the house, she thought idly, and those from lack of sleep rather than grief.

'Junius isn't the killer and you know it.'

'I'll ask again. Where is he?'

Ten seconds ticked past. 'He's running an errand for me, if you must know. He's due back any minute.'

'Now, that wasn't too painful, was it?' He helped himself to dates. 'What about this Tanaquil and her brother?'

'She's a two-bit hustler. One whiff of trouble and those two are off faster than chalk on a chariot wheel. Can I go now?'

'One more question.'

He sank his teeth into an apple, and she was forced to listen to the sounds of crunching for a full half-minute before he followed up.

'What brings you all the way from Rome to Sullium?'

'Business.'

It was irritating, the way that single eyebrow lifted like that, as though it didn't believe her.

'Would you mind telling me what sort of business?'

'That's two questions.'

'Humour me.'

'Well, in case it slipped your sharp investigative mind,' she replied through a mouthful of almonds, 'let me remind you that seven weeks ago I inherited a sizeable business from my late husband, and that Eugenius Collatinus is also a wealthy businessman.' She waved her hands in an expansive gesture. 'There are certain . . . certain links and . . . things.'

'You're in wine, he's in sheep – and you talk of links?'

It was getting bloody warm in this room, someone ought to open a window.

'Naturally.'

Take the bones out of that.

'Nothing to do with the fact that you might be living beyond your means in Rome?'

'Good heavens, where did you hear that ridiculous rumour?'

I never live beyond my means, Orbilio. Not when I can borrow.

'And nothing to do with the fact that Sabina was passing herself off as a Vestal Virgin? For which purpose, incidentally, she would need an accessory. Ideally a woman.'

'You *have* heard some funny stories.'

'But you knew she wasn't a real Vestal?'

'I did?'

'Come on, you spent over two weeks in her company and that bridal dress is brand new. Don't tell me the retiring priestess ordered a new dress to show off at home.'

'You're slipping, Orbilio. Losing your touch.'

'Oh?'

'Sabina was due to be married. To Gavius Labienus. At the end of November.'

'Oh.'

He looked about seven years old at that moment, despite the hollow eyes and roughened chin, and Claudia wondered why she should find Marcus Cornelius Orbilio so damned attractive. Well he wasn't, of course. She was just desperate.

'It still doesn't add up,' he said, prizing himself off the table and sauntering over to the window. 'I mean, if you know she's an imposter and I know she's an imposter, how come we're the only ones?'

'You're the policeman, you work it out.'

'The family obviously believe she *was* the retiring Vestal.'

'And you haven't put them straight? How noble.'

Orbilio shrugged. 'I don't see what good can come of disillusioning them,' he said. 'After all, it's not as though it was a motive for murder.'

'Personally, I wouldn't go around making sweeping statements until I knew who was responsible,' she said, surprised to find more astringency in her voice than she bargained for.

'That's no problem,' he said simply, turning his gaze back on Claudia. 'I know who killed her.'

X

The yellow sandstone of the old Pharos, grating slivers off Claudia's backbone, was perversely comforting as she sat watching the sun cast a cloak of molten copper over the landscape. Using her palla as a cushion instead of a wrap, she stubbornly refused to acknowledge the nip in the air. The strong, powerful wingbeats of a pair of cormorants whirred overhead. Below, white frills laced the deserted shoreline.

She picked up one of the fallen stones from the crumbling, abandoned edifice and lobbed it, but the peninsula was deceptive and the stone bounced off a boulder before slithering pitifully into the sea.

Where the bay opened out, tightly packed pines whispered softly to each other in the breeze, and beyond them, in the hills, a solitary bleat reminded her this was sheep country, not cornfields. Yet Eugenius had once been a prosperous wheat farmer. Why the switch?

Not that she cared. She was leaving in two days, she should have her answers by then, it would just cost a bit more, that's all – paying several men to do the job swiftly, instead of one or two at their leisure. Worth it, in the long run, though . . .

'Idiot!'

She hurled the largest stone that would fit into her fist. It fell woefully short of the water.

'You know the seas close down in October. Why didn't you think, you silly bitch?'

Another brick followed. Then another, then another. Gradually her temper cooled, and she could forgive the fact that four and a half years of soft living as Gaius Seferius's wife had eclipsed memories of those early years – years a very different Claudia spent in Genua, living off her wits. Well, it was too late to start scourging herself. She'd jumped in without thinking and had to pay the price. Eugenius expected her to stay the winter, but frankly, the prospect of hanging on, where laughter and compassion were as abundant as hairs on a pickled egg, was too dire to contemplate.

Claudia slipped off her armlet and began to twiddle it round her finger.

It irritated her that Orbilio should have thought the problem through when she hadn't, and had arranged for a grainship to drop anchor in the bay on Friday. It irritated her even more that the sea situation pressured her into accepting a passage back with him.

No one likes a wiseguy.

And Marcus Cornelius Orbilio was the very worst kind. He was rich and handsome and debonair with it.

Worse still, she didn't need him cluttering up her life. He was like some noxious disease, cropping up once and just when she thought herself cured, up pops a second bout. Without so much as a by-your-leave, he took her raw emotions and swirled them around in a colander so they came out in tiny droplets, a jigsaw puzzle which took forever to piece together again and left you bruised and bleeding without cause. That was on top of everything else.

Still, her young Gaul should have all the answers by Friday. He was a good boy, Junius. Trustworthy and discreet. And if what he turned up was the worst news possible, plans would have been laid to deal with the situation once and for all.

Which, if she'd had an ounce of common sense, she'd have done in the first place. From Rome!

Goddammit, Sicily had been a mistake. It had turned into a right bloody mess and the more distance she put between herself and this godforsaken island the better, because just now the last thing Claudia wanted was her own name trawled through this. For gods' sake, the whole idea was to sneak in and sneak out. Would nothing go according to plan?

'Are you all right, madam?'

Claudia and her skin parted company and the armlet bounced off the stones. 'Kleon! For gods' sake, what do you think you're playing at, creeping up on people?'

'I wasn't creeping, madam, it's the grass, it dulls the—'

'It dulls your bloody senses. Pip off.'

The Cilician looked uncomfortable. 'I'm your bodyguard—'

'Then obey orders. Get lost.'

'There's a murderer on the loose.'

'I know that, Kleon, I found the body. Now run away like a good little Assyrian.'

'Cilician.'

'Assyrian, Cilician, Sicilian, I don't bloody care. Just vamoose!'

'But it's getting dark and Master Orbilio told me—'

The pitch of her voice dropped several octaves. 'Kleon, unless you want to end up as fishbait, I strongly suggest you do as I tell you. *Go away*!'

She watched the twilight swallow him up.

'Kaak.' A hooded crow alighted on a boulder nearby, and cocked its head on one side. 'Kaak, kaak.'

Claudia stared it straight in its yellow eye. 'And you can sod off, too.'

Where was that damned armlet? Claudia bent forward to retrieve it. It was gold, in the shape of a snake which coiled itself four times round your upper arm. She carefully polished the green jewelled eyes with her hem, then continued to twirl it round her finger.

Who the bloody hell does he think he is, she thought, giving orders to my bodyguard? Let me tell you, Master Smartarse Orbilio, if I choose to sit out here and get myself butchered by marauding maniacs, I'll bloody well do it, do you hear me? And just what are you playing at? Coming all the way out here, swaggering around and pretending to solve murders? You've no idea who did it. When I called your bluff this morning, you probably smelled your own goose charring. Remind me what you said so smugly. Ah, yes. *I know who killed her.*

So what happens when I ask, 'Who?' It all changes, doesn't it? Nothing but bluster and blubber.

'I need proof,' you said.

'You're the Security Police, I thought you beat the proof out of the poor sods?' I said, then a blond head popped itself round the door and saved your miserable skin.

'Claudia, the ceremony's about to begin in the

garden— Oh, sorry!' Realizing it was interrupting, the head promptly withdrew.

Orbilio's eyebrows arched slowly. 'Who's the gigolo?'

Claudia had felt her colour rising and turned away, ostensibly to pat her bun into place. 'That young man,' she'd said loftily, 'is Diomedes, the family physician. Now if you'll excuse me, the Meditrinalia is about to begin. What a shame you weren't invited.'

With a toss of her head, she flounced out of the room in the direction of the garden, wondering why it felt uncomfortable, Diomedes seeing her in such close proximity to this oily patrician weasel.

For obvious reasons, the annual toast for health could hardly take place in the atrium. Not in the presence of Sabina's stiff and mutilated body! Now in Rome they made a real event of this, with the priest of Mars heading a flamboyant and boisterous occasion. In the Collatinus household it had every appearance of turning into something solemn and dreary – even allowing for the recent death.

Which, apart from the inconvenience of cluttering up the atrium, seemed to affect no one in the slightest.

And again Claudia wondered where Sabina could have been these past thirty years. Thirty years! It was hell of a long time. Was there somebody (a man?) pining for her, as yet unaware what the Fates had in store . . . ?

The family was beginning to gather in earnest now, their black mourning clothes and gaunt faces making them look more like vultures than human beings. Two strong slaves arrived, carrying Eugenius towards his special Head of Household chair, beautifully carved and inlaid with ivory, and shaded by a bay tree. The accident, a riding accident by all accounts when he fell off his horse and broke his back, had left him paralysed from the waist down, but he'd at least retained full mobility of his arms. The blatant stare he bestowed on Claudia's breasts belied his seventy-seven years. As did the twinkle in his eye when it met hers.

Immediately he was settled, Actë moved into action, pulling a blanket over his knees and tucking it round, knotting a light woollen scarf round his neck and smoothing the wisps of hair on his head as an aged claw slid up her thigh. Claudia wondered what would happen to Actë, should anything happen to Eugenius. The family clearly resented the fact that the old man consulted with slaves on matters about which he didn't even consult them, and twice now Claudia had seen Actë resisting Aulus's advances. Really, she thought, the best Actë could hope for was that Eugenius lived for another twenty years!

Eugenius was patently enjoying the fuss being made of him. Aulus shot a look of blatant disgust down his long nose.

'Get on with it, man!' he ordered, but Diomedes, with barely a glance at Eugenius, reminded him politely they were still waiting for Master Fabius. Claudia wondered whether the old man had caught the drunken slur in his son's voice.

As sandals were shuffled, sighs let loose and yawns stifled but with still no sign of Fabius, Claudia's thoughts returned to Sabina. She was definitely not one of Vesta's priestesses, yet she'd timed her return carefully, ensuring it coincided with the retirement of the real senior Vestal. Which meant – assuming she was a Collatinus – she had deliberately deceived her family, one and all, into believing she had been in service for those last thirty years. Why?

'I'll tell you this much, you'll not catch me wearing one of those nancy-boy tunics.' Fabius's voice preceded him into the garden.

'Isn't it customary for patricians, the longer tunic?' The second voice was light and high, which made it Marius, Linus's younger son. Hero worship was written on his face. Linus's other son, Paulus, was dragging his feet behind them.

'Customary, my arse. Poofs, if you ask me, wearing skirts almost as long as a woman's.'

Good old Fabius. Spent twenty years in the army where they wore their tunics high above the knee and obviously he still enjoyed the air whistling up his thighs, bless him. Claudia thought she ought to be able to draw a conclusion from that, but for the life of her she couldn't think what it might be.

'Bit late,' he said by way of apology. 'We've been practising our drilling, the boys and me. Got carried away by the time.'

Ungrateful lad, that Paulus. Didn't look at all like one who'd been carried away by the time. More like one who'd been counting off the minutes . . .

The ceremony got under way with Diomedes filling glasses from the jug on the left and passing them round.

'From the old wine we drink,' he intoned solemnly in that thick, delicious accent, 'and from the old illnesses may we be cured.'

If he noticed any irony in the fact that here was a qualified physician banishing disease by the simple action of drinking wine he didn't let on, but calmly poured wine into clean glasses from the jug on the right.

'From the new wine we drink,' he said, 'and from the new illnesses may we be protected.'

There followed sufficient hear-hear-ing and enough your-health-ing for Claudia to feel she could slip away quietly, but Eugenius beckoned her over.

'I'm going to my room,' he said. 'I'd appreciate some intelligent company.'

What could you say to the man whose house guest you were?

'I was hoping you'd invite me,' she said silkily.

Sod it.

Out of the corner of her eye she saw Fabius clap a hand on Paulus's shoulder as the boy was set to make his escape, and heard his voice boom out.

'Can't stand sloppy drill. Sloppy drill meant a crack from my cane and the man on barley rations for a week.'

So he *was* a centurion, then. Strange! Wealthy equestrian ranks, like the Collatinus clan, usually put a son in the army as a junior tribune as a stepping stone to a decent career in administration. The treasury, civil engineering, the usual stuff. Why should Fabius sign on as a legionary, an out-and-out footslogger, serving six or seven years before he could even qualify for promotion? She wondered whether she'd ever understand this family. Or frankly whether she was interested enough to bother.

Back amongst his own possessions and his dirty pictures, Eugenius seemed less frail, more the tyrant she knew him to be. Actë went through her paces once again, tucking and folding, pouring and serving, silently but not subserviently attending his needs, which she did without having to be told.

'Here's your alum water.' She placed a glass on the table beside his couch. 'This time you drink it.'

She turned to Claudia. 'Keep an eye on him, will you? I found out yesterday he's been tipping it under the bed.'

The old man's mouth turned down at the corners. 'Horrible stuff. Why can't I have wine?'

'Diomedes says it's good for the paralysis.'

'I haven't noticed any improvement.'

Actë shook her head. 'I don't hear you moaning about the massage he ordered, and that hasn't made a scrap of difference either.'

Her eyes, when they met Claudia's, said 'Honestly!' and Claudia smiled. She liked Actë. How old would she be? Twenty-eight? Thirty? There was a rumour circulating that she was still a virgin.

The room seemed a lot emptier without her.

Picking up the alum water, Eugenius began to sip. 'I've been talking to that Orbilio fellow.' He pulled a face and replaced the glass on the table. 'Seems very young.'

'I fear he's seen the porticoes of the Senate House, Eugenius. He's running a direct course.'

'Good luck to him, then. Patrician stock, should do well.'

'They usually do,' she replied caustically.

Eugenius made a sucking sound with his teeth. 'You're telling me! Look at Agrippa! The Emperor gave him half the plains of Katane after the war, and you've never seen more fertile soil.'

Claudia knew he wasn't referring to the terrible civil wars which had racked the Empire, he meant the war for independence when Sextus, youngest son of Pompey the Great and commander of Augustus's naval forces, rebelled and took control of the island.

As with most wars, of course, no one came out a winner. Although Sextus occupied Sicily for nigh on eight years before Augustus managed to recapture it, the cost to both was immense. Sextus cut off grain supplies to Rome, creating a famine and almost (but only almost) bringing her to her knees, but as a result the wheat farmers had no one to buy their harvests and the island lost much of its prosperity. Augustus retook Sicily around the time Claudia was born, but the province had never recovered. Augustus immediately showed his mettle by finding additional sources for grain (his people would never go hungry again!), and by granting vast tracts of prime Sicilian land to his army veterans, thus keeping it in the family, as it were. Agrippa, his friend and general, fared particularly well.

A thought occurred to her. 'Sabina went to Rome around the time Sextus took Sicily, didn't she?'

He seemed surprised by the question, rather than ruffled by it. 'She did,' he replied, 'and I can remember it like last week. That was the year after the Divine Julius was murdered. I was forty-seven years old and a prosperous wheat farmer, when along comes some snotty-nosed upstart ordering me not to ship my own grain to the motherland!'

'So you sent your granddaughter instead.'

A glint of cunning crept into his eyes. 'Took some palm-greasing, I can tell you, since they have a preference for patricians, but yes, I sent Sabina. Sextus and his ragbag followers were after the whole Empire, see, not just Sicily, and even scum like that understood the value of the Vestal Virgins.'

Crafty old sod! Torn between two masters, and Eugenius Collatinus managed to keep sweet with both! One thing was clear, though. He saw no reason to doubt Sabina's authenticity.

There was a long pause, and Claudia did not fool herself into thinking his mind was wandering. Finally he said, 'Fabius has been something of a disappointment to me.'

'Really?' Only Fabius?

'His father never showed an aptitude for business I rather hoped the son would do better. Since he was always playing soldiers as a boy, I suppose I thought if I let him join up, he'd quickly tire of it as a man.'

'Instead he took to it like a duck to water?'

It went a long way towards explaining why Eugenius kept such a tight control on the reins, but it was interesting what he'd said about Old Conky. Claudia had got the impression (admittedly from Aulus) that Aulus was practically running the show.

'Twenty years I've waited for that boy to come home.' The old man shook his head. 'Twenty years – and most of them in this bed.'

'And he's not showing any aptitude for sheep rearing now he's home, is that what you're telling me?'

Eugenius looked up sharply. 'Not unless you call route marches an interest.' He tugged at his lower lip. 'On the other hand, now he's back in the fold, ha-ha, I feel that if he had a suitable wife it might be different.'

A faint flame of intuition began to glow. 'Strangely enough, Eugenius, I am tempted to agree with you.'

She picked up the glass of alum water and walked over to the wall.

'Don't drink that,' he said, 'it's vile.'

Claudia shot him a glance which said she believed it as she poured it straight out of the open window. With any luck, Orbilio would be sitting underneath eavesdropping.

'It's coming up to noon,' she said gently. The slaves would be back any moment to convey him to the litter which would accompany Sabina's funeral procession.

'It's funny,' he said absently. 'Sometimes I think the years have dragged, being crippled and bedridden, then I think to myself, hold on. Last January you were bouncing your grandson on your knee and now here we are in October and he's got four children of his own.'

Claudia smiled to herself. They were all the same underneath, weren't they? Soft men inside rock hard shells.

Now, from her perch beside the old lighthouse, she noticed the last vestiges of daylight were almost extinct. High in the hills, lamps and lanterns shone from the houses in Sullium; closer to hand, torches flickered at the Villa Collatinus and oblongs of yellow thrown from the windows gave a honey glow to the courtyard. But with dusk the chill had intensified and could no longer be ignored. Claudia threw her palla round her shoulders, but made no move to pick her way home.

Sabina's funeral this afternoon had made for a good turnout. For a small town, the wailing women weren't bad, although Claudia would have preferred to see a bit more ash plastered about. Also the undertaker leading the cortege tended to give the impression he was more important than the dear departed, but on the whole it went well, the men with black togas drawn over their heads, the women with their hair dishevelled. Indeed, a stranger might have been fooled into thinking they cared.

Fabius shone, quite literally, in his uniform so that whenever the sun caught it, anyone looking his way was positively blinded. Even Claudia had to admit he cut a dashing figure with his broad chest and gleaming bronze armour. The red crest on his helmet, running side to side to reflect his centurion status, ruffled in the breeze in the most stately and dignified fashion, drawing the attention of many a maiden along the route, yet even as she recalled the procession, she could think only of another man, a patrician, in the scarlet tunic and hammered breastplate of the tribune. Not that his would need to be beaten out to exaggerate the muscular development of the professional athlete . . .

Dammit, that man gets on my whiskers!

Claudia pushed thoughts of Orbilio's torso to a dim and distant recess of her mind and concentrated on the funeral cortege as it filed slowly through the streets. As they were entering the Forum, the wailing women almost drowning out the trumpeters, she spotted Utti in the crowd, his ugly mug practically obliterated by the bodies of two small children, one perched on each shoulder for a better view. Before Claudia had had a chance to identify Tanaquil, another familiar form had sidled up.

'You'll help me find her, won't you?' The rings under Hecamede's eyes were darker, the hollows in her cheeks deeper. 'Only you promised.'

'I did no such thing!' Praise be to Juno, both breasts were tucked up safely!

'You did, you give me your word.'

Two of the Collatinus slaves pulled her roughly away and frogmarched the pitiful figure out of sight. Diomedes moved up beside Claudia.

'What was that about?'

'Oh, nothing, really. The woman's touched. Thinks someone's stolen her child and tried to point him out to me, but there was nothing there except some bloody great spider. She said he – whoever he might be – was collecting them at the time.'

'Aristaeus, you mean?'

'Pardon?'

'Aristaeus. The man who collects spiders' webs.'

Claudia faltered, nearly tripping over her hem. 'Say that again. You mean there really is a man who goes around collecting spiders' webs?'

'Of course. Didn't you know?'

Failing to see how anybody could possibly make a profession out of something like that, Claudia shook her head.

'Strange man,' Diomedes continued. 'Lives up in the hills. A – what's the Latin word? – recluse.'

Child molesters would be, wouldn't they?

As she began to follow the white line of the path along the peninsula, Claudia's mind pictured this seedy individual, this raptor of little girls. Middle-aged, pot-bellied, probably more hairs coming out of his nostrils than left on his head. No doubt he stank like a drain, too. She thought of Hecamede, driven out of her wits because this sordid specimen had run off with her little Kyana and no one giving a damn, simply because they were dirt poor. It touched a raw nerve and she felt her breath catch in her throat.

Claudia knew what poor was like.

Claudia grew up poor.

Claudia knew that poor didn't count for shit.

And she knew something else, too. She knew she'd never be poor again. Ever.

More overpowering than the smell of cinnamon and myrrh as Sabina's pyre burned was that earlier image of Hecamede – one breast lolling out of her tunic as she wept in the filthy gutter. Now, as the night noises from the mountains began to fill the air, the cry of a screech owl, the bark of a fox, she resolved that Aristaeus wasn't going to get away with his filthy practices any longer.

'Claudia Seferius is on your case, my lad,' she said aloud. 'Make no mistake, your time's up.'

It would take her mind off the Agrigentum business. A means of passing the time until Friday, when she had that boat to catch.

Even if the voyage did entail being cooped up with that smarmy investigator for a whole week or more.

XI

The man Melinno threw down his pack and leaned forward, hands on his knees, until his breath came back. He'd thought that climb up Mount Tauros was tough – by Janus, this bugger made Tauros look like a pimple. He wiped the sweat from his brow with the back of his hand and took a swig from his canteen.

Strictly speaking, it weren't his canteen, mind. He'd swiped it from a legionary who'd passed out cold back in Zankle. It had been full of that cheap sour wine them footsloggers seemed so fond of, but Melinno had flushed out the field flask and filled it with sweet, fresh mountain water. He shook it and replaced the bung. Getting low, but he'd passed enough streams, there'd be another one shortly. Wouldn't there?

Defiantly he shook some into his cupped hand and sluiced his face. Howay, man, there's bound to be water up here. Stands to reason. Mountains? Water? Why, aye.

Melinno hefted his pack on to his shoulders and resumed his trudge along the narrow path. It were only a goat track, slippy and slidy, and he'd only another hour of daylight at best. Frustrating for a man who needed to cover ground, but that was the price you paid for October. There was more hours of dark than day, and it were worse up here, because for much of the afternoon the sun had been blotted out by the Great Burning Mountain on his left. It were doused at the moment, this forge of the fire god, but a bloke could never tell. Word was, nineteen summers back and just before sunrise, some old shepherd actually saw with his own eyes the mighty Vulcan hobble up to his forge and start fanning the flames. The whole mountain had burst into fire, rivers of living red hell burning everything in their path. Aye. Well. Melinno didn't want none of that. The quicker he did his business and left, the better, as far as he was concerned.

As the light began to fade, his footsteps became more urgent, his eyes more vigilant. He wanted to make his shelter down there, in the valley, where there were trees and where there'd be water. Water and safety. Turning the corner, he heard himself gasp. Right in front of him was this huge cave. He dodged back. It could be, you know. It were big enough.

Mouth dry, he peered round the corner, but as his eyes adjusted to the gloom, he realized that what he had mistaken for a cave was nothing more sinister than the shadow of an overhang. It was the way these rocks was up here, you'd think a bloke would've gotten used to them by now, wouldn't you? Nevertheless, his heart was pounding as he passed underneath. And he didn't feel daft, neither. Cyclops lived in caves up here, them giant one-eyed cannibals what kept sheep, and Melinno knew they were close, he could hear bleating.

A bush of yellow broom blocked his way and he had to tread warily not to slip over the precipice. Aye, he were a fool to come this way, thinking he knew best.

'Take my advice, lovey,' the fuller's wife had told him,

running plump hands invitingly over her hips, 'follow the coast to Katane, *then* cut across. It's safer.'

His eyes had lingered on her tits, which seemed fit to burst from her tunic. Big, ripe, floppy tits, more than a man could hold in one hand.

'If I go round the Great Burning Mountain,' he swallowed the build-up of saliva forming in his mouth, 'it'll save time.'

She laughed in the back of her throat. 'Ooh, I like a man in a hurry,' she said, handing him the string of her girdle. 'But you'll make good time on the coast road.'

'Talking of good times . . .' he'd said thickly, with a sharp tug on the string.

She charged eight asses, but he'd given her ten on account of the way she pouted her lips; aye, that were a mistake, because she were older than she made out and her tits weren't so much floppy as sagging like half-empty flour sacks – and he'd forgotten, till he mounted her, that the way fullers cleaned clothes was by treading them in vats of stale piss.

The memory of the way that old whore stank was as good a reason as any to do the opposite of what she said, but Melinno thought he knew best and could save time cross-country. Then he found himself in the Lands of the Cyclops . . .

With little light left to see by, he was forced to make his descent without even the goat track to guide him. Hey now, he weren't no more superstitious than the next man, was he? Had he been scared by them fields of bubbling mud, them entrances to the underworld? Nah. And hadn't he crossed the pastures where the Oxen of the Sun grazed without trouble? But let's be reasonable. Them Cyclops do enjoy the succulent taste of human flesh, it made sense to steer clear of them.

Suddenly his foot slipped and he tumbled noisily down the mountain, thirty or forty paces before he righted himself, and when he did, his left foot was paining him.

'Fuck!'

He dropped the pack and rubbed his ankle.

'Fucking, fucking rocks!'

There was no way he could walk, he'd have to spend the night up here. He daren't risk starting a fire in case it were seen and there wasn't much by way of cover either. Great! No cover, no fire, and unless he was very much mistaken, it would rain within the hour. Winds were piling up the clouds at an alarming rate – he'd be drenched to the skin in no time.

'Fuck! Fuck! Fuck!'

By accident his good foot sent a boulder crashing down the hillside. Janus, would nothing go right for him? He limped painfully across to a hummock and hunched down as far as he could, back to the wind, his ears alert for the sound of the Cyclops. He opened his pack and found only a few hard biscuits and a bit of bacon. Better than nowt, he supposed. Better than nowt.

The rain began almost immediately, driving icy trickles down the back of his neck. His cloak was useless. Absolutely bleeding useless. Being wool, it soaked through in minutes, about as much use as a pen to a blind man. What he needed was a beaverskin cloak. Aye, like he'd seen in, where was it, Ostia? At the time, mind, it seemed bloody expensive. Another fucking mistake, and he was wrong about something else, too. The only water up here was bloody rainwater.

Shit, his ankle was throbbing. He ought to put a poultice of some sort on it, only he didn't know what. Sulpica used to slap bonemeal on to bring out a bruise, but he'd never twisted a joint before. Not since he were a bairn, anyroad. Melinno looked at the biscuit in his hand. Aye. Well. Why not? He didn't know how sodden it ought to be, but he softened two more, enough to make them pliable, and plastered them round his ankle. She used plantain, too, but he didn't know where plantain grew and it was too dark to look. In this rain, with his weak ankle, he might end up down a ravine. But fennel was everywhere, so he wrapped that round the soggy mess and tied it in place with his handkerchief before hunkering down as low as he could, trying not to think of the shelter down in the valley. Or the fact that, had he taken that old whore's advice, he'd have been halfway to Sullium by now.

'Fuck!'

Oaths came easy of late. He knew why he did it, to spit in the eye of them three old crones, the Fates, because on the odd occasion when he swore at home, Sulpica would laugh and say, 'Melinno, was that a swearie word I heard?' and he'd remember where he was and beg a hug of forgiveness. Sometimes he'd swear just for that and oh, those hugs! He'd wrap her in his arms and she'd say, 'You can squeeze me tight, pet. I won't break, you know,' and he'd squeeze and she'd squeeze until all the breath had come out of them both. Then they'd sit there by the fire, talking of all the things they wanted to do together, how many bairns they'd have, whether Melinno ought to open a bigger shop for his baskets – and then they'd catch each other's eye. Sulpica would come over and sit on his lap and she'd whisper, 'Why don't you blow that candle out?' and he'd reply, 'I want to see what I'm getting', so she'd inch up her tunic and ask, 'Is that enough?' and he'd say no, and this would go on till she had no clothes left and they'd both be rolling naked on the floor, and even when it was over, they'd be panting for more.

To Melinno's surprise, although the rain had stopped, his face was streaming with water. He blew his nose with his fingers and blinked the rest of the tears back inside.

Now, because of some murdering bastard, Sulpica was cold and in her grave.

Melinno felt himself tense. Janus, that bastard would pay dear, mind. Slow and painful, if he could, but death for a death it would be. He owed her that.

He knew the killer's name, knew he were an important man and that he moved around a lot, but he didn't know where to look until an armourer told him the bloke had gone to Sullium. It had cost Melinno time, his basket-making business and every ass of his savings and even then, more often than not, he'd been reduced to stealing. Worst of all, when it got really bad, he turned to whores. Fat whores with huge hips and yellow hair. Older women who looked nothing like the girl with dark, springy curls and breasts like small, sweet figs who was his wife. Had been his wife.

Dawn had not broken when Melinno wrung out his cloak, broke his fast with the last of his bacon and biscuits and drained his canteen. He was not surprised, as he untied his handkerchief, that his ankle was fully recovered.

Sulpica never let him down in life – she'd certainly not let him down in death.

XII

The trouble with rain is that it's so bloody depressing. You tend to take warmth and sunshine for granted, then suddenly the skies darken and before you know it, your boredom threshold is rising in direct proportion to the drip of the water clock.

Claudia pulled faces at herself in the mirror. There was only so much time a girl could spend on the essentials – the bath, the manicure, the hair – even though Pacquia had done a marvellous job on her legs, shaving them so gently with the hot walnut shells that Claudia hadn't suffered one single burn.

But by mid-afternoon the minutes were starting to drag heavily. It was utterly impossible to venture into the hills in this weather, but Old Conky assured her it would be fine again tomorrow, ample time to tackle Aristaeus before catching the boat back to Rome.

Claudia had rummaged through her jewellery box until she found the right phial. Belladonna. Lace that pervert's wine and the world would be a better place for everyone. Oh yes, everything was working out *perfectly*. Junius had returned from Agrigentum with good news, in fact, the very best. Claudia's future was absolutely watertight. Which reminded her. Supersnoop had the hump.

'You lied to me about Junius,' he said. 'You knew damn well he wasn't due back when you said he would be.'

'You knew damn well he wasn't under suspicion,' she had retorted. 'That makes us even.'

Tut, tut. She really hadn't taken Orbilio for a grudge-bearer.

'How many times do I have to tell you, Claudia? Murder is not a game. Why do you take everything to the wire?'

Good question. One she'd often asked herself. But a gambler is a gambler. We take everything to the wire, Marcus.

But that was last night, when she'd had too much to drink and was feeling benevolent. Why else would she have mentioned seeing Utti at the funeral? Hell, he probably knew the whereabouts of those two deadbeats anyway.

'You're up to something,' he'd said, totally ignoring the Utti thing. 'I can smell it.'

Bully for you, she thought. But you'll never know what, because it's finished with. Over. Gone. Forgotten. Yessir, what I found in Gaius's papers, what I chased halfway round the world for, hasn't a shred of evidence to its name. And on the strength of that, she'd honoured Bacchus a little too heavily. The headache this morning had been a real blinder.

'I'm warning you, Claudia. If I find you're breaking the law, I'll clap your fanny in irons, regardless of what's between us. Do I make myself clear?'

There was only one response you could make to a sanctimonious statement like that and Claudia made it.

She put her tongue between her lips and gave him the loudest raspberry this side of Mount Etna.

It had been easy to avoid him at breakfast this morning, but returning from the bath house she'd seen little Vilbia playing in the atrium. So there she was, Claudia, rolling around on the tessellated floor, singing:

> *'Pat-a-cake, pat-a-cake, baker's man,*
> *Bake me a cake as fast as you can—'*

when a man's voice cut in.

> *'Take the ingredients down from the shelf—'*

Claudia's eyes were staring at a familiar pair of patrician boots. With one fluid movement she bundled up little Vilbia, still chortling and chuckling, jumped to her feet and thrust the squirming tot into Orbilio's arms.

> *'Sod off, said the baker, cook it yourself!'*

Whether this wasn't the finish line he'd learned in the nursery Claudia didn't know, but for a seasoned representative of the Security Police he seemed somewhat inexperienced when it came to handling the more junior members of society.

'The mouth goes to the top,' Claudia had offered helpfully.

Vilbia's response to his indignities was to turn bright red and scream, although Orbilio had stolen the honours on colour. His anguish was ended only when the child's nursemaid snatched her charge from his arms with a glare that, in lesser men, would have turned their hair snow white. Sucking in her cheeks, Claudia marched off to her room.

'Wait.' He dodged in front of her. 'I have a few more questions about the family.'

'I thought you'd solved your case?'

'I have, but a bit of background information never goes astray.' He made a brave stab at a grin. 'You know me. Always like to soak up the atmosphere.'

'Dreadfully sorry to disappoint you, Orbilio, but the role of informant doesn't appeal, thank you very much.' She flashed a devastating smile at Diomedes, passing through the far arch on his way to give Eugenius his massage, and continued talking through her teeth. 'As it is, I strongly resent you following me out here, invading my privacy—'

'I did not.'

'You damn well did.'

He watched the rain drip steadily from the roof-spout into the pool. 'I didn't follow you. I followed Sabina.'

Claudia suddenly felt like the fish who'd swallowed a fly, only to find it was on the end of a hook, next stop the boiling pan. A lead weight thudded into her stomach, she could hardly breathe. *You followed Sabina?*

'Why?' That thin little voice sounded a million miles away. 'If you knew she wasn't a Vestal Virgin?'

He didn't even have the decency to look her in the eye.

'I followed her *because* she wasn't a Vestal,' he said, jutting his chin out. 'It . . . seemed odd, her pretending to be one when she wasn't. Especially when the family thought she was. If you see what I mean.'

Claudia did not see. She did not want to see. In fact, the only thing Claudia wanted at that particular moment was to pass right through the wall and into her bedroom. She couldn't use the door, Orbilio was blocking the way.

Tell a lie, there was one other thing she wanted. A very stiff drink.

Dear Diana, how could she have let herself believe he'd sailed halfway round the world after her? Claudia Seferius, you really are a silly bitch.

'What do you know about Old Bedroom Eyes?' he was saying.

Claudia felt her colour rise. 'Who?' she asked sharply.

By Juno, she'd be in that doctor's bed tonight, come hell or high water. She'd put that mattress through its paces.

'Come on! Ever since I got here, it's been Diomedes this, Diomedes that. Has he cast a spell on the Collatinuses, for gods' sake?'

'If he has, it's a bloody sight better than casting aspersions the way you are.'

'Claudia, I know for a fact—'

'That's another thing, Orbilio. I'm sick up to here with the patter of your tiny feats, get out of my way.'

And that was when she received a second bombshell – because he did, goddammit! He bloody stepped aside!

Claudia stared at the rain hammering hard against the window and ran her finger up and down the glass until it squeaked. Well, she thought. That arrogant patrician is nothing to me. What did it matter if he had more sex appeal than you could shake a stick at? There were other men. Better looking. Younger. Blonder, even . . .

That was another thing about Supersnoop. By rights

she ought to take him with her to Aristaeus's, except he'd only insist on dragging the man off for trial. In fact, with only Hecamede to give evidence against him, Aristaeus could be out in no time, free to ply his evil trade on other little girls. Oh no. Keep Orbilio out of this and let Belladonna do the work.

But Aristaeus was scheduled for tomorrow, Diomedes for tonight – and in the meantime, Claudia was bored.

Bored, bored, bored.

All four kittens lay piled in one contented, snoozing heap on top of their mother, who half-opened one protective eye every so often, but couldn't be bothered to move on a wet day like this. Claudia gave her a few strokes between her ears, but the purrs were obviously an effort, so to pass time she decided to inspect the redecorated banqueting room.

Eugenius had ordered new friezes, garden scenes of peacocks and finches, waterfalls and nymphs, but the workmen, who had all but finished the job, apparently couldn't get over in the rain. The room was deserted. Claudia cast her critical eye over the walls. They looked great from a distance but could they stand close scrutiny? To her surprise, the detail was as skilful as the overall picture. Maybe more so, because once you started looking closely, the eye was drawn to finer and finer detail. Some of the plants were quite astonishing and she wondered whether the painter carried the same honesty through to portraits. Not if he wanted further commissions, she thought.

On a table in a corner, fresh fruit stood piled on a silver tray, apples, nectarines, grapes, figs. There was one peach remaining, and she selected it.

'That's my peach. Put it down.'

Examining the skin for blemishes, Claudia turned slowly. A small child, no more than eight, stood in the doorway. A pretty child in all probability, with her raven black hair and slender form, but at the moment she was scowling too ferociously to tell.

'I said, that's mine. Put it back!'

Small hands became small fists.

Claudia regarded the child carefully, then held the peach to her nose, testing it for ripeness. Small brown eyes blazed with temper.

'If you eat my peach, I'll take that pot, I'll throw it on the floor and then I'll tell Mama you broke it.'

Her name was Popillia, she was Linus's and Corinna's third child and this was her normal disposition.

'So?'

'So,' she said haughtily, 'it contains Mama's new perfume, the one she sent for from Syria. She was showing it to Grandmama, only she left it behind by mistake.'

She advanced purposefully across the room and stretched out her hand.

With delicacy, Claudia picked up the ceramic pot, lifted the lid and sniffed appreciatively. 'Expensive,' she murmured.

'*Very* expensive,' the child corrected.

Claudia smiled. 'All right, you win,' she said, waiting for the light of triumph to fill those little nutbrown eyes before adding, 'Pity though.'

She opened her fingers. There was a crash and immediately a pungent aroma exploded in the air. The child's jaw dropped in amazement, her whole body frozen in surprise.

Claudia bit deep into the peach, seemingly oblivious to the juice dribbling down her chin.

'Don't forget to tell your mama, will you?' she said, stepping over the broken shards.

In the atrium, as she licked the last vestige of fruit from the stone, she decided that her first encounter with Popillia had not been the most auspicious of starts. Oh well. Claudia let the stone fall noisily on to the mosaic floor then, with a judicious kick, sent it winging into the pool. The resulting plop was more than satisfactory.

'You'll do as you're fucking told.' The voice of Aulus Collatinus was unmistakable. 'Don't think you can come back after farting around for twenty—'

'You call that uprising in Pannonia farting around? I nearly lost an eye, and when—'

'Don't change the bloody subject. I'm telling you now, boy, you can forget coming home with big ideas about taking over.'

'Taking—? I was only checking to see how much wool had been carded up.'

'Bollocks! You know sod-all about the spinning process, you're out to undermine my position.'

'The old man asked me to do it.'

'Oh! So now you're sneaking off to him, are you? Trying to worm your way round the old man so you can take over when he pops off? Well, I'll not have it, d'you hear me?'

Claudia listened at the door for another few moments, but since the exchange was going nowhere, a series of oh-yes-you-are, oh-no-I'm-not's, she moved on. They were an argumentative bunch at the best of times, this family, but the rain made them ten times worse.

Orbilio came in, tunic and toga soaking wet, hair plastered over his face, his legs streaked with mud. Claudia said, 'Still soaking up the atmosphere, I see,' to which he gave a very-funny-I-don't-think grin as he squelched across the tiles leaving a long line of drips in his wake. She hoped he got pneumonia and died.

Fabius and his father were still at it hammer and tongs but, two doors along, altercations of a different kind were in progress. Linus, disgust heavy in his voice, was berating Corinna, this time about her hair. Claudia leaned her ear to the door.

'You're making a fool of yourself, all those curls piled up. You look like mutton dressed as lamb.'

'It's the fashion, Linus. You said I should keep up with it.'

'Well, you haven't been, have you, you silly bitch. Remus, can't you do anything right?'

'I try, Linus, really—'

'The hell you do. You've only got to look at Claudia to see what a pig's ear you've made of it.'

'Her maid's sick, that's why she's wearing a bun.'

'You make *me* sick, you know that? The old man's got you tutors for the children, he's got you nannies and nursemaids coming out your ears – you can't complain you haven't got the time.'

'That's another thing, Linus, I never get to see my own children.'

'For gods' sake, woman, all I ask is you keep yourself smart, be a credit to the Collatinus name, and you can't even do that right.'

'I do, Linus. I am. I mean . . . but the children, I hardly ever—'

'Then what's that ridiculous confection stuck on your head? You look like a common tart.'

Claudia shook her head. If there were prizes for being a berk, Linus would win the crown. Given time, he could probably make it an olympic event.

It was because she was at the far end of the colonnade, listening at Portius's door, that Claudia failed to catch the rest of what passed between Linus and his wife.

'You do it on purpose, don't you, you selfish cow?'

The back of Linus's hand lashed against Corinna's cheek, sending her reeling against the table.

'You embarrass me on bloody purpose.'

Corinna struggled to her feet. 'Linus, that's not true—'

'Shut up, bitch!'

A fist cannoned into her stomach and she fell, doubled up, on to the floor. His foot rammed into her lower back and she screamed out in agony.

'Do that once more, you worthless cow, and I'll give you the hiding of your life.'

Linus directed another kick into her ribs, then pulled her to her knees by the hair. He hit her hard in the mouth. Not once, but twice.

'You show some respect for the family name.' He jerked her roughly towards him and bent to look at her, a grimace contorting his face. 'Croesus, you're ugly.' He recoiled. 'Ugly and scrawny and lazy and stupid. No other man would take you if I divorced you – which I could, you know, any day I choose. So what do you say?'

Corinna swallowed the blood in her mouth.

He twisted her hair so hard, a clump came loose in his fingers. 'I asked you a question.'

'Th-thank you.'

A balled fist thudded into her breast. 'Louder, you ungrateful bitch.'

The room swam and went dark, but Corinna forced herself to rally. She daren't pass out. Not right now.

'I s-said th-thank you, Linus.' The words were slurred from the swelling on her lip. 'I'm g-grateful for everything you've done f-for me.'

Linus let go of her hair and straightened up. 'So you bloody should be.'

Corinna began to sob uncontrollably, her muscles convulsing, as Linus brushed his hands together and finished off the last of his wine.

'Well, that should teach you a lesson,' he said conversationally, as he stood over her and began to untie his loin cloth. 'Now let's have a bit of fun.'

XIII

The deluge might have stopped, but the clouds were still low and threatening as Marcus Cornelius Orbilio slipped unobtrusively out of the slaves' entrance. For warmth this evening he'd opted for a long cloak rather than his toga, since freedom of movement was essential for the job in hand, and to that end the bulk was thrown over one arm with the weight at the other shoulder taken by a brooch. He was fully aware he looked less the professional on the job, more a young man on the razzle.

He paused in the shadows to sniff the air in the same way a dog will. All too soon the rich scents of Mother Earth would be overwhelmed by the more customary smells of sheep and their by-products, so he filled his lungs with the cool, fresh air. When bleaching started again, when it was dry enough to stretch the wool in the open, the air would be foul with sulphur and some of the pigments they used in the dyeshed stank abominably. He'd enjoy this while he could!

He winced as a solitary drip from the gutter spout trickled down his neck. Long after he'd wiped it away, Orbilio could still feel its icy track. In the kitchen behind him a pot crashed to the floor and a quarrel broke out, inciting that mangy guard dog Cerberus to damn near bark his head off. Didn't take long, he thought, for the peace to be shattered in this household.

Keeping to the shadows, he ducked under each window, whether lighted or not, pausing again at the corner. In Rome this routine was second nature, this checking and double-checking, but tonight he was simply honing his skills. It was one way to take his mind off things and, under the circumstances, he couldn't think of a better.

There was a scuffle to his left and Orbilio spun round to see a black rat disappear into the nettles. Mother of Tarquin, he was twitchier than he thought! He desperately needed a drink, but he'd been a good boy since he got here, hardly touched a drop. He looked up at the heavy bank of clouds. His drinking had got out of hand lately, trying to get that Seferius woman out of his mind, but he wasn't stupid. He needed a clear head for this job – if only to impress his boss.

The very thought of Callisunus made him break out in a sweat. On the one hand it was a hot sweat, because he was furious with his boss for sending him off to Ostia in order to take the kudos himself for solving those gruesome murders. And on the other hand it was a cold sweat, because in his haste to track down Claudia and find a passage to Sicily, Orbilio had completely forgotten about making his report. In fact he was a full five hours into his voyage before Callisunus even entered his head – which meant that he was by then precisely two hours late for the meeting.

Since that left a high-ranking tax inspector hanging unnecessarily under a thundercloud of suspicion, Callisunus would have Orbilio's cobblers for kebabs unless he could redeem himself, and the surest way of doing that would be to bring in a murderer red-handed. Red-handed and *single*-handed! It might not be enough to set his career back on track for the Senate, but it would be a damn good start. Oh yes, he could picture it now.

'Clever fellow, that Orbilio. Sniffed trouble right from the outset.'

'I know! Amazing, isn't it, the way he knew the Seferius widow was in danger, and what with that Sabina creature passing herself off as a Vestal Virgin, well!'

'Saved the poor widow, he did, and when the imposter was murdered, he caught the chap right away. Shrewd fellow all right. Should go far.'

Except that if he wasn't careful, Callisunus would have him flushing out drains instead of flushing out criminals.

He played at adjusting the cloak over his arm, lifting and dropping the soft, scarlet wool into folds. Danger! He ought to have known better, imagining Claudia Seferius to be in danger!

Kidnapped and held to ransom for her inheritance, that's what he'd thought. Ha-bloody-ha. The man who tried that would need his brains examining – it was safer rolling naked in a viper pit. Juno's skirts, you're a fool, Marcus! You knew she was in debt, you should have realized she'd be working some sort of scam.

Don't blame me, a little voice argued back. I've been busting my balls all bloody year, first on that murder business, then in Ostia, I was too tired to think it through properly. Tired . . . and frustrated. He slumped against the wall, letting his head rest against the cool of the stone. Croesus, I need a woman! I can't go on like this much longer. I'm twenty-four, for gods' sake, it's not bloody natural.

Aulus had sent him a slave girl, a pretty little thing, but she was only fourteen and quaking like an aspen, so he politely sent her away again. No, what he wanted was a real woman. One with firm, ripe breasts to tickle and tease him. One with long, dark curls to make a tent round their faces. One who breathed fire and passion. Electricity sparking in the night. Heat. Craving, begging, clawing fury.

And for him, Marcus Cornelius Orbilio, there *was* only one woman.

'You're a damned fool,' he told his shadow. 'Why all that shit about clapping her in irons? You know you didn't mean it. And why say you followed Sabina? Why not tell her the truth?'

He knew why, of course. Not only the way that bastard Diomedes ogled her, blue eyes lingering blatantly (and Orbilio felt a stab in his gut whenever he thought about it), but Orbilio was no fool. He'd seen the looks she gave that bloody quack. He'd watched her whenever Diomedes's name cropped up. Well, he was damned if he was going to tell her what really brought him to Sicily. A man had his pride, goddammit.

He ran both hands through his hair. He'd make her take that boat tomorrow, if he had to carry her down the gangplank over his shoulder. That slimeball wouldn't lay one finger on her, not one damned finger.

He passed under the dining room window, empty now, except for tantalizing smells of goose and hare and the inevitable mutton and heard his stomach growl.

In many respects, the timing of his arrival was perfect

– the very day Sabina had been killed – allowing him to inspect the body within hours of the murder, though interrogation had been one hell of a task. Collatinus had so many slaves, it was like being back in the army and Orbilio couldn't be sure they weren't breeding faster than he could take statements, because for every one on his list, three turned up at interview.

He paused to listen to the chirrup of crickets in the undergrowth and congratulated himself that hard work and diligence paid off. He had worked out who had committed this disgusting crime, but he had to have proof. Conclusive evidence to bring this bastard to justice, because without that, where was he? Grovelling to Callisunus, that's where!

The local magistrate would be none too happy when he discovered the Security Police tramping his territory, but he'd have to bloody well lump it. Orbilio was only a few months away from his twenty-fifth birthday, the date he legally became eligible for the Senate. Time was not on his side, there was no room for politics. Not at this level.

Orbilio's palms began to sweat. He was really beginning to need that drink.

One thing he couldn't fathom was Claudia's involvement. Money had to be at the core, but what did she hope to gain from passing an imposter off as Eugenius's granddaughter? She was clever, he'd give her that; no one in the family suspected a damned thing. But what happened to the real Sabina? Was she dead? And why wasn't Claudia upset that her partner had been killed? And in such an inhuman way?

Holy shit, the thought of raping a woman who was

paralysed made his gorge rise, but to do it while she lay dying was too disgusting to contemplate. What sort of pervert did that?

Orbilio's hand patted the dagger in his belt. Chances are he wouldn't need to use it, and even if he did, he'd have no compunction at killing the evil sod, his only regret would come from not taking him back alive.

Squaring his shoulders and straightening his neck, he turned his mind back to the job in hand. With the evidence he had gathered, there was only one man who *could* have killed Sabina, and to get the proof he needed, a search of the man's room was required. That was why he'd chosen tonight. Everyone was out of the way.

Fabius was visiting an army pal in Sullium, Linus was drowning whatever sorrows he might have in a wineshop in Fintium, Portius was hobnobbing with his clique of so-called intellectuals, and Aulus was out checking wool stocks with his father, who'd suddenly demanded to go over them. (Why he'd chosen this time of night when he could have chosen any time he liked and when the light would have been better, Jupiter only knew. But that was Eugenius for you. Liked to keep them on their toes!)

Plus it was Senbi's night off, Diomedes was moonlighting, Dexippus was stuck with totting wool stocks, which left only Antefa, Senbi's son, who'd been allocated to act as Orbilio's manservant and Orbilio had sent him off on an errand. Oh, and Piso, who liked to frequent the local brothel on a Thursday evening.

He had the place to himself.

The time for playing games was over. Stepping purposefully out of the shadows, Orbilio threw his cloak over his shoulder with a flourish and strode across the tiles.

The shutters were closed, as would be reasonable on a night like this, and there were no yellow lines round the door to suggest a lamp burning inside. Nevertheless, his dagger was in his hand as he threw wide the door.

Empty.

Closing the door quietly behind him, Orbilio fumbled for a light. The room was bigger and more opulent than he expected, the friezes quite remarkable. He had set down his lamp in preparation for the search when he heard footsteps. Light footsteps, those of a woman. Dancing footsteps, those of . . .

'Well, well! If it isn't our friendly neighbourhood snoop hard at work as usual.'

His heart began to pound, though he couldn't tell whether it was from pleasure at seeing her or from jealousy at why she was here.

That was not an outfit one wore for darning one's slippers.

She was wearing a stola of the very finest cotton. Midnight blue with midnight intent. It was girdled below the breasts to fall in delicious folds, clinging to her thighs and draping delicately over her feet. That alone could drive a man wild, never mind that the upper edge of her garment, the bit that fell from neck to elbow, had not been sewn but was pinched together at small, enticing intervals by a series of gold brooches. So many, a man could be sent insane unclipping them slowly, one by one, and kissing the place they'd been keeping. And that would be after he'd removed every bracelet, every anklet, every armlet, every pendant she had deliberately and desirously draped over every inch of bare, soft skin.

When he tried to speak, his voice failed him and he

resorted to a sickly smile, only to be skewered by the sort of glance that kills the shine on polished bronze.

'Enjoying yourself, are you, poking around in other people's secrets?'

He shrugged. It was his job and she bloody well knew it.

'Your trouble, Orbilio, is that you've got no one except yourself *to* enjoy. In fact, I hear they call you Bedspread these days, you've been turned down so often.'

He could feel his lips twitch and turned away before they let him down completely and showed teeth. She was angry, he could tell by the flush on her cheeks and the flash in her eyes, but Jupiter be praised, he was confident now of getting her on board that grainship tomorrow. He didn't mind admitting, either, he was going to get a real kick out of bursting her bubble.

He'd have to tread carefully – not only because she was softer than she made herself out to be, but burst it too quickly and she'd never forgive him, he'd be back where he started. The knack was to make her understand for herself. And if there was someone there, close at hand, a shoulder to cry on, during that long, long voyage back to Rome, was it Orbilio's fault he just happened to be that person . . .?

He noticed her finger was trailing the edge of the cupboard beside her.

'Good quality furniture,' he said quietly, wondering where to begin his search. The room was packed with shelves and cupboards for all his paraphernalia, the instruments, the apparatus, the drugs, the palettes, the balances.

'Why not? Physicians are worth their weight in gold pieces.'

Especially Greek ones. They were reputed to be the best in their field, although Orbilio had scant regard for these so-called skills. It was all too easy to bury your mistakes.

'You obviously think so, to be troubling him this time of night. Couldn't you sleep?'

He realized his mistake the instant the words slipped out, and unable to help himself his eyes jumped from her tantalizing outfit to the broad couch in the corner. How many times had she been here, he wondered, as red hot irons began to wrench his guts apart. Diomedes, blast his balls, must have set to work straight away and what a smooth operator he turned out to be. She'd been here only a week.

Claudia shot him a brittle smile. 'I've always found that early to bed, early to rise, my dear Orbilio, was the most wonderful piece of advice I was ever given the chance to ignore. Too many good times would have been utterly ruined otherwise.'

He pretended not to hear. Dammit, when he sailed halfway round the Mediterranean, he'd expected her to be in danger. He didn't expect her to be in some stranger's bed.

'What are your greasy little fingers looking for, anyway?'

Orbilio forced his mind back to his search. No doubt there was method in this wild disorder, but for the life of him he didn't know what, and he had to be careful not to show anything had been disturbed.

'A scalpel.' If he didn't find it tonight, he'd try again in the morning. '*The* scalpel, actually. The one that killed Sabina.'

Her mouth turned down in disgust. 'How revolting! How do you know it was a scalpel?'

He was back on level ground now. 'I examined the wound carefully. The blade that made it was sharp, thin, and the cut so precise it verged on the professional.'

She tipped her head on one side. 'Oh dear, have you been sniffing the hemp seeds again? I mean, you can't seriously suspect Diomedes?'

He closed one cupboard carefully, opened another. He lifted the lid of a tin and inhaled warily. It reeked of stale animal fats.

'Who else?'

He tried not to sound too cheerful. Means, motive and opportunity. Find that weapon and he had him bang to rights.

'Well for a start, he was with me when Sabina was killed. Or do you have me down as an accomplice?'

'I wouldn't put anything past you.' Orbilio shook a copper vessel, heard the liquid inside swish and untied the bung. Vinegar. 'But not on this occasion. However, by his own admission, Sabina had been dead between two and three hours. Ample time for him to nip into town and establish an alibi. Especially if she'd been dead, say, an hour longer. Just remember who showed you that short-cut in the first place.'

Claudia began to play with some little white pills Diomedes had been rolling and Orbilio realized she was thinking it through. Wonderful! Because when she did speak, it wouldn't be some trite remark about doctors being supposed to save lives rather than take them, it would be a remark worth waiting for. Several minutes ticked past as he continued rifling. Boxwood containers with papyrus labels. Limewood boxes preserving scented flowers. Bowls, scrolls, scoops and spatulae. Finally Claudia put down the marble palette and he shot her a quizzical look.

She picked up a pair of forceps with long, slender handles, hollowed jaws and interlocking teeth and waved them menacingly in his direction.

'If you're so clever,' she said, 'answer me this.'

'Mmm?'

'What are these for?'

XIV

Old Conky had been right about the weather. All traces of rain had vanished when Claudia opened her shutters on Friday morning, and it was back to bright sunshine and vibrant blue skies. The sea, calm and clear, brushed the sands below, while a gentle breeze rustled the leaves of the pines and the oaks and the spurge bushes. The most perfect of days for the hundreds of water-blessing ceremonies that took place, not only on Sicily but throughout the Empire in veneration of the goddess Flora. The most perfect of days to sneak off to see to that cockroach Aristaeus without anyone being the wiser.

This was a day of so many local ceremonies that she could be attending any one of them, watching sacred garlands consigned to the waters or posies laid around the tops of the wells.

The breakfast table looked suitably festive, bedecked with flowers and ribbons and, best of all, Claudia had the dining room to herself. But not for long. Matidia threw herself down, confiding she was in a real froth about what to say, because it was her turn to lead the procession. She wanted to make a speech, a really wonderful speech, better than all the speeches the other wives had given over the years.

'Flora won't give a brass fig,' Claudia said, flicking a

grape pip across the room. 'I think you're wasting your time.'

Matidia couldn't have looked more shocked had Claudia announced she'd spent last night humping every slave on the Collatinus estate and was going back for seconds. The atmosphere was broken when Portius swept into the room. There were more ringlets in his hair than tendrils on a vine and he'd rather overdone the antimony round his eyes. He looked like a polecat.

'Mother, I've solved the problem,' he said eagerly. 'Listen!

She prayed, and all her sister nymphs,
The three hundred nymphs that guard the groves,
The three hundred nymphs that live within the streams.
Three times she splashed the glowing hearth with wine,
Three times the flame, renewed, shot up to heaven.'

'Darling, that's brilliant. Oh, you're such a clever boy, Portius, what would I have done today without you!'

Claudia nearly choked on her plum. Did he never learn? Another straight quote! Still, he was on to a sure-fire winner with that little gem, combining the water-blessing with a reference to Sabina in her role as a Vestal, and it was unlikely the good matrons of Sullium knew enough about Virgil to trip him up.

Her ears blocked out the praise being heaped upon Portius's beautiful curls and she concentrated on what she had to do today. Orbilio said the grainship would drop anchor mid-afternoon, but she'd decided against breaking the news of her departure to the family until the last minute. It was, she felt, none of their damned business.

Therefore she'd packed her own boxes, quietly if not particularly efficiently. By now Cypassis was well on the mend (thanks to Diomedes), although she was still weak in the legs. Leaving Cypassis to rest but allowng Pacquia to believe her maid was with her, Claudia had managed rather well on her own, she thought.

As she was draining the last of her breakfast wine, Old Conky came thumping in, his face as black as yesterday's thunder.

'That's all we bloody need, half the workforce out.'

Matidia didn't even glance up from her speech. 'Hmm?'

'Some local kid's wandered off and our slaves have taken it upon themselves to search the ravines and gullies roundabouts.'

Claudia narrowed her eyes. 'Whose child was it?'

Aulus tutted. 'Who cares? What I want to know is, how am I supposed to meet production targets when half the bloody workforce has done a bloody bunk? Where's Linus?'

'What does the old man say?' asked Portius. 'About the search?'

Aulus tapped his temple. 'Going senile,' he replied. 'Said let them get on with it. Can you believe that? Look, where's Linus? I need him in the yard.'

In the privacy of her bedroom, Claudia slipped the belladonna in to the folds of her tunic, sending up a silent prayer to Jupiter, Bringer of Justice, that there was sufficient of the drug in her phial to lay that son-of-a-bitch Aristaeus flat in his grave. If she hurried, she might, just might, be in time to save the life of another little girl.

With her room at the front of the house, it was

impossible to miss that familiar ring of laughter as Orbilio exchanged pleasantries with Fabius. More boys' own army jokes, no doubt, but she waited until it fell silent before slipping away.

It had come as a complete shock last night, seeing Supersnoop standing where she expected to find Diomedes, and it rankled that merely looking at him brought on a strange tingle which left the Greek a very limp second. The tendril of a blue vetch entangled itself in Claudia's shoe and she paused to free it. Lust, my girl. Decent, honest lust. Accept it for what it is, then the quicker you'll find someone else to lust after. Because it didn't matter to Claudia that Orbilio wasn't interested in her. Why should it? If he had other fish to fry, what did she care? Dressed to the nines and absent from dinner last night, there was only one conclusion to draw. He'd been in some harlot's bed before snooping round Diomedes's room. So what? A small smile lifted one side of her mouth. So she hoped the bitch had crabs, that's what!

Nevertheless, seeing him there had taken her breath away. But it was only for a moment and perfectly understandable, amid that gruesome array of saws, chisels, clamps and catheters casting eerie, flickering shadows in the lamplight. Not to mention that half-size statue in the middle of the bloody room! So you see, it had nothing to do with Orbilio, it would have been the same no matter who.

Our master sleuth did not, of course, unearth the Secret Scalpel duly encrusted with dried blood from its hidey-hole. Honestly, it beggared belief that anyone would be stupid enough to set aside a special scalpel purely for butchering women, and after a while he looked where

Claudia would have looked in the first place. Amongst the other scalpels. Which was as unproductive as she expected it to be, too. Diomedes kept one full set in a special hinged box, but a whole host of back-ups and spares in the corner. Really! What did Orbilio expect? A knife with the word '*me*' written in dried blood?

By coincidence, they'd bumped into Diomedes in the hall shortly afterwards and he'd given them both such an odd sideways look that, had Claudia been in possession of such a trivial thing as a conscience, it might have made her feel guilty about going through his papers while Orbilio searched for mythical clues.

Much of yesterday's rain had drained away, but here and there – on blades of grass, in flower cups or in spider's webs – small drops clung on obstinately, twinkling in the sunshine like precious jewels of red and white and gold. Despite the lateness of the season, with the dust washed off the leaves, the vegetation, high as it was, still contrived to look fresh and vibrant. Even the parched grass looked more like a miniature cornfield at harvest time.

For obvious reasons, Claudia made her climb alone. It was the only way to tackle Aristaeus, and she'd left so many contradictory instructions that it was impossible for anyone to know exactly where she had gone or with whom. She scanned the horizon. Not that the trireme would come early, but the gesture brought Rome that little bit closer. Great! There were so many things to do there. A girl could get away from people she wanted to get away from (people like debt collectors and oily investigators), she could enjoy the Senate debates, the odd funeral oration (hypocrisy is a marvellous thing), the games and the races. Claudia totted it up on her fingers.

A speedy passage home would deliver her right at the start of the Victory Games. I ask you. Could life be sweeter?

The terrain up here was rugged, open and windswept, scrub and rock. Limestone, someone said. As if she cared what bloody rock it was! Her lungs were wheezing like a pair of faulty bellows as she stopped to examine the track. In theory the path she'd been following should have led her straight to Aristaeus. So why, suddenly, was there a choice?

She glanced back. The villa, Fintium, even Sullium – they were all out of sight now. Talk about remote! She looked again at the fork in the path. Both tracks led over peaks, and you could see woods on the other side. These southern slopes, of course, had been stripped of trees to make Sextus's warships during his seven-year battle for independence and the land had never recovered. It was stony and arid and sheep was the best you could do up here. But over the rise waited a different, cooler world where umbrellas of oak and beech and birch shaded and refreshed you with their dazzling display of autumn colours. Sweet chestnut trees scattered their shiny bounty across the forest floor, mushrooms and fungi adorned branches and boles. The red breast of a robin flashed across the path, the harsh churr of a jay rang out from the canopy.

Claudia chose the right-hand fork for no other reason than a green spotted lizard lay sunning itself on a stone and up here any company was better than no company. But it didn't take long to realize it was the wrong path – she was heading too far east. Damn! There wasn't much time to play with, either. Juno, suppose Aristaeus wasn't there? Suppose he was out, pretending to hunt for the missing child? She'd just have to lace his wine and pray no one else swallowed the wretched stuff. Hell, he was a recluse, wasn't he? Who else would there be to drink it?

'Lost, are you?'

Claudia nearly fainted with shock. She hadn't heard him approach, and with the crackle of twigs underfoot, still bone dry despite yesterday's downpour, that was quite some feat.

'Do you take me for a fool? Of course I'm not!'

She had to lift her head to see him clearly. Bearded, dark-haired, going grey at the temples, he wore the leather leggings of the huntsman. To prove the point, he carried a small, sinew-backed bow in one hand and a brace of coneys in the other.

'I was looking for a man called Aristaeus.'

'Then you be looking in the wrong place.'

His Sicilian brogue was as broad as they came. The huntsman stepped past her and set off along the track at a cracking pace, a quiver of arrows joggling on his back.

'At least have the decency to tell me where I should be looking!'

'I thought you said you wasn't lost.' He neither slowed down nor bothered to look over his shoulder.

'Disorientated. Look, can you help me?'

His sole response was a casual 'Nope.'

Claudia slapped her forehead with the heel of her hand. Men! She called after him. 'You know that girl who went missing in Sullium—'

'Nope.'

She was having to shout now. 'Aristaeus was the last person seen talking to her,' she lied. 'Do you know where I can find him?'

The last word she heard as he rounded the bend was another infuriating 'Nope.'

Claudia was out of breath by the time she caught up with him. He was in a small clump of pines, heading towards a clearing. Two shaggy dogs ambled up out of nowhere, their tails wagging as they stuffed their wet noses into his hand. Only then did she notice the square hut built into the hillside on the far side of the clearing. She fell back against the red, fissured bark of a pine.

'Holy shit, you're Aristaeus!'

She hadn't realized she'd spoken aloud until he said, 'So?'

Without pausing he disappeared inside the hut and she could see him hanging the rabbits on a hook on the wall. Shit! If she'd known the local huntsman was also the man who collected spiders' webs and was also the man who abducted children, she'd never have shown her hand!

The queasiness in her stomach made her search for some kind of makeshift weapon, and it came as something of a relief to note that he'd divested himself of his bow and arrows. On the other hand, she was able to see the dagger in his belt more clearly. Oddly enough, she didn't remember seeing it there before . . .

Claudia sidled over towards a pile of logs. There was a handy looking chopper embedded in that wood!

'So . . .' she began, 'tell me. Is that a statue of Diana over there?'

He was supposed to turn his head, she was supposed to yank out the axe, he was supposed to say 'Why?' and she was supposed to clonk him over the head.

Instead he said, 'Yep.'

It made sense, Diana being patron of the hunt and all that, she was bound to protect her own. Now what?

'Ooh! Is that a figpecker I can hear?'

Figpecker? *Fig*pecker? Up here? Claudia, are you nuts?

'I shouldn't think so, no.'

He was giving her a damned funny look, so she smiled. Show lots and lots of teeth, Claudia. Put the man at ease. He's frowning, so come on, more teeth. Dammit, she had no more left to show and he was still frowning. It was probably his special child-molester frown.

'What on earth's your dog doing?'

That did the trick. The second his back was turned she was yanking on the axe, trying to work it loose.

'Let me do that.'

A broad, brown hand closed over the handle and out it came, like a hot knife through honey. Aristaeus pushed his face towards hers. His eyes narrowed as they bored into her own, and Claudia shivered involuntarily. A cold sweat broke out on her back as she realized she was powerless under his glare. Mesmerized. Paralysed. Suddenly he swung the axe in the air and let out a gigantic bellow.

Claudia's eyelids snapped shut. Her senses were in sharp relief now. She could smell the woods on his tunic. Sharp. Bitter. The tang of leather, the sickly smell of blood. Rabbit's? Child's? She heard the swish of the axe, felt the whoosh of parted air. Time stood still. The blade crashed down. Crunch! She felt a sharp pain in her cheek. Terrified, her eyes opened. A pungent smell of sawdust hit her nostrils.

Aristaeus shot her another strange look as his thumb flicked off the splinter which had embedded itself in her cheek. Then he picked up one of the split logs and chopped that in two, before reaching for the other half. He repeated the process twice more before piling them into Claudia's shaking arms.

'You best put them on the fire.'

Claudia opened her mouth to protest, but no words came out.

'There's a pheasant in the pot, just needs warming up.' He shoved her not ungently towards the hut. 'Go on.'

She ought to refuse, she ought to confront him – but with a dagger in his belt and an axe in his hand, Claudia knew this wasn't the time. She had the belladonna. She could afford to humour him.

The fire sprang into life almost immediately, the pot sending out tantalizing clues to its contents. Pheasant, salt bacon, beans, onions – what the hell! So what if Aristaeus dies with a full belly?

The fire was blazing majestically but, despite the warmth of the day, Claudia couldn't help hunkering down right in front of it, rubbing her arms and her legs. She was cold to her marrow, as though, like the nymph Arethusa in Syracuse, she had been turned into icy cold water. The flames crackled and spat. The two dogs came up, panting and wagging their tails, and she absently tugged on their ears. They were strange creatures, long-haired, big-jowled, flop-eared, a type she'd never encounted before.

'Celtish, them.' His frame filled the doorway, blocking out much of the daylight. 'I calls 'em Chieftain and Druid and they helps me hunt boar.' He rolled up his sleeves before adding, 'Ugly buggers, aren't they?'

The smile transformed his craggy features and suddenly Claudia couldn't quite picture this man raping and murdering little girls for want of anything better to do. Still, who's to say what goes through a child molester's head? She watched him dish the stew into the bowls, pour beer into two cheap but attractive goblets. There were two of everything, she noticed, including beds, stacked one on top of the other like army cots. The woodsmoke was distracting. Cherrywood, unless she missed her guess. He beckoned her to eat. She could hardly refuse . . .

'Are you Celtish?' she asked, forcing her vocal chords to perform normally.

'Me?' He didn't look up. 'Never been off the island.'

'But you do . . . collect spiders' webs?'

'Yep.'

Claudia remembered Sabina's funeral – Hecamede being dragged away, her body limp and unprotesting but her eyes imploring justice. Justice against the man who collected spiders' webs. Justice against the man who killed her five-year-old daughter. Justice against the man Aristaeus. Who now sat across the table from Claudia, wiping his beard with his sleeve, pushing away his empty plate. Watching him top up his beer, Claudia didn't trust herself to speak. However, she had ample time to tip the belladonna into his goblet when he turned to prod the fragrant logs.

Had she wanted to.

'Why do you collect them?'

He shrugged as he sat down. 'I bottles 'em in vinegar.'

Well, you would, wouldn't you?

'Drink your beer,' he urged. 'I brewed it myself, so I knows it's good.'

Claudia wanted to say she didn't touch beer, it was a

thin, unwholesome drink brewed by Egyptians in the east and Celts in the west. (Hence her earlier question.) But there was an intensity in his eyes which was impossible to ignore and she took a tentative sip. It was bitter, as she expected. Perhaps *he* was trying to poison *her*? Codswallop. Snap out of it. But she couldn't. Nothing seemed real. Time had no meaning. The experience was weird, dreamlike, as though she was in a different, alien world and to her surprise, she found herself drinking deeply. And at that moment Claudia knew that, as strong as she was, her destiny lay in this man's hands. She would not, could not, fight it . . . and the feeling was as intoxicating as the beer.

'Why do you bottle spiders' webs?' she asked.

'They stops up small nicks.'

'Like shaving, you mean?'

'Yep.' He reached for the jug. 'I ships 'em to Syracuse. There's a good market when the fleet's in.'

She glanced at the two beds. 'Do you live alone?'

The jug came down on the wood so hard she thought it would crack. 'Why?'

It required considerably less mental agility than Aristaeus possessed to make the leap from this question (and he'd seen her eying up the cots) to her earlier remark about missing girls.

'Idle curiosity,' she said blandly. But somehow it sounded like an objectionable vice.

It was getting late. She had to be leaving if she was going to catch the boat. She rose, relieved he made no effort to stop her. From the corner of her eye she noted the square jaw, the set of his chin. Handsome? Not exactly. But confidence oozed out of every pore. The slow deliberation in his movements, the strength, the rugged magnetism. She realized suddenly that she was drawn towards this man, this recluse. This child molester?

But then everything today was topsy-turvy.

Maybe Hecamede was mad after all. Claudia visualized a love affair, its passion long spent. A woman spurned by the man she thought had loved her. Who left her pregnant. Years later, as her wits evaporated, every slight had become intensified until Aristaeus represented a walking personification of all things evil, a scapegoat for the worst crime she could imagine when her darling Kyana had gone missing.

Outside she noticed it was later than she thought, and with the race down the mountainside a sense of balance, of normality, was restored. More than once she ricked her back. Every jolt threatened to loosen a tooth, every boulder threatened to turn her ankle. Puffing profusely and red in the face, Claudia raced across the plateau to check the grainship in the bay.

What grainship?

The bay was empty! The bay was bloody empty!

She slithered down the hill to the villa, skidding across the atrium floor as she flung open Orbilio's room. That, too, was empty. His chest was gone, the table bare. Nothing to show he'd ever been here.

She grabbed hold of Senbi as he passed. 'Master Orbilio?'

'He left, madam.'

'And the ship?'

'That left, too. Were you hoping to catch it?'

She shot him a glare. 'Don't be ridiculous, I love it here.'

Behind her, Vilbia gurgled and giggled beside the pool under the careful eye of her nursemaid, pushing on the tiny wheeled trolley she used as a walking aid. Claudia brushed the hair from her eyes. Well, she thought, it's been that sort of a day. I got nowhere with the child molester, I missed my ship, I'm stuck with a backbiting miseryguts of a family and there's a sadistic killer on the loose. Still. She puffed out her cheeks. It isn't all bad. I've got four kittens to amuse me and there's the little one to play with.

She walked over to Vilbia and knelt down. 'Peekaboo!'

The tot looked up, broke into a sunny, gappy smile and held up her finger.

'Claudie, look!' she lisped. 'Vilbi got a bogey!'

XV

The letter which arrived the following morning did nothing to lift Claudia's spirits. It was from Leonides, warning her that he thought Master Orbilio might be on his way to Sicily . . .

She scrunched it into a ball and tossed it into one of the frankincense burners as she marched towards the peristyle. Call this a garden? A few poky cypresses, a handful of measly shrubs and a bit of statuary do not make for a place of rest and relaxation. You need chirruping birds, the heady scent of herbs, a knockout display of floral colour and a fountain that boils and bubbles all day long. *That* was a garden!

Through the arch Claudia could see the vegetable garden and the walls of the orchard beyond. Cypassis, her big-boned maidservant, was emerging with a boy as young as herself, possibly younger, and whereas her face wore the bright-eyed bloom of sated love, the lad had a glazed expression in his eyes and a stupid grin on his face. One didn't need to be a genius to deduce this was his first time.

The shadow of Diomedes fell over Claudia. 'That girl shouldn't be on her feet so soon after the fever.'

Claudia grinned. 'I don't actually think she's been on her feet, but I'll pass on your concern.'

In his hands he held a tray from which only Eugenius would consider eating – boiled fish, cucumber sauce and a bowl of some sort of milky gruel. Claudia grimaced and Diomedes laughed.

'Light diets for the invalid,' he said, 'though he's always complaining the food's too tough or not fresh enough.'

Aren't we all?

'I – I thought you might have been leaving us yesterday,' he added.

'Me? Good heavens, no. Whatever gave you that idea?'

She gave the physician another once-over. His eyes, blue and as measureless as the ocean beyond, danced with warmth and light as he watched her. His nose was finely chiselled, his mouth exactly the right size – and the way his hair fell neatly into place was unbelievably sexy. With Orbilio out of the way, she ought to give him another chance. She studied his hands. They were small, for a man, with long slim fingers. Another thought occurred to her. Doctors had to be ambidextrous – it would be interesting to see how that affected bedside techniques . . . Again she felt a stab of longing. Yes, indeed, it had been a very long time.

Whatever Supersnoop had insinuated, Claudia felt perfectly safe with Diomedes. One or two of his patients might well end up under the earth, but it wouldn't be intentional. Call it instinct, call it experience, she did not believe a man could look at a woman the way he was looking at Claudia right now and in the blink of an eye turn into a slavering, bloodthirsty ghoul.

However, if Cleverclogs wanted to bark up unsuitable

trees, who was she to stop him? Her personal opinion was that the killer was a local man, from Sullium or maybe Fintium, and assuming Orbilio was right and the murder weapon did turn out to be a scalpel, heaven knows there were enough physicians and apothecaries with access to one – not to mention the cutlers whose job it was to make the blessed things. Any old bod could get his paws on one.

Diomedes was saying how he thought she might have caught that trireme yesterday though he was jolly glad she hadn't, when Marius and Paulus came charging down the colonnade, yelling at the tops of their voices. Brandishing wooden swords, they lunged and thrust, dodging and darting, through the arch before attacking the vegetables beyond. No radish was safe as they rampaged across the neat, orderly beds. A trail of decimated leeks and quaking spinach leaves quivered in their wake.

'Nice boys.'

'Marius is all right.' The thick Greek accent was utterly beguiling. 'He's fallen under Fabius's spell, can't wait to join the army himself.'

'Eugenius must be thrilled.'

Diomedes grinned. 'The boy's only nine, he'll grow out of it.'

'Fabius didn't.'

'Fabius is an exception.'

True. Soft living and privilege are rarely given up voluntarily, and not for the first time Claudia wondered what had caused Fabius to turn rebel.

'Paulus, by contrast, is a right little b.s.t.d.'

That was what he did, Paulus, he abbreviated words to form a kind of code you had to crack to converse with him and Claudia knew it drove Eugenius up the wall, tutors coming and going like nobody's business. Because there was no continuity, problems were exacerbated rather than reduced and Piso's recent appointment aggravated the matter even further. His obsessive predilection for the cane had concerned more families than you could count and he had moved from pillar to post in consequence. Yet it was that very quality which Eugenius felt might, quite literally, whip the children into line. Time would tell . . .

'He's not alone,' she replied. 'Paulus thinks because he's born rich it gives him all sorts of rights. He—'

Eugenius's door opened. 'Diomedes,' Actë hissed, beckoning frantically. 'He's going spare in here!'

'Coming.' The Greek pulled a face of reluctance and carried the now congealed meal in to his patient.

Claudia's mouth twisted in displeasure as she thought of her steward's letter. Orbilio wasn't the only subject Leonides had raised. Rollo, the bailiff up at the farm, was after his instructions; should he start dunging the fields, cleaning the cellars and fumigating the wine press? Cocalus, the banker, had called twice, wondering what had happened to the 200 sesterces he lent Mistress Seferius for the weekend, and there was bad blood brewing between two of the slaves, an Iberian and a Parthian, which was causing friction throughout the whole household. Finally, he couldn't be sure, but Leonides had a feeling someone was syphoning off the household funds, since fifty silver denarii were unaccounted for.

Bugger.

From behind the laurel Claudia was aware of a door opening a mere fraction. It was such a furtive movement in such a bustly house that aroused the very curiosity it was undoubtedly trying to avoid. She bobbed back behind the bush. Cautiously, a woman covered head to foot in stone-coloured cotton tiptoed out and darted down to the bath house. Intrigued, Claudia counted to thirty then followed. The sight that met her eyes took her breath away.

'For gods' sake, Corinna, what happened?'

Her face was puffed up like a pig's bladder. Somewhere in there was an eye, she supposed. Corinna made a grab for her clothes, but not before Claudia had seen the vast expanse of purple bruising on her body.

'Has Diomedes seen this?'

Corinna shook her head.

'Well, he's in the house now, I'll call him over—'

A strangled cry cut her short. 'No!'

'Corinna, for pity's sake, you need medical help!'

'I'm fine. Really. I'm fine.' She tried so hard to smile. 'I – I went for a walk in the rain the other night. I tripped, I lost my footing and I fell down the hillside.'

Of course she had. 'How often do you . . . trip down the hillside?'

Corinna's shoulders sagged. 'Please, if you want to help me, keep this our secret.'

Claudia had been happy to dismiss her as a mouse – well, more a mole, really, since she rarely surfaced – and had she been the one with a claim to invisibility, rather than Sabina, Claudia could have understood it. Now it made sense, the stooped shoulders, the self-effacing colours, the downcast gaze.

'Give me one good reason.'

Tears welled in Corinna's eyes. Eye! 'Just promise me, Claudia. *Please.*'

She suppressed a shudder. What Linus would do if he found out she'd been talking, she didn't dare think about. The beatings were bad enough, but what he expected her to do afterwards was revolting. And it was getting worse. With increased frequency, he was finding new and more humiliating sexual practices to inflict upon her.

'I'll do no such thing. Your husband uses you as a punchbag and you expect—'

Corinna gripped her arm with both hands. 'You don't understand,' she wailed. 'It's *my* fault.'

'Balls.'

'It is, it's my fault, I'm a lousy wife, I know I am—'

'Corinna, stop blaming yourself for this.' Claudia picked up a sponge and began to bathe the bruises as gently as she could. 'You need vinegar compresses on those swellings and balsam where the skin's split.'

'I don't keep balsam.' Corinna didn't seem to have noticed that no promise was given.

'I'll get you some. Then, when you're better, you pack your things and leave.'

'I can't,' she said. 'I've got four children—'

'Take them with you.'

'Eugenius will never let me. He's got plans for them, plans in the business.'

Claudia steered Corinna into the warm water. A long soak would ease matters considerably, especially if she could put some chalk or something in it. She'd have to check with Diomedes – she could do it at the same time she picked up the balsam.

'When Eugenius dies, Aulus takes over. Aulus is still under sixty, so by the time he pops off, Fabius will be in his mid-, maybe even late fifties, probably with sons of his own to take over.'

'But—'

'But nothing, Corinna. Go back to your family, divorce Linus – ssh! I know it's difficult, but it's not unheard of and I'll stand witness for you.' Hell, she'd stand up in court and give such a graphic account of Linus's brutality, half the Collatinus fortune would end up settled on Corinna. 'It's the only solution.'

She wondered how grateful Corinna would be. In terms of gold pieces, that is. After all, she was still on the right side of thirty and if she put some weight on the old bones and smiled a bit, she could bag herself a catch in next to no time. She left her thinking it over.

Since only Pacquia and Cypassis were allowed in her room – that was Drusilla's decision, not Claudia's – she decided to pick up some titbits for the cat and was just heaping a plate with chicken, duck and sardines when a buzz of excitement went up.

The huntsman is coming, the huntsman is coming.

Claudia practically threw Drusilla's dinner at her. She didn't stop to consider what dangerous compulsion motivated her going into the hills with a man so big he could strangle her with one hand, a man whose hut was so remote her body could be picked clean by vultures, devoured by ants. All she knew was that there was something exciting, scary, intoxicating about a man who controlled you with his eyes and with his actions.

A huge boar covered much of the floor space. There was a pile of birds – quail, pheasant, partridge, songbird – and a few hares. No venison, which was a pity, although the last lot was as tough as old boots. In fact, it could well have been a pair of Fabius's. Smoothing her hair and straightening her tunic, Claudia picked her way to the outside door, where the kitchen slaves had congregated, plying him with wine and honey cakes. Her cheeks were flushed, her heartbeat rapid as she approached the huntsman.

Who was short and squat and approximately ten years older than Aristaeus.

Dammit, she should have realized there'd be swarms of the little beggars.

The pines offered shade and a delicious, heady scent. They also offered company. Magpies hopped and chattered in the branches, a squirrel noisily nibbled the seeds of the large, round, stalkless cones, fishing terns splashed into the waters. Claudia scooped up a handful of white sand and let it drift through her fingers. Against her will, the image of a tall, handsome, willowy woman formed itself in her mind, an image which it took considerable effort to dissolve until, finally, all that remained were a few fragments of blue glass.

Claudia shivered. At the Villa Collatinus, it was as though Sabina hadn't existed. Tears had not been shed, her name was never mentioned, her unsettling mannerisms never broached.

There is a formula for clearing your mind of difficult encumbrances. You tell yourself jokes, you sing dirty songs, you count to a hundred and fifty then you repeat one word twenty times. Claudia was on the second round of joke telling when she became aware of a small shadow beside her. Popillia, red in the face and desperately trying to suppress tears of anger, radiated so much heat you could have lit a bonfire with her.

'I hate you!'

Claudia pulled up her knees and hugged them. 'You resent having your bluff called,' she corrected.

'Do so hate you. Piso spanked me on my bare bottom and in front of my brothers, too. I hate you more than Piso!'

Claudia waited for the fire to burn itself out.

'It's not fair. I told Piso it was you who broke the pot then—'

'Then Piso spanked you for that, as well.'

'How did you know?' The blazing fury had been replaced by sullenness.

Claudia smiled. 'That's grown-ups for you. Still, you've learned one valuable lesson.'

'Yes I have! Never tell the truth.'

Claudia's grin broadened. Well, that too, but what she meant was: 'If you want something in future, try asking nicely. Blackmail never works.'

'It works for you, I heard you with Orbilio.'

Wow. This child has potential.

'I hate my brothers, too.' Popillia began to scuff the toe of her little leather shoe against the rough bark of the tree. 'They talk Greek and climb trees and Fabius has given them wooden swords to fight with. I only get dolls, it's not fair.'

It was the second time she'd said that in less than a minute.

'I regret to tell you this, young lady, but fairness is a myth. It's up to you – and you alone – not only to even unfair odds, but turn them round and make them work in your favour.'

'How?' It wasn't quite as sulky as previously.

'First things first. Greek's taught to boys, I know, but if you want, you can pick it up by asking Diomedes to teach you, can't you?'

Tentative nod.

'Same with trees; you can learn to climb those yourself. Start with a yew or something, they fork close to the ground. That'll get you admitted to the Boys' Club, won't it?'

Nod, nod, nod.

'Except that's not enough, is it?'

Popillia, who clearly thought it was, shook her head very, very slowly.

'Ideally you'll need an extra qualification, some advantage to make them so envious of you they'll beg you to join.'

Eyes grew big as fingerbowls.

Claudia patted the rock beside her. 'So why don't you and I share this,' she opened her handkerchief to reveal a luscious assortment of honeyed fruits, 'while I show you how to make a catapult?'

XVI

'Bite on this.'

Diomedes placed a stick between the child's teeth before rubbing the mixture of salt, saltpetre, wine and vinegar into the wound on his shin. The boy's eyes watered, but he didn't murmur even when Diomedes began to set the fracture with palm fibre splints. Behind them, the boy's mother hovered like a broody hen, clucking and soothing her chick and throwing out a big, brave smile every now and then, and although it wasn't her intention, it was she who was largely responsible for the boy's courage. He'd have gone through surgery without poppy juice before letting his mum know the doctor was hurting him.

Diomedes tied the last knot in place. 'And next time you play blind-man's-buff, stay away from the cliffs. That could have been a jolly sight worse, you know.'

He ruffled the boy's hair and, taking pity on the pinched, white face, popped a pastille into his mouth. He used them in the main for the expulsion of bladder stones, but they were flavoured with honey and wouldn't do the lad any harm.

'Take half a cup of this twice a day—'

'Cor, that stinks!'

It was the first time the child had flinched and Diomedes wasn't surprised. The root of the white mandrake had a stench which alone was often quite sufficient to put a person out. Even Diomedes had not grown inured to it.

The boy's mother pushed herself between her son and the physician. 'Thank you, sir. Thank you very much. He'll take it, sir, twice a day, like you said.'

'Be careful with it, it's very strong. No more than half a cup. Once in the morning, once at night.'

'Yes, sir. Thank you, sir.'

The slave woman backed clumsily out of the room, the boy already feeling the painkilling effects as he hobbled off on his bandaged leg, his mind busy with what capital he might make out of his injury among his peers.

Diomedes closed the door behind them. At least it made a change from the usual toothaches and stomach problems he was presented with. He wiped his hands on a towel and began to mix up a saffron salve for Gelon's inflammation. Gelon was the head fuller and Diomedes didn't know why those slaves who worked in the fuller's yard had more eye problems than those in the weaving sheds, or why the dyers seemed to suffer more from hardening of the limbs than anyone else, and frankly he didn't care. Collatinus ran so many slaves – far more than he had realized when he accepted the job – that it was tough enough simply keeping abreast of the coughs and colds, sores and swellings. Now there was an outbreak of whipworm to contend with, an intestinal parasite he was having serious trouble controlling. Zeus forbid it ever got into the house, his head would be on the block for that. The old man wasn't renowned for swingeing acts of forgiveness and he'd already made no bones that he hadn't wanted Diomedes here in the first place.

'Waste of bloody money, all you know is blood letting.

I could have bought my own doctor from the auctions for a fraction of what I pay you.'

Diomedes had continued to massage the wasted muscles. 'An unqualified slave with a few quack remedies is no good,' he pointed out. 'Look at the trouble the last one gave you.'

The old man had snorted. 'Cured my warts, didn't he?'

Diomedes turned him over. 'What did he prescribe when you had the fever, eh?' Cat dung and owls' toes tied to the body of a cat killed just before the moon waned!

Would Eugenius accept he'd recovered naturally? 'Pah! I tell you, if physics were any good, there wouldn't be three of the buggers buried up in Sullium – and not one of 'em a day over thirty.'

Diomedes had long since concluded it was Aulus who had pushed for his appointment, but Aulus would have no sway if the whipworm spread any further... and Diomedes didn't fancy moving on again.

Not yet.

Not alone.

Not since Claudia Seferius walked into his life.

He ceased rubbing saffron into the beeswax. She was beautiful and no mistake! A straighter back he'd rarely seen and she moved with the grace of a panther. She had a reputation for being prickly, but he'd only ever found her witty and charming. Then again – he recommended his mixing – she had a reputation for that as well. She was reputed to have charmed half the men in Rome, and Diomedes found that very easy to believe.

He transferred the ointment into a small ceramic pot, set it aside for when Gelon called during his meal break, and began measuring milk into a cup. Claudia was waiting for something, but to ask outright would mean showing his hand and he'd made one terrible mistake already. He ought to have remembered she'd recently been widowed and would still be grieving for Gaius. Zeus, he shouldn't have tried to kiss her last Tuesday! On the footpath in broad daylight, what was he thinking of! At the time, though, she appeared so full of life, so full of laughter, that he thought the signals he'd picked up were from a woman not just wanting to be kissed, but expecting to be kissed. Diomedes, he told himself, you're a fool to think you could rush a woman like Claudia Seferius.

In the corner a small bronze container bubbled on the brazier. Diomedes lifted it off and poured the boiling water over a pile of crushed peppermint leaves, oblivious of the aromatic scent. When it was cool, he would strain it and add it to the milk and, with any luck, there should be enough of the mixture to cure a week's worth of indigestion in the Collatinus household. Ordinarily he would have passed the half hour's waiting either reading or catnapping, but today there was too much to catch up on and he set about making another infusion, this time of horehound with wine for the cook's cough.

He'd spent as much time as he could with Claudia over the last few days, more time than he should, in fact, but it was important to him. Dare he risk a second kiss? Progress was good – look how grateful she'd been because he'd nursed that floozy Cypassis back to health. She could have taken that grainship yesterday. Why hadn't she? She hinted her stay concerned business with the old man, but Diomedes knew that wasn't the whole truth. From what he'd overhead, Eugenius's business with Claudia (and no one except the two of them seemed privy to exactly what this entailed) was pretty well concluded to the satisfaction of both parties.

Could her reluctance to go, he wondered, his heartbeat increasingly rapid, have any connection with himself?

There was one other hint, the most solid yet. If she wasn't interested in him, why spend so much time in his company?

Flimsy excuses. First she needed balsam, then she was back to enquire as to the efficacy of chalk in bathwater. She'd even demonstrated a close interest in the tools of his trade, selecting a pair of forceps with long, slender handles, hollowed jaws and interlocking teeth and asking, 'What's this for?'

When he told her they were pilecrushers, it was truly comical to note the speed with which she dropped them.

Another time she said, 'They found that child, you know,' and he pretended not to know about the missing kid. That way she was forced to spend yet more time with him as she recounted the story of the child – a boy, as it turned out – who had been frightened by the storm, ran for shelter then got himself hopelessly lost. He was eventually found over in Fintium by an old fisherman whom he cajoled into taking him out next day, little suspecting there was a storm of a very different kind awaiting his return.

Diomedes had smiled at the way she'd ended the story by saying, 'I'd have scalped the little bugger if he'd been mine.' She injected such energy into things!

Had he been born either wealthy or aristocratic, it would have been easy. Instead, as a Greek, he was acutely aware of the disadvantages weighed against him. Setting the cook's horehound infusion to one side, he moved across to his desk and opened an envelope of papyrus. Shaking a dozen or so tiny oval seeds of fenugreek into his mortar, he began to pound them with his pestle. In a poultice, they should sort out Antefa's boil once and for all. Yes, if only he'd been born patrician!

His lips pursed instinctively whenever he thought of Marcus Cornelius Orbilio. Everything about the man screamed class. Class and breeding, and he hadn't realized Claudia knew him so well until he saw the two of them together on Thursday night – Orbilio in his fancy scarlet cloak, Claudia in that sensuous midnight blue creation.

Impossible to find words to describe the sense of loss, of failure, that he experienced in that split second. They were two of a kind. Same class, same background – what chance did a Greek physician stand?

That night Diomedes had prayed to Aphrodite – oh, how he had prayed – for help, and to his utter astonishment the goddess dismissed Orbilio the very next day, demonstrating in that one Olympian gesture that there was no stigma attached to being a doctor. It's a respectable profession, Aphrodite was telling him, requiring skill and qualifications well beyond the abilities of the average man. You should not feel shame.

Thus his spirits lifted and his confidence soared with them.

But however buoyed up he was by Aphrodite's support, Diomedes appreciated it was far too soon to moot the subject of marriage. Nevertheless, he worked on it as skilfully as he worked on his remedies. Claudia was young, beautiful, suggestible even, and Diomedes more than most understood the immense power of sex. It could pull a person against their will, draw them like a fish on a line – and women, especially, were susceptible. His Claudia would be no different.

Content with progress on both his love life and Antefa's troublesome boil, he decided it was time to stretch his legs. Automatically patting the little stone statue of his healing god, Asklepios, he turned left to follow the dusty track up the hill. The view from his quarters might not be the worst in the world, but even a physician grew sick of certain smells and the stink of urine from the adjacent fuller's yard was one of them.

The scenery was breathtaking, the air redolent with pine and spurge and wild rosemary. The African Sea, today as blue as forget-me-nots, tickled the sands under a cloudless sky while sheep bleated contentedly beneath the noonday sun. He would miss this land, he thought, but come spring it would be time to move on. To move on, the way he had always moved on, forever seeking his sacred goal. So often in the past he had been on the point of giving up, fearing his aim to be as unattainable as immortality itself – but now, since meeting Claudia, he was not so sure. He felt his fists clench. If only—

The raucous cry of a jackdaw cut in and he paused to look down on the villa, its red roof dwarfed by the distance between them. Miniature figures dashed hither and thither, always at someone else's beck and call. So many of them! When he took on the job, Diomedes had no conception of the size of the Collatinus empire, nor that he would be required to doctor the entire contingent of slaves single-handed. For the most part, his previous positions had entailed little more than pandering to the problems of over-indulgence by prescribing fresh air and exercise and a decent diet. Well, excess was no problem in this family, quite the contrary, but he hadn't expected to have to earn his living as a slave doctor. Diomedes plucked a blade of grass to chew on and continued his climb.

These rocks, these coves, these shrouded mountain ridges seemed to him more Greek than Roman, even down to the reserved and sombre townspeople, and he felt very strongly that the island ought to have remained in his countrymen's hands. Instead it had been wrenched from their grasp, and it was unfortunate that the very people who had founded democracy should have taken this rugged and beautiful island from the Sicels and then promptly allowed it to be ruled by a succession of tyrants. As a result it fell under Roman dominion and now his own land, too, was a Roman province. He was taught as a child to be proud to be a part of the Empire. Well, he wasn't. He was Greek, and as such he was viewed by Romans – especially Romans like that arrogant bastard Orbilio – as second rate. Diomedes pursed his lips. We shall see, he thought. We shall see who's top and who's not.

A fat, stripey bee came buzzing up to check whether this newcomer was a walking pollen factory, decided he wasn't and buzzed off elsewhere.

One thing had been bothering him these past two days. A small matter, but it nagged him like an obstinate itch.

Someone had been in his room.

In the few months since his arrival, Diomedes had become aware that someone was regularly filching one of his eye drugs. Minute quantities were being taken at a time, but he had quickly noticed that one particular copper vessel was getting gradually lighter and now he weighed it once a week on his balances to prove it. This didn't bother him. Someone in the house had poor eyesight but possessed nous enough to correct it and stealth enough to ensure no one else found out. Sooner or later the supply would run dry and the culprit (he suspected it was Senbi) would be forced into the open. Here Diomedes was content to wait.

This other business was altogether different.

It was Thursday, the day it rained. He had been in Sullium on a private commission, checking on the leadbeater's daughter who had swellings in her neck. During his absence his room had been searched.

The minute he returned home, he knew he'd had a visitor. The rain had cleared the air outside, sharpening his sense of smell, and the instant he opened the door his nostrils picked out the recent burning of lamp oil over and above the usual and familiar medicinal scents. The eye-drop thief called only during the daytime but it was possible an exception had been made, so Diomedes had weighed the little copper container on his balances – and found no change. Immediately on his guard, he checked his drugs and poisons before moving on to his instruments, but these were where he had left them, neatly facing outwards or upwards to suit his requirements.

It was only when he opened the box in the corner that he made his discovery. His old (and indeed blunt) double-ended scalpel, the one with the bronze handle, was lying upside down. It could not have been a mistake on his part – he always laid his instruments in a precise manner and since this was a dissection scalpel, never used, its position never varied. The handle end doubled as a spatula, and as such faced up. The person who had gone through the box was a layman and would be unaware of this when he replaced it . . . spatula down.

No, there was no mistake. The question was, what should he do about it?

As he paused to catch his breath, Diomedes realized he was almost upon the exact spot where Sabina had been killed. The flattened grass, parched and yellow, had sprung up again after the rain, there was absolutely nothing to suggest anything sinister had taken place, yet in spite of himself and his profession, he shivered.

Claudia was of the opinion that the family were not touched by their kinswoman's death, but she didn't know them the way he knew them. Sabina had been away for thirty years, they had practically forgotten her existence and when she did return they neither liked nor understood her. They might not be driven by grief, but they had been undermined by another emotion. Fear.

Fear of what, he didn't know. Fear that because Sabina's sanity had left her, the same might happen to them? Fear of a monster on the loose? Perhaps just fear of the unknown? Even as their doctor he was unable to plumb those intimate depths, but the Collatinus clan did what many families do in times of crisis.

They pretended nothing had happened.

To his right, a small bird warbled from the top of a thorn bush. He ought to be getting back, he thought. One of the weavers was calling about his infected toe, Dexippus had promised to repay those two denarii, and the Penates ceremony was scheduled for dusk. But the

Greek's eyes remained fixed to the place where Sabina had died.

Many people had seen the corpse in its raw and shocking state, not only himself and Claudia, but when the news was out, the entire family clambered up here to gawk.

Yet there was something very wrong about Sabina's corpse.

Diomedes wondered who else had noticed the discrepancy.

XVII

The ceremony of the Penates was an annual event, a sacrifice to the gods of the household store-cupboards who watch over and protect the stocks for the winter. In Rome this took the form of a morning ceremony up on the Velia, after which families gathered for private celebrations. A quick check of the kitchen, a generous toast; on to the grain stocks, a generous toast; down to the cellar, a generous toast. By the time it came to making the actual sacrifice, everyone was pretty well oiled and it ended up a wonderfully festive occasion hugely enjoyed by one and all, if the hangovers were anything to go by.

Claudia had no idea why, in the Collatinus house, it should be celebrated at dusk. If celebrated was the word, and she had her doubts here.

She tapped her foot impatiently. There was still a half-hour to kill, and she categorically refused to spend more time with these people than was necessary. Dear Diana, a girl daren't set foot outside her own room these days for fear of tripping over hovering physicians. Then there was Portius poncing on about 'his' poetry, Matidia banging on about those bloody cushions for the banqueting hall or else it was a summons to Eugenius.

Eugenius! Any more stories about that damned war and she'd scream. All right, so the island had been in decline for the last quarter century and maybe its towns and villages *had* decayed into nothingness, but you couldn't blame Sextus for every crumbling ruin or every bankrupt landowner.

'He incited the slaves to rise up,' Eugenius had argued. 'Without that, we'd all have remained prosperous.'

Whinge, whinge, whinge. Good life in Illyria, the man was as rich as Midas, what more did he want? He'd come through the war unscathed, which is more than many could boast. Penalties for supporting the wrong side were harsh – in many cases, whole towns were razed – and as for the slaves, could you blame them for fighting for freedom? They had prayed to Feronia, goddess of liberty, and believing she'd sent divine help in the form of Sextus's rebellion, they flocked in their droves to Sicily. But, Juno, how wrong could you be! When Augustus clawed his province back, some thirty thousand fugitives from the mainland were rounded up and returned to their owners, leaving a staggering six thousand unclaimed. Six thousand souls on whom Feronia turned her back.

They had been impaled, every last one of them.

And Eugenius Collatinus had watched.

In fact, he'd turned it into a right bloody picnic and taken the whole damned family along.

A gong clanged in the atrium outside her door, frightening the kittens and alarming their mother. Claudia spent twice as long soothing them as was necessary, indeed anything to postpone the time when she would have to stand among these ghouls and smile and be polite and witty and charming. When, finally, she could no longer put off the evil moment, she found the whole family assembled on the far side of the pool. Lamps flickered, bringing the farming friezes to life. Lambs gambolled, bees swarmed, corn was threshed. Rich unguents scented the room, herbs were strewn on the floor.

There was Linus, his distinctive forehead shining in the artificial light, looking bored. Portius, weighed down with jewels, nibbled a broken nail. Matidia, in yellow wig and crimson stola, looked like a candle and you could hardly see Corinna for cloth – it was draped up her neck, down her arms, over her head, presumably to hide the bruises from children who showed no interest in her whatsoever. Paulus amused himself by pulling Popillia's hair out of its clips. Marius stood proudly to attention beside his uncle Fabius, who today wore a scowl to match Popillia's.

Eugenius was apparently unwell and couldn't attend, so it was Aulus who clapped his hands, took one majestic step forward – and stumbled. His eyes were glazed, his jaw loose. Claudia reckoned he must have been drinking solidly since daybreak.

Behind him, the slaves, factory as well as household, hung back in the shadows. They stood stiffly, exchanging the occasional glance, biting the occasional lip. Considering Sabina had been murdered on Tuesday and buried on Wednesday, it was hardly surprising they were still jittery on Saturday. Gossip was rife enough – a maniac lurking in mountainous crevices, waiting to pounce on helpless women – without Marius pitching in with tales dear old Uncle Fabius had told him. Like how in one battle the centurion had thrust his sword deep into a barbarian's throat, up through the top of his skull and blood had gushed out of his eyes . . . dear me, who wouldn't have dropped the sacrifice?

It was only a tray of corn and lentils, spelt and honey and, yes, she had to admit that it made one hell of a sticky mess, but Aulus went ape. The slave had done it on purpose, he insisted. A slur on himself, his family, his ancestors and his household gods. Deliberate sabotage of this most solemn of occasions.

The boy shot a haunted glance towards Eugenius's quarters. 'But the Master—'

That, although he couldn't have guessed, was his undoing. Whether it was the drink or the build-up of years of frustration from constantly deferring to Eugenius, Claudia would never know, but Aulus exploded.

'*I am the Master*!' he roared. 'Do you hear me? I'm the Master, and I'll teach you to fuck up my ceremony, you clumsy bastard. Everybody! Outside! I'll have no blood spilled on my floor.'

Blood?

Aulus clapped his hands. 'Antefa, take this piece of filth out of my sight. You, fetch some torches and light up the yard.'

The boy's face had gone white. 'Wh-what are you going to d-do?'

Aulus mimicked his slave's quivering. 'I'm going to chop your bloody thumbs off, boy, that's what I'm going to der-der-do!'

A gasp rose from the slaves before they filed silently towards the rear of the building and into the square. Aulus barked an order to his steward. Claudia glanced round the rest of the assembly. Dexippus had a strange light in his eye. Actë looked sick. Diomedes was pushing his way towards another exit, presumably to fetch his case. Linus had a hand on his eldest son's shoulders, propelling him towards the orchard. Fabius whispered something in Marius's ear. Finally, only Claudia and Aulus remained in the atrium. Senbi passed by, weighing an axe in his hand, wearing the sort of grin that a man wears when he particularly enjoys his work. The splash of the fountain made her feel queasy, but Claudia kept her face expressionless.

'What's your problem?' The contempt in Aulus's bellow could be heard in Sullium. 'Think it's too harsh, do you?'

'I do, yes,' she replied slowly, 'but more importantly I think if a man feels the need to establish his supremacy in such a brutal manner, then he's totally failed to hit his target.'

The point was further emphasized when the boy watched his thumbs fall from his hands without so much as flinching – though whether Aulus realized his servant had retained moral superiority Claudia very much doubted.

XVIII

'Who are you writing to?'

Claudia surveyed the small round face which thrust itself in front of her. Marius might well be nine going on ten, but he had yet to add character to his features, which remained typical of rich boys everywhere who have been given everything they want in terms of toys, education, attention and flattery. Everything, that is, except the one thing they truly need. The love and attention of their parents. Perhaps it was no bad thing he'd latched on to Fabius with a single-minded obsession. It might yet be his salvation from a world of sycophants and sybarites, which was the way his other uncle, Portius, was heading.

'My sister-in-law,' she replied.

In fact she was composing a reply to Leonides, for nothing in the world would have induced her to write to that frightful old windbag Julia.

'I don't know why girls bother to learn to write.' He gave a superior sniff. 'It's not as if they do anything with it.'

Claudia ignored him.

'I speak Greek, you know, and I'm only nine. Even boys in Rome don't start to learn Greek until they're eleven, do they?'

Claudia decided not to dignify that with an answer

either. She just hoped she was around when Popillia trotted out the two sentences she was so earnestly learning by heart.

'Not that I'll need Greek in the army.' He stood stiffly to attention, shoulders back, chest out, chin up.

Claudia's pen scratched over the parchment. '*I appreciate your attempts to conceal my whereabouts from Master Orbilio . . .*'

'Bet you don't know how to make camp.'

She laid down her pen. Did this boy say *bet*?

'How much?' she asked.

A calculating look crept into Marius's eyes. 'My bulla against that ring there.'

The boy knew his precious gems, then. Claudia eyed up the amulet round his neck, the little golden globe given to him at birth which was supposed to protect him until he was old enough to go it alone. It would weigh at least an ounce.

'You're on.'

Claudia held out her hand and when he did the same, she made his eyes pop by clasping his wrist, warrior-style. Before he could recover from the shock, she was reciting as fast as she could.

'Find a place which offers grazing and fresh water, but without cover where an enemy might be able to hide. Mark out the corners with coloured flags before digging first the outer defence then the inner. Only when that's completed can you pitch tents, erecting the centurions' tents at either end of the horseshoe.'

She held out her hand, palm upwards to receive the bulla. Spanish gold. Nice.

Marius stomped off, his face like thunder, and Claudia

slipped the bulla into her tunic. Was it her fault her father had been an orderly in the army? But back to the letter-writing. Poor Rollo. She had absolutely no idea what he should be doing up at the farm, but if he wanted to start dunging fields and fumigating presses, let him have his bit of fun.

'Is that a l.t.r. to R.m.?'

Dear Diana, what was it about the garden this after-noon? Usually the place was deserted, but so far she'd had to fob off Diomedes (who was fast beginning to resemble a limpet), then Matidia, then Marius – and now Paulus.

'Y.?'

Paulus shrugged. 'Just w.d.r.d.'

'Then wonder elsewhere, this is private corre-spondence.'

Claudia hoped that if she ignored Paulus he'd find someone else to annoy and she concerned herself with what Leonides could say to mollify Cocalus the banker concerning the 200 sesterces of his she'd invested on that charioteer in the Circus Maximus. It was a cumulative bet, that one, and she was all set to win a full 600 on the Red faction – until Blue put a hub through the spokes of Red's chariot on the last-but-one turn. Bugger.

'Are you going to the t.t.r. in A.g.t.m. tomorrow?'

'Paulus, unless you move p.d.q., you'll feel the full force of my foot up your a.r.s. Now hop it!'

Odious child.

' . . . *therefore suggest you tell Cocalus* . . .'

Hang about, what did Paulus say? T.t.r. in A.g.t.m. Theatre in Agrigentum. *Theatre?* Claudia clenched her fists with joy. Theatre! She blew a mental kiss to Hercules, patron of the arts and leader of the Muses. Fun and pantomime, laughter and music. The crush of the crowd, the colours of the tunics, the blare of the trumpets, the click of the castanets. People. Milling, spilling, fighting and thrilling. She could almost smell the freshly painted scenery, hear the rattles of the sistrum. Thank you, thank you, Hercules, how can I thank you enough! Tomorrow – Tuesday – Claudia Seferius will be there. And the change of scenery won't hurt Drusilla, either. She comes from Egypt; her blood must be used to travelling.

Only first that damned letter to Leonides. '... *tell Cocalus I'm very sorry, but the money is locked in my room and—*' And what? Think, think. '... *and unfortunately I seem to have come away with the key.*' Well done. '*Sell the Parthian, he's been nothing but trouble...*'

'Mind if I join you?'

Claudia's pen slid from her hand, leaving a thick trail of black ink right the way down her pale blue tunic. She could feel teeth grinding together.

'Eugenius, what a charming surprise.'

Bugger, bugger, bugger.

Two burly slaves deposited their bantamweight burden in his special ivory chair. Actë tucked the blanket round his legs and over his feet before heading off to supervise the preparation of her employer's meal. Again Claudia acknowledged the dignity with which she went about her duties, carrying herself straight, her face composed and tranquil, as though she was mistress of the house rather than a slave.

'Love letter?' Eugenius asked, 'accidentally' brushing the curve of her breast.

'Not exactly,' she replied, landing a stinging slap on

the wizened hand, and eliciting a throaty chuckle from its owner. How did Actë cope with the groping? Probably didn't notice, it happened so frequently.

'I'm writing to my sister-in-law to enquire about the health of my dear stepdaughter, Flavia. Such a sweet girl, I miss her dreadfully.'

Like hell. If I never see that miserable little frump again, it's still too soon.

'Wasn't she jilted at the last minute?'

Claudia did not wish to discuss Antonius Scaevola. Not now. Not ever. Neither did she intend to allow the conversation to turn itself on to the subject of marriage, which it invariably did whenever Eugenius was present, the crafty old sod.

'Eugenius, there's something I wanted to ask you.' She smiled so sweetly, he couldn't possibly take offence at the sudden change of subject. 'That blue dye of yours, the one that comes out the colour of wild anemones, I was thinking about using it as a livery for my slaves.'

That should set tongues wagging in Rome. Having all your servants dressed in the same colour was by no means uncommon, but a blue as arresting and vibrant as this should send more than one patrician cross-eyed with envy. Including Eugenius? He clearly prided himself on his bleaching techniques, even the family wore white – but then it's cheap, isn't it, you miserly old buffer?

Eugenius sucked his teeth. 'There's enough fleeces in the clipshed,' he said at length. 'I'll arrange for some to be spun into cloth and dyed – providing,' he laid his hand over hers and squeezed, 'you accept it as a gift. From an old friend of your husband's.'

A bribe, you mean. And actually, Eugenius, this is the

first time you've mentioned Gaius – and I've been here nearly a fortnight.

'I'd be honoured.' She leaned forward and tapped him playfully on the knee. 'And in return I'll send you some of our finest vintage wine.'

One taste and you're hooked, my old son. My livery is a one-off, whereas you . . . You'll be placing orders for my wine year after year after year.

'Did you say something, my dear?'

Claudia shook her head. 'No. Why?'

'It sounded like "gotcha", and I wondered whether it was another of those strange local oaths.'

She trusted bending down to recover her reed pen would account for the rush of blood to her face. The ink had run out to form a black, tarry puddle right in the middle of the path.

'I never got the hang of the local patois.' Eugenius had his eyes closed. 'When Aulus was born, I was employing translators because at that time no one on the island spoke Latin, it was a straight choice between Greek and Sicilian.'

Here we go. First it would be how he came here with his pregnant bride at the age of nineteen because he could see Sicily was losing its old identity and he wanted to get in at the beginning of the new one. Then it would be how this wasn't an easy island to grow fat on.

'Not that this was an easy island to grow fat on.'

'You surprise me.' Now how far had she got with that letter to Leonides? Had she covered Cocalus the banker yet?

'Oh no. Augustus might have solved the language difficulty, but he created problems of an altogether differ-ent kind when he gave away prime tracts of arable land to his war veterans. That didn't concern me, of course, I'd seen this coming, which is why I exchanged my grain fields for pasture.'

'Had you?' Yes, she'd covered Cocalus.

'Then there was the tax situation. Five per cent on everything that comes in, five per cent on everything that comes out.'

'Really?' Ah, she was sacking the Parthian, that was it.

'My biggest problems, though, came about when Augustus scrapped the tithe system in favour of stipends, because these were then assessed on landholdings.'

'Terrible.' No doubt the trouble was over a woman. That stupid Parthian couldn't keep his dongler to himself if his life depended on it. Which in the case of the Iberian, it well might.

'So we have to send cash instead of goods, and he's levied a poll tax on top.'

'Never!' However, if Leonides kept his mouth shut about the reason behind the sale of the Parthian, it ought to raise five hundred sesterces.

'Did I tell you Augustus came to Sicily eight years ago?'

The first stop on his tour of the Empire. 'No.'

'It was his first stop on a tour of the Empire . . .'

Faced with the prospect of liquidating five hundred lovely sesterces, Claudia switched Eugenius off completely. With a sum like that she could repay her most pressing debts, although it would be foolish not to set aside a hundred, because if she was back in time for the Victory Games she could double her investment. There was always a mock battle or two, and she'd never put her money on the wrong side yet. So if she kept, say, two hundred to one side . . .

'. . . which nets me only 3 per cent, whereas you'll be netting nearly 10 per cent, won't you?'

Claudia was on the point of admitting she frankly had no idea of the profit margin, when what he was saying sank in. Seferius wine brought in an annual profit of 10 per cent.

Ten per cent.

Profit.

She would need an abacus to work out exactly what that meant in terms of bronze sesterces, but she didn't need an abacus to know it meant a lot.

'Eugenius!' She jumped up from the bench, threw her arms round him and kissed his papery cheek. 'Have I ever told you how wonderful you are?'

XIX

High in the hills, rain was falling as sleet and the man Melinno shivered under his cloak. He'd got a fire of sorts going but it didn't throw out much heat, it was all he could do to keep the rain from dousing it. He clutched his pack to his stomach, for comfort as much as for warmth, and found neither.

He'd fucked up again. It was all he were bloody good at, fucking up. Fucking up and making baskets. Aye, he could weave a good basket, could Melinno. His father had made them for an olive grower, such good baskets that the merchant gave him his freedom. Aye, first generation freeborn and nimble with the withies was Melinno, and his da was real proud of him. They worked side by side until the wasting disease claimed him, then Melinno turned his hand to weaving mallow fibres as well. Howay, who'd have thought them fish baskets would sell so fast? Like iced wine in summer they went, just because they could drain the whey out of curdled milk and save buying a separate basket. Business was booming when he met Sulpica. They wed and everything was grand – until *he* killed her.

There's no justice, Melinno thought, coughing into his hand, no fucking justice. That bastard's still living the high life.

Melinno couldn't believe the gods were not on his side – no, the problems he had right now were his own making. What with the weather and all, he'd been so busy watching out for them one-eyed giants that he'd completely missed the turn-off to the east. Trudged right round the Great Burning Mountain, he had, and it were only thanks to an old goatherd he'd missed Hadranum. Aye, that were a close call. That were the town where Vulcan's sacred shrine stood guarded by a thousand slavering hounds from Hades. They welcomed pilgrims, the goatherd said, but sniffed out disbelievers and tore them to pieces. Melinno shuddered. What a way to go, eh? Well, he were certainly no pilgrim, and if he'd got any closer, they'd have sniffed him out and no mistake. Then who'd have avenged Sulpica?

Sulpica. The very name drove a pain through his belly like the rip of a knife. The Fire God had foreseen the murder of the Divine Julius, hadn't he, and he'd spewed his flames ten miles into the air as a warning. That were nineteen summers back, the same time Sulpica's mother had brought her into the world. Melinno scrubbed his eyes with the heels of his hands.

'Fuck you, Vulcan!' he shouted, but the Fire God wouldn't be able to hear in this wind. As he well knew.

Once clear of the Lands of the Cyclops, he'd made better time, but it had taken him far too long just to reach Henna here – leastways, as close to it as he ever wanted to get. The navel of Sicily, they called it. Melinno thought that if Sicily ever got piles, Henna was where it would get them.

Perched like an eagle's eyrie right up on the island's highest point, all its buildings were of coarse and pitted tufa, making the town as grey and unwelcoming as any grave. Why, no; he were better off down here and he hadn't much fancied mixing with them dour Sicilians neither. You couldn't understand a word they spoke, so how could you trust them? He lifted his head and looked across the lake to the hilltops hidden by raincloud and spat. Janus, what he'd give to leave this hell-hole!

He spread his fingers over the fire in an effort to warm them, but the wood was green and he was in danger of choking long before. The outdoor life wasn't for him. Basketmakers were townsmen, he were like a fish out of water up here. Waiting for this latest bout of coughing to subside, he counted the days. Three, now, since his sputum turned brown.

To take his mind off the ache in his chest, Melinno rummaged in his pack for that chunk of bread and sheep's cheese. He'd been filling his canteen down in the river Chrysas, by chance hidden by one of them big, grey boulders when a shepherd strolls up. As luck would have it, the bloke got caught short, so while the poor sod squatted with his back turned, Melinno filched his lunch. He bit into the bread, but it tasted like sawdust and he shoved it back and re-sealed his pack.

It were odd, that. He'd not eaten for two days, yet he didn't feel the least bit hungry. He just kept shivering all the time, and that were long before this fucking sleet set in. A wolf howled from the far side of the lake.

'Sod off!'

Shouting don't deter wolves, but it didn't half make Melinno feel better. More in control.

He rested his head on his knees. In control, eh? That were a joke. He couldn't control this shivering and shaking, he couldn't control the tears which coursed down his cheeks. Or this bloody cough. It racked his bones and left his lungs peppery, and he wished it'd go away.

Janus, he was tired. It were all this travelling, he supposed. Mind, away from the slopes of the Cyclops, the terrain had got easier, the hills rolling and rounded rather than steep and savage, with streams and rivers and sweet, fresh pastures. You'd have thought he'd have felt less tired, wouldn't you? That his legs would've not felt so wobbly and that, perhaps if he'd had more strength in them, he might have braved that hilltop town on a night like this.

Howay, it'd look better in the morning, after a kip. As the wolf howled again, he looked out across the lake, pockmarked with silver spots of driving sleet, then his ears picked up a scraping sound close by. His hand flew to his dagger.

'Mind if I join you, mate?'

The stranger hovered at the far side of the clearing, which meant he was either unsure of his welcome – or he was checking out the camp. Either way, Melinno wasn't bothered. His funds had run out long ago, maybe this bloke had something worth nicking.

'Feel free.' He beckoned him over to the fire, and saw he wore a stout, old-fashioned goatskin cloak. Better protection than his own useless wool thing.

Settling himself beside the flames and chafing his hands together, the newcomer was in his teens, brash and cocky. 'You on the run an' all?'

'No.'

'I am.' The boy nodded in the direction of Henna and

his face split into a grin. 'Give the rozzers the slip, I did, and cor, you should have seen the chase I give 'em.'

'Why?'

'Well I didn't wanna get caught, now did I?'

'I meant, why are you on the run?'

'Oh that.' The grin became a grimace. 'Yeah, well. I'd stopped to ask this geezer if he'd like to give Socrates his money, see.'

'Socrates?'

'Yeah, Socrates.' The reflection of the flames flickered and flashed on the steel in the boy's hand. 'And he kinda says no, so – well, you get the drift, eh?'

Melinno felt his gut lurch. Far from being in a position where he could steal the boy's cloak, he was more likely to end up jackal fodder.

Think, man, think! He wondered what Sulpica would do, but Sulpica was no longer with him, he couldn't feel her spirit in this hostile place.

'So what you on the run for?'

Melinno was poised to say, for the second time, that he wasn't on the run, when he realized that the gods had sent him a message. A fellow criminal would be treated as a friend.

'I'm not . . . why, aye, I can trust you, can't I, seeing as how we're both in the same boat, like?'

'Betcha sweet life, mate.'

More than likely.

'I'm wanted for . . .' he couldn't think what he might be wanted for ' . . . murder.'

'Oh, yeah?' The insolent sod was picking his nails with his knife. 'Who d'you kill?'

'Propertius, the brickmaker – oh, you'll have heard

about it.' He jerked his head in the direction of Henna the same way the stranger had.

''Fraid me and Socrates haven't had much time to listen to gossip lately.' This boy didn't see Melinno as a desperado.

'No?' His mind was swirling. 'Well, it were like this. Propertius was popping my wife, see, so—'

'So you what?' No, the boy saw Melinno as another friend for Socrates!

'So I skinned him alive.'

'Say that again!' The boy dropped his knife. 'You skinned this geezer *alive*?'

'Oh aye.' For a simple basketmaker, you have one hell of an imagination, my lad. 'I've got his hide here in me pack, d'you want to see it?'

'No! No, mate, that's fine, I'll take your word for it.' He backed swiftly towards the trees. 'Well, the rain's eased off, reckon I'll be on my way, then.'

'Right.' Melinno felt his body shudder with relief, but he couldn't help himself from saying, 'Before you go, though . . .'

The boy jumped like a startled hare. 'Yeah?'

'I was wondering, like . . .'

'What?'

'Well, whether you might want to swap cloaks with me, if I throw in a bit of supper as well?'

The young thief's eyes darted to Melinno's pack and back again as he made a few quick mental calculations.

'Forget the supper, mate,' he said, swinging his water-proof cloak off his back. 'Let's just swap gear, eh?'

He hadn't realized what a difference the goatskin would make, keeping the sleet out. Warmer, too. Melinno snuggled down and closed his eyes and dreamed of Sulpica. Her tiny, tight breasts, her shiny bright nipples. He dreamed of kissing her, caressing her, parting her thighs and hearing her moan. He dreamed of her arching her back beneath him as the wind blew in scents of roses and thyme.

Then suddenly the roses shrivelled. They turned black, and the thyme was putrid. Sulpica was still arching her back, but this time it was taut as a bowstring. Her smile had become a death rictus and her convulsions were of agony not ecstasy.

Melinno awoke, shaking and drenched with sweat, under a pink and cloudless dawn, but the gentle wooded slopes of the mountains no longer looked beautiful. They were harsh and raddled and whispered of betrayal. As well they might, because this was Lake Pergus, where Proserpine had been betrayed. Snatched into one of them dark holes round the lake and dragged to Hades to live among the ghosts of the dead, away from the sunshine and the flowers . . . as he, Melinno, was condemned to do without Sulpica by his side.

Suddenly them things he'd told that young thief last night didn't seem that despicable after all. Skinning alive was just what the fiend who killed Sulpica deserved.

XX

This was more like it!

Agrigentum's theatre was throbbing with bodies several thousand strong, pushing and shoving, laughing and joshing, as they made their collective way forward, and Claudia experienced a buzz of excitement at being back amongst the crush. Sullium, the bay and the villa all reminded her very much of frieze paintings. Beautiful – but lifeless. Here, your senses were assaulted on every front, from the smell of the wine and saffron sprayed on the floor (but which clung to your tastebuds like barnacles) through the thin, reedy tunes from the pan pipes to the cheers for the snake-charmers, the jeers for the alms-seekers. All this frolicking just for some pedestrian local deity whose name began with a P or an N or something. Good life in Illyria, what would they do for Minerva their patron?

Despite grey skies and a wind from the north, the city lost none of its splendour. High on its precipice, honey-coloured walls, built to protect and intimidate, served only to enhance its dignity. Lofty temples stood testimony to its prosperity.

Claudia's driver negotiated a path through the out-stretched cups and cans of the beggars hovering round

Golden Gate in the south wall. This wasn't the fastest route to the theatre, but Claudia had a detour to make.

Covering her head with her palla, she mounted the steps of the temple of Hercules. Vast and majestic, it soared into the clouds, a far cry from that poky little affair in Rome. Of course, in Rome he had two, one as leader of the Muses and one as patron of commerce, so perhaps that made up for it. Then again, they did everything on an ostentatious scale in Agrigentum, didn't they? On the top step she nodded to Junius, who then began the back-breaking process of lugging two large amphorae of wine up to the vestibule.

Bearded like Aristaeus, his head cocked slightly to the right, Hercules was a handsome devil and no mistake. To allay the suspicions of the precinct priests, Claudia, with a fluttering feminine gesture, laid a lyre at his feet as though in honour of the Muses and the priests retreated, satisfied no sacrilege had been perpetrated. Fools. Claudia lifted her palla to show Hercules the crown of laurel she was wearing, so he'd know the real reason for her visit. His commercial role required a men-only approach – rules, she assumed, made because women didn't run businesses. Yet.

'You understand, don't you?' Of course he did. If Claudia Seferius was to retain her wine business and make money at it, she needed proper backing.

Two amphorae, a tithe against future revenue. And he wouldn't mind that it was Collatinus and not Seferius wine, would he? It was top quality after all!

Pausing in the doorway, Claudia looked back. It was the angle of his head, surely, but for a split second she thought Hercules winked. Laughing, she pulled off her laurel crown and sent it skimming across the marble floor, where it came to rest before the sacred sandals of a young priest who couldn't have looked more horrified had he been gang-raped by five male lepers.

As she descended the steps, shaking bay leaves from her hair, Claudia wondered if she oughtn't to make a second sacrifice. It was all very well having Hercules behind her, but shouldn't Bacchus be kept sweet, too? Selling the wretched stuff wasn't enough, was it? A girl needed to be assured of a continuous market . . . However, she could do that any old time. Right now there was a play about to start, its audience assembling in earnest.

The backdrop of the stage had been painted to represent a street scene of three housefronts and you could almost cool yourself on the marble columns or contemplate buying one of the statues in the niches, they were so lifelike. Judging by the colours of the tunics, the rainbow had been torn apart and scattered to the winds and the air vibrated with a thick mix of Sicilian brogues, Carthaginian cadences and the excited squeals of the children. Fruit sellers were rushed off their feet and Claudia found it wasn't so much a question of finding a seat as requiring medical insertion. Then, finally—

'I've always maintained,' she said, squeezing herself in next to the young man at the front, 'that if a chap has a face that long, he ought not to be allowed out of doors with it.'

Marcus Cornelius Orbilio turned abruptly, his face suffused with colour as well as an emotion she found difficult to pinpoint.

'Don't worry,' he said. 'I make a point of never looking

miserable in public for longer than I make love in private
– and since my seven seconds are up . . .'

Put it down to the jolly atmosphere in the theatre, it
was impossible not to laugh with him.

'I thought you'd gone back to Rome.' He was forced
to shout. With an increasing threat of rain, huge canvas
awnings were being cranked over the seats.

I thought you had, too.

'What?' she shouted back. 'And miss out on a good
time?'

'With the Collatinuses?'

'You know what they say, never look a gift horse in
the mouth.'

Orbilio leaned closer. 'Then you don't know much
about horses,' he said. 'I think you've been looking at the
wrong end.'

The guy ropes were secured, the awnings tight against
any shower which might interrupt, and therefore spoil,
the play. Sicily had retained so much of its Greekery,
Claudia feared they were about to inflict some dire tragedy
upon her. It would go with the mood back in Eugenius's
household. In fact, Oedipus would really hit the spot at
the moment.

'Let me introduce you to my friends.' He was able to
speak normally again. 'Julius Domiticus Decianus, city
prefect and . . .'

That explained the front row seats. Patricians were
entitled to good seats, but the best were reserved for civil
servants.

' . . . his wife, Urgulania.'

They were a charming couple. Genial, middle aged,
the very people who would insist on a young aristocrat

189

taking advantage of their hospitality while he was in the area. Claudia felt very comfortable about inviting herself to the feast afterwards.

'Do you play Countryman?' asked Julius.

Do I? It's why I came to Sicily, to play games indoors and out, attend feasts and pageants, watch the bear-baiting, the cock-fighting, the rope dancers . . .

'Like a native.'

Providing they'd got a good supply of balls. Claudia did have a slight tendency to whack too hard and knock the feathers out. Especially when she was in a bit of a mood.

'And knucklebones?' asked Urgulania.

'And knucklebones,' she confirmed, closing her eyes in ecstasy and wondering whether she could ask another fifty for that Parthian.

'Ah, here she is!' exclaimed Julius. 'What kept you, my dear? Claudia, allow me to introduce my lovely daughter, Mucia.'

He slid along to let his daughter slot in between himself and Orbilio. Eighteen years old, fair, tall and slender, Claudia hated the girl on sight.

'She's had a hard time of it lately,' Marcus whispered. 'Her fiancé jilted her for an heiress in Parma.'

'Shame.' Claudia tut-tutted in sympathy. 'I can see it's turned her hair quite blonde with worry.'

He began to splutter so badly that Mucia gave him her fig and Claudia was incensed to see Orbilio actually sink his teeth into it. She hoped the pulp splashed down to stain his dazzling white toga right where it showed the most.

Oh yes, this was definitely the day for Oedipus!

Two horn players, their cumbersome instruments wrapped round their middles, marched on to the stage, positioned themselves at either wing and let out three long blares, which brought instant hush across the whole auditorium. Just in case someone, somewhere had missed the point, they blasted out another earsplitter. To the roll of unseen drums, the doors to each false house opened and out tumbled three actors. They skipped across the stage, performed a series of headrolls and cartwheels before jumping to an abrupt halt in perfect synchronization, arms outstretched. The audience was on its feet, clapping and cheering and whistling and, dammit, who needs Oedipus when you can have a show like this?

It was a touring company Claudia had never seen before, and they were truly amazing. The way they walked in their thick-soled buskins deliberately exaggerated the points they were making, their cork face masks helped to project their voices so even the poorer people up in the gallery had no need to strain their ears.

The theme of the play was the old, old story of three neighbours – a young soldier, a young girl and an old man. The girl was having a passionate affair with the handsome soldier whilst trying to hook the old man in marriage by pretending to be a virgin, desperately trying to make sure the other didn't know what she was up to. What made this company unique, however, was their magical and innovative use of music. When the girl was pretending to be a virgin, the flute warbled a few rising, fluttering notes. When she was with the soldier, the earthy horn gave a short, sceptical honk. And whenever there was a punchline, the cymbals would crash together. Needless to say at the finale, when flute, horn and cymbal were all going at once, the audience was doubled up, ensuring everyone was in the right frame of mind for a night of feasting and dancing.

Julius's impressive residence was a mere two minutes' walk from the theatre and no one seemed to notice the steady drizzle which had set in. Claudia walked beside Urgulania, who didn't care one jot that her companion hailed from the equestrian class, rather than a patrician family like her own. She was an interesting woman, as far removed from the likes of Matidia as the moon, discussing the local political situation, the changes and developments her husband had been and was intending to introduce, and Claudia decided that if more women were like Urgulania, she might actually begin to like the species.

Urgulania had really done Julius proud with the banquet, serving so many of Claudia's favourite dishes that she was in danger of becoming a veritable martyr to indigestion. Figpeckers in pastry, peahens' eggs, snails (which had been milk-fed, unless she missed her guess), and venison in a pepper and lovage sauce. Was this living, or was this living?

Between courses, a snake of dancers and musicians dressed as woodnymphs and satyrs wound their way between the dining couches and the meal was interspersed with poetry recitals to calm things down or fire-eaters to liven things up. The evening was going well, even at the point where Urgulania said:

'My husband is hoping to talk Marcus into signing a marriage contract with Mucia, and as one who knows him, I'd really value your opinion.'

Claudia was not offended. Urgulania held no prejudice against equestrians, but so entrenched were the class divides that, without even realizing it, she'd automatically drawn a line of distinction between Claudia and Orbilio. There were some chasms that were simply never bridged.

It explained why Urgulania genuinely felt able to seek independent advice.

And it explained why Claudia had had to forge her own identity in the first place. Gaius Seferius would never have dreamt of offering marriage to a dancer and erstwhile prostitute from the lower orders.

'My dear Urgulania, Marcus will make Mucia a wonderful husband,' she gushed. 'Providing she doesn't want children, of course.'

Urgulania frowned. 'Oh? Doesn't he like them?'

'Marcus? He *loves* them, would have a houseful of the little beggars – if only he could.'

'Well, that's easily settled. A healthy young girl like Mucia will be pregnant in no time.'

'Uh-uh,' Claudia said. 'I mean . . .' She held her hand out horizontally, then let it fall limp. 'He *can't*.'

Urgulania looked puzzled. 'But surely—'

'That's why,' Claudia cut in quickly, 'his first wife threw herself in the Tiber.'

'Are you certain of that? He told us she ran off with a common sea captain.'

Claudia gasped and clapped a hand over her mouth. 'Yes, yes, of course she did.'

The older woman's lips pursed. 'Do you mean he invented that story to cover up his wife's suicide?'

'Urgulania, please. If that's what Marcus says, I insist you take his word for it.'

'Mmm. Excuse me a moment, my dear, I'd like a quiet word with my husband.'

Orbilio, as was due a fellow patrician and potential son-in-law, had been given pride of place beside Julius on the top table. When he glanced over at Claudia, she noticed a slight crease in his brow. She smiled and raised her glass to him. It was entertaining the way his frown didn't go away. It merely deepened – the way a frown would, if it suspected you were up to something behind its back.

Claudia beckoned over the slave with the wine jug.

'Fill this up,' she said, holding out her glass. 'I feel like celebrating.'

There seemed no end to the festivities, and what started out as refreshing hedonism quickly descended into profligacy. There were only so many flamingo tongues one could eat, so many oysters one could swallow, and after twenty-four hours, the rattles and the pan pipes and the horns began to grate. At least, that's how it was for Claudia; the others were revelling like there was no tomorrow.

'It's barbaric,' she told Drusilla, slipping her a morsel of sucking pig. 'They eat till they're sick, they drink till they're sick, and then damn me, they go back and start all over again.'

She and Drusilla were lucky, having a bedroom to themselves with this horde milling round the house, but for some strange reason none of the other women had fancied sharing.

'I just pity the poor slaves whose job it is to mop up the vomit.'

'Mrrr.'

These excesses reminded her of Diomedes's lament about how the wealthy made themselves ill by constant over-indulgence in fatty foods and vintage wine. He'd have made a good living here in Agrigentum, she thought, with his purges and his bloodletting – why take a job at the Villa Collatinus? What did he mean when he said he'd found peace there?

'And I tell you something else,' she said to Drusilla, as one of the kittens burrowed under the flounce of her tunic, 'there'll be a good influx of babies nine months from now.'

Hardly a slave girl passed unmolested, most of them taken in the shadows of the prefect's pink marble pillars with the same delicacy his guests showed towards their other physical needs. Claudia pursed her lips. Randy old goats she could understand. Hadn't she spent her teenage years pandering to their sexual fantasies? They wanted. They paid. Fair enough. But these girls were treated like herd animals, and suddenly Claudia was sick of Sicily.

Sick of its decadence, its over-the-toppery, its fat cats creaming off the goodies in a way Roman citizens, no matter how rich or privileged, would never dream of. She was sick of the brooding superstition which clung to the island, she was sick of the Collatinuses and the callous way they ignored the violence of their kinswoman's death, almost as though it was a way of life for them.

The kitten began a death-defying climb up the north face of her tunic. Claudia would never know, now, where Sabina had spent the past thirty years. Her original theory, bunking up with a distant relative, was knocked on the head as she remembered the sun-darkened skin, the dirty nails. No relative would expect (or indeed allow!) her to work for her keep. On the other hand, Sabina did not give the appearance of a woman who'd had to graft in order to survive. What happened when she went to Rome all those years ago? Why continue the pretence of being a Vestal Virgin? It didn't surprise Claudia that none of the family had visited, they were far too absorbed in their own lives, although Matidia mentioned a regular exchange of letters. The most curious point, however, was why Sabina chose to return at the precise time the real senior Vestal was retiring. Why not stay where she was?

'Too late now,' Claudia said aloud to no one in particular. Drusilla was chomping on a flatfish, and Slingshot here was on the horns of a dilemma. Should he continue the ascent or quit while he was ahead?

Cypassis flung open the door and began dashing round. 'I'm sorry I'm late, madam.' She collected Claudia's tunic and sandals and put them away, refilled the water bowl and lit four more lamps all more or less at the same time.

Claudia unhooked the squealing mountaineer and placed him amongst his siblings, who were blotto on the blanket. 'Slow down, slow down.'

She was in no great hurry, anyway. There was, after all, a limit to the number of castanet-clacking Arabian dancers a girl could cope with over dinner and frankly, that last lot of breast-wobbling came too close to her custard for comfort.

As Cypassis began to heat the curling irons in the brazier and ease the pins from her mistress's hair, Claudia noticed a silver bangle round her wrist.

'Where did you get that?'

'One of the magistrates.' The Thessalian girl's cheeks

darkened to the colour of half-ripe bilberries. 'Did I do wrong?'

Claudia let out a throaty chuckle. 'Let's just say you didn't do badly. Now for gods' sake, get those bloody tongs out before they get too hot to handle.'

Of all the revelries which Julius Domiticus Decianus had planned, tonight's feast was to be the pinnacle. Urgulania had ordered everything from peacocks' brains to ostrich steaks, bear cutlets to stuffed crane, and entertainments ranged from full-blown political satires to high camp female impersonators. It promised to be quite a night.

'I'll wear the white.'

The hairpin froze in Cypassis's hand. 'The white, madam?'

'Does silver make you deaf? I'm talking about the outfit I bought today.'

She knew what was going through the girl's mind. Slaves wore white. Noblemen wore white. Noblewomen, most assuredly, did not wear white. Especially not to a banquet given by a city prefect. But since when did etiquette count? All that concerned Claudia was that, when everyone was reclining on the couches, eyes would be exactly where she intended them to be. On the widow of Gaius Seferius, now the owner of a large and prosperous wine business. When transaction time came (and it would) Claudia wanted to be absolutely certain they remembered her.

She ate little and drank less as she scanned the hall for potential clients, but each time her eyes made the tour they were caught by the intensity of one young man in particular. He was wealthy, you could tell from the cut of his tunic, the rings on his fingers, although he was neither patrician nor equestrian or he wouldn't have been stuck at the back. You couldn't say he was good-looking – his brow was too low, his eyes too small – but in any case, the look he gave her was not sexual. Just unblinking. Hell, the whole idea was to get noticed, she could hardly complain . . .

The heat in the banqueting room was fast becoming intolerable and she excused herself to take a walk in the peristyle. Darkness had fallen and yesterday's drizzle had turned into a steady downpour, but there was no breeze and the colonnade offered shelter enough from the elements. The rain hammering on to the herbs sent up a heavenly waft of bay and rosemary, lavender and roses, while the fountain gurgled and chuckled in the darkness. The statuary here was exquisite, far superior to anything Gaius had commissioned, and she was admiring the compact marble buttocks of a naked warrior when a familiar voice broke the silence.

'You haven't savaged me once today. I'm beginning to think you don't love me any more.'

Marcus Cornelius Orbilio was holding two glasses of wine. When he passed one across, she pretended not to notice the twinkle in his eye.

'And you practically betrothed to that Mucia trollop!'

She saw his teeth shine in the darkness. 'I'll have you know, Claudia Seferius, a lot of women will be sorry when I get married.'

'Good god, just how many are you planning to marry?'

He laughed softly. 'Put it this way, I don't know what you told Julius, but I'm very grateful.'

Wait until you find out what it was.

There was a long silence in which Orbilio leaned one arm against the pillar and propped himself up with it. Claudia continued to scrutinize the white statue.

'Why aren't you in Rome?' he asked eventually.

'Why aren't you? It was your damned grainship.'

Tell me about it, he thought. Callisunus will have my balls on a bellpull for that, and my plans for the Senate have swirled right down the gutter. But when it came to the crunch—

'It was every bit as criminal for me to walk away as it was for the man who murdered Sabina in the first place.'

'Gone off Diomedes, then?'

'Oh, no,' he said quickly. 'It's him all right. I just needed proof.'

'Which, naturally, you have by the bucketload?'

He jerked his head back so hard it hit the pillar. 'No,' he snapped. 'No, I bloody haven't.'

The whole purpose of coming to Agrigentum was to find out more about that Greek quack, but no one knew a damn thing about him. Not one damned thing. Still, at least it had established that the manner of Sabina's murder was – at least on Sicily – quite unique. Evidence, albeit circumstantial, was mounting.

Claudia walked her fingers up the leg of the warrior. 'That's not entirely surprising,' she said. 'Considering you've got the wrong man.'

'So who's your money on, that bumbling great oaf Utti?'

Do me a favour. When I bet, I bet on winners. Well, most of the time. 'No way. He's forever playing What's

199

the Time, Mr Wolf with the slave children, giving them piggy-back rides and playing hide and seek.'

Whatever plan he and Tanaquil had hatched, butchering Vestal Virgins wasn't part of it.

'Tell me something,' he said softly. 'What were you and Sabina up to?'

'Orbilio, you'll travel to the Senate a lot faster if you get your damned facts straight.'

'You're saying there was no collusion?'

'You're the detective. Detect.'

A long silence followed, in which the drumming of the rain on the tiles played accompaniment to the splash of water in the fountain. The scent of pinks filled the cool night air, and a large-winged moth took advantage of the shelter to find nectar in a mallow. Whatever response she might have imagined, it wasn't to hear him tell her:

'Your curls have come loose again.'

'What?'

'They always do when you shake your head like that.'

This man was so irritating! 'Come to the point, Orbilio.'

'Ahem.'

The sound startled them both. Orbilio straightened up and nodded politely. Claudia had to peer round the warrior's hips to see the intruder. The boy from the banquet? How odd.

'Claudia Seferius?' he asked.

She looked him up and down before replying. There was no emotion on his face, only that strange intensity. 'So?'

Her reaction didn't throw him. He merely stepped one

pace forward and she could see a small mole on his chin. 'Might I have a word? In private?'

Claudia drained her glass and positioned it carefully, end up, on top of a clipped laurel. 'You can talk in front of Supersnoop here. He'll only be eavesdropping in the background otherwise.'

Again no jolt to his confidence, not even a glance at Orbilio. 'I thought it was time we were acquainted,' he said casually.

'Oh, and why's that?' she asked.

'Because my name is Varius Seferius,' he said. 'I'm your late husband's son.'

XXI

The rain might have moved on, but the air stayed thick and heavy, the clouds low and oppressive. The windows were wedged open, their hangings fixed back, yet still no breeze found its way to Agrigentum. Every minute of the night threatened to suffocate her and by morning Claudia's shift was soaked through. Even the wine was warm.

She leaned over to fan Drusilla. The kittens, eyes rheumy like old men's, were heady with their recent transition from wiggling to wobbling and were transmitting squeaks which ranged from smug look-at-me's to frantic helps and back again, all within the space of five seconds. Their mother was content to let them learn the hard way. Claudia was not.

'Come on, Smallfry, back to mum.'

She scooped up a little lost wanderer and placed the squirming, bleating bundle on the blanket, where he homed in on a warm, secure teat. Claudia swore Drusilla poked her tongue out deliberately.

'What about that Varius insect?' she asked, flapping the ostrich feathers over the cat.

'Meowr.'

'No, not a real insect, poppet, pay attention. I'm talking about that little creep who thinks he can pass himself off as my stepson.'

His visit last night had shaken her to the core, although she was far too experienced a trooper to let it show.

'Why, that's wonderful.' Fountains and spring water couldn't gush more profusely. 'Did you hear that, Marcus? My dear, dear Gaius didn't die in vain, he has a son to carry his name and father his heirs. Oh!' She dabbed at her eye with her handkerchief. 'I'm quite overcome, you must . . . (sob) . . . excuse me.'

Now *that* was acting. None of those wild, extravagant gestures made in the theatre, where it's merely a question of throwing your voice and adopting the odd mannerism. This was the genuine article.

'The question is, what do I do about him?'

Drusilla began to wash Smallfry's ears as roughly as she could to teach him a lesson for wandering. Claudia could hear the rasp of her tongue on his tiny head and felt for Smallfry, the way he was jerked up and down, poor soul.

'Mrrrr.'

'That?' Drusilla's ears had pricked up at the scraping sound outside the door. 'That's just Urgulania's slaves dragging the extra tables back out of the banqueting hall.'

She didn't envy them their job of clearing up, and although the festivities might have peaked, they showed no signs of abating. All this for a local deity whose name began with a C or an F or something.

Cypassis returned, staggering under the weight of a large jug of fresh water. Juno be praised, it was cool. Claudia tipped the whole lot over her head.

'What's scheduled for this morning?' she asked, drying her hair on a towel.

'Hopscotch and darts, madam.'

The very thought of watching a large party of portly folk playing hopscotch with tunics hitched to their thighs and sweat pouring down their bloated faces, was too dire to contemplate.

'Shall you be going in to breakfast, madam?'

Claudia pulled on a mint green sleeveless stola. Her face did not show the revulsion her stomach felt at the prospect of food, or the churning inside from her fear of what Varius might do. Think, girl, think! Blame the heat, blame the humidity, blame the noise of moving furniture, whatever the reason, Claudia's brain had died and gone to heaven. Only the heart-thumping, gut-churning, sweat-inducing fear remained.

'You stay here and fan Drusilla.' She picked up Smallfry and kissed him noisily between his spiky, bedraggled ears.

'Oh, madam! You're not going out alone?'

'I shall have Junius and I shall have Kleon,' she snapped, replacing the kitten amongst its siblings. 'I shall hardly be alone.'

'But without a female attendant—'

'Another word and I'll slit your tongue clean up the middle.'

'It's not decent—'

'And then rub in salt to stop it knitting together.' She snatched up her purse, but the drawstring wasn't tight and coins spilled over the floor. 'Now look what you've done!'

Marching down the atrium, she had to clap twice before her bodyguard materialized.

'And you two,' she hissed, smiling graciously at Urgulania as she passed, 'will be cleaning toilets if you can't move faster than that.'

'I'm sorry—' the Cilician began, but Claudia cut him short.

'Get out there and hire me a car. Here!' She fished a silver denarius out of her purse. 'A nippy, two-wheeled job, Kleon, and make sure it's not pulled by some sullen nag with a bent back who can barely lift a hoof. And tell the driver to take the tilt off. I want to feel the wind in my hair. Dear Diana, are you still here?'

Kleon blinked rapidly, thought to ask a question and then thought better of it. He was back so quickly, Claudia wondered whether he'd turfed someone out of a passing vehicle and, if so, resolved to promote him the instant they returned home.

'Get that awning off!' she commanded the driver.

'I'm afraid it's not detachable, milady.'

'Do you want the damned fare or not?'

The driver stood his ground. 'I do, milady, but I'm not prepared to wreck the vehicle for—'

Claudia drew a small knife from the folds of her stola and cut the rope. The tilt collapsed at the same speed as the driver's expression. 'Hop on,' she instructed her slaves.

The driver held out his hands. 'Please, milady! There's only room for me and one passenger.'

Claudia studied the vehicle. 'They can sit on the bar at the back.'

'The car would tip over,' he said querulously, 'the mule couldn't pull—'

Claudia jumped in and adjusted her skirts. 'Junius! Kleon! Take the day off! And you—' She turned to the driver, his face contorted with misery. 'Get some speed up.'

The last thing Kleon heard as the car rattled down the street and out of sight was his mistress shouting, 'Faster, you idle oaf!'

'Wouldn't fancy changing places with that poor sod,' he said, jovially. 'D'you reckon she was serious?'

'What about?'

'The day off, you daft bugger.'

The young Gaul kept his eyes on the road. 'You're new,' he said, 'so the quicker you learn Mistress Seferius means precisely what she says, the easier life will be.'

'Yeah?' He rubbed his hands together. 'Well in that case, I'm not hanging around this bleeding street any longer. What do you fancy?'

Junius shrugged. 'I'm not sure what to do,' he said, staring in the direction the car had taken.

Kleon nudged him in the ribs and pointed. 'There's a tart in that tavern who looks tasty. All long legs and big tits. Fancy a nibble?'

'Not me. Thanks all the same.'

The Cilician leaned closer. 'Go on,' he urged. 'I've heard about her, she's good. Charges ten asses, but she'll do us together for fifteen.'

'No. Really.'

'It'll be fun. They say she'll do *any*thing, so if we use our imagination . . .'

'What?'

'You know.' Kleon gave an exaggerated wink and nodded back towards the house. 'We can pretend it's Miss Snottyboots.'

He didn't see the punch which laid him out.

XXII

The problem of her virginity was one which had occupied Actë's mind for most of her adult life, but now, she thought, closing the orchard gate behind her, the matter was finally settled. And while the prospect of marriage at any age is exciting, a proposal at her age – coming out of the blue – made it ten times more thrilling.

She paused at the clipshed, deserted this time of year apart from its recent occupation by the fortune teller and her brother, but resisted the temptation to slip inside. Oughtn't she to distance herself from the house? Find space to think? To make sense of this enormous change in her circumstances?

In a matter of days she, like Miss Sabina, would be able to wear the bridal veil, the betrothal ring, the saffron-coloured sandals, the Knot of Hercules. Her heart skipped a beat. Except she would be free to discard hers afterwards, and wear two bands in her hair instead of one.

Pinching her nose against the sulphurous fumes as she hurried past the bleaching yard, resembling a giant beehive with its circular frames over which the whitened wool had been stretched, Actë thought that virginity was probably the only thing she'd had in common with Miss Sabina. Especially since Miss Sabina remained a virgin through service to Vesta, whereas Actë's circumstances were pretty well unique in the whole of the Roman Empire. Women, even slaves, were seldom allowed to remain single, the marriage laws being what they were. It was only through the Master's intervention, his rigid enforcement of the Chattel Rule (which said a man's slaves were his possessions, he could do what he liked with them), that she wasn't foisted off on some uncouth lout as breeding stock.

Giving the dyeshed as wide a berth as possible, Actë turned her eyes to the ground. She'd left the Master having a massage with Diomedes, so the small amount of time she had to spare was precious. She couldn't afford to waste it on chitchat if the inevitable happened. Which it did.

'Got a minute, Actë?'

The voice of Nikias, the foreman, carried across the yard and she felt bad about pretending she hadn't heard him. He was a nice man, Nikias – a widower, solid and dependable – and she supposed she could have married him, had she wanted. There was nothing to stop her from choosing a husband of her own, only—

From the corner of her eye, she saw his mouth twist in disappointment. Too bad. Today his arms were black to the elbow from the privet dye, last week they had been yellow from the rowan bark. Sure, Nikias was nice. But who wants a man with multi-coloured arms in their bed at night?

Actë's first choice today would have been Pharos Point, but since it took a full half-hour to reach the lighthouse she turned left instead. To every other slave, going to the birch grove was tantamount to visiting a leper colony, a place to be avoided at all costs on account of how it was haunted. Actë despised them for their narrow-mindedness, but chose never to disabuse their talk of ghostly apparitions walking and moaning and generally doing their damnedest to spook people. It guaranteed her privacy there – and privacy, for a slave, came second only to freedom.

The climb was energetic, the heat intolerable, and by the time she reached the grove her tunic was sticking to her skin. The clouds were low, trapping the heavy, humid, sultry air. She could barely breathe. The leaves, thin and papery and yellow, hung limp. Mostly the grove comprised silver birch, graceful and airy, but theirs was not an exclusive colony. Cobnuts, for instance, had fallen around the smooth brown bole of the hazel, red shiny fruits hung on the haw. Spotty red toadstools fed off the roots of the birch. Actë settled herself against the grey, scaly bark of the solitary charcoal-oak, its evergreen canopy incongruous among the falling leaves of its fellows. A blackbird flew in and began systematically to strip the berries off a rowan.

In the middle of the copse, the flat white rocks of this limestone outcrop lay like so many fissured tables waiting to be set for a picnic. Actë used her fingertips to pull her damp tunic away from her body and began to flap it like a fan. Fancy thinking this place was haunted! True, a man, a Collatinus slave, had been killed here some years ago. Stabbed in the back by his jealous lover, a girl from Sullium, freeborn and with the finances to buy him his own freedom, and Actë spared little sympathy for the man who had squandered everything for a roll in the hay with a kitchen maid. Except . . . well, maybe it said something for his qualities as a lover, and since she had no experience on that score, perhaps she oughtn't to judge him so harshly?

Occasionally (but only occasionally) she'd been tempted herself to indulge in a quick fling with one of the men – and weren't there some handsome devils about? – in order to learn what it was the other women enjoyed so vocally and she was missing out on. Except too much was at stake. Suppose she got pregnant? The Master demanded total commitment, and Actë would not put her job at risk, although often over the years she had regretted not forming a romantic attachment. It was an unfortunate by-product of the education the Master had given her that she saw the workers for what they were – coarse, ill-mannered, uneducated bumpkins. Fifteen years ago they might have been for her, but not any more.

Thus the conundrum persisted, and long nights passed dreaming of a man to hold, this terrible ache for the touch of a hand, the brush of a kiss, the whispers, the glances, the ecstasy. Well, the problem was solved now. Maybe not the way she'd hoped for and certainly not the way she'd expected, but solved it was. And what a thrill! What a change!

Her ears picked up a rustle on the autumn floor and she peered round the trunk of the oak.

'Hello?'

The blackbird, fully gorged on rowan berries, flew past her and Actë smiled. Fancy a bird making you edgy! She was getting tense, the very thing a bride shouldn't do. She'd have to snap out of it before she faced the Master, because she intended to stay calm and collected when she told him about her decision. Heaven knows, it wouldn't be easy!

Sixteen years ago, when she arrived, she'd been terrified of him. Daily his leonine roars threatened to shake the very foundations of the villa and she, little more than a child, had been forced to cope alone. Matidia, just turned forty and no less vapid than she was now, was clueless when it came to handling a situation whereby the Master was still master of everything except his body and Aulus was no help to anyone. He made it clear from the outset that as far as he was concerned, it was a disaster the old man hadn't been killed by the horse that threw him; his only consolation lay in the hope that his father's days might be numbered in single figures.

All this Actë had picked up within her first few weeks before she gradually realized the Master's bellows were born not of temper, but of frustration. This still-handsome and vigorous man had, by one cruel stroke of the gods, been reduced to the level of a turtle locked inside an immobile shell, and she began to recognise that his insults and his rantings were simply rage against himself.

Imperceptibly, the roles began to change until it reached the stage where Actë supervised his diet, his medicine and his rest periods with unprecedented strictness, while spending every waking moment as his companion, his eyes and ears to the outside world. In return Eugenius taught her to read and to write, to discuss philosophy and politics, to appreciate art and music and poetry and literature.

He had, in his way, set her free.

Not, she reflected wryly, that it was all plain sailing. All too often he'd pinch her bottom, tweak her nipples, slide his hand up her skirt, and because she was a slave and therefore unable either to refuse or to retaliate, she found recourse in pretending not to learn the lessons he so painstakingly taught her. Of the two, his sexual frustrations proved less important than his intellectual frustrations, and so Eugenius Collatinus made his choice and the pornographic friezes on his wall became his compromise. Here he could indulge his passion for past appetites, his imagination doing the work his poor manhood could not.

When, later, the groping began again, Actë had frustrations of her own and the next time he cupped his hand round her breast, they both knew her protests were more for propriety than for anything else. Lying alone at night, desperate to feel the pulsations of love inside her, she wondered how it was that this old man, with his crinkled face and papery hands, could bring her to the brink of heaven just by fondling her breasts and kissing her nipples?

Not that it went further than that. She made it clear, when he first tried parting her thighs, that he could touch her only through her tunic, she wouldn't let him play with her as he wanted. At the time she didn't quite understand why (it certainly wasn't from a moral standpoint, there were times she'd have given her right arm for gratification!), but her instinct had guided her well. Had she given in, she'd have had nothing left to bargain with – and above all Eugenius Collatinus was a businessman. Negotiation was a currency he understood.

A crackle of twigs on the far side of the rocks interrupted her thoughts. It was probably a snake, sluggish and sleepy, heading back to its hole, but—

'Hello? Who's there?'

Not even a leaf rustled in the heat and the stillness, and Actë's ears strained for sounds.

'Hello?'

It's all that talk of ghosts and haunting. And the thought of facing the Master. She sighed. Diomedes would have finished the massage, the Master would be asking for her.

Yes, the Master had done much for her over the years, far more than just teaching her the arts and fine manners, and Actë's obligations rested lightly on her. Until the Master's eyesight had began to fail. She never let on, but from time to time slipped into Diomedes's room to syphon off small quantities of drops without the doctor being any the wiser. Neither was the family. With her help and connivance, Eugenius pretended to read the letters and study the reckonings, and to compensate for his shortcomings he'd make unannounced spot checks, to keep them on their toes.

Then when those other pains began, the pains that doubled him up and which he likened to a red-hot claw tearing out his liver, her loyalty was pushed to its limit. The Master had made her promise not to tell a soul, not even Diomedes – and that was the hardest promise she'd ever had to make. It was Actë who had talked the Master into hiring a proper physician, which was well overdue, but in spite of Diomedes's skill in massage and so on, the Master still wouldn't allow him to know about the pains. It wrenched her apart to watch him writhing in agony, knowing she was helpless. But the Master was adamant. He wanted to retain all his faculties, he said. Didn't want to be drugged to the eyeballs, wanted to be in charge and coherent right to the end.

Which they both knew would not be that far away. The Master would not see the spring.

Actë wiped a tear from her eye. She loved the Master. With all her heart she loved him, and when, this morning, he told her it was time he took care of her, she had no inkling of what he meant.

'I'm talking about marriage, Actë. You and me.'

The suddenness of it all, the sheer unexpectedness, had taken her breath away. She'd had to sit down.

'You won't get much money,' he said, 'and the business will pass to my son, but it'll give you a decent status after I've gone. You'll nab a good husband as my widow.'

'I – I can't!' she had stammered, but he was adamant.

'I'm not asking, I'm telling you,' he said. 'And anyway . . . he slid his hand up the inside of her thigh and tickled his finger between her legs, 'I want to do *what* I can *while* I can,' he'd added with a chuckle.

Actë Collatinus! Matidia's . . . oh dear, Matidia's mother-in-law!

Actë Collatinus, virgin no more. Eugenius (she'd have to learn to call him Eugenius now!), he couldn't make love to her as a proper man could, but he'd promised her all manner of delights. And the end to her virginity was one of them!

The snap of a branch made her spin round. This was no mouse, no reptile. She saw a flutter of leaves as they fell to the ground. Saw a flash of white. Actë felt her mouth go dry. It was true then, the stories. The haunting. A band tightened round her chest. Trembling, she climbed to her feet. A man she could fight. But a ghost? Her throat was gripped in ice. Then . . .

'Oh, it's you!' she said.

Her knees went weak with relief and she leaned her hand against the broad span of the charcoal-oak to let her legs regain their strength. She felt silly. Ghosts, indeed! When all the time, it was only—

She didn't see the blade until it was too late.

There was no pain. No time to cry out. No chance to struggle. In an instant she'd lost control. Could feel nothing. Could move nothing.

She knew from the angle of the trees that she'd been caught as she fell. Knew she was laid on a limestone slab. She saw him toss her tunic aside. Then her breast band. Then her thong.

She knew, because his mouth was moving, that he was shouting at her, calling her names. Filthy names. Undeserved names. But she couldn't hear him. Her ears were filled with a fearful hammering.

The sheer helplessness of it overwhelmed her. Never again would she feel the warmth of the sunshine, the bite of the frost – the softness of the babies she would undoubtedly have birthed from a second marriage.

Panic cut in. She was dying. She was being murdered. There was nothing she could do. Couldn't fight, couldn't scream, couldn't leave clues. He was killing her, and he was getting away with it.

She tried to pray, but couldn't.

She knew, from the way he was pounding, pumping, ramming, that he was inside her. That at last, and in the most foul manner imaginable, she was losing her precious virginity.

She saw him laughing.

But it was the last thing Actë did see, before a red mist flooded her eyes.

She heard a roar, an explosion.

Before the silence.

XXIII

'For gods' sake, man, I could have harnessed snails to this bloody car and got more speed up.'

The driver negotiated a tight turn before replying. There was sweat on his brow and on his upper lip. 'This is a built-up area, milady. Someone might get hurt.'

'You, unless you crack that bloody whip.'

'We practically overturned back there, when you jerked on the reins.' He was wondering how his wife would take to widowhood and decided she'd probably love it, the hypocritical old cow. 'To go fast, we'd have to leave the city.'

'Which is the nearest gate?'

The driver grinned. He had a feeling the day might not turn out so badly after all. 'Gela.'

Claudia unpinned her hair. 'Then let's put a bit of froth round this nag's mouth.'

An hour at full pelt was quite sufficient for Claudia's head to clear. Whatever was she thinking of, letting scum like Varius needle her? Claudia Seferius wasn't going to be displaced. No way. And certainly not by that verminous object.

'What's your name?' she asked the driver.

'Theocles, milady.'

'Well, Theocles, I've got what I came for. Let's head

for the coast. And for heavens' sake, drop that milady business, it makes me sound like an arthritic old matron.'

Unfortunately it was such a grubby, scrubby coastline that Claudia had no desire to linger. What next? The mule was too tired to gallop, and in any case she'd done that once. It was time to find fresh flowers to pick. Theocles was apologetic. He was used to driving men, he had no idea what to suggest to a lady seeking excitement. A man, now . . .

'Where would you take him?'

'For a wager, you mean?' He still only half-believed her. 'The fight, I suppose.'

Even as they drew up outside the village, he hadn't really expected her to dismount, but Claudia bounded down and elbowed her way through the crowd towards a clearing sprinkled with sand. It was purely a local bout, nothing on the scale of the matches staged in Agrigentum, but Claudia's experienced eye weighed the men up and realized immediately that this was a grudge match.

'Put ten sesterces on him,' she instructed Theocles. 'The one with his hands on his hips.'

'Alypius? I'd go for the other one, me. Look at his face, you can see how many battles he's won.'

Yes, Meno's face was pitted from studmarks, his nose squashed to a pulp and both ears had bits missing and yes, he made Utti look positively handsome – but the other man, this Alypius, looked dangerous. Whereas his opponent had worked himself into a blazing temper, puce in the face as he stomped up and down shouting abuse and shaking his fist, Alypius stood stock still, his mouth a thin white line. The clincher, for Claudia, was the red puckered scar which ran from ear to mouth. It was that disfigurement which had probably given him his temperament – and men who contain their anger are men to be reckoned with.

'It's three to one against,' advised Theocles. Who could miss the high spots of colour on her cheeks or the way her tongue flickered nervously round her lips? She was squeezing her hands as though in grief and he felt responsible, milady losing ten sesterces, seeing as how this was his suggestion and all.

'Is it indeed?' Her eyes glistened as she delved into her purse. 'Then you'd better make it thirty.'

It was a deflated and defeated Theocles who finally placed the bet as the bout started. It was to the death, the umpire announced, bringing down his rod of office to signal the start. Let honour be triumphant.

Claudia had no idea what score these two men had to settle, but from the first it was bloody. Alypius waited for his opponent to lunge, stepped smartly aside then jerked at his ear. Blood spurted into the front row of the crowd. With a roar, Meno brought up his foot and, with a vicious kick to the knee, sent Alypius flying off balance. Squaring up, they charged again, Meno bellowing like a mad bull, and Claudia nodded. She was right to bet on Alypius. Only amateurs yelled.

For a good ten minutes she sat, knuckles white, lips pursed as they slugged it out, their bodies slippery with blood as they bit and gouged and tore at each other. Then to her disgust, Alypius threw a wild and clumsy punch at Meno's ribs, which any fool, never mind a professional like Meno, could see coming and Alypius's knuckles crunched on to the metal studs in his opponent's belt, impaling themselves in the process. It was the only garment either man wore and the crowd groaned in unison when Alypius's other fist closed round Meno's testicles and twisted. A sweet shock of realization shuddered through Claudia and her heart began to pound. Alypius had deliberately sacrificed his hand for the greater good, because while Meno was distracted by the excruciating pain, Alypius wedged his knee into his opponent's back and looped his damaged arm round Meno's neck. Quick as a flash, he released Meno's testicles and locked both wrists together.

The crack that rang out as Meno's neck snapped sent a momentary hush over the crowd, then cheering and clapping and whistling broke out which was probably heard in Libya. Claudia tossed a denarius in the air and Theocles caught it.

'I can't take that, milady.' It was a whole day's pay. 'The repairs to the tilt will only cost an ass or two.'

'What are you babbling about? What tilt? Just fetch me a mug of beer – yes, beer, man, are you deaf? – and let's get going before it's too dark to see the damned road.'

The grand house of the city prefect still echoed with drunken laughter and girlish squeals as Theocles pulled up, and Claudia groaned. Deal me out, she thought, and marched straight past the two bronze pillars flanking the front entrance towards the slaves' door round the corner. It was pure misfortune that the first person she bumped into was that ferreting investigator emerging from the kitchen with a plate piled high with chicken, eggs, celery and onions and a long crusty loaf tucked underneath his arm.

'Good evening,' he said pleasantly, licking the grease off his fingers.

'Drop dead.'

Orbilio ignored the invitation and matched his pace with hers. 'How's the new stepson?'

Claudia turned sharp right into the Cretan-style labyrinth and gained two paces. Of all the people she wanted to avoid, this man topped the list. By Jupiter, the gods must have had a field day when they watched Varius drop his little bombshell in front of Orbilio. Good life in Illyria, hadn't the whole point of this wretched exercise in Sicily been to neutralize the threat against her inheritance – discreetly?

Back in Rome, rummaging around for dealings with Collatinus, she'd unearthed a letter from some bawd by the name of Livia Maximus who was living in Agrigentum and who claimed to have given birth to Gaius's bastard. At the time of writing, the boy was fifteen and if Gaius wanted him to have a good marriage, etc., etc., etc. . . . The letter was clearly a bid to get him to part with money, but there was no record of his reply, which was unusual. Gaius kept meticulous records. Thus Claudia had used Eugenius's offer of a holiday as a cover for finding out once and for all whether this Livia creature really did have a son by Gaius. She'd sent Junius on exhaustive missions and it had cost her an absolute fortune in bribes to well-placed civil servants and other lowlife to establish that the answer was a resounding negative.

There was no Livia Maximus. There was no son. There was no pretender to the House of Seferius.

All this way she'd travelled, through storms and saddle-sores, misers and murders, to find not only this little cockroach crawling out of his dung heap, but making his announcement in front of Supersnoop to boot.

'Claudia, you're chilling me out so much I'm getting frostbite.'

'Somewhere painful, I trust.' She swerved to the path on the left, and was delighted the torchlight was bright enough to see two onions roll into the night. A second swerve, also to the left, took care of the eggs. 'Ouch!'

She spun round to see him grinning where he'd whacked her on the bottom with his loaf. 'Now I have your attention,' he said, 'perhaps we could retire to the peristyle. Walking Indian-file is hardly conducive to conversation.'

'That's the Cretans for you. Probably never spoke to each other from one year to the next.' Lucky devils.

She ducked to the right so fast he overshot, but before she had the chance to take another path, a firm hand had closed round her arm.

'The peristyle, Claudia,' he said sternly.

Carefully placing the remains of his dinner on the sundial, he continued, 'If you stand still long enough, you might realize that, with my contacts, I'm actually in a position to help.'

I'd rather die than take help from you, she thought. Then be cremated, just to be on the safe side. She smiled sweetly and patted his hand.

'In times of trial, it's a real comfort to know you're there for me, Marcus.'

The side of his face twisted up and there was a wicked glint in his eye, but his voice remained level. 'In times of trial, Mistress Seferius, you should be aiming for an acquittal.'

It was damned hard not to laugh, but by grinding her heel on to her toe Claudia managed it. She wondered why she made no effort to move away and put it down to the relaxing sound of the fountain gurgling nearby. The music from the banqueting hall, which was hitherto providing pleasant background noise, had been replaced by the sort of guttural laughter associated with blue comedians. Why men found bodily functions amusing was beyond her, but in the days when she earned her living as a dancer, she made damned sure her own act followed the dirty jokes. That way you could count on good tips.

An elderly man, round as a marble and clad only in goatskin leggings, came tottering down the side of the peristyle. When he saw them, he made a wobbly detour in their direction.

'Claudia, we're playing sylphs and satyrs next. Come and join ush.'

'Not if you paid me!'

When he moved in closer, the overwhelming stink of stale wine and turnips was scary. 'Come on—'

'What are you goggling at, you disgusting little man?'

'I expect he's wondering why you've got bloodstains all over your stola.'

'Rubbish, he's staring down the front of it.'

'I am,' the man said cheerfully. 'I'm shtaring down the front of it. Hey, we're playing sylphs and satyrs next. Why don't you join ush?'

'I told you before, you malodorous little pusboil, I—'

'Sounds great!' Orbilio clapped the drunk on the shoulder and propelled him down the path. 'We'll be along in a minute, there's a good chap.' He watched him totter out of sight before saying, 'Tell me about Varius.'

Credit where it was due, he didn't let go, this boy.

'What's there to tell? We meet by chance at Julius's

banquet and he realizes I'm the same Claudia Seferius his father married.'

'With an inheritance like yours at stake, chance doesn't come into it. As you know.'

When Claudia bent down, it wasn't so much to pick a marigold as to decapitate it. The best course of action, she decided, was to charm his patrician boots right off him.

'At least Varius is a bastard by birth. You, Orbilio, you're a self-made man.' She lobbed the marigold into the fish pond. 'Anyway, it's none of your damned business. You investigate murders, remember?'

'Oh, I'm investigating. So much so, this is – ' he weighed the sadly misshapen loaf – '*was* my first meal of the day. I've been chasing . . .'

The kerfuffle in the corner diverted him. It seemed more intense, more serious than the usual scuffles in the peristyle, which tended to be of a carnal rather than an argumentative nature. Suddenly a woman in a dark-coloured tunic broke free of the small knot of slaves and, as she raced past a torch, Claudia recognized the fuzz of red hair.

'Tanaquil! What on earth are you doing here?'

The girl seemed bemused, and then Claudia realized that Tanaquil had come in search of Orbilio, not herself. Well, of course she had, because no one at the villa knew where Claudia was staying. But the irritating thing was, if Tanaquil knew Orbilio's address, how come Claudia hadn't known it? That would teach her blithely to assume he'd sloped off back to Rome.

'Marcus, something terrible's happened! Terrible! You must come quickly.'

Oh, it's Marcus, is it? You a lowborn hustler, him a patrician policeman, and you call him Marcus.

'Everything's under control.' Orbilio waved away the anxious slaves. 'Now, Tanaquil, calm down. What's the matter?'

Her face, which was chalk white to start with, now had a greyish tinge to it. It was swollen from crying and her eyes were red.

'It's Actë,' she said. 'She's dead!'

Claudia felt an icy wind blow through the peristyle. Not Actë. Sweet Jupiter, tell me it's not Actë. Not at the hands of that butchering lunatic.

The muscles on Orbilio's face tightened, the only sign of emotion. 'What happened?'

Tanaquil dug her fingers into his tunic and made fists of them. 'Oh, it was awful. Just like Sabina. Only that's not the worst of it.'

Claudia and Orbilio exchanged glances.

'No?'

'Eugenius is beside himself, he doesn't know what he's doing, you've got to come, it's awful, I think he'll do it, he says he will and I believe him, you've got to hurry—'

'It's all right,' he said gently, placing a hand on each of the girl's shoulders.

'Oh, but it's not, it's not, you don't know what Eugenius is saying, he's beside himself, I told you, he means it.'

Orbilio applied slight pressure with each hand and shook her gently. 'Tanaquil, you're not making sense. What does Eugenius mean to do?'

The redhead began to cry. 'Utti,' she wailed. 'Eugenius means to kill him.'

XXIV

Orbilio led the distraught Tanaquil to a marble bench, sat her down and patted her heaving shoulder. Claudia picked up a chicken leg from his plate on the sundial and absently began to gnaw.

'Your brother's a free man,' he was saying. 'Eugenius can't act outside the law, you know that.'

Oh, she knows that, Orbilio. And any minute her head will find itself on your shoulder, and if I were you, I'd check for hair dye on your tunic.

'He will, Marcus,' she sobbed. 'Eugenius means to do it, even though Utti's innocent.'

'Now, Tanaquil,' Orbilio said sternly, 'pull yourself together. Collatinus can do what he likes with his own slaves, he can execute the whole damned lot of them if he feels it's justified, but trust me, there's nothing he can do to a freeborn citizen.'

'Really?'

'Has your brother got his cap of freedom with him?'

'Yes, of course.'

'Then neither of you have anything to worry about.'

'You honestly think so?' The tears were conveniently under control. 'He loves people, Utti does.'

For breakfast maybe, Claudia thought, crunching into a stick of celery.

The redhead sought affirmation. 'Claudia, you saw him with Sabina, they were both the same, weren't they? Childlike in their different ways. Besides,' she blew her nose on Orbilio's proffered handkerchief, 'if he'd killed Sabina, we'd have left the island long ago.'

'Why didn't you?' Claudia asked innocently, and received a hurt look in reply.

'Tell me about Actë,' Orbilio said. 'Who found the body, and when?'

'Me.' Tanaquil spun round on the bench to face him. 'Marcus, it was horrible, just the same as Sabina. There's a birch grove about a half-mile up the hill from the villa, only nobody goes there because it's supposed to be haunted—'

'So what were *you* doing there?' There was a certain sharpness in Claudia's voice, and she was not surprised to see the girl blink several times before answering.

'I – I, well, I was just out for a walk, that's all. We'd been staying in Sullium and I fancied a bit of fresh air and—'

'Never mind that.' Orbilio admonished Claudia with a glare. 'What time did you discover the body?'

'Around noon. It's been a hot day, hasn't it, which might have something to do with it, but . . .' A violent shudder shook her whole body. ' . . . but her flesh was still warm.'

Which meant the murderer might still have been in the vicinity. Claudia wondered whether Tanaquil realized how lucky an escape she'd had.

The way she described finding the body, so meticulously yet so impersonally as though she was recounting someone else's story, brought the reality of Actë's death into sharp focus. The poor little bitch had been laid out on a limestone slab, her tunic covering her nakedness and anchored in place with her hands. As she said, just like Sabina. At first, because she seemed so peaceful, Tanaquil thought she was merely unconscious, but when she lifted Actë's head and saw the spreading stain on the white rock below, it was obvious she was way too late. But the action of moving the body had dislodged Actë's tunic, and Tanaquil saw that the insides of her thighs were bright red and sticky, and that's when she'd panicked and screamed.

Orbilio scratched his chin. 'She hadn't been . . . mutilated?'

Tanaquil shook her head. 'She'd been raped, but there weren't any of the bites and bruises like on Sabina.'

The celery stick fell from Claudia's fingers. Had Tanaquil interrupted the killer before he'd finished his work?

'Why should Collatinus think it was your brother who killed Actë?'

Tanaquil spread her hands. 'He said that since we arrived, two women had been murdered in the same foul way and he didn't believe in coincidence. What's more, he seemed to attach some significance to our leaving straight after that horrid business with Sabina.'

Don't we all! thought Claudia.

Orbilio rose to his feet. 'Look, you clean up, have a rest . . .'

His eyebrows rose enquiringly and Claudia found an imaginary knot in her girdle needed adjusting. No way! That light-fingered con artist could doss in someone else's bedroom!

'Use my quarters,' he said, with excruciating politeness. 'First past the shrine, on the right.'

Bugger. It was too late to intervene.

The redhead began to sob into Orbilio's handkerchief. 'They're going to kill him, I can see it.'

Claudia snorted. If further proof was needed that Utti's future was secure, that was surely conclusive. In fact, on that basis alone, he'd probably make eighty.

'I can,' Tanaquil gulped between sobs. 'I *can* see things. Only I don't always see the right things.'

You're telling me!

'You remember I saw your ship and I saw danger, except I thought it was for you,' she said to Claudia. 'I didn't realize it meant Sabina. Not until it was too late!' She began to convulse again. 'Nobody took her seriously.'

'Can you blame them? She was completely off her onion,' Claudia said reasonably, but, to her surprise, the fortune teller jumped to her feet.

'Don't say that about my friend!' she said hotly. 'Sabina just saw things from an unusual angle, found it hard to express herself.'

'She called me a cat.' Claudia's eyes defied Orbilio to say one single word. 'Told me I could see in the dark.'

'Cats are graceful,' Tanaquil explained. 'Seeing in the dark meant intuitive – well, you are, aren't you?'

Claudia remembered Sabina discussing these cat-like ways – the chase, the play, the pounce – and decided this wasn't a subject she'd particularly care to pursue. 'In Syracuse, she was babbling about fresh water in the sea.'

'The Spring of Ciane, you mean? The one that's hard by the Spring of Arethusa?'

Yes. Well. I knew that. She heard a sound from Orbilio, which might or might not have been a stifled laugh. You couldn't tell, the back of his hand was covering his mouth and he was looking over his shoulder to check the hang of his tunic.

'Sabina said drinking the water turned you white,' Claudia said accusingly.

Tanaquil produced a cross between a sob and a giggle. 'That silly religious cult, where the priestesses daub themselves in white clay and call themselves the Silver Nymphs of Ciane?'

Good grief! Assuming Sabina wasn't such a fruitcake after all, had she dropped some clue to her whereabouts these past thirty years? Incredible, but it wasn't as though it could have saved her life. Or Actë's.

Orbilio, who had begun pacing up and down the peristyle, his face tense with thought, asked, 'How did you get here so quickly?'

'I borrowed a horse from Eugenius's stables,' she said. 'Once I realized Utti was in danger, I rode like the wind.'

'Then you'd better get some rest.' Orbilio nodded towards his bedroom. 'We'll leave at first light, I promise you. Only for gods' sake stop worrying about your brother.'

He's big enough and ugly enough to look after himself, Claudia added silently.

Midnight was stalking up. Julius's revelries showed no signs of diminishing, the racket from the banqueting hall was as raucous as ever, but this end of the peristyle remained a haven of peace and relative tranquillity. The fountains and ponds absorbed much of the heat from the oppressive night air, and the various tinkling and bubbling and gurgling sounds made it as relaxing as was possible under the circumstances. A well-built but totally naked maenad came squealing down the path, zigzagging between the laurels and the sweet-smelling myrtles, pursued by a lecherous satyr. In the parts not lit by torchlight, he tended to lose sight of his quarry until another girlish giggle gave him his bearings. He eventually brought her down on the marble bench where Tanaquil had been sitting, leapt straight on top of her and began to knead her breasts. As foreplay went, Claudia thought it was on a par with a military charge.

'Do you mind!' Orbilio said. 'This is a private conversation.'

The satyr was either too drunk or too engrossed to grasp the message. 'You can have a go next. She won't mind.'

Probably grateful, Claudia thought. She was old enough to be their mother.

In response, Orbilio grabbed hold of the satyr's goatskin leggings and hauled him off the seat. 'I said this is private, now clear off.'

A kick up the goat's tail helped the young man along the path, and the woman sobered quickly, oh-my-godding under her breath as she scuttled into the shadows, undoubtedly computing the odds of either of these people knowing her husband.

Orbilio crashed his fist into a sandstone column. 'It's my fault,' he said bitterly. 'Actë would still be alive if it wasn't for me.'

There was no point telling him otherwise. Not yet.

'I shouldn't have left that bastard alone up there, I should have known he'd kill again.' Red blood dribbled down the grooves of the column. 'Mother of Tarquin, I'm a fool!'

'No one could have predicted a second murder so

quickly, Marcus. It's only eight days since Sabina was killed.' Officially the family still had one day left of mourning. Unofficially they never started.

'I should have arrested him on the spot instead of prancing round Agrigentum in search of proof. I could have done that while he was under lock and key.'

'You're not still on about Diomedes?'

'Claudia, I know you rate him, but listen. I've tried tracing the references he gave Collatinus, and they're false. Every last one of them.'

Her eyes challenged him. 'You condemn everyone who's forged their own past?'

'Dammit, Claudia, why can't you admit you're wrong about this bloody quack?'

She smiled and dipped her handkerchief in the bubbling fountain. 'I may have my faults, Orbilio, but believe me, being wrong isn't one of them. Wrap this round your knuckles.'

'Who else could it be?' He absently bandaged his bleeding hand. 'Who else has that precise medical knowledge?'

Claudia shrugged. 'How do I know? Someone who's spoken to him in the past? Another physician? An apothecary, pedlar or cutler? Could even be a lucky strike and now the killer's found a method, he's sticking to it.'

'This isn't about luck and the sooner this pervert's executed, the better. Are you coming with us to the villa tomorrow?'

That was one very intimate 'us'. And let's not forget she calls you by your personal name. 'Someone has to stop you putting the wrong man in chains,' Claudia said.

'Come on, who else is there?' he asked. Orbilio picked up the battered loaf and pulled a chunk off.

'You don't go along with Eugenius that it might be Utti?'

'Uh-uh,' he mumbled, his mouth full of bread. 'The proverbial gentle giant, him. I don't know what game Tanaquil's playing, but I don't think her brother's a party to it, which is why I'm in such a hurry to get back and knock some sense into the old man.'

There was a silence as the musicians took a well-earned break and the revellers paused for the last course of the banquet, probably fresh, sticky honeycombs. Little else would keep them so quiet.

'Two virgins, two murders,' he said eventually, brushing crumbs off the front of his tunic. 'What sort of maniac is this?'

'I hate to disabuse you, Orbilio, but there's a problem with your arithmetic. Sabina wasn't a virgin.'

'Not a Vestal, I know—'

'No, I mean she wasn't a Vestal *or* a virgin. I saw her body before it had been cleaned up, remember? Bruised, battered, semen on her thighs – but no blood. Wherever Sabina had been for thirty years, she hadn't been sticking to a vow of chastity.'

'Croesus!' Orbilio combed his hair with his hands and began to pace up and down again. 'You know, one of the lines I followed up was to see whether a Sabina Collatinus had ever been called to initiation and guess what? She turned up all right, six or seven years old, but before she could be ordained, she ran away. Naturally a full-scale search was organized, but before the holy sisters could contact the family, word came back that Sabina had been killed in a traffic accident. As far as the Vestals were concerned, the matter was closed.'

'How does that tie in with Matidia writing to her daughter, care of the Vestals in Rome?'

'It means the letters were intercepted.' Orbilio cupped his hands in the fountain and briskly sluiced his face with the cold water. 'The pieces are beginning to come together at last.'

They are? 'It still doesn't answer whether the woman I met was the real Sabina Collatinus or an imposter.'

'No it doesn't, but it's proved one thing. You weren't in on it.' Orbilio let out a loud and throaty chuckle. 'Juno's skirts, you were after Varius all the time. You bloody came after Varius!' This time he drank the water cupped in his hands.

'I came for a holiday,' Claudia replied coolly. 'Chaperoning Sabina was all part and parcel. Who's your money on now for her accomplice?'

'Take your pick, anyone's as likely – or as unlikely – as another. But one thing is without doubt. The bastard who killed Sabina and Actë is no novice. Someone, somewhere, has been butchered in the same way, I'll lay money on it.'

XXV

The sun beat hot on his back as Melinno stumbled along the road, pushed and jostled by the throng of pedestrians and donkeys and handcarts making their way to market. Children jeered and mimicked his apelike shuffle, catcalls rang in his ears and more than once he'd been on the receiving end of a lash.

He knew what he looked like – clothes torn and ragged, hair long, beard matted. He probably stank like a hoopoe's hole, only he'd lived with himself too long to notice. Tears streaked the grime on his face. Sulpica would be ashamed of him, it were pitiful. No longer able to walk upright, he clutched his aching chest, shuffling like a stroke victim, barely strong enough to cough up the dark phlegm in his lungs.

He were dying.

He knew it – aye, as sure as the sun rises in the east and the Trojan horse were made of maple – and it didn't bother him none. Soon he'd be with Sulpica. Together for ever. It drove a sword in his heart that he could no longer picture the precise colour of her eyes or recall the way she spoke, but soon – very soon – he'd be able to see for himself.

But before he could go to her, he must avenge her. How could he face her otherwise? He had made his vow on her deathbed and by Janus, he would keep it. It were this oath what drove his body, lending him the strength and cunning to leap aboard the wagon of an itinerant pitch seller, a Corsican, bound for Agrigentum from Henna. The strong resinous smell of his cargo disguised the presence of the stowaway and after just three days the wagon was rumbling through the high arches of the Gela Gate.

Within minutes, almost, the Corsican were descended upon by hordes of farmers, desperate to melt his pitch into tar to preserve their timber and put in their sheepwash, mark their corn sacks and smear on their wine corks. Unseen, Melinno slipped into the crush. Agrigentum. Half a day from the Villa Collatinus. Cough or no cough, he were within an ace of his quest. Retribution would be his.

He reached down to pat his knife. It were gone. He spun round, losing his balance. His knife, his cloak, his pack, his canteen! He'd left them on the wagon! Oblivious to the blood coursing from his knee, he hauled himself up from the gutter and pushed through the crowds, first this way, then that, until all hope of finding the Corsican was lost. He fell against the stone wall of a spice dealer, too tired, too spent to swear. Not that he'd sworn much of late. Sulpica didn't like it, and he wanted to be more the man she loved and remembered when they met up.

'Oi, you! Clear off!' The spice merchant prodded him with a cattle goad. 'You're bad for trade.'

Melinno reeled round the corner. In his confusion, he realized now, he'd been blundering in the wrong direction, He was back at the Gela Gate, which was closing for the night. Now what? He tried begging, and received only clouts. Being neither blind nor lame nor deformed, people mistook him for a common drunk, shivering and delirious with the DTs. Turning right, where the wall fell away so many hundreds of cubits it made him dizzy, Melinno chanced upon a flight of steps cut deep into the rock. He slipped and slithered, hoping to find a roost for the night, and found instead they led to a narrow chamber, which in turn led to two great caverns lit by torches. This were a shrine, most likely Ceres judging from the offerings, but if he kept to the shadows he could pass the night here and maybe get healed a bit. There were springs in the caves, springs of sweet, fresh water which fed the basins in the little courtyard, and some of the pilgrims had left bread for the corn goddess.

At first light, before he could drink the water or eat the bread, the priests had found him and thrown him out by the scruff of his neck, splitting open the cut on his knee. Now, well clear of the city and shambling along the Sullium road, he found the local traffic had thinned and his ears picked up the sound he'd been waiting for. The sound of hooves clip-clopping along the paving blocks. Turning, his weak eyes nearly blinded by the sun, he saw he were right. Two mules, a covered wagon for long distance travel. Stepping into the middle of the road, he flagged it down.

'I need a ride,' he pleaded. 'To Sullium.'

It were gentry on the wagon. A young noblewoman, tall and beautiful, surrounded by slaves and a girl with red hair.

'It's a matter of life and death.' He were stuttering, only he couldn't help it, it were the fever.

The noblewoman stood up. 'It would be for us, you walking pestilence factory. Out of the way.'

Melinno held out the only treasure he had left. Sulpica's betrothal ring. 'I can pay.'

The young woman's nose wrinkled. 'I don't want your trinket, you verminous little man.'

Their eyes met momentarily and hers looked away first. When she spoke, her voice was softer. 'You can take this, if you like.' She nodded to one of the slaves, a black man, who offered a water flask by its leather strap held at arm's length.

Melinno's eyes blinked his understanding. He were a fool to think gentry'd have him, and were grateful beyond words for the water. As he leaned forward to take the canteen, the mules already being chivvied, he heard a cat snarl and a soothing voice saying:

'It's all right, poppet, our kittens won't catch anything nasty from him.'

Claudia yawned and massaged her ankle where her left foot had gone to sleep. Junius was riding on the buckboard with the driver, an extra pair of eyes to watch for bandits, leaving Claudia with the other three bodyguards in the back. Safety was not a problem. She yawned again and rubbed her eyes. Dammit, she hadn't slept a wink all night. Not that she was jealous of Tanaquil bunking up with Orbilio. Good heavens, no. Those images of writhing limbs and sweat-soaked bodies which kept her awake were mere irritants, nothing else. Who cared what they got up to?

All the same, if Fancypants was such a hot-shot lover, how come Tanaquil had been uncharacteristically silent all day? She, who wouldn't talk for five minutes when half an hour would do, had done nothing but hold her head in her hands since boarding the wagon. Orbilio, of course, true to his word, had set off at daybreak on Tanaquil's horse, so Claudia got no clues from that quarter.

Her own progress, meanwhile, consisted of one delay after another. First came the legion on the march, clanking six abreast, bronze greaves dazzling in the morning sunshine and there was a slight argument in which the wagon driver, Rupi, put the case for pulling off at the approaching post station and Claudia put the case against, followed by a full-blown argument when Claudia put the case for skinning the wagon driver and Rupi put the case against.

The cavalry, protecting the baggage, led the van followed by the legates and the tribunes and the prefects and the escorts, a myriad of scarlet cloaks swinging in unison. Then came the eagle bearer and the standard bearers wearing their animal skins, wolf and lion and leopard, followed by ten thousand crunching hobnail boots. Finally the doctors, the secretaries, the blacksmiths and the orderlies brought up the rear. Somewhere, too, were the musicians – horn blowers, drummers, trumpeters.

The sound was not dissimilar to a million bronze sieves and saucepans being repeatedly dropped from a great height, yet in years to come, the master of this particular post station would swear, hand on heart, that he had witnessed a miracle. The 8th Legion had filed past in silence, he swore. All anyone could hear was the heated argument between one young noblewoman and her driver.

To Claudia's disgust, the sun had moved considerably across the heavens before the last orderly had jangled off and Tanaquil still had her face buried in her handkerchief.

Well, let's be accurate here, it wasn't *her* handkerchief, was it? It was a patrician handkerchief, and one could only hope he had something infectious to pass on.

Clambering back on board, she thought of that dung-beetle Varius. Attractive as it seemed, it was no use having him turn up in the river with a blade between his ribs, she'd be prime suspect – and anyway, who could she trust? Junius, she knew, would give his life for her; which was not the same thing as taking one for her.

For some strange reason, instead of staying in Agrigentum to sort the problem out, here she was, trotting back to Sullium and making as much headway as a sleepy slug on an oiled pole. Shortly after the cohorts had marched past, they were delayed by some filthy tramp with a bleeding knee trying to cadge a ride, if you please. On the face of it, she ought to have sent him away with a flea in his ear (although he probably had a whole nestful of them there already), yet there was that momentary flicker when his eyes held hers and she saw, not the drunken beggar, but the young artisan he once was – straight of spine and keen of eye – and in that brief flash of communication, she had wondered what circumstances had reduced him to this pathetic level.

Claudia had encountered many beggars in her time. They clotted round city gates like flies on a sore and sometimes you dropped copper and sometimes you didn't. But they never expected you to look in their eyes, and thankfully you never were tempted.

That, though, was mid-morning – yet here, two hours on and the far side of Sullium, the wagon was once more at a standstill! Goddamit, was there no justice?

Claudia nudged the canvas aside, more for air than

the view, yet it was the view which startled her. They were on the western highway, less than a mile from where the road to the Villa Collatinus branched off, giving a fine view of Eugenius's estate.

Had she really been gone only three days? It had changed out of all recognition!

The blue of the African Sea was as bright as ever and sparkling like glass, and the red tiles and white walls of the villa itself still shone like gemstones on a granite slab. You could even see the tops of the birch grove where Actë had met her fate, and the serpentine trail that was the short-cut she had taken the day she found Sabina. Then it had been the epitome of solitude and rural tranquillity. Today it swarmed with life.

Sheep, hundreds of them, had been brought down from the hills and packed into hastily erected pens. Shepherds who, for most of the year, were tough, self-sufficient, solitary creatures, clustered together with their fellow shepherds and the sea breeze carried the bleating and the pan pipes and the gossip and the laughter, even at this distance. Closer to the building, and more curiously still, half a dozen cows were gathered in a smaller pen, gormless creatures with dewlaps flapping, horns glinting, brushing away flies with a desultory swish of the tail. The occasional low filtered up, a baritone among the bleating sopranos.

Claudia decided the delay had gone on long enough. Small clouds of dust rose from her feet as she walked round the cart. There was a strong smell of wild celery in the air, and rosemary and spurge. She stretched her arms, stiffened after the journey. 'What's the problem?'

Junius pointed. 'The old man,' he said. 'Said he was

here first, he's too old to shift, but Rupi can't move over because of the camber.'

Typical, she thought. Rupi gives way to a couple of soldiers and then refuses to help an old man.

'I'm going uphill, I've got right of way.'

'You've got no rights, you stubborn old sod, shove off.'

Seven donkeys, laden with baskets bursting with seaweed the old man had collected to enrich his exhausted patch of soil, stood mournfully in the middle of the road, while pack-man and driver traded insults. They had just reached the stage where their mothers' sexual proclivities were being aired when Claudia tossed a denarius into the seaweedy air. Instantly the old man's eyes homed in on the silver and a claw swooped down. Faster than you could say 'That'll buy one week's meat and grain for a month', the denarius had disappeared and five of the donkeys were already treading grass. Not so difficult, was it?

Claudia had hardly got herself comfortable when she heard the driver shout, 'Whoa!' and felt the mules slow down.

'*Now what?*' She jumped from the wagon and marched to the front. She would have a word with Eugenius, really she would, leaving a man like Rupi in charge of a vehicle. He was incompetent. Downright dangerous in fact, and she was in the middle of telling him how she would have him roasted on a spit with artichokes and lovage when Junius butted in.

'I think he's trying to tell you the rider has signalled us to stop.'

'What rider?'

'You can't see him from down there,' Rupi replied

with no small amount of satisfaction, and magnanimously offered her a hand up.

Tempted to snatch the whip out of his hand and beat him to a pulp with it, Claudia refrained. The buckboard was narrow and uncomfortable, but you sure could see well. A rider was pushing his horse hard up the incline, head bent forward, as the hooves kicked up swirls of umber. She could only surmise, because Rupi seemed to understand it, that his frantic arm-waving was some sort of recognized signal to halt. Reining in his horse, as handsome a grey as you got on this island, the rider became visible through the subsiding dust clouds.

'Good grief, it's the cavalry.'

Marcus Cornelius Orbilio gave a mock salute and shook the hair out of his eyes. A small, powdery halo formed and was quickly dispersed by the salt air. A second rider was hard on his heels, and Orbilio greeted him with surprise:

'Linus?'

'Marcus.' As an afterthought, Linus turned to acknowledge Claudia. 'Have you told her yet?' His eyes, shining, were back on Orbilio.

'No. Look, I'd be obliged—'

'But it's great news,' Linus said, his face splitting into a grin. 'We've caught him.'

'Who?' Claudia asked, aware that Tanaquil had left the wagon and was standing wringing her hands. Was this for Orbilio's benefit or for Linus?

'My sister's murderer,' Linus said, attempting to cover his baldness with his gingery hair. 'We've got him, it's all over.' He manoeuvred his horse into a victory circle. 'Isn't that great?'

She glanced at Orbilio. He clearly didn't think great was the word, and she could see what had happened. Collatinus was holding Utti prisoner and proud of it, a scapegoat to hold up to the world, and until he brought down higher authority, Eugenius was milking it to the full. He would know, as Orbilio would know (and indeed had probably told him till he turned purple), that it would never get to trial without evidence, and this wouldn't bother Collatinus. He'd be getting enough publicity to last his great-grandchildren's lifetimes. The Security Police had got nowhere, the local magistrates not even as far as that. He would be a hero, and when the real killer was caught, he could hold his hands up and cry, well, he was an old man, what do you expect, and Utti would . . .

Aha! Yes, Utti would also be a hero. Claudia began to see Tanaquil's angle. Cunning little bitch, she'd been planning this all along. Those powers of hers, off-key and infrequent as they were, had served her well here, because when Utti walked free, everyone on the island would want to watch him wrestle. Coins would change hands, his fame would spread, they would move to Rome, where greater denominations would change hands. Claudia took her hat off to the redhead. She *did* know how to make a packet out of the Collatinuses – and without them coughing up one single copper quadran of their own. She looked at Tanaquil out of the corner of her eye, face hidden behind a white, linen blob. A white, patrician, linen blob.

She had taken so long in answering Linus that he was guiding his horse on a vociferous celebratory canter round the wagon, much to Rupi's annoyance. It was getting his mules' rag up and, as we all know, when it comes to mules, rags don't have very far to travel.

'You're talking about Utti, I presume?'

Linus seemed to have lost interest in Claudia and was asking Marcus whether he fancied coming to the pothouse tonight. Orbilio, she noticed, was trying to speak with his eyes to Claudia while answering with his mouth to Linus. Neither communication seemed to be getting through.

'Giddy-up,' she said to Rupi, squeezing herself between him and Junius, 'let's get these nags some hay.'

Linus was whistling, at least she presumed that's what it was meant to be, as he wheeled his horse round. 'Race you back, Marcus.'

Orbilio hadn't moved. His gaze was directed straight at her now. Claudia felt a blast of cold, intuitive air. It wasn't Utti at all. Holy Mars, they'd collared Diomedes! You bastard, she thought. You cold-blooded, calculating bastard. False imprisonment for a physician would ruin his career, he'd be begging on the streets within a year. Eugenius would turn him out, innocent or not, because mud sticks, even when you spread it yourself. And Supersnoop had let him do it. Correction, Supersnoop had actively encouraged it.

His gaze didn't waver, neither did hers. An innocent man arrested for murder, because you see the doors of the Senate House opening in front of you. An innocent man ruined, because you can't see beyond your own filthy ambitions.

As Linus galloped off, Claudia's eyes ground into Orbilio's. Well, if you can't do your damned job, then I'll bloody well do it for you. I'll catch this pervert, Marcus Cornelius, and I'll do it the only way I know how. I'll set myself up as bait. I'll have you looking so small, they'll have to pick you up with tweezers.

He inched his horse forward. 'I'm sorry—' he began.

By rights, ice should have formed on his eyelashes, snow should have fallen on his brow. Claudia's glacial expression didn't waver. This man didn't know what sorry was. Yet!

His face was lined and drawn, his mouth pursed. The twinkle in his eye was reduced to a glint of pain. A stone mallet thudded into Claudia's stomach. Oh no. Oh no, please, no . . .

'What have you done to Diomedes?' she asked stiffly.

His expression flickered. 'Who?'

'What?' She was puzzled, too. 'I'm asking what's happened to Diomedes.'

Orbilio's expression changed several times then hardened. He squared his shoulders before speaking. 'I'm sorry,' he said, in a voice generally reserved for superior officers and inferior lowlife. 'I thought you were interested in Utti.'

'Utti?' Tanaquil darted over and placed a hand on his knee. There was, Claudia noticed, no tunic covering that particular area of knee. 'What about him?'

Orbilio covered her hand with his own, and Claudia felt a pang of something she couldn't identify.

'They've arrested him, haven't they?' Tanaquil made to run off, but Orbilio leaned down from his horse and held her back.

'It's worse than that,' he said gently. 'I am so sorry, Tanaquil.' His face was twisted with pain. 'Collatinus has impaled him.'

XXVI

Claudia did not know where to direct her anger.

From a hundred miles away she heard Tanaquil ask, 'When?' and Orbilio reply, 'Yesterday, at dusk,' then the sickening reality set in.

Utti. Impaled on a stake. A big man, a tough man, a fighter. Utti, who for those very reasons would have taken hours and hours to die. She imagined the scene, scores of slaves crowding round. *Is he dead yet? Is he dead yet?* Utti, the wrestler, with his great ham fists and his flattened nose and his cauliflower ears. Utti, the children's favourite. Utti, impaled on a stake, roaring like a wounded bear, crying like the baby he really was. Alone. Frightened. Unable to comprehend.

Orbilio had dismounted and was doing his best to comfort Tanaquil, who stood as stiff and motionless as a statue. Junius, Kleon, Rupi the driver – everyone was open-mouthed and silent.

Claudia leaned against the great wheel of the wagon and was quietly, tidily, efficiently sick. Then, when the shaking subsided, the anger began to grow, intensifying, magnifying, getting hotter and hotter with each passing second until the volcano could contain it no longer.

She wanted to slap Tanaquil, tell her this was *her*

fault, her stupid scams, her stupid brother, couldn't she see where it would lead?

She wanted to pound her fists into Orbilio, tell him this was *his* fault, if he'd done his job properly, Utti would be alive and well and so what if it meant living in poverty, at least he'd be alive.

She wanted to shake Eugenius until his eyes rattled, tell him this was *his* fault, he should have consulted the magistrates, followed proper legal procedures instead of jumping to half-baked conclusions.

She wanted to scream at Aulus, Fabius, Linus, Portius, tell them this was *their* fault, why didn't they challenge the old man for once, stuff the law which demands a father's orders be obeyed, even at the expense of an innocent man.

But most of all, Claudia wanted to claw her fingernails down her arms and draw blood, to watch it drip into the dusty soil and turn brown and harden. This was not her fault, yet she could not rid herself of the guilt.

Before she even realized it, she was slithering down the slope towards the villa. Somewhere in the area – maybe in Fintium, maybe in Sullium – lived a man. A man who killed defenceless women, raping them while they lay paralysed, their lungs unable to supply the air they needed to breathe. A slow, agonizing death. The same man who, now thought he had got away with it.

Well, he hadn't. Not by a long chalk.

There was only the porter at the front gate, and Cerberus who came loping up, wagging his tail, straining on his chain to greet her. Claudia paused to rub his ears and pat his neck. It was sufficient time for Junius to catch up.

'I didn't realize you'd gone, madam.' The words came

out stilted because he was out of breath. Sweat poured down his forehead.

Claudia couldn't speak, even if she wanted to. She wondered whether her face was as pale and pinched as his.

'May I make a suggestion?' Junius? Making a suggestion? Well, why not? 'That you wait a bit before tackling Master Eugenius?'

She gave him a look that told him it was none of his business, but the young Gaul stared so earnestly that it clicked her brain back into action. And Claudia Seferius knew better than most that to succeed in this life, you follow the head, not the heart. And that sometimes it was hard.

She laid her hand on his arm and squeezed gently and didn't speak. He was right. She had to separate grief from outrage and, to be in any way effective, to channel her anger in the right direction. Towards the man responsible for murdering Actë and Sabina.

It did not occur to her to ask the boy how he knew she intended to confront Collatinus.

You'd think nothing out of the ordinary had taken place. Slaves with buckets scrubbed the floors, polished the statues, dusted the tables, chairs and couches. A smell of sprats and cabbage and poached plums filtered through from the kitchen, and someone was singing a song to which Claudia sang different words. Marius and Paulus lay flat on their stomachs, prodding a wooden boat back and forth across the pool. Vilbia sat, tongue between her teeth in concentration, playing with her favourite knitted doll.

Claudia crossed to the garden, alive with the crunch of sand against stone as paths were swept, laurels were clipped and plants were watered. Eugenius's room was at the far end, but before she could reach it, a blond figure intercepted.

'Claudia!' He was slightly out of breath, his hands hidden in an unsightly lump beneath his pallium. 'You look as ravishing as ever.'

It was true. Between them, Claudia's make-up box and her natural instinct to hide her emotions had veiled every trace of the turmoil within.

'I . . .' The beguiling accent hesitated. 'I have something for you. A gift.'

From his pallium he revealed his secret. Claudia blinked several times.

'Why, um, thank you.' *A pigeon?* 'Diomedes, that is . . . Well, what I mean to say is . . .' She gave what she hoped was a light, silvery laugh as he pressed the fluttering bird into her hands. 'You've no idea how much this means to me.'

'Really?' His cheeks flushed.

'Oh yes. Really. I shall . . . treasure it. Always.' Dammit, the bloody thing was already pecking her finger, but Diomedes looked so happy it seemed churlish to throw it back at him.

To her infinite relief he said, 'I must go now,' and his eyes, surprisingly, were moist.

Claudia's smile was both practised and perfect, and the instant his back was turned, she stuffed the pigeon into the hands of the slave collecting the clippings. If it was going to poop, let it poop on someone else. She shook her stola, mint green and flattering, leaving a sprinkle of white feathers in her wake. She did not wait for Eugenius to reply to her knock.

'Welcome back, my dear.' The old man sat in his chair behind a desk, papers spread in front of him. Dexippus sat to his right, Fabius and Linus stood before him. 'Enjoy the celebrations?'

For one absurd moment she thought he was referring to Utti, then remembered the festivities in Agrigentum in honour of some local deity whose name began with a K or an F or something, and which seemed years away, rather than hours.

'Splendid.' He hadn't waited for an answer, the response was automatic.

A small shiver ran through Claudia as her senses sharpened and her brain clicked up a gear. She was about to witness the real Eugenius in action. Not the sanitized version he had allowed her to see up till now, the old-man-reminiscing version, the old-man-with-his-family version, which, whilst not actually exuding warmth and affection, was not cold or wooden either. No, the gloves were off and the self-same instincts that fired the inveterate gambler in Claudia were aroused. Her heart beat just that little bit faster, her eyes were just that little bit sharper, her mouth just that little bit drier.

Eugenius started laying into Linus, leaving Claudia with a sackful of mixed feelings. It was unquestionably satisfying, watching him wither and wilt under the onslaught, shrinking with each verbal missile, but Linus was not the type to let it rest. He would vent his anger and frustration later. On his wife.

'How many times have I told you, you fathead, I don't want cattle on my farm. I'm a sheep farmer, not a bloody cow man.'

'But—'

'Those brutes are neither use nor ornament. How much did you pay for them?'

'About—'

'You were ripped off. The buggers are too old to breed, and if I've told you once, I've told you a million times, good cattle have thick necks. Janus, I could wring one of those in my own puny fist!'

'I wanted—'

'Get out.'

Linus opened his mouth.

'I said, get out!'

Linus's face was dark with indignation, but Claudia noticed the door closed quietly on its hinges. Dexippus's thick lips smirked openly as Eugenius turned his attentions to his favourite.

'And you, boy, I expected better things from you.'

Fabius had drawn himself up to his full height, shoulders back, staring straight ahead, two decades of army training standing him in good stead.

'Yessir.'

'White rams, I said, and what do you bring me? White rams with – what, boy?'

'Black tongues, sir.'

'What did I tell you about black-tongued rams?'

'They breed black-spotted lambs.'

'And do I want black-spotted lambs?'

'No, sir.'

'Then get rid of them.'

'Yessir.'

That was Fabius for you. Nerves of steel and a brain to match. It was interesting, she thought, as he reached the door in three long strides, to see the sprig of bay clipped to his tunic. She had learned much from her father, the army orderly. Admittedly he wasn't home very often, but you picked up a lot in the short time he was there. Like, for instance, how soldiers wore bay to sanctify them from the blood they had spilled . . .

Her mind was busy digesting this when Eugenius rounded on his secretary. 'And you, you idle oaf, get off your fat arse and chase up that bitumen shipment. You know damned well I can't dip my sheep until it arrives.'

'I checked yesterday, Master.'

'It should have been here yesterday, you dithering fool, now get out there and see what's holding it up.'

The smirk on Dexippus's face had given way to an expression dripping with obsequiousness. 'I'll see to it straight away, Master. You can rely on me, Master.'

He backed out of the door, and Eugenius swept the papers on his desk onto the floor with a backward flip of the hand.

'Where's Actë?'

The question startled her. 'She's er—'

'Dammit, I don't know what she's up to lately, didn't even bother to bring me my breakfast this morning. Have you signed that contract yet?'

Claudia felt she was walking on quicksand. 'Contract?' She was stalling and he knew it.

'You know damn fine what I'm talking about, young lady, and I want to know when—'

He stopped, realizing that he was in danger of overstepping the mark. This was the very reason he hadn't shown his true colours before, and he wouldn't risk spoiling his chances now.

'Pour us both a drink,' he said, 'and tell me whether you think that position there is humanly possible, or whether the woman would need to be double-jointed.'

Claudia did not look at the pornographic frieze he was pointing to, neither did she pour the wine.

Eugenius Collatinus knew a challenge when it was dangled in front of him, and his eyes twinkled appreciatively. 'I like you,' he said.

'It's not mutual,' she replied, but there was no sting in her voice.

'You'll make a good team, you and – Alieee!' His face contorted and his hands flew to his stomach.

'I'll fetch Diom—' she began, and got no further.

'Stay!' There was no mistaking the authority, even through the pain. 'It's just the colic.'

Claudia waited until the pains abated before pointing out, purely as a matter of interest, that she had seen colic.

He winced as he gave a short laugh. His face was grey and beaded with sweat. He drank the wine she poured, and they both pretended it was alum water.

'I like sheep,' he said eventually. 'I dip them, I brand them, I clip them, I lamb them.' He looked very small and shrivelled in his ivory chair. 'I don't have to bother about plagues of thistles or how bad the blight will be this year.'

'Why did you kill Utti?'

'It's my poor neighbours who have to worry about weevils in their corn sacks, I just let my sheep graze in their stubble fields.'

'Let me rephrase the question. Why did you kill Utti?'

'Where's Actë?'

'Who are you covering up for?'

The accusation rattled him. 'Eugenius Collatinus doesn't cover up for anybody, my girl, and you'd do well to remember that.'

He drained his glass so fast, wine dribbled down his chin, staining his tunic crimson. Claudia waited. As so often happened with this old man, she met with the unexpected. He banged a wax tablet several times on the table, and a slave came running.

'Did I hear that red-haired trollop has returned?'

'You did, Master.'

'Clap her in irons then.' When the slave had gone, Eugenius turned to Claudia. 'You want to know why I executed that ugly, fat bastard? Because he killed my granddaughter.'

A paper-thin hand drummed gnarled fingers on the woodwork. Claudia's eyes followed them up and down, up and down.

'Those filthy hands of his had been all over her, he got what he deserved, which is more than my Sabina did.' The drumming stopped and he leaned forward. 'She rode in carriages, you know. Fine, fancy carriages whenever there was a special festival.'

'How do you know?'

'Eh?' He looked at Claudia as though she was stupid. 'We got letters, of course.'

'Of course. You were saying?'

'Sabina devoted thirty years of her life to Vesta, that's a hell of a long time to spend doing nothing except offer sacrifices and make sure the Eternal Flame never whitens to ash. She deserved better.'

'I agree. You haven't answered my question.'

Again the change in direction. 'You were right, it's not colic. I've got ulcers in the intestines, and sometimes it feels like red-hot claws tearing out my liver.'

'Why won't you tell the doctor?'

He looked up sharply. 'None of your damned business! Where's Actë, have you seen her? Didn't bring me my breakfast, y'know.'

This was odd. Extremely odd. Surely someone had told the old man about Actë . . .?

'Eugenius, look, I'm not sure how to say this—'

'Probably excited. I'll let you into a secret, Claudia, just between you and me. I've asked her to marry me.'

What? 'Have you told the family?'

'She knows how to look after me, I don't need a bloody charlatan poking about in my innards.'

Claudia was having to absorb so many different shocks, she was in danger of having mental indigestion. To play for time, she bent down and gathered up the rolls and scrolls from the floor.

'That's very kind of you, my dear.' So many shifts of mood, no wonder he was a devil to do business with. He began to arrange them neatly on his desk. 'I like to keep my accounts in good order,' he said, 'and naturally I've made provision for Actë.' He leaned forward and whispered. 'Another year's the best I can hope for, but she makes me happy. Don't tell Dex.'

Still this present tense . . .

'Why not?'

The old man cackled. 'He's jealous of her, so I wrote the will myself. Find it for me, will you?'

Claudia shot him an old-fashioned look, but was glad of the opportunity to rifle through his papers. Unfortunately there was nothing startling or contentious among them, and she handed him the paper making provision for Actë.

Did he, or did he not, know she had been killed? Had his grief-stricken mind blocked out what it couldn't bear to face? It happened all the time, but the question was, did it happen to a man like Eugenius Collatinus?

'I'll get it witnessed later,' he said, glancing through the document. 'You can sign your own contract at the same time.'

'Oh, can I?' she asked smoothly, settling herself in the seat Dexippus had vacated.

Eugenius laughed appreciatively. 'You're a clever woman, Claudia Seferius.'

She widened her eyes ingenuously.

'Didn't take my hint of dismissal,' he explained unnecessarily. He pretended to fiddle with the scrolls in front of him. 'You want to know about Utti?'

'Right.' At last. We are getting there at last.

He ran his hand sensuously over the lionhead carving on his chair. 'Let's start with that little trollop claiming to be his sister.'

'Claiming?'

Eugenius shrugged. 'Who knows? Who cares? She stole a horse of mine.'

'She went to fetch help.'

'Pah! This has happened before, mark my words. Trace their footsteps and you'll find a score of butchered women, just like my Sabina, and every time that little whore's covered up for him.'

'How do you know?'

'Tell me what she was doing there yesterday.'

'Where?'

'Said she was out for a stroll, but why weren't they together? How come Utti's already there?'

'Where?'

'The birch grove, where my little Sabina was killed.'

Claudia waited a moment, marshalling her thoughts and resisting the temptation to state the obvious. Finally she said, 'How do you know he was there?'

'Utti? Someone saw him.'

'Who?'

'Can't remember.' He saw the expression on her face. 'Does it matter?'

Claudia's eyes continued to bore into his.

'All right, Marius saw him there. But you can't convince me it wasn't that big bastard, because I know it was. Two women have been murdered, both in exactly the same . . .'

His voice trailed off and the look he gave her was of inconsolable bereavement. He had remembered. What he had spent the day trying to block out had come back to him. Tears scoured his thin, papery cheeks.

'Actë,' he wailed. 'Actë!'

He was still rocking himself when Claudia closed the door behind her, wondering why she felt no pity for the old man, only contempt. In spite of the fact that he'd held the will upside down and pretended to read it.

XXVII

It was Junius who discovered the man, delirious and barely alive, on the road above the villa.

'You're kidding!' Claudia said, when he told her. 'The same chap?'

The young Gaul nodded.

'Well, I'll be damned. I presume you haven't left him there?'

'No, madam. I carried him down to the clipshed.'

The more I hear about you, Junius, the less I know you. The clipshed. Deserted this time of year. In other words: 'So no one else is aware of his existence.'

The Gaul gave a sheepish grin. 'He's in a bad way, though.'

'Hmmm.' Claudia placed her palms together and pressed her fingers to her lips. 'Look, you go and disinfect yourself, you're probably crawling with lice, and I'll send Diomedes to look him over. No, hang on. What was it you wanted to tell me about Dexippus?'

She listened, and it was clear to Junius that she didn't like what he had to relate. It did, she confided, tie in with a rumour she'd heard earlier, explaining why she'd taken such pains to transport Drusilla and co. to Agrigentum which, at the time, was planned as only a day's visit. She dismissed him, wondering what strange motivation drove the boy to be so utterly conscientious. He was, after all, only a slave and did not, as far as she was aware, have a lover. His job was his life, it seemed, and if that was the case, good luck to him. One day he'd find out there was more to life than work, but in the meantime, this was all to Claudia's good.

The physician's mouth turned down at the corners as he straightened up. 'It's difficult,' he said. 'I'll know a lot more, of course, once I've got him cleaned up, but right now? A fifty–fifty chance. Do you know who he is?'

Claudia shook her head. 'When Junius found him he was mumbling some girl's name, Sulpica I believe, and whilst our friend may be dirty, I don't think underneath those scabs and incrustations we're likely to find a woman's body, do you?'

Diomedes grinned. 'Probably not. As I say, I'll clean him up and see what he looks like, but basically those are superficial wounds he's carrying. The main problem area is the chest. I'm afraid his lungs will need the cautery.'

Claudia winced. What drugs cannot cure, the knife can. What the knife cannot cure, the cautery can. And what the cautery cannot cure, cannot be cured . . .

Leaving him at it, she made her way round the walls of the villa. A window had been broken, it looked like the glass of the newly decorated banqueting hall. From inside, harsh words were being addressed to a very quiet individual. She listened.

'Your impertinence, I assure you, will be reported to your father.'

'It wasn't me!'

Claudia heard the swish of the cane, grimaced as it connected with tender young flesh.

'Children who tell lies have to be punished. What is this?'

'A stone, sir.'

'A very small stone, and see that trajectory? This is the work of a catapult.'

'I don't—'

Swish, thwack. 'Less of your backchat, young man!'

Young *man*? Claudia's eyebrows arched involuntarily and when she turned round, Popillia was standing beside her, mischievously swinging the device in question. Claudia threw back her head and laughed aloud.

'You are one quick learner, young lady.'

'Marius is a pig,' Popillia said haughtily. 'I'm just getting my own back. What were you doing in the clipshed with Diomedes?'

'Not what you think, madam.' Precocious brat.

'He's taught me my Greek.' She swung into step alongside Claudia. '*That apple had a maggot in it* and *Boys are sillies, because they've got willies.*'

I'll go along with that, thought Claudia.

Popillia broke into a skip. 'You like him, don't you?'

'Who?'

'Diomedes.'

'Of course. Doesn't everyone?'

The child screwed up her nose. 'I don't.' She jumped round 180° and began to skip back up the path. 'He tells lies.'

Marius was out of breath by the time he reached his favourite perch. He liked climbing trees. Oaks and cedars were best, and the stone pines down by the beach. They had broad boughs close to the ground, you could swing like a monkey, balance like a rope walker, sit astride and pretend you were on a horse. He liked this tree best, though. It was a walnut with really thick branches and plenty of cover to hide. His favourite branch overhung Great-Grandpapa's room and sometimes Marius could watch him put his horrid old hand down Actë's tunic. Once he saw a nipple.

Normally he could clamber around for ages without puffing, but then normally he didn't get punished for things he hadn't done. Small hands reached up and grasped the rough bark. Who was firing from a catapult, that's what he wanted to know? He'd find the boy and thrash him like Piso had thrashed *him*. Marius tenderly probed his sore stripes. He'd knock that boy's teeth down his throat, he would too. He'd rub his face in a cowpat and then he'd hold his head under the sheepdip and then . . .

The flash of gold made him lose his grip and he'd slithered two handspans, grazing his elbow, before he could steady himself. He was right. It *was* gold! Marius licked his little pink lips. Treasure! He'd found treasure! He remembered Jason and his Argonauts on their quest for the Golden Fleece. They found it, after all those adventures, in the Garden of the Hesperides and now here, in his very own garden, was another golden treasure swinging gently back and forth, catching the dazzling rays of the setting sun.

Flash.

And flash.

And flash.

Mesmerized and excited, his eyes followed it. He came

here so often, how come he'd not seen it before? Had it been here all along, hidden among the gold autumn leaves? He reached out. Nearly... Nearly... He stretched his arm to its limit, his cheeks puffed out like round, shiny apples in a monumental effort of concentration. Then he saw what it was. A small globe on a chain, spinning, spinning. Just as his fist made to close over it, his treasure shot up in the air.

'Hallo, Marius.'

Claudia, lying along the length of the branch above, dangled his Spanish gold bulla from one fingertip.

His eyes were as wide as colanders. 'You can climb trees?' It was a whisper of awe.

'Oh, yes, Marius. I can climb trees.' The amulet continued to oscillate, small eyes riveted to its arc. 'I presume you'd like your bulla back?'

He nodded silently. On finding Marius had lost this valuable and essential asset, Piso had caned him and then reported the matter to his father, who promptly caned him again. One thing Fabius had taught the boy, though. Never snitch. Claudia admired the lad for holding out.

She lowered the chain and Marius reached up. Again it was whisked away.

'It's yours,' she said, 'for a price.'

Marius thought long and hard, and eventually pulled his wooden sword from his belt. 'This is my most favourite thing,' he said, twisting his lip. 'You can have it, if you like.'

Claudia forced herself not to laugh. 'No, Marius, you keep that. I just want a little chat.'

'What about?' he asked warily.

She released the chain. Marius caught the bulla in mid

air. It was carefully examined before being slipped round his neck.

'Just things,' she said casually. 'Like what you saw at the birch grove yesterday.'

Marcus Cornelius Orbilio was frustrated. In fact, he was frustrated on so many counts, he had actually lost count. Taking them point by point, and not necessarily in order of priority, they looked grim. Put them together, and the outlook was bleaker than a Gaulish winter.

He could kiss his career goodbye. This evening he'd called on the local magistrate, a redneck equestrian called Ennius, and the meeting got off on completely on the wrong footing.

'You're interrupting my devotions,' the man had said irritably.

Orbilio had difficulty in controlling his runaway eyebrows. Whatever goddess Ennius was worshipping, she wore cheap scent and left long, dark hairs on his tunic, which he hadn't had time to belt properly. Orbilio apologized and offered to call back when it was convenient, but Ennius took this as a slight, the nobility patronizing the lower classes as usual, and insisted he conduct his business on the spot. To emphasize both point and authority, he meant it literally and Orbilio was faced with the embarrassing position of outlining the facts on the magistrate's doorstep.

Ennius already had strong views regarding the Security Police stomping over his territory and showed Orbilio the letter of complaint he'd sent to Callisunus. When asked politely what he, as magistrate, proposed to do about

Utti's illegal execution, Ennius lost no time in telling Orbilio that he backed Collatinus to the hilt – clearly the fellow was guilty as hell.

'This is nothing short of cold-blooded murder,' Orbilio pointed out reasonably.

Ennius jabbed his neatly manicured finger into the younger man's chest. 'Don't lecture me on the law, you insolent puppy. In Sullium I am the law – and the law backs Collatinus. Now get the hell off my doorstep.'

Orbilio found himself raising the subject of Tanaquil's illegal imprisonment to a bronze door-knocker.

So! Ennius had put in a less than favourable report and Callisunus, that wily politician, was unlikely to consider the subtler aspects of a matter which fell outside his jurisdiction. It would have been different (oh, how it would have been different!) had Sabina genuinely served as a Vestal Virgin, but of course she hadn't. Instead, an innocent man had been executed and the whole affair had turned into nothing short of a fiasco.

He could not see a way out. He could not arrest Diomedes, there was insufficient evidence to go to trial – largely because, between them, Ennius and Collatinus would ensure the case against Utti was rock solid. Providing Diomedes didn't kill again, he was free to move on and murder away to his heart's content. Which he'd probably been doing for years and years.

As the law stood – Roman law, as opposed to Ennius's law – a murderer need not stand trial providing (a) he confessed or (b) he was caught red-handed. Diomedes was no fool. A man had been executed for the crimes he himself had committed, he would not risk his neck by killing again in the same area.

Orbilio did not relish the prospect of losing his job (and thereby his shot at the Senate), but he bitterly regretted his loss being caused by a man who had, quite literally, got away with murder.

He began to pace the room in frustration, not all of it connected to work. Common sense and logic told him to bed the first woman who came along and there had been plenty. The prefect's mansion in Agrigentum was packed to the rafters with pretty girls and his ears still rang with their offers, and yet he'd held back. It made no kind of sense and was something he'd never encountered before, even when married.

He rubbed his back muscles. The tension started in his neck and continued to his loins. Here he was, in the wee small hours, unable to sleep for frustration. He urgently needed release, he was as taut as a bowstring, but what? He would wear a groove in the mosaic if he kept pacing up and down. Weights! That was it. In Rome he frequently worked out in the gymnasium, why not here? Two small statues stood on the desk, one of Castor, one of Pollux; they would do very nicely. He stripped off his loin cloth and systematically flexed every muscle in his body. Placing the statues at his toes, his hands closed tightly round them.

'You don't expect to see a full moon on a night like this.'

Orbilio spun round. 'Croesus, Claudia, don't you knock?' He lunged for his tunic and held it in front of him as Castor rolled under the bed.

She had a wicked, wicked grin on her face. 'Ssh! There's something I want you to see.'

'Do you know what time it is?'

'Too long after supper and not long enough to break-fast. Come along, you'll enjoy this.'

He stared, inhaling her spicy perfume. She was wearing a night shift, diaphanous and white. Her hair hung loose, luscious thick curls framing her face and tumbling over her shoulders. He could see the firm points of her nipples moving up and down as she breathed.

'I'm not dressed,' he said pompously.

She cocked her head to one side and let her eyes rest on the bunch of material he was gripping in front of him. 'Orbilio, are you coming or not?' she said innocently, and he found himself doing something he hadn't done for over ten years. Marcus Cornelius Orbilio blushed to his roots.

Claudia watched while, with unconscious masculine grace, he donned a fresh tunic before letting the other fall to the floor. She thought back to the marble warrior in the garden of Julius Domiticus Decianus and compared it to the figure in front of her. Lithe and lean with hard, rippling muscles and dishevelled hair that fell into his eyes. How many women, she wondered, had succumbed to the urge? She doubted whether he could keep count, or even if he wanted to. Then she remembered Tanaquil and the hand on his knee . . .

'For gods' sake, Orbilio, we haven't got all bloody night.'

But by then, Marcus had caught up with his equilibrium and he merely raised one little eyebrow in response.

'Sssh!' She placed her ear to the door and opened it carefully. 'Be very quiet,' she whispered.

He followed her on tiptoe across the shadows of the atrium, their bare feet making no sound. The only noise came from Cerberus, snoring loudly by the front door.

'See?' She spoke so softly, he could barely hear and it was dark, he had to squint. Then he saw what she was pointing at. Aulus. Pacing barefoot up and down a mosaic of Apollo in his chariot, spitting something from his mouth and glancing furtively round the hall.

'What's he doing?'

Claudia strained to catch the words. 'Black beans,' she hissed back. 'Listen.'

'With these beans I redeem me and mine.'

Aulus popped another one in his mouth, sucked it a bit, then *ptwee*. Out it popped and he repeated the phrase. Finally he poured a small trickle of water over his hands in a symbolic cleansing ritual, picked up two bronze kettles and closed them very, very quietly together.

'Ghosts of my fathers, be gone!'

He gave a low bow, then walked softly across the hall towards his bedroom. Claudia and Orbilio filed back to Marcus's room, since it was closest.

'What do you make of that?' she asked, settling herself on his bed and drawing up her knees.

'I'm not sure. Some sort of death ritual?'

'Like the rites you give a loved one's spirit to help it on its way? I mean, the same bronze kettles, the nine beans and all that, but – did you catch his words?'

'And what about the symbolic cleansing?' He found Claudia's excitement contagious.

'Do you think what I think?'

He nodded. 'The ceremony for the undead.' Orbilio shook his head in bewilderment. 'What were you doing lurking in the shadows at this time of night, anyway?'

'I was hungry.'

They thought everyone had the appetite of an ant in

this house. The only one who looked properly nourished was Fabius, and when you compared Collatinus grub to army rations, it might well explain why he joined up.

'So there I am, rummaging around in the black of night for a bit of cheese or a cake, and blow me down, what do I hear? Old Conky droning on. I thought at first he was sleepwalking, then . . .'

Orbilio poured wine into a glass. It was the only glass, and Claudia wondered why she felt a brief flicker of pleasure at sharing. He sat down on the couch, keeping a horribly respectable distance, although she noticed his pupils were fully dilated. Which, of course, they would be in the darkness, they needed all the light they could get.

'The undead, eh?' Orbilio's mouth turned down. 'I didn't know they still believed in wandering spirits out here.'

Personally Claudia didn't believe in the undead either and, until now, didn't know any self-respecting Roman who did. Well, not one who admitted to it. But there was no doubt Aulus was deadly serious; he was stone cold sober.

'Backward lot, these Sicilians,' she said. 'But my point is this: is Aulus expunging his guilty conscience? After all, he wasn't exactly broadcasting the ritual.'

Orbilio leaned back, head against the wall, and gave it some thought. 'I suppose if his father was against it, he might resort to secrecy, but it doesn't seem likely. Not from what I know of the man.'

There was an even longer silence as he stared at the painted peacocks on the wall opposite, then he said, 'The real issue is whether a man would – *could* a man – rape and mutilate his own daughter. I don't think so, somehow.'

'Me neither.'

A light flickered in his eyes. 'I beg your pardon? Did you actually agree with me for once?'

The look she gave him could have stripped summer leaves from a willow.

Suddenly he sat up. 'Hang on,' he said. 'What day is it today?'

Claudia had lost count. 'Let me think. Yesterday was Lustration Day, so that means we're into the early hours of . . .' she totted them up on her fingers, 'the twentieth of October.'

'Well, there you are!' Orbilio snapped his fingers. 'Today would have been Sabina's thirty-seventh birthday.'

Another fine theory washed out to sea.

'Besides, I've told you often enough, it's Diomedes.'

'What about Fabius? Maybe it was a little trick he picked up in Outer Pannonia or wherever it was he went legioning.' Triumphantly, she told him about the sprig of bay he was sporting.

'Sorry,' Orbilio said cheerfully, topping up the glass. 'You said it yourself, yesterday was Lustration Day. Soldiers all over the Empire wear bay to cleanse themselves of the blood they have spilled, whenever they spilled it. Even retired army veterans.'

Bugger, yes. She'd forgotten that.

'Linus is capable.' She told him about Corinna. He told her that was just wishful thinking. Which it was.

'All right, then, how about Senbi?' Claudia described the look on his face as he chopped the slave boy's thumbs off, and how he enjoyed beating the slaves, needing only

the smallest excuse to reach for the bullwhip. 'Or Antefa.'
Like father, like son.

'Claudia, stop. I'm not saying these men are paragons
incapable of violence, but you have to weigh up facts.'

'You don't.'

Indignation flooded his face. 'I beg your pardon—'

'Right from the start, you've had it in for the Greek,
just because he's a smoothie. What about Piso?'

'Anyone else?' he asked patiently.

He wasn't taking this seriously, dammit. 'No.' Why
did that sound sulky?

Orbilio grinned. 'Well, thank goodness you've let poor
old Dexippus off the hook.'

'Marcus Cornelius, must I do your job for you?'

His grin broadened. 'Is that an application for the
post of my assistant? In which case, please be advised that
interviews will be held next Tuesday, although female
applicants stand a better chance if they attend the sleeping
couch preliminaries on the Monday.'

'In your dreams, Marcus. In your dreams.'

'I'm not proud,' he said. 'Wherever you like. My only
condition is you tell me about Dexippus first.'

The flirtatious smile dropped from his lips when Claudia told him how Eugenius's secretary was partial to a
spot of puppy crucifixion and dismembering cats while
they were still alive. Why else, she said, would she have
uprooted Drusilla and her kittens for what was originally
to be a day's outing to the theatre? Leave them at Dex's
mercy? No bloody fear! Rumour also had it he'd blinded
a newborn lamb once, although it was never proved or
he'd have lost his job, but she knew for certain he was
prone to snaring small animals for his 'experiments'.

A greyish light had begun to infiltrate the darkness, and a cockerel crowed. It was a damned silly time to be drinking wine, it went straight to your knees.

'There's something else, too.'

'Oh?' He leaned forward, but only to top up the glass.

'That birch grove. The day Actë was killed, Tanaquil was there, as we know, because she found the body. But Marius was also there. Apparently there's an ash tree on the edge of the grove and he wanted to make himself a bow—'

'A what?'

'Fabius is teaching him how to shoot arrows, so for any quail in the area, now's the time to strike camp. Marius wasn't there, of course, when Actë was killed – in fact he didn't even see her – but guess who he did see?'

'I am preparing to be astonished.'

'So you should. Fabius. Bet that took you by surprise?'

'Marginally.'

'That's not all. Dex was there, and so was Piso.'

'And?'

'What do you mean, *and*? And nothing. Good life in Illyria, I've done half your work for you, all you've got to do is arrest the guilty party.'

'Who is?'

She hit him with a cushion. 'You're the policemen, you fathom it out.'

Orbilio snatched the glass out of her hand and drained it. 'I don't understand,' he said ruefully, combing his hair with his free hand. 'Can someone please tell me why, when the grove is supposed to be deserted on account of it being haunted, the whole world and his wife just happen to be up there the very day Actë is killed?'

Claudia snatched the glass back and frowned when she saw it was empty. 'That's easy,' she said. 'The slaves avoid it, which is the circle Actë moved in, and don't forget the only spare time she got was when the family were gathered round Eugenius. It wouldn't have occurred to her that the family mightn't believe in ghoulies and ghosties. They often congregated there. I know something else, too.'

Birds were singing, dogs were yapping, suns were rising, skies were clearing – and policemen were groaning. Groaning. I ask you! Claudia cheerfully recounted the old man's proposal of marriage, but it seemed he'd heard the story, which was a shame, really, because she'd saved that titbit till last.

'So the only person who wasn't in the grove was Diomedes? How very convenient. Ouch!' He ignored the kick to his shins and pressed on. 'Is this because Dreamboat's been showering you with love gifts?'

Thick, dark curls shook in confusion. 'Not me, I'm afraid.' She was sure she'd have noticed gold bangles or British pearls lying around.

'Then what do you call that white dove?' Was he talking about the pigeon? 'Among Greeks, it's a token of undying love.'

Claudia clapped her hand over her mouth. 'Oh-oh!'

'What have you done with it?'

'I . . .' She burst into giggles. 'I'll tell you what I did with it. I ate the bloody thing.'

Orbilio began to splutter. 'You what? You ate it?' He threw his head back and roared.

Her eyes were watering, too. 'Damn right. With mushroom and parsley sauce.' She stood up and walked to the door, clutching her aching stomach. 'And I'll let you into another secret. It was absolutely delicious.'

His laughter, echoing through the still morning air, was as refreshing as the water in the atrium pool and it was singularly unfortunate that the first person she bumped into in the colonnade outside Orbilio's room happened to be a Greek physician with blue eyes and obedient blond locks.

XXVIII

It doesn't matter whether you live in the centre of Rome or the outer reaches of the Empire, every eighth day is market day and that's that. Hides are traded, cheeses are sold, gossip is embroidered and fashions are admired by stallholders who set up stands long before the first rays of dawn clear the hilltops or shadows lift from the ravines.

Claudia was too fired up to sleep and in any case it was too noisy. Bitumen, it seemed, was an essential element of sheep dip. Eugenius already had enough watery olive lees to float a warship, sulphur from his fullers' yards and sufficient hellebore and squill to fill the Pharos. What he did not have was bitumen, and without bitumen sheep could not be dipped. Instead they were crammed together in makeshift pens, bleating and baa-ing every god-given moment, clearly preferring ticks and footrot and scab to pressing flesh (or rather fleece) with their neighbours and you could tell they were not going to be mollified by the odd feed of broom and willow. Moreover, you couldn't take a walk without tripping over a shepherd, they really did clutter the place up.

She eyed them closely. Young men, mostly. Rough, tough, sure-footed; men able to withstand all manner of hostile conditions and that didn't just mean the weather. Loneliness must be a problem. Maybe a real problem for some of them. And maybe, just maybe, an uncontrollable problem for one of their number . . .?

Orbilio believed the killer was Diomedes, Claudia thought it more likely to be a local resident – but had anybody considered the shepherds? Well used to rough terrain, they could move quickly over ground most of us would struggle with, which could explain their rapid disappearance after the event.

How often did they see a woman? How often did they take a woman? How did they feel about the prospect of a soft virgin? They were strong men, accustomed to fighting off mountain thieves and wild animals – and they carried small, sharp knives about their persons. Claudia studied each weatherbeaten face carefully and decided they all looked capable of this heinous crime. She hoped the bitumen would arrive shortly.

In the meantime, it was market day in Sullium.

Portius climbed into the car beside her, the gems on his fingers looking like gaudy knuckledusters. 'The old man's taken a turn,' he said cheerfully. 'Gone right downhill.'

Claudia refrained from telling him she knew all about it. That's where Diomedes was off to at dawn, to visit his patient. There was time, though, to ask him about the tramp in the clipshed, and although he admitted it was really too soon to tell, he did think the prognosis looked good.

He looked strained, she thought. His eyes stared past hers at Orbilio's closed door, as though something was bothering him.

'I must see Eugenius,' he said, without any great emotion in his voice. 'Can I call to see you on my way back?'

That, she thought, was as good a reason as any to nip into Sullium.

Since Pacquia was still officially assigned to Claudia, she'd left the girl playing with heated cauteries, chamber pots and goodness knows what, on the strict understanding that it was to be a secret between the three of them, Claudia, Diomedes and Pacquia, and that she was to report to Claudia the minute the tramp said anything sensible. At present he was alternating between sleep and incoherent ramblings, but one thing they had discovered. He had a name, Melinno.

It didn't mean anything to anyone.

'I'm sorry about your grandfather,' she said.

'Father will be pleased,' Portius was saying, fanning himself with the most ostentatious band of pink and blue ostrich feathers. 'He and Linus rub along well enough, they'll be happy for Fabius to go off and work his own lands.'

She was thinking about Melinno and nearly missed it. 'I beg your pardon?'

Portius licked his middle finger and wiped a smudge of antimony away from his left eyelid. 'Fabius was given a parcel of land in Katane when he left the army and, being a centurion, the old so-and-so's done rather well for himself.' He coiled a ringlet back into place. 'It's just up your street.'

'How so?'

'Didn't you know? The old man made him plant vines on it.'

'Made him?'

Portius's mouth puckered and his eyes rolled theatrically. 'You should have heard them! Big Brother knows nothing about grapes, wanted to grow wheat like every-one else in Katane, but would the old man wear it?' He leaned over conspiratorially. 'Between you and me,' he said in an exaggerated whisper, 'I don't see Bacchus getting much veneration from it, Fabius hasn't a clue about wine.'

Who had? But it certainly explained one thing.

'What about you?' she asked. 'Where do you fit in?'

Why were they talking about the business as though Eugenius was already dead?

Portius laughed. 'You must be joking. When Father takes charge, I'm off.'

'Rome?' Claudia found her fingers were crossed.

'Capri,' he said, and she sent up a silent prayer of gratitude. 'Rather more to my eclectic tastes, don't you think?'

Claudia laughed aloud. 'Hence the Virgil quotes?'

Portius assumed a tortured artist pose with his hands. 'Please don't say that!' he mocked, then added seriously, 'My parents don't know the difference between Virgil and valediction. That poetry is my escape, Claudia. Father thinks it's genius – which it is, of course, except it's not mine. It's my ticket to Capri.'

Only a couple of miles off the mainland, its high cliffs and dense greenery made the island an impenetrable haven for pederasts and paedophiles, sycophants and orgies, where prying eyes did not see the 'games' enacted there nor ears catch the splash when, occasionally, those 'games' went wrong and there was a body to dispose of . . .

Gooseflesh rippled up her arms. Portius? She looked at him again, peeling off the veneer of antimony and carmine, jewels and unguents. Underneath was a boy, a *man*, eighteen years old, strong and healthy which was more than his appetites appeared to be. How unhealthy were they? It was a point to bear in mind.

Pulling up in the Forum, the driver watered his mule and Claudia disappeared into the crowd before Portius could finish describing the steep, grey cliffs of Capri and the delights awaiting him. Many of the streets were narrow and without pavements, packed shoulder to shoulder with men, women and children, their legs buckling under the weight of market produce. Blackberries, duck, pottery, ivory, ointments. She heard the clip of iron scissors on hair, the clap of wooden plates from the beggars. The air was filled with hot, spicy sausages and rich, spicy wine. A salt seller sawed lumps from his block, acrobats tumbled, and along the street a fight broke out between two women at the communal oven. Babies squawked, children played chase, their grubby little fists clutching tunics and stolas and togas as they darted between your feet. Donkeys brayed and women haggled and backstreet barbers, eager not to miss out on the trade, brought their chairs and their wares into the square, grating their whetstones and scraping the chins.

It was, Claudia thought, as close to heaven as mere mortals get.

Searching for a place to eat her slab of honey bread, still steaming and rich with the scent of the wood-fired oven, she turned away from the Forum, past the law courts towards the temple of Minerva. Recalling how Minerva didn't exactly favour Claudia Seferius, she decided against tempting the goddess by nibbling her bread on the temple steps and followed the street down the hill. It was unpaved, and just to prove this was a poor area, shopping baskets contained more beets and less meat, lentils rather than cheese. Shops became booths, plaster peeled away from the buildings and the wooden overhangs looked rickety and dangerous. Sharing her honey bread with a small urchin who could have been boy or girl, Claudia watched a funeral procession pass by the lower road. How different from Sabina's. No hired mourners, no hired musicians, no hired torchbearers to light the path of the soul.

'That's Hecamede,' the child said, helping itself to another chunk of the hot honey bread while still chewing on the first.

'Kyana's mother?' Claudia was shocked.

'Yep.'

The urchin crammed in so much bread, its mouth couldn't close properly. To avoid a close-up in mastication, Claudia stared down the street. 'What happened?' she asked.

'Topped herself.'

'How?'

No answer, and when she turned round the child had gone, along with the rest of the honey bread and a gold brooch set with carnelians. It was left to a passing crone with three dark hairs sprouting from a mole on her chin to explain that Hecamede could finally take no more. On the anniversary of her daughter's disappearance, she cut her wrists and bled to death.

Claudia pictured her last hours. Lost and lonely, inconsolable in her grief. Did she think of Aristaeus? Or were her last thoughts focused solely on little Kyana, five years old and full of mischief? Little Kyana, who disappeared the day Aristaeus went to collect spiders' webs.

Claudia raced after the funeral procession, intercepting the undertaker at the second block of tenements. When he reached the pyre, she said, he must do it properly. He must deliver the funeral oration personally, extolling Hecamede's virtues as a mother and then afterwards ensure a sow was sacrificed to Ceres with all the pomp and ceremony he would bestow upon a wealthier patron. Pop-eyed, the undertaker agreed, mentally noting that the ring he had been given in payment would look particularly nice on his mistress's finger.

It was only later, approaching the villa, that Claudia remembered seeing something that was important, if only she could remember what it was. Damn! So many people milling around, so many sounds and smells compounded by the mental confusion and shock surrounding Hecamede's suicide, was it any wonder?

Doubtless, though, it would come back to her at some stage.

Providing it wasn't too late.

Marcus Cornelius Orbilio had spent much of his morning listening. Listening and following.

It intrigued him to watch little Pacquia, dark-skinned and thin as a billhook, weaving back and forth between the villa and the clipshed via an extremely convoluted route which took in the dyesheds, the bleaching yards and the orchard. Sometimes she carried water in a bowl, sometimes cloths, sometimes objects hidden by cloths, but each time she was whistling, as though her errand was of no importance.

What on earth, he wondered, running an ivory comb through his hair, was Claudia up to this time?

His spirits unexpectedly fell when he realized he was mistaken. One of the shepherds had fallen sick and Pacquia was running errands for Diomedes, which possibly explained the tortuous route. For here was the shepherd convalescing in the clipshed, probably because he had something contagious which the Greek didn't want bandied about.

Leaving the man tossing fitfully in his sleep, Orbilio went to check on Tanaquil. Eugenius had been completely closed to reason when he spoke to him yesterday evening. The girl had stolen a horse, Collatinus said, and theft was a civil matter which, as Orbilio knew, was tried in the magistrate's court.

For magistrate, read Ennius, Marcus thought irritably. He'd find her guilty and order her to make restitution. She might argue that she had returned the horse, which was only borrowed in the first place, but Ennius would be deaf to her appeals and insist she sell herself into slavery to cover the debt. No prizes for guessing who'd snap her up.

'Don't look so bloody sanctimonious, man,' Eugenius had snapped. 'Haven't you ever hankered for a full-breasted redhead to warm your toes once in a while? Spirited little filly, I like 'em like that.' He swirled wine round inside his mouth. 'Don't you?'

Arguing with a bigot was like arguing with stone and Orbilio gave up. Collatinus appeared to have forgotten Actë pretty damned fast, and for a girl who'd given sixteen years of her life pandering to the old sod, it was bloody unfair. When he'd heard the old man had been taken ill in the early hours, he was actually rather glad.

Tanaquil had been locked in a shed which at present was empty, but which would shortly be filled with bracken for the sheep's winter litter. Orbilio felt he owed it to the girl to tell her her fate before she found out from anyone else, and to tell her also that he intended to outbid Eugenius. Not that he expected to win, Ennius would see to that, but by Janus, he'd bloody well try.

The presence of four guards was unnecessary. Tanaquil couldn't hope to escape, the shed was stone built – and how could she hope to reach the thatch without a ladder? But Eugenius was going to make as much capital as he could out of this, and so the guard was for show more than anything else. Approaching from the clipshed, it was the voices which stopped him in his tracks. Low-pitched, they were embroiled in heated argument, although he was unable to make out the words. When he turned the corner, the last person he expected to see with his lips to the crack in the stonework was Fabius.

'Holy Mars, you gave me a fright!'

'So I see.' He'd jumped like the proverbial scalded cat.

Orbilio waited, but Fabius said nothing, either to him or to Tanaquil through the gap. He simply nodded and strode off, his face suffused with anger.

A single green eye blazed its fury through the crack. 'I'll kill him. When I get out, so help me, I'll kill him.'

'Fabius?'

'Eugenius,' she spat.

Orbilio rattled off a few platitudes to calm her down before finally breaking the news about the impending trial.

She didn't enquire as to his motives for outbidding Collatinus, neither did she thank him for his efforts.

'I'll have his guts for my girdle,' she hissed. 'He had no right to murder Utti.'

'You didn't tell me Utti had bloodstains on his tunic.'

'Well, of course he did,' she snapped. 'He came running when I screamed and helped me turn Actë on to her back again. Whose side are you on, anyway?'

'Tanaquil, why *were* you in the birch grove on Wednesday?'

'I told you, I went for a walk.' It sounded petulant.

'What was Utti doing there?'

There was a long pause and a longer sigh. 'He was following me,' she said. 'Only I didn't say, because I didn't want to incriminate him.'

'By lying, it appeared you were covering up for him, you realize that?' Of course she realizes that, you stupid oaf! The knowledge is eating her alive! He quickly moved on. 'Why was Utti following you? Was he worried something might happen to you, a woman alone?'

'Yes!' She said it too quickly, as though she was pouncing on the idea. 'Yes, that's it, he wanted to protect me.' She began to cry. 'What's going to happen to me, Marcus? Suppose they kill me, too?'

'They're not going to kill you, Tanaquil.' Not in the sense you mean.

Injustice seethed within him and he decided to have one more go at Collatinus. Instead, the gigolo blocked the doorway, stressing how ill the old man was, how frail.

'Bit sudden, isn't it?'

'He's eluded Death for sixteen years,' Diomedes said.

'But now Death's picked up the spoor, he's not going to let go.'

'How long?'

Diomedes shrugged insolently. 'Who knows?' he said, in a manner which made it clear to both of them that he did know and wasn't telling. Orbilio resisted the urge to smash his fist right between those blond-lashed eyes.

But that was this morning. Since lunch . . .

Since lunch, he wasn't feeling so well. He was cold, so cold he was wearing his toga on top of his tunic and was still shivering. An open charcoal brazier burned in the corner. Beside his couch, a portable water heater stood on its tripod. He lay down and pulled the bedcovers up to his chin, using the cold as an excuse for knees which weren't functioning properly. He was certain there was a draught in the room, but he'd closed the windows and drawn the hangings. There was a noise, too. It was, he decided later, the sound of his own teeth chattering, an unwelcome accompaniment to the constant drumming inside his cranium.

Weakly he propped himself up on one elbow and tried to call for assistance. Instead he was violently sick.

Returning from Sullium, Claudia walked into a house which had a surprisingly festive air and she had to check the calendar nailed up on the wall beside Cerberus to confirm this wasn't some spurious Sicilian holiday she'd forgotten about. Tossing Cerberus a joint of mutton – all bone and gristle, that hound – she was puzzled. No local deity to honour? No local custom to celebrate? It was left to Senbi to explain, as he handed her a letter.

'It's the Master,' he said. 'He has taken a turn for the worse.'

Claudia stopped in her tracks. 'Bit sudden, isn't it?'

Senbi shrugged. 'That's not for me to comment,' he said, with what appeared to be a mouthful of oil. 'I do know, however, that Master Aulus has already spoken with the undertaker.'

Like circling vultures, Claudia thought as Senbi padded off, each member of the family looking forward to Eugenius's death with purely selfish interests.

Matidia would, at long last, be mistress in her own house; it would be her duty, not Actë's, to line up the slaves of a morning and dish out the orders. Aulus would have the power he had waited fifty-eight years for, the power of initiative, of life and death, even of selling his entire family into slavery if he so desired. Portius would have his precious ticket to freedom and Fabius could farm his lands in Katane, ripping up his ailing vines and planting wheat in the rich, fertile soil, much to Linus's delight, who would then be second in command to Aulus.

Really, the atmosphere in the house seemed to say: you'd think Eugenius would have done the decent thing and popped off long ago, wouldn't you?

Diomedes waylaid Claudia in the peristyle. 'The old man was asking for you earlier,' he said quietly, his eyes brushing her face. 'Wanted to know whether you'd signed . . . the contract.'

'Sod that for a lark.' That had never been her intention.

'Which, er, contract might that be?' Diomedes asked mildly, wondering whether her bad mood had any connection with the letter Senbi had just handed her. He heard her sigh.

'I suppose I owe it to him to tell him,' she said. 'How bad is he?'

'Bad,' the doctor replied. He stepped in front of her and looked deep into her eyes. 'Claudia, there's something I want to say to you.'

He had to move fast. Aulus had collared him just a few minutes ago and pointed out in no uncertain terms that it was that bitch Actë who'd pushed for his appointment, but since Eugenius was shortly to join her in the Underworld, their influence was finished. Aulus was telling him now, he wanted no truck with mountebanks, Diomedes could bloody well sling his hook. And don't think he didn't know about the fucking whipworm, because he fucking did, and Diomedes's fucking wages would be docked because of it. When they came back from the funeral, he wanted Diomedes gone or he would have him forcibly removed.

He spread his accent thicker to catch her wavering attention. 'Claudia, I want to ask you—'

'Later, Diomedes.' She brushed past him. 'I'll speak to Eugenius first.'

'Of course.' With effort, the Greek swallowed his disappointment and ushered her into the room. 'Although I doubt he can hear you.'

The first thing that hit her was the smell. They say you can smell death, but until now Claudia hadn't realized it was so sickly-sweet, so pungent, so utterly repellant. She resisted the urge to hold her handkerchief over her nose as she crossed towards the bed.

The man who had held the Collatinus family in his

hand for seventy-seven years, playing with them like pieces on a board, controlling their lives, their marriages, their children, had finally relinquished his grip. His eyes were hollowed, his temples sunken, his nose sharp and pointed as happens immediately prior to the Great Reaper gathering his harvest. The skin of his forehead was hard and tight and translucent, and it was difficult to imagine the man behind the little walnut face terrorizing family and servants, clients and buyers with his bullying and his railing and his insults. Around her, the pornographic friezes shimmered and wavered in the light of the torches which had been lit, the leers ugly and repulsive, and you could almost hear the lewd laughter from the cripples and hunchbacks and lepers. From the figure on the couch, small as a child, came a series of harsh rattles in the throat. She would never know whether Eugenius had been genuinely grieving for Sabina or merely mourning the loss of a prized asset.

She feared it was the latter, and couldn't wait to pack, to get away from this house. The villa, the inhabitants, the whole place made her sick to her stomach.

'Claudia, I need to talk to you.'

'Later.' She waved the doctor away and made for the bath house. Cold water. Give me cold water to wash in. As cold as you can make it.

Now about that lowlife Varius, she thought later, towelling herself dry. Insolent little turd. She glared at the letter, innocently rolled up on top of her stola, but which had been burning a hole in her hand from the moment Senbi delivered it. In itself, it wasn't so much an affirmation of the reasons behind his claim to Seferius blood, more a means of informing Claudia that he knew her whereabouts. Implicit was the threat that should Varius come to harm for whatever reason, others might be made aware of the circumstances.

Bugger!

But life isn't always unkind and it was pure providence when, heading back to her room, Claudia heard a frantic scuffle and turned just in time to watch Senbi go flying on a mysterious patch of grease near the front entrance. There was a satisfying crunch as his outstretched armbone gave way at an unnatural angle.

Fluttering footsteps approached across the atrium floor. Corinna, fully made up and looking almost pretty, was smiling.

'Claudia,' she said, laying a hand on her arm. 'Could you spare me a moment?'

'Well . . .' When you looked closely, you could see it was all make-up. Beyond the carmine smile and ochre cheeks, Corinna's eyes were dead. 'I am rather busy.'

She really wasn't in the mood for Corinna's custody plans.

'Oh, but!' Corinna gave a light laugh, the first Claudia had ever heard from her. My, my, there was nothing like a death to cheer this family up, was there? 'You see, it's Linus . . .'

Claudia rubbed her aching temple. 'What about him?' she asked wearily.

'Well, you see, I've killed him,' she said, with a self-deprecating gesture. 'Stabbed him in the stomach with a knife.'

XXIX

Being Corinna, of course, she was wrong on both counts. Linus was neither dead nor stabbed in the stomach.

She'd got him in the left-hand side.

Claudia's first instinct was to fetch Orbilio, because if this could be hushed up, so much the better. His two-year stint as an army tribune and subsequent service in the Security Police would give him as fair a knowledge of first aid as was necessary, but unfortunately it appeared Supersnoop had succumbed to a bout of food poisoning. Serve him right, he should eat proper meals at proper times, instead of scoffing whenever he felt like it.

Diomedes, fresh from setting Senbi's arm, was unfazed by Claudia's account of how Linus had been larking about with his sons, slipped and fell on his knife. The wound wasn't serious, he assured her, the blade had missed the vital organs; give him a week and he'd be as good as new. What surprised him was Linus's silence throughout. Presumably he felt an utter prat, falling on a knife in front of his sons and Diomedes rather enjoyed prodding the wound as he cleaned and stitched it.

'Claudia,' he said quietly, drawing her to one side. 'I need a word with you.'

'Yes, yes, Diomedes. But later, eh?'

Good life in Illyria, what was it with this man? If

there was such a thing as reincarnation, the Greek should come back as a barnacle. Claudia slammed the door on him and rounded on Linus grey and pallid and with dark circles under his eyes.

'Listen to me, you scumbag, that was just a warning.' She had sent Corinna out of the room long ago. 'Your wife has had it up to here with you, the beatings and the whoring.'

'It was only—'

'Next time, she said, it'll be your balls she takes the knife to.'

Linus winced.

'I'm glad you understand.' Claudia folded her arms across her chest. 'These are her terms.'

She rattled a dozen straight off, with Linus nodding to each condition with every appearance of compliance. Corinna might have been fooled, Claudia was not. His true colours shone clear when she drew out of her gown a neatly written document requiring only his signature.

The painkillers had kicked in long before he finished reading the terms. 'This is outrageous,' he spluttered.

'No more than being a eunuch,' she replied reasonably. 'Sign the paper, Linus.'

Linus signed the paper, cursing under his breath. Jupiter in heaven, life was a bitch. The minute you were free of one miserable tyrant, another came along to turn the screws. And when it was your own wife, what chance did you stand?

'Here.' Claudia caught up with Corinna in the atrium, cuddling Vilbia so tight the toddler's face was changing colour.

She examined the contract with wide eyes. 'You got

him to sign this? Unlimited access to my children? Sack Piso? A monthly clothes allowance? Linus only goes out once a week? Claudia, he'll tear it to pieces.'

'For pity's sake, Corinna, you place it with a goddam lawyer. And if he turns on you again, look serious with that knife.'

'But I couldn't,' she protested. 'I wouldn't fight back again.'

'I know it and you know it,' Claudia said, 'but thankfully Linus doesn't. Don't throw everything away at the next confrontation. Stand up to him just once more and the occasion won't arise again.'

Whether Corinna would have the guts was another matter but Claudia had done all she could for the silly bitch, it was up to her from now on.

Corinna crumpled. 'I love Linus,' she said, burying her face in Vilbia's curls. 'I didn't mean to kill him, but he kept taunting me. Said . . . said Vilbia wasn't his.'

Bastard. Pity she hadn't made a thorough job of it.

Since there was nothing more to say, Claudia left Corinna by the pool and threw herself down on her own soft bed. It had been one hell of a long day, she was exhausted.

In the corner, Drusilla began to stir. Light was fading, temperatures were falling, mice would be scampering, moths would be fluttering. A family was fine, she decided, languidly washing her forepaws, but by gum, they were a tie. Her whiskers twitched impatiently. What she wouldn't give for a stalk through the long grass, to hear the rustle in the undergrowth, catch the scent of a musk beetle. Reluctantly, she turned her ablutions to the kittens.

Claudia scrunched Varius's letter into a ball, bounced it off the ceiling and called for Cypassis.

'Have you seen Kleon lately?'

'Now that you mention it, madam, I haven't. Not since yesterday.'

'Me neither.'

Funny that. Damned funny, in fact. Junius she had sent to Sullium, the Nubians were engaged on another little scheme of hers. Kleon, though, should have been here.

Where in heaven's name was he?

Diomedes slipped quietly into his patient's room, pausing in the doorway. There was a stillness in the air, a calmness. He closed the door behind him and padded across to the window. The hangings were tight, blocking out every chink. Lighting the oil lamp, he considered the figure on the bed. His colour was high, his breathing rapid. Diomedes checked the pulse. It was faint. Very faint.

Laying his box on the table, he set out his medicines one by one. The cautery had gone well, he thought, encouragingly so, considering it was one of the few operations safe enough for the softer organs. He had successfully drained the empyema from the membranes, cleaned the superficial cuts and left Melinno in a haze of soothing aniseed looking for all the world like this was the first proper sleep he'd had for months.

The late October dusk was falling fast. Diomedes heard the loud trumpeting call of a crane going back to roost, the caw of the rooks and the constant bleating of animals protesting at such enforced intimacy. Supper was under way, he could smell the beef roasting on the spit.

He moved across to the couch. It was damp from sweat, the blanket in a huddle on the floor, apart from one corner which had caught on an ankle. He laid a hand on his patient's forehead. Red hot.

'Not long to wait,' he whispered soothingly.

In the looking glass he caught a glimpse of the scene, saw his own serious expression framed by a halo of blond hair. Gently he laid the mirror flat on its face. Death was never a pleasant episode to watch. He patted his patient's hand twice, then selected a feather from the top compartment of his medicine box. It was a goose feather, robust and rigid.

Where would he go next, he wondered? It all depended on Claudia, didn't it, whether his dream, his golden goal, could finally be realized? Yes indeed, so much hung in the balance. When he looked down, the feather between his forefinger and thumb was shaking. Stop it, he ordered, control yourself. Soon, very soon, she will give you your answer. Soon, Zeus be willing, she will be your wife.

He waited until the hands that had so painstakingly removed ingrowing eyelashes, explored fistulas and extracted bladder stones had stopped trembling, then turned up the lamp and removed the top from a small ceramic pot.

As he leaned across his patient, a hand closed round his wrist with surprising strength.

'Kill me and you're finished.' The voice was barely audible, a croak.

Diomedes looked directly into the eyes of Marcus

Cornelius Orbilio. 'You're delirious, my friend,' he whispered.

Orbilio's eyes mocked him. 'That feather is dipped in poison.' He spoke with difficulty. 'An old dodge.'

Diomedes made to interrupt, but the patient forestalled him. 'A report is lodged with Ennius,' he said, 'a second's on its way to Rome. I repeat, kill me and you're finished.'

'Marcus, Marcus, you have a fever—'

'Which you gave me, you bastard.'

'Sssh. Drink this.' He tried to put a cup to his patient's lips, but the grip on his wrist was like an iron shackle. 'It's only water,' he said. 'You're not thinking straight.'

'Neither are you.' Marcus slumped back on to the couch. 'I'm her legally appointed guardian, did you know that?'

Blue eyes narrowed. 'You're what?'

The man on the bed managed a short laugh. 'I think you know what that means, but just so we don't have any misunderstanding on the point, let me explain.'

The eyes were bright – too bright – and the voice ragged, but he pressed on.

'In legal terms, her money is my money, anything she wishes to spend has to pass my approval.'

'But . . . She never mentioned it.'

The grip on Diomedes's wrist weakened as the muscles fell slack. Children ran squealing past the door. 'She's a very independent woman, but the law is the law when it comes to guardians. When I die, that money goes straight to my next of kin, a brother stationed in Egypt.' Sweat was pouring down his face. 'Then it'll be up to him to look after Claudia Seferius until she remarries.'

'The fever's affected your brain, Marcus, I'm not after her money. Lie still and—'

He could barely form the words now. 'Take your feather, Diomedes, and get out.' He began to gasp for breath. 'Only for gods' sake, open that bloody window on your way.'

With a slow, sad shake of his obedient blond hair, Diomedes watched Orbilio sink into oblivion. He scratched at an itch behind his left ear for several minutes, staring at the motionless form on the couch before shaking his head again and slowly replacing his medicines in their compartments.

'Oh, Marcus,' he said softly.

Finally he picked up the oil lamp and held the goose feather to the flame. He swept the ashes from the table into his hand and funnelled them into a rag before closing the lid of his box.

Almost as an afterthought he unhinged the shutters to let in the cool, healing evening breeze.

'Good morning!'

Claudia plumped herself down on the edge of the couch and dangled a bronze manicure set from her right index finger.

Marcus Cornelius Orbilio opened one eye. 'What's that for?'

'Well, it was difficult to know what to give the man who has everything and virtually all of it contagious.'

He gave a sickly grin. 'Thank you.'

She dropped the manicure set on the bed. 'You can

play with your toys later,' she said airily. 'I came to update you on the news.'

Since he'd declined the offer of grapes, Claudia placed the bowl in her lap and began to strip the bunch one by one.

'Around dawn, Eugenius finally did what Old Conky's been praying for these past sixteen years. Collatinus, like the reptile that he was, sloughed his mortal skin and slithered away to join his ancestors.'

'There'll be a sign up,' he said. ' "Under New Management".'

'You're not well, Marcus. Leave the jokes to me.' She decapitated another grape. 'I also have to report that Linus, as of today, is a reformed character.'

Unlike Diomedes, Orbilio found his imagination stretched to its very limits picturing Linus, purely by chance, falling horizontally on to a vertical fruit knife, but wholeheartedly agreed that it couldn't have happened to a nicer chap.

'What else?'

'Sarcasm doesn't become you,' she said, turning the bunch over to attack the grapes from the other side. 'Lots of things have happened while you've been idling away in your pit. Tanaquil, for instance. Antefa went to give her her supper and guess what he found?'

Orbilio struggled to prop himself up on his pillow. 'Don't tell me, let me guess. Four guards unconscious, door open, Tanaquil gone.'

Claudia's mouth pursed. 'Have you heard this before? Swear it?'

He swore it.

'Then how did you know?'

A sparkle danced in his eyes. 'I'm a policeman. What was I supposed to make of two big strong Nubians hanging round the litter shed? The puzzle is, *why* did you let her go?'

The grape about to enter Claudia's mouth was brandished like a weapon. 'Who said I let her go? Don't get me wrong, Orbilio, I'm not saying I'm sorry she's free, but why you suspect me is a mystery. Are you sure you don't want a grape?'

'And deprive you of the last four?'

'Oops. Sorry about that. Anyway, that's not all, guess who's vanished?'

'Surprise me.'

'Diomedes.' She started in on his dish of figs. 'Upped and went last night without a word. What do you think of that?'

'Astonishing.'

'Then sound like you mean it. They'll track him down, of course, he won't get far.'

'Who wants to track him down?'

Claudia spread her hands in an exasperated gesture. 'You, for one. Ever since you arrived.'

'Ah. I have a confession to make. I was wrong about Diomedes.'

'No, I was wrong about Diomedes.'

'No, I was.'

'Orbilio, I said I was—'

'Diomedes didn't kill Sabina or Actë, he—'

'Rubbish, he's as guilty as hell—'

Orbilio banged his head three times on his pillow. 'Dammit, Claudia, listen to me—'

'There's a chap in the clipshed called Melinno—'

'The shepherd?'

'Marcus Cornelius Orbilio, will you shut your mouth for thirty seconds and use your damned ears for a minute?'

The instructions were so utterly absurd that they both fell into fits of laughter. Then the figs slithered to the floor in one sticky heap and the manicure set slipped elegantly off the bed to land right in the middle, like a cherry on a custard. You could have fried a dozen flatfish in the time it took them to calm down.

'I'm serious, Orbilio,' she said, mopping her eyes. 'There's a boy in the clipshed, his name is Melinno and he came here to kill the man who killed his wife. And that man was Diomedes.'

'Did he tell you how his wife died?' He was the policeman once more.

'Not in so many words, no . . . Don't look at me like that, the boy's had his lungs cut open, what do you expect? But all the time he's been calling her name, Sulpica, and crying because he can't remember her face clearly, and promising to kill the man who killed her.'

'Diomedes?'

'Put it this way. When I told him the name of the man who had cured him, he put his head back and roared like a wounded elephant. Let me demonstrate.'

Claudia tipped her head back and yelled at the top of her voice. Ignoring Orbillo's claims of permanent deafness, she gathered up a handful of raisins. 'And I'll tell you another thing, that girl didn't die peacefully in her bed. Melinno talks of a slow death in excruciating agony.'

'Sabina and Actë didn't die in excruciating agony, though. Not in the way he seems to describe.'

'You're in no physical condition to split hairs, Marcus Cornelius.'

'Maybe not, but my theory . . . Could you pass me a drink of water while there's still some left? My theory is that Diomedes killed her by negligence. It wasn't murder.'

'What makes you think that?'

'It's a long story,' he said, wiping his mouth with the back of his hand. 'I'll tell you some other time.'

He should have known better. Within minutes, she had prized the whole sordid tale out of him, how Diomedes had flitted from rich family to rich family, ingratiating himself by first making one of the more influential members fall ill and then 'curing' them. Each time his goal was wealth. Each time he had set his sights on marrying one of the daughters, and each time his proposal had been rejected, because although he might be a valuable asset as a family physician, as a bridegroom he didn't pass muster.

'There aren't any marriageable daughters here,' Claudia protested, and then remembered Sabina. 'What about Labianus, who was lined up in pole position?'

'I think the plan was to make Sabina fall sick and work back from there. Probably couldn't believe his luck when the retiring Vestal came home with a full suitcase but only half her wits, and when Diomedes saw she'd brought along a wealthy young widow, well! Two bites at the cherry.'

Claudia's nose wrinkled in scepticism. 'As much as I am tempted by your theories, especially as they dovetail with previous theories of my own and you know how I hate to be wrong, it doesn't explain why he's done a runner.'

Orbilio looked away. 'You remember your conversation with Urgulania in Agrigentum?' He began to pleat the bedsheet. 'Let's just say, I've evened the score.'

'Do you mean to tell me that you, Marcus Cornelius Orbilio, the pillar of every Roman community, actually *lied*?'

'I'm sure my account to Dreamboat was as truthful as yours to the good matron.'

Claudia had learned her manners from her mother, who, when sober and not prone to suicide attempts, had quite a repertoire, having once served as a rich man's courtesan until he dumped her for a younger model. It was therefore from her mother she had learned that snorting was vulgar. On the other hand, there are times when vulgarity is vital to a girl's well-being. Claudia let rip the kind of snort your average hippo would be proud to own.

'I didn't know you did warthogs as well as wounded elephants,' Orbilio said mildly, and received a slap on his arm for his pains.

'The invalid is so tired he's starting to hallucinate.' Claudia stepped daintily over the figs. 'Oh, I nearly forgot.' Liar! 'The reason for my gracious visit to the sickroom was to let you know I'm leaving this afternoon.'

All things being equal, his expression should have changed – fallen, ideally – and he should have asked what time, how was she travelling, what were her plans. In fact, any number of possibilities presented themselves except the question: 'Before the funeral?'

Damn you to hell. 'The quicker I get away from this place, the better, but first I have a call to make.' Her hand was on the door when she asked, 'Incidentally, you haven't seen Kleon, have you?'

'He's not in here with me,' Orbilio said, pretending to

search the bedcovers, 'although you're welcome to check for yourself.'

'I'd prefer to sit through a swarm of gadflies.' The hell she would.

The air hung heavy between them. She waited for him to speak but nothing happened.

'See you around, then.' For some ridiculous reason her throat was tight. Of course, there was still time to call her back. She'd be across that room like oiled lightning . . .

'Right.' She was halfway across the threshold when he whispered under his breath, 'By the gods, Claudia, you are beautiful.'

She daren't turn round, her eyes were cloudy. 'What was that?'

'I – I said, "By the gods, Claudia, do be careful." ' He smiled wanly. 'Later. When you go out.'

XXX

The climb was no less steep than she remembered it, the terrain no less rugged, the path no less slippery, and yet it was difficult to reconcile the fact that she'd made this climb a mere eight days previously. Reality seemed to have been bounced on its head and made to turn somersaults. Was it really only four weeks since she left Rome?

Claudia leaned against a limestone crag jutting into the pathway to catch her breath. The sea shimmered and sparkled below, and on a day like this you felt you could almost reach across and trickle the sands of Africa through your fingers. It was warm, but not too warm, breezy without being windy, enough puffs of white cloud to break the brilliant monotony of the sky. Probably as close to perfect as you could get on this island. And Claudia was thoroughly glad to be going home.

In four weeks, little progress would have been made on the emperor's massive restoration programme, the building and renovation of temples and libraries and law-courts and gateways, even less at her villa and vineyard now the harvest was in and the wine busy fermenting. But suddenly it seemed imperative she return – to settle the kittens, catch up on the gossip, witness the grand finale of the Victory Games, employ a few more prevarication tactics on unsuspecting creditors.

How she had become embroiled in a murder mystery on this superstitious island was beyond her! In a few short weeks she'd been practically shipwrecked, dumped on a family of mealy-mouthed misers with a pea-brained fruit-cake posing as a Vestal Virgin. Two women had been murdered, an innocent man had taken the rap, there was a child molester on the loose and because of him, a grief-stricken mother had committed suicide. The man who wanted her wasn't the man she wanted, and the man she wanted wasn't interested. Let us also not forget that behind all this was cast the long shadow of a money-grubbing scumbag called Varius, claiming to be her husband's bastard.

Claudia sighed as a pair of blue rock doves passed by, wings whirring in flight. Junius had been a pain in the backside about this visit, insisting he accompanied her. Threats to mash his face like a turnip hadn't worked, neither had her proposal to dangle his nutmegs from his ears like jewellery. In the end, she'd resorted to the age-old tactic of promising faithfully not to go anywhere without him, but meanwhile, would he mind just running an errand to Sullium? Yes, yes, of course she meant what she said, she had given her word, hadn't she, now run along, there's a good boy. Oh, before he went, though – had he seen Kleon lately? No matter, it wasn't important.

Cypassis was almost as bad, although it was easier with her. Tell her you're going to Sullium with Junius and she's to get on with the packing and simple honest soul that she is, she falls for it.

Claudia continued up the steep path, wary of the small rocks which crumbled and gave way beneath her feet, of the dust clouds raised on these deforested slopes, of the limestone crags jutting into the pathway. No longer could she hear the bleating from the sheep pens, only the single cry of a hovering eagle searching out snakes and frogs and lizards. The overpowering smell of prospective mutton cutlets had given way to fresher scents of juniper and furze and wild rosemary. Purple asters bloomed in the valleys, arbutes and hazels clung precariously to the crevices. She paused on the ridge.

So Diomedes turned out to be a lady-killer in the accepted sense of the word? Of course, *she* hadn't been fooled by those measureless blue eyes, the devastating fall of his hair; his accent cut no ice with her. (I ate the pigeon, didn't I?) With hindsight it occurred to her that if little Popillia had rumbled him, surely she should have done – especially when he'd used the same trick on Cypassis to get to her as he'd used on Matidia, who – heaven knows – had gone on long enough about his curing an illness she'd contracted virtually before he'd finished unpacking.

To his credit, though, Diomedes was a good doctor – got Melinno sorted out in no time. Pity he did his flit before he got a chance to look at Supersnoop. He'd have had him back on his feet in a twinkle!

Once over the rise, the canopy closed in like a hug from an old friend, cooling, comforting, refreshing. Flocks of finches – green, gold and haw – fluttered between the branches, enticed by the new season's beech mast. A blackbird foraged noisily among the deep, decaying layers. Claudia felt the same strange feeling creep over her that had thrilled her the last time. This sweet, unsettling lack of reality. This sense of magic, of illusion, of fanciful notions. The sun cast a golden glow through golden leaves on to a soft golden floor as though the beechwood had become the Palace of Midas where everything you touch turns to gold. Her toe took careful aim at a puffball. Clouds of spoor shot high into the air, but they did not descend as gold dust. *Silly bitch*.

From the corner of her eye, she caught a flash of white. A magpie? The rump of a deer? Different senses were suspended. She felt a thumping in her chest. There it was again, and one thing was sure, it wasn't that damned pigeon come back to haunt her. This was linen.

She stood stock still, rueing her choice of iris blue cotton instead of the buttercup yellow which would have made her damn near invisible under this autumn canopy. She hardly dare breathe. Where is he? Has he gone? Damn the leaf litter! It was so deep, footfalls were muffled. Of course, there was no reason to suppose he'd even seen her . . .

'Spying again?'

The breath caught in Claudia's throat. 'F- Fabius!'

The shock of seeing him was surpassed only by the sight of the narrow blade in his hand. The knuckles gripping it, she noticed, were white.

'I wasn't . . .' Calm down, you've nothing to fear. Take it easy. She cleared her throat and drew herself up to her full height. 'I was not spying.'

Even at her full height, he towered over her, his face dark with anger. 'Interfering busybody, I've seen you creeping around, listening at keyholes. Watched you sneak into Diomedes's room—'

'You were supposed to be in Sullium!'

He leaned forward and so did the knife. 'Think you know everything, don't you?'

Numbly she stared at the point of the blade and shook

her head. Words were useless. Fabius's eyes blazed with manic fury, his mouth a thin, pitiless line.

'I know your game.' He spat the words at her, and she flinched at every one. 'Drive a wedge into my family, marry me for my money—'

'You've got it all wrong—'

'You were after my vineyard.'

Those paltry acres? Claudia took a step back, and stumbled over a huge root. For gods' sake, there was a warbler singing!

'It was Eugenius,' she babbled, 'he wanted me to marry you, that's why he sent for me, he wanted to get his hands on Gaius's fortune—'

'Lying bitch!'

Trembling, Claudia clambered to her feet. She put out her hands behind her back and inched backwards until they met resistance in the form of a towering beech. Bugger! She was trapped. 'It's true, I swear it! He drew up a marriage contract, wanted me to sign everything over to him—'

'Shut up!'

Mighty Mars, help me! Help me now! 'Fabius, please—'

'I said, shut up!'

Lions snarl. Wolves snarl. Claudia had never before seen a man snarl – and what little strength was left in her legs blew away like the spoors of the puffball.

'Got shot of two husbands and thought to make me the third, did you? You and that loony imposter.'

'No!' In panic, she cast around for a means of escape, but the steel was wavering, glinting, a mere hand span from her ribcage. One false move . . . 'She was your sister, Fabius.'

'Are you trying to be funny? There's no insanity in *my* family.' He shot her an odd look. 'Claudia, seriously. Do we strike you as barmy?'

'No.' Titter, titter. 'Of course not.' The forced laughter was in danger of becoming hysterical.

'Damn right. You'll never convince me that woman was anything but an imposter.'

Claudia felt her strength seeping back. 'Oh, but I can,' she said evenly, wrenching her gaze from flashing blade to flashing eyes. 'That woman really was Sabina Collatinus.'

A chill wind passed between them as, unhurriedly, she gave her reason.

She'd expected her revelation to unsettle him, disconcert him so she could run. But he stared at her. Just stared at her. Even then, there was the possibility he might relax – step aside – let her go . . .

His arm came up. '*No*!' He buried the blade in the smooth, grey bark. '*No-o-o-o-o*!' It was a howl of pain and anguish, of hopelessness and despair.

Claudia tried to dart forward.

'Why didn't you tell me?' His hand, closing round her neck, flung her back against the tree. 'Why didn't you fucking tell me?'

In his fierce volcanic anger he was oblivious to her struggles, the kicks to his shins, the punches to his chest.

'She's not my sister,' he raged, pinning her tight to the bark. 'She's not my fucking sister!'

Over and over he repeated it and with every roar, his grip tightened until her struggles became pitiful, reduced to the flutterings of a wounded bird. She heard a rasping sound, a rattle, and realized it came from her own throat.

There was a darkness, a fuzziness round the periphery of her vision, then suddenly her head was falling forward and the noise in her throat had stopped. Choking, she tried to make sense of what her eyes were telling her: Kleon and Fabius rolling in a cloud of dust and leaf litter, arms and legs flailing – and, lumbering down the embankment, the limp but recognizable figure of Marcus Cornelius Orbilio. She weighed up the protagonists. Fabius was fighting (appropriately enough) like a madman, thrashing and roaring and kicking, his workouts and route marches standing him in excellent stead. Orbilio, hollow-eyed and distinctly grey around the gills, didn't look as though he had the strength to wrestle a fieldmouse, much less a seasoned campaigner. And as manful as Kleon's effort was, this had every appearance of being Fabius's game.

Orbilio paused to examine the bruising round her neck. 'Are you all right?'

'Are you?' she croaked. He looked ghastly. Purple hollows under his eyes, deep crevices in his face. His breathing was shallow, his pallor grim.

He held up one hand, palm outstretched, which could have meant anything from yes to don't ask, and shuffled across to pitch in. And in that instant, Claudia instinctively knew she was wrong. Diomedes *had* visited Supersnoop. Except the minute dose of poison he normally administered had been a tad stronger than usual . . .

The rock that came crashing down on Fabius's skull was intended for a blond Greek, but the soldier crumpled and lay still.

Orbilio gave a twisted smile. 'Thanks,' he said, sinking on to a tree root.

'My pleasure.' Truly it was.

The Cilician, still on his knees and badly winded, was wiping blood from his mouth and Claudia tried to ignore the jagged thorns that seemed to be tearing at her stomach. Dammit, why should she feel guilty? Looked at from her point of view, he was new to the staff and within weeks two women lay dead. What was a girl supposed to think?

'Kleon, where the bloody hell have you been?' She felt a lot better for snapping at him.

Five-year-old eyes looked out of a twenty-five-year-old face. 'I . . .'

Orbilio struggled to his feet. 'He was acting on my orders,' he explained. 'At first I thought I'd contracted a chill, then food poisoning and then I finally realized—'

'Diomedes was a fully paid-up member of the Hemlock Society.' Claudia finished it for him.

'You know?' He was making a valiant effort not to sway, she noticed. 'Well, it occurred to me that it was just possible, after what I'd told Lover Boy about me and your inheritance, that he might have fancied a spot of revenge, hence my asking Kleon here to follow him, confident – ' he shot her a sardonic grin – 'Junius was guarding you.'

He untied his belt and offered it to the Cilician, who used it to bind tight the makeshift bandage he'd torn out of Fabius's tunic.

'When Kleon reported back to say our doctor friend had hitched a ride aboard a northbound wagon this morning, I came to tell you. Instead I walked into a raging argument between Junius and Cypassis, each blaming the other for your disappearance.'

Fabius's blood began to seep through the white linen. His face was grey and the bodyguard's attempts to slap him back to consciousness failed abysmally.

'How did you find me?'

'Melinno saw you from his sickbed. That blue stola stood out on the plateau and that was our starting point. It was only when Fabius began bellowing we knew exactly where to aim for.' He gave his chest a rueful pat. 'Only Kleon is that bit fitter than me.'

As though to prove the point, Kleon slung the limp form of Eugenius's favourite grandson over his shoulders as though it was a sack of cabbages and took off in the direction of the villa. He didn't need to be told Fabius needed medical attention – and quickly.

When they were alone, Orbilio asked, 'Care to tell me why our friendly centurion chose to use your head as a hammer?'

Claudia crossed her arms as though she was cold. 'He'd added two with two and made seven.' She still sounded like a frog with tonsillitis. 'But I think it goes deeper than that. I think he killed them.'

The policeman's eyes popped. 'Sabina and Actë? Croesus, I hadn't had him pegged for that!'

Me neither, thought Claudia.

Orbilio ran his finger slowly over the hilt of the knife embedded in the beech. 'Raped his own sister.' The incredulity in his voice had a slight catch in it.

'In his defence, he thought she was an imposter.'

Orbilio's mouth turned down at the corners. 'Who didn't?' he said, more to himself than to Claudia. There was a long pause, in which you couldn't fail to notice the pallor of his face, the deeply etched lines, the purple shadows under his eyes.

It came almost as a surprise to hear him ask, 'How were you planning to get back to Rome?'

'Syracuse.' There were always ships in and out of the capital.

'Fancy a freighter from Fintium? It docks in about –' his eyes turned up to scan for the sun – 'three hours.'

Damn you, Orbilio. Sometimes a girl could forget you were a policeman with contacts, an aristocrat with connections.

'I'll think about it,' she said stiffly.

He laughed. 'You do that. By the way, I was right about Melinno's wife. She died of lockjaw. Trouble was, Diomedes guaranteed a cure and Melinno handed over all his savings for what was effectively snakeoil.'

'Poor chap.'

'Save your sympathy for the Greek. Melinno's already itching to follow him.'

She looked him square in the face. 'I daresay someone mentioned the northbound wagon?'

'I daresay.'

'And slipped him enough funds to see him through?'

He grinned. 'Quite possibly. Listen, I want to be around when Soldier Boy wakes up, hear his side of the story. Coming?'

'Not yet.' Claudia tentatively probed the bruises at her throat. 'There's someone I want to see first.'

'Up here?'

'Up here.'

They stood listening to the sounds of the woodland.

The warbler was still warbling, possibly its very last warble before it moved on to its winter quarters. Or perhaps it was recounting recent events to other birds in the area, the tits and wrens and tree-creepers.

'Don't worry about Varius,' he said eventually, pushing his hair back from his face.

Claudia stiffened. 'Who's worried?'

'Gaius made a will, didn't he?'

'You should know, you busted your ballistas in an effort to quash the bloody thing.' What was so damned funny about that?

'Exactly.' His patrician tunic hung even longer without the belt.

'Am I missing something?'

'Look around you, Claudia. The beech trees are so densely packed, you can't see there's oak and birch and pine in the woodland.'

She made a great show of tucking a runaway curl into place. Dammit, she really was a silly cow! If Flavia couldn't get her hands on it . . . And suddenly it was obvious. The money was Claudia's, whether Varius's claim about being Gaius's son was true or not. (Which it wasn't. Her husband's tastes ran in an entirely different direction.)

'Write him a nice, polite letter,' Orbilio was saying. 'Remind him of your legal rights and I very much doubt he'll trouble you in the future.'

Varius, you bloodsucking leech, touch me for money again and I'll chop you into pieces and personally feed them back to you.

Was that polite enough for Supersnoop? She watched his slow and obviously painful progress up the embankment, and it was only when Marcus Cornelius Orbilio was over the rise and out of sight that she whispered, 'Thank you,' under her breath.

She looked round the cavernous beechwood. There was nothing left of the magic. No Palace of Midas, no touch of gold, no fantasies, no illusions. Only a knife buried to its hilt and a handful of small, shiny, black, egg-shaped berries scattered underneath.

Claudia bent down to examine them.

And frowned.

XXXI

It was still there, the hut in the hillside. Built of stone and as wide as it was high as it was deep, this dwelling wouldn't crumble from wind or rockfall or even fire; the surprise came from its being there at all. So strange had been her previous encounter with the huntsman Aristaeus that sometimes Claudia wondered whether she'd dreamed the whole affair, and half of her expected the clearing to be a figment of her imagination, along with the hut and the dogs and the wooden statue of Diana.

Smoke coiled from the hole in the roof. Chieftain and Druid heard her approach and lifted themselves, reluctantly, from their slumbers and dry, sleepy snouts were pressed into her hand. If they caught boar, she mused, it must be because they charmed the miserable buggers to death. She leaned her hand against the door and it swung open, not on a hinge but on a primitive pivot. Claudia accepted the tacit invitation and walked in.

There were two of everything. Two wooden platters, two goblets, two knives set out on the table, two carved chairs drawn up. The fire, a permanent necessity for any isolated, humble dwelling, glowed faintly and gave off very little heat. The chest on the far wall was made of oak, plain and functional. Moreover, it was unlocked.

'I knew you'd be back.'

The lid crashed down, echoing monstrously in the tiny hut.

'Oh.' It seemed woefully inadequate, but it was difficult to know what to say when your hands were full of that person's shirt.

The heavy frame of the huntsman filled the doorway. The hounds' wagging tails, their snuffled greetings, belied the silent menace.

And then he grinned. 'Find anything of interest?'

'No.' It was too late for politeness, so she gave him the truth. 'I didn't have time.'

The grin creased his face into thick, leathery lines. He shrugged off the quiver of arrows and laid his bow against the wall by the door. Either he'd been unsuccessful or his quarry was too large to bring in. Of course, anything larger than a pheasant probably wouldn't fit.

'Sit down.' It was gruff but well-meaning. He wiped his hands down the sides of his leather leggings and poured beer into the goblets. 'Hungry?'

'Famished.'

It was one of life's revelations. You stare death in the eye and, incredibly, it sharpens the appetite.

'Do you know what these are?' She dropped four shiny black berries on to the table.

He gave them barely a glance. 'Baneberries.'

Not much of a conversationalist, was he? 'What can you tell me about them?'

'They smells foul and they're poisonous.' He'd drained one goblet and was now dividing his time between sinking a second and cracking eggs, hundreds of them, into a bowl. 'Drop one down that pretty blue tunic of yours and you'll never get the stain off.'

'A black dye, in other words?'

'Yep.' He was adding honey and almonds and oil and milk to the eggs.

'And your spiders' webs. They don't all go to Syracuse, do they?'

'Nope.'

He lifted the pan off the fire and threw in the egg mixture, agitating it with his hunting knife. Funny how, when you don't have many possessions, the ones you do own become multi-purpose. Claudia laid down her beer and delved into the folds of her gown.

'Recognize this?' She laid a garnet ring on the table.

'Nope.'

'What about this?' The second item stopped him in his tracks, but only momentarily.

'What about it?' He stirred the eggs.

Claudia tapped her fingernail on the blue glass. 'Sabina kept her soul in a flagon identical to this.'

You could hear his breathing above the scrape of steel on iron. 'Where did you get the ring?' He still didn't look at her.

'Syracuse. She gave it to Minerva for safe conduct from Rome.'

Aristaeus laughed, a rich, brown laugh that matched his rich, brown features. 'Wrong,' he said. 'She gave it to Minerva because I told her to.'

Two plates of sweet, scented eggs materialized on the table. Claudia blew on hers to cool it, but Aristaeus shovelled his straight in, confirming his insides were as weatherbeaten as the exterior.

'How—'

'Eat your eggs,' he said. She did, and they were delicious.

Finally, when the plates had been polished by the dogs and the goblets refilled, Aristaeus leaned back in his chair. He was not, she realized now, a day over thirty-five, it was the grey at the temples which made him seem older. That, and the dark brown, outdoor skin.

'Knew you'd be back,' he said slowly. 'I kept the table ready.'

'This was for me? You couldn't be certain.'

'You knows my secret. That's what brought you up here in the first place, and you ain't the type to let things rest.'

I knows your secret. Claudia settled her spine against the back of the chair. Do I, Aristaeus? Do I really? She sipped her beer, watching him over the rim of the goblet. 'I know you taught Sabina to dye her hair with walnut juice.'

His eyebrows arched in surprise, but he merely said, 'My mother used it.'

It was the day of Sabina's funeral, when Claudia was in the atrium smoothing the orange bridal veil, that she noticed the roots were a different colour to the rest of her hair. It was virtually all grey, which made her Matidia's daughter all right. No question of it.

'And you intercepted the letters.'

'I bribed the messenger, if that's what you mean. Gave him meat, which he couldn't otherwise afford.'

Claudia picked up the ring and examined it. Aristaeus had instructed Sabina to give it to Minerva. Why? And why pick Syracuse? Why not Rome? Then, slowly, the pieces fell into place.

Sabina hadn't been to Rome.

Yes, she was on the *Furrina*, but now Claudia realized Sabina had been shipped there and, just like cargo, transferred from one boat to another before being ferried back to Syracuse. Lest someone recognize her, she had been under orders not to disembark until the very last moment. Which posed something of a problem: how could she make her offering to Minerva? Hence she had slipped away and had, quite simply, got lost. There was nothing sinister about two wagons converging on a narrow street and the sailors were just sailors, drunk and soft and not really meaning any harm. It was a lark, a prank, which spun out of control.

'Sabina Collatinus lived with you, didn't she?'

Aristaeus blinked rapidly. 'I thought that was why you were here?'

'One of the reasons,' she said carefully. 'Care to tell me how it came about?'

The story was astonishing. Wilder than any theories she'd tried stringing together herself, yet coming from this rough, tough mountain man, it seemed as normal as clipping your toenails or putting the cat out. The sort of thing any decent chap would do, placed in the same position.

Thirty years ago, said Aristaeus, a man called Faustulus was hired by Eugenius Collatinus to escort his six-year-old daughter to Rome where she was to be ordained as a Vestal Virgin. At the time, Collatinus was a prosperous wheat farmer working lands to the east and Faustulus a hunter in the hills above, renowned for his integrity and dependability.

'It was the father what was supposed to hand the

daughter over,' Aristaeus explained, 'but we was at war with Rome. Sextus agreed to Sabina's ordination but he wouldn't agree to Eugenius leaving, whereas Faustulus, being Sicilian born and bred, knew ways.' He tapped the side of his nose knowingly.

'Faustulus handed her over to the Vestals, then the next thing he knew, she'd run away. He found her at the wharf, hysterical and desperate to find a passage to Sicily, saying the Holy Sisters wanted to bury her alive.'

Claudia was fully aware of the tale of the recalcitrant Vestal who had forsaken her vow of chastity. Her lover had been whipped to death in the Forum, but she, poor cow, had been interred alive.

'So the young novice had nightmares?'

Aristaeus toyed with his plate, tapping his knife against the wood. 'You must understand,' he said eventually, 'that Sabina was only six, and what she told Faustulus he believed.' He threw down the knife. 'She said she couldn't go back to the temple, because she was . . . unchaste.'

'Surely he—'

Aristaeus cut in firmly. 'Sabina told him her daddy had done to Sabina what her daddy had done to her mummy. Do you understand?'

Claudia gulped, and nodded.

'Right. Faustulus believed that, six years old or no, they'd bury her alive because Vestals have to be pure. Not just free of bodily defects, pure right through.'

'Rubbish! They simply wouldn't have admitted her!'

The huntsman held up a restraining hand. 'I know,' he said. 'But Faustulus didn't understand, he thought she'd been ordained and that if he took her back, that's what would happen. So he told the Sisters she'd been killed in a traffic accident and that, for them, was the end of it.'

She knew Orbilio had tried tracing Sabina's chaperone, but after three decades the leads were too cold. 'What happened next?' She was almost scared to ask.

'Faustulus brought her back to Sicily and raised her as his own. What else could he do? Couldn't hand her back to Aulus, not after that. So we pretended she was ordained. Who's to know? Not that lot, they're too busy looking after Number One.'

Claudia slowly shook her head. Aulus. Old Conky. Assaulting his own daughter . . .

Not long after, Aristaeus said, Sextus began stripping the hills for his warships and Eugenius was having financial problems from not being able to offload his wheat stocks. When Collatinus moved west, Faustulus followed. Sabina could keep tabs on her family, and in any case the pickings were good above Sullium.

'Faustulus was your father?'

'Yep.' He swung out his arm and lifted another jug of beer on to the table. 'On his deathbed, he made me swear to look after Sabina for the rest of her life.'

Claudia made rapid calculations. 'How old were you?'

'Fifteen.' The word was almost obscured by a gulp. 'Both sisters long married and my mother two years in the ground.'

'It doesn't sound like Faustulus,' she protested. 'It was unfair. I mean, why for life?'

'Oh, Sabina always had clouds in her mind,' he said, as though half the population were batty. 'From the outset we knew she was . . .'

'Mad?'

'Special.'

'Because of what Aulus had done?'

He didn't reply, but set cheese and radishes on the table. Claudia watched him slice off a fist-sized piece of bread and chew on it.

'You loved her?' she ventured.

His eyes rose and bored into hers. 'I *cared* for her,' he replied, wiping the crumbs from his beard. 'But I told her straight. We'll keep up the pretence, but when your thirty years is up, you go home. When the Senior Vestal retired, I sent her back.'

Claudia thought back over the things Sabina had told her. About seeing mountains split asunder, spilling rivers of blood. Etna, erupting nineteen years ago. So obvious. Just like Varius. Why couldn't she see the things that were under her nose?

'Last year I built this hut. There's no room for two, she knew I meant business.'

'Did you sleep with her?' After what had been aired today, the question didn't seem impertinent.

Aristaeus took a deep breath. 'A man has to relieve his frustrations, don't he?'

Claudia hoped her expression was suitably ambivalent.

His fist thumped down on the table. 'Croesus, she just lay there. I was eighteen years old, red blood coursing through my veins, and it's not as though I didn't ask if . . . I could . . . you know. But she just lay there, staring up at the roof. Then I saw it – the blood – and that's when I knew . . . I knew . . .'

'She'd been lying.' Claudia finished it for him.

The huntsman's face was distorted with pain. 'I asked her. I said, why didn't you tell me you was a virgin? Why say them terrible things about your father – and you know what she said? She said, "But he did. Daddy kissed me." ' He gave a hollow laugh. 'I sacrificed twenty years on account of a *kiss*.'

There followed the sort of silence that seems endless and yet, at the same time, seems no time at all. The sort of silence you feel sacrilegious about breaking.

Finally, Aristaeus picked up the ring. 'This was my mother's, it was all she had. I wanted to give it to Minerva, to atone for my shame.'

'There is no shame, Aristaeus.' Only irony. Bitter, bitter irony. But he needed, desperately, to assuage his guilt. 'Why don't you give it to Diana?'

He used his hunting knife to slice through the wooden hand to create a finger and solemnly slipped the ring on to it. Again, the sense of unreality was aroused. He patted the statue reverentially and stared deep into its carved eyes.

'It wasn't just that once, either.'

Claudia heard the wind whispering in the leaves, a distant woodpecker drumming. There was a faint mushroomy smell in the air, mingled with sawdust and woodsmoke. She could sense the searing pain inside him, even though she struggled to catch the words.

'But I beseech you, Diana of the Forests, not to judge me harshly.'

She won't! 'Sabina was a selfish woman, Aristaeus. She came from a selfish family.'

'Said she didn't mind me doing it, because she was invisible.'

Sweet Jupiter, no man deserved this on his conscience. 'If it's any consolation, they've got the man who killed her.'

Pained eyes left Diana's. 'Who?'

'Fabius.'

He shook his head in wonderment. 'By Apollo, they're an evil family.'

I'll drink to that! Claudia thought.

'How did you find out she lived here?'

Claudia explained about the blue glass flagon. How she was in Sullium on market day and noticed a barber mopping a cut with a spider's web which he drew from the bottle. Preoccupied with other matters, it didn't sink in at the time and only later, when the memory returned, Claudia realized that the chances of two such flagons appearing in one town were remote, to say the least. She sent Junius to track down the barber, who confirmed he bought his webs from Aristaeus, and the Syrian glass-blower, who confirmed he had indeed supplied a stock for the huntsman.

She braced herself to ask the next question. 'Do you know a woman named Hecamede?'

'I know *of* a woman called Hecamede. Killed herself, didn't she?'

'Yes. Yes, she killed herself.'

Her knees were weak as she made her way across the clearing. She did not say goodbye. She did not look round.

She certainly did not tell him that Hecamede's suicide was her fault. That, again, if only she'd seen what was in front of her nose, Hecamede would be alive today, coming to terms, albeit painfully, with what had befallen her little

Kyana but at least having the satisfaction that justice was served at last to the man who'd abducted her.

Because that was the second thing she'd sent Junius to check out.

Stand in front of the harness maker's, she told him, three paces from the corner, then turn and look over your left shoulder. What do you see? Take a wax tablet and a stylus and note down everything. *Everything*.

He'd followed her instructions to the letter. Harnesses, hooks, customers, shopkeeper, coins, strips of leather, a painted sign, a spider in its web, the side street, kerbs, gutters, a poulterer on the other corner, the barber's next door to the poulterer . . .

Exactly. The barber's next door. Had Claudia's eyes not been riveted on the spider, her own survey would have taken in the shop over the road. She'd have realized earlier that not every barber pays for pre-vinegared spiders' webs. That now and again, they go and collect them themselves.

So simple. Hecamede was a local woman, she'd have been concerned only with local issues.

Claudia passed out of the cool, leafy canopy into a blast of dry, dusty air, surprised to find herself weeping. Not for poor, blighted Aristaeus, whom she had nearly killed in the belief he was a child molester. Not for Kyana and the other little girls who had been abducted, tragic though it was. Not even for Sabina or the long-suffering Actë, despite their obscene murders.

Claudia was weeping for Hecamede, whom she had failed. Hecamede who was slum poor, and whose accusations against a seemingly respectable barber fell on a bigoted magistrate's deaf ears. Hecamede, one breast lolling out of her tunic, driven wild by grief until, finally, she was driven to suicide.

Hecamede. Who had cut her wrists the way Claudia's own mother had cut her wrists.

Claudia had failed her, too.

XXXII

It was over. Finally, it was over.

Physically drained and emotionally exhausted, Claudia halted on the plateau. Below, a molten silver streak cleaved a path towards the shimmering ocean beyond and suddenly she was impelled to immerse her whole body in this river of forgetfulness. A cold plunge which was no luxury, but a necessity.

There was much to forget.

The raw injustice big ugly Utti had been given, and the dreadful truth confronting Aristaeus after he made love to Sabina. Alas, it said much about Aulus that Aristaeus, Faustulus, even Claudia herself, believed him capable of the charge laid against him, but the unpalatable fact was, a grim brutality simmered underneath the surface in that family which was as sickening as it was incomprehensible.

Linus, knocking his wife into next week; Aulus, chopping off thumbs left, right and centre; even the viciousness of Senbi, Piso and Dexippus. It seemed Fabius had felt justified as long as the vacant creature calling herself Sabina wasn't related . . .

Claudia slithered down the slope, using rocks as footholds and tree roots as handholds. Far in the distance were the whitewashed walls and red shimmering tiles of the Villa Collatinus, surrounded by small, bleating puffs of white. A peaceful scene, and utterly uninviting.

She listened to the babble of water as it raced over the stones in its excitement to reach the sea.

Orbilio had believed Diomedes the killer, since who but a doctor would have the precise medical knowledge? There had been no 'trouble' before he arrived. And yet the same criteria applied to Fabius. Army life would teach a man how to kill, maim and immobilize. Did it, then, desensitize him to such a degree that he could plan the cold-blooded killing of two women? Cut their spinal chords, leave them paralysed – helpless and desperate for air – so he could rape them?

Like the beechwood earlier, precious metal turned to base as the silver became nothing more exotic than water, yet it was no less appealing. She sat on a rock and pulled off her sandals, thinking of the murder weapon embedded in the tree trunk. In time, no doubt, the bark would grow to envelop it, obliterating all traces of this hideous crime, but despite the warmth of the sun trapped in the valley, Claudia shuddered.

She waded into the middle of the river, her iris blue cotton darkening to blueberry, and sat facing downstream, hands outstretched on the river bed behind her, head tilted towards the sun. The icy water washed over her, floating her skirt and numbing the bruising on her neck. Stay here long enough and it'd wash away the guilt and the horror and maybe, just maybe, the fear of waking in the night and seeing the hollow eyes of Hecamede staring back at her.

It was over. Praise be to Juno, it was over. She was stupid to have come to Sicily in the first place, but in a matter of hours that freighter would be whisking her back to Rome and life would continue as normal. Well, not Rome exactly, she thought, hauling herself upright, amazed at the weight of her wet stola. It'll drop us on the mainland and we can cover the coastal route by road, picking up the Via Appia which will be a damn sight quicker than fighting headwinds. I can't wait to get back to the—

'Dammit, Aulus, you made me jump!'

Pervert. Still, he wasn't the only man in the world who got turned on by watching women bathe and by wet cotton clinging to feminine curves.

'Ooh, you made me jump,' he mimicked. 'Oooh, Aulus, you made me jump.'

Claudia wrung out her skirt, wondering how much satisfaction she would feel when Old Conky heard his eldest son was a depraved monster. She picked her way towards her sandals, trying not to let him see how painful the jagged rocks were on bare feet, and she was gripped by an exhilarating surge of mischief.

'Aulus,' she said, heaping on the sympathy. 'I know who killed Sabina and Actë, and I'm afraid it . . . wasn't Utti.'

'Oh?'

Claudia smiled to herself. String him along a little further and the blow would fall the harder. 'But I know who, and I know how, and I know why.'

'You do?'

The bolt shot home, you could see the emotions race across his face. Anger, hatred, resentment, possibly even respect. A strange light burned in his eyes and Claudia nonchalantly reached down for her sandals.

'Pity you won't have the chance to tell, then!'

It was the venom in his voice that made her look up, but it was the scalpel in his hand which held her eye.

Oh shit!

'Orbilio knows,' she said quickly, not daring to take her eye off the blade.

'Is that why he left you alone?'

'It's a trap. I'm the bait. He's up there, waiting . . .'

It sounded feeble, even to her own ears. 'You'll have to do better than that, soft sod can hardly walk – and don't think your servants can save you either, they're busy lugging boxes over to Fintium.'

Claudia kept her eye on the scalpel. To slice her spinal chord, he'd have to get behind her.

'You won't get away with this!' Is that what Sabina and Actë had said? Were those their last words?

'Maybe I will and maybe I won't.' He took a step closer, Claudia took a step back. 'I'm knocking sixty, yet my father treated me like a schoolkid. No responsibility, no nothing. You've seen that brainless cow I'm married to – the old man even picked her, because it was a good match. Good for him, he gets a good dowry, but what do I get?'

'I—'

'I'd learned everything there was to know about wheat. How to combat rust, the optimum yield from threshing, the best way of burning stubble – everything there was to know and you know what he does?'

'No.' It came out a squeak.

He took another step closer, she took another step back. The sharp point of a rock against her instep drew blood.

'He sells up. I'm thirty-three years old, and he doesn't

even consult me. I tell him the war'll be over soon, he tells me to mind my own business. He tells me I should count my blessings that I, an equestrian, have a daughter serving Vesta. Had it not been for the war, they'd have had their pick of patricians.'

'Sabina—'

'After a lifetime tilling the soil, I have to forget about wheat and learn about fucking sheep. I don't even *like* sheep! But he's my father, I do what he tells me.'

He took another pace, Claudia backed up, her eye still on the blade. As long as he was talking, she was safe.

'Aulus, listen—'

'Finally the old man tells me he's given permission for my son, *my* son, to join the army. I told him, I've got a girl lined up, the dowry will mean we can live better – because by then, he'd spent all his bloody money building that damned house. Got to impress the locals, he said. Let them know who they're dealing with. No one messes with Eugenius Collatinus.'

'Look—'

'He was right. No one did mess with him, except the one person he never suspected. Me! For sixteen years, I've been ripping him off and he didn't suspect a thing. Not one damned thing. The day he had that riding accident, that was the day I began. Even bedridden, the old bastard wouldn't let go of the reins, but I prized them away without him even knowing.'

'Aulus, please—'

'How? I'll tell you how. His eyesight was bad. That little cow Actë thought she was the only one, but he couldn't fool me, I knew what was going on. Dexippus is in my pocket, did you know that? Found him doing things to lambs you wouldn't ask a butcher to do, and I went spare – but then I realized this gave me a hold over him. Through Dex, I could manipulate the old man. Write letters, keep ledgers. I controlled the whole bloody shooting match.'

'Surely—'

He made a slashing movement with the scalpel, the sinister swish audible even over the burbling waters. 'Then things went wrong! Don't ask me how, maybe I made a few bad investments, all I know is, the business began to go downhill.'

Comprehension dawned. The food (or lack of it), the sparsely planted garden, the household economies. These were at Aulus's instigation, and because he had pared them down to the bone gradually, no one had noticed. Only a visitor would comment and visitors, as she knew from experience, were unwelcome.

'Do you know what a shock it was to find Sabina was coming home? Just didn't seem like thirty years. The old man waits till the day she arrives to tell me he's agreed a dowry with Labienus. Eight thousand sesterces. Croesus, we didn't have eight hundred in the coffers, let alone eight thousand.'

He'd calmed down, but Claudia knew she wasn't in the clear yet.

'Thank the gods when Sabina announces the old sod's ravished her. Turned her head, I thought, holy orders. Actually felt sorry for the little mare – I mean, chastity isn't natural, is it?'

Claudia remained mute.

'I said, it's not natural. Is it?' He was shouting and

waving the scalpel, and she felt the hairs on the back of her neck prickle.

'No.' She cleared her throat. 'No, Aulus, it isn't natural.'

'Damn right, and you listen to me when I'm talking to you.'

'Yes, Aulus.' She was suddenly the downtrodden and dutiful woman he expected. 'Sorry.'

'What was I talking about?'

Had he genuinely forgotten or was this a test? 'Sabina's dowry,' she said quickly.

'Oh, yes. Well, she turns Labienus down, then damn me if the fucker doesn't do a deal with the old man. For *twenty* thousand he'd be prepared to take her, daft in the head or not.' Aulus snorted derisively. 'Twenty thousand. No bugger's worth that.'

'So you . . .?'

'Tried to reason with the silly bitch, told her what the score was, that we were broke. I was totally honest, explained everything to her. Offered her all the money we had to run away, disappear, start a new life. I begged her, I actually went down on my knees and begged the little cow not to ruin my life and do you know what?'

His face was in the grip of strange contortions.

'What?'

'She'd never been a bloody Vestal. She'd run away once, she said, and didn't like it. Spent thirty years in a hovel without servants, and now she was home she liked it.'

His eyes were staring past Claudia. She wondered whether she dare make a move, but the scalpel was close enough to slit her throat – and Aulus had nothing to lose.

Dammit, surely the ship was in by now. Why wasn't someone out looking for her? And then she realized that, in reality, very little time had passed. Her gown was still dripping, the shadows had barely moved round with the sun.

In that instant, Claudia knew with a chill certainty that she could not carry the strain much longer. After the physical fight with Fabius and the emotional encounter with Aristaeus, she was drained almost to her limit.

It was too far out for the Collatinus slaves. Aulus was right, Orbilio was dead on his feet with the poison and the exercise. She was on her own.

Tears of helplessness welled up.

He was talking about that fateful day (was it really only twelve days ago?) when he met Sabina on the path. Claudia forced herself to listen, it was her only chance.

'What do you mean, run away? I asked, and she said it was because of what I'd done to her when she was a child. What, I asked, and she . . . Janus, she said I did to her what I did to her mother. How sick can you get?'

Claudia could not bring herself to state the obvious. Instead she said, 'So you killed her?'

He made a sound of impatience. 'You won't believe this, but it was an accident. I always carry a scalpel, it comes in useful in the dyesheds, in the clipshed, collecting berries and bark for the dyes. Like today, collecting bane-berries. What you call all-purpose. Sabina turned her back on me. Just like that!' He snapped his fingers. 'Turned her back and started to walk down the path. I grabbed her hair and, as Jupiter's my witness, I swear I meant only to cut it off to teach her a lesson. She jerked . . . and the blade sliced the base of her neck.'

He shrugged. 'I realized then she'd made me kill her. I tried to punish her, hitting her and hitting her, but she was dead, there was nothing I could do to hurt her the way she'd hurt me. She'd made me kill her, and now she was getting away with it. But guess what? It gave me a hard-on. It gave me a bloody hard-on. So I did it. I did what she accused me of doing when she was six. I fucked the bitch!'

Claudia was trembling. 'What about Actë?'

Aulus produced a gleeful slurping sound Claudia never wanted to hear again. 'Got what she deserved, did Miss High-and-Mighty. Turned me down so often I lost count, yet I saw the old man putting his hands all over her, sucking on her, and her, the conniving bitch, egging him on so she could get her hands on my business, tricking me out of what's mine.'

Claudia's legs could barely support her. The bank was too high, the riverbed too jagged, and all the time the scalpel was wavering in front of her. Her nerves were so stretched that, when Aulus did make his move, she wondered whether she'd have the reaction time she so desperately needed.

'It was fun with Actë.' He was laughing! Actually laughing! 'I knew by then that Sabina didn't die immediately, that she was aware she'd had to be punished for what she'd done, and so it was better with Actë.'

'You didn't beat her, though?'

'Why should I?' He seemed genuinely puzzled. 'She didn't need to be punished. All I gave her was what the old man had been giving her for years, but the best joke of all was, he hadn't! Actë was still a virgin! I tell you, it was all I could do to stop myself running in and telling him that, for once, I'd got somewhere before he had!'

Claudia swallowed hard. 'Then you poisoned him?'

'No one can blame me for that. He'd had his run, it was time for the next generation to take over.'

'What about me?' It was the question she'd been dreading to ask, but it needed to be said. She had to know what was in store.

'Ah, yes, the lovely Claudia. Since Utti killed Sabina and Actë, we can't have you going the same way, can we? Let me see.' He waved the scalpel up and down to taunt her. She refused to let him see it was working. 'Are those bruises I see round your neck?'

Instinctively her hand shot up to cover her throat. 'Fabius knows about them,' she said. 'He put them there.'

Aulus clucked his teeth. 'Perfect. When I hold you under this lovely clear water, he'll be able to swear they were made earlier and put his old father in the clear.'

Shit!

'They'll know it was you!'

'Me?' His face was a picture of innocence. 'I'm out collecting berries.'

'Wasn't Fabius collecting them?'

'My son doesn't know his baneberry from his bum. They grow in damp places yet he goes searching the woods. I am surrounded by fools.' His tone changed. 'This has gone on long enough.' He made a beckoning gesture. 'Come here.'

'Go bugger yourself!'

'Claudia, Claudia. Why fight it?' he said reasonably. 'Drowning's quick, it's painless and, believe you me, there are plenty of other ways. I could even do to you what I did to the others, providing I bury you deep.' Manic eyes swept over the blue cotton clinging to the curves of her body. 'You're a beautiful woman, I could really take my time.'

'We could do a deal?' Feeble, Claudia. Very, very feeble. 'I have money.'

'Too late, I'm afraid. You could have married Fabius and come to live with us, but you had to go and spoil it, didn't you? You had to worm out my little secret?'

A spark of irritation flared.

'It's been the day for people's little secrets, Aulus. Don't feel privileged. Look!' She pointed. 'Up there!'

'Bitch!'

She had run into the river, it was her only chance. Hampered by bare feet and waterlogged skirts, she aimed for the middle. Swim to safety. A hand reached out, but her arms were wet and his grip wouldn't hold. Splashing like a hippopotamus, Claudia zigzagged towards deep water, ducking and twisting to escape him. She could hear his stertorous breathing, see his shadow on the clear, babbling water.

Then she was free! Launching herself into the current, she felt the icy water on her cheeks, one stroke, two—

The grip on her ankle was of iron. In a frenzy, she tried to kick, but the twisting and writhing served only to wrap her skirts round her legs like bandages. Aulus, panting, was dragging his quarry to the far bank. She held on to rocks, but he was stronger, they cut into her hands, grazed her arms, she had to let go. She picked up a boulder.

Yesss!

His hands flew to his face. The stone had broken his

nose, that big, long nose. Blood streamed everywhere, he was trumpeting like a bull elephant.

'Shit!'

Her foot slipped, her ankle twisted and rocks fell inwards to trap it. She tried to claw free, but the boulder over her foot was huge.

'Got you, you bitch!'

Too late she realized he'd come up behind her, and for the second time in one day a vice clamped round her neck, dragging her head backwards and under the water. She saw him, grinning, as her arms flailed. A pebble, that's all I need, a pebble to blind the bastard! Her leg held fast, the knee twisted and sending out waves of excruciating pain. She saw weed, thin green strands of it, trailing in the current. She heard a roaring in her ears which wasn't water, and now the picture of Aulus, face twisted with hatred, had red tinges round the edges. With one monumental surge, she pushed herself out of the water, spluttering in the warm sunshine.

'Oh, no, you don't!' Before she drew breath, he'd thrown her back under.

Fingernails clawed. At his hands. At his arms. She could see red trails spiralling in the current, saw strips of flesh flapping in slow motion, saw the white flash of bone. With her last remaining effort before oblivion, Claudia forced back his middle finger. Back, and back – and snap!

Aulus, roaring with pain, let go. Gasping, Claudia jack-knifed towards the bank, kicking at the boulder pinning her ankle. With a second mighty jerk, she twisted again, freeing her trapped leg while her arms pulled on her stola.

'Bitch! You've broken my finger!'

Choking, she threw her sodden gown over his face, hoping the weight and the wetness would confuse him while she pelted him with stones. She had forgotten how weak she was. Like raindrops, they bounced off and he easily shrugged off the soggy cotton.

On the bank lay a branch, swept down in the spring floods but stranded when the waters receded. Coughing water, Claudia hurled herself towards it. She'd break his bloody leg! Hurry, hurry . . . Over her shoulder, she saw Aulus was gaining. Faster . . . Willing the strength into her body, she heaved herself out of the water. Sweet Jupiter! His hands, his arms, his tunic were saturated with blood and where fingernails had clawed, gobbets of flesh flapped loose.

Six paces. Five. Four . . . Too late she discovered the ordeal had left her too weak. She fell to her knees. Somewhere a girl was whimpering. She was shocked to find it was her. Crawling, the gravel cutting her knees to shreds, Claudia stretched out an arm. Oh no. It was still out of reach! A shadow fell over her. A cry lodged in her throat. Aulus, dripping with blood as though he'd been peeled, eyes blazing with fury, raised his scalpel.

Then, above the gurgle of the waters, Claudia heard a twang. Aulus jerked, astonishment written clear on his mangled features. She rolled herself into a ball, hoping to minimize the target, but Aulus stood there, wobbling, a vacant look on his face. As he pitched forward, she rolled out of the way.

For a moment she thought it was a ruse, a ploy to tease and torment her.

Until she saw the arrow in his back.

On the far bank, at roughly the point where she clambered down from the plateau, stood the gigantic figure of a man.

By the time Aristaeus had made his way down, Claudia had watched her iris blue stola drift on the current until it was out of sight. She wished the shaking would stop.

Aristaeus handed her his tunic. It came to her ankles, smelled of cherrywood and fresh sweat and you could have fitted a whole troupe of Syrian dancing girls inside.

'Good shot.' He couldn't make out the words, they were still a gargle from the throttling, but he probably got the gist.

Confident his quarry was dead, the huntsman pulled his arrow free and rolled the corpse over. Claudia backed away, covering her nose with her hands. The stench was vile. Aristaeus pointed to the black stain oozing over the front of Aulus's tunic.

'Looks like he fell and crushed his baneberries,' he said with a grin.

Later, when the joke about baneberries had worn off and the pain in her throat had eased to a throbbing, she thanked him properly.

'I tracked you,' he explained, 'to give you this.'

He held out a golden filigree net, as light and insubstantial as gossamer.

Claudia took the gift in trembling hands. It was a hair snood, the sort women wear when they're alone – or with their lover. When their hair hangs loose and they have no need of curls or ringlets or ribbons. In the centre was a single, golden ornament.

'It's beautiful.' One of those items which is both inexpensive and yet utterly priceless. 'Thank you.' It wasn't necessarily the bruising round her throat which was the problem at the moment.

Eventually, when the mist cleared from her eyes, she explained why Aulus was trying to kill her.

'I'm glad it weren't Fabius,' Aristaeus said. 'They makes a good pair, him and that readhead.'

'Fabius and *Tanaquil*?' The hustler who dyed her hair and padded her breastband?

'Thought, after the way those two hit it off in Syracuse, you'd have known about them love trysts in the birch grove? When I heard of this second murder I assumed it was her, not poor Actë.'

'Tanaquil and *Fabius*?' In love? In Syracuse?

'Real upset he was when her brother died, terrified she'd up and leave him because of it. Tried to stop the execution, but, course, the old man never budged on nothing.'

Which explained this morning's tantrum. Discovering Sabina really was his sister, he was petrified Tanaquil would leave him in case insanity ran in the family. Fat chance; that redhead had Fabius just where she wanted him. From now on, Fabius would follow *her* orders, it was what he did best, and as for Tanaquil, not only had she fallen on her feet financially, she'd slotted Fabius into the role her brother had played.

'Don't reckon they needs to run off to Katane, now he's got this lot to see to.'

'Do you know why he joined the army as a footslogger?' That, like the reasoning behind Sabina's blue flagon, had been nagging away at Claudia for ages.

Aristaeus wiped the blood off his spent arrow. Perhaps he wanted it as a souvenir, most likely he wanted to destroy evidence of his involvement.

'Fabius was fifteen when Eugenius forced him to watch the impaling of six thousand fugitives. He believed there was a better way to serve justice by fighting men face to face, and I'm inclined to agree with him.'

He snapped the arrow shaft in two and threw the pieces into the water.

Claudia thought of the little freighter bobbing in Fintium bay, of the man waiting on board. 'I have to go,' she said, and the huntsman nodded.

'Safe journey.' She thought his voice sounded gruffer than usual.

He began the arduous ascent, the quiver of arrows slung across his nutbrown back, showers of red arbutes raining from the branches he used to lever himself up. Soon, she thought, it will be winter. The leaves will fall, there will come a bite in the air which is welcome for the olives but not for the rest of us. The asters will blacken, and snow will cover the mountains and drive down the wolves.

She trickled the snood through her hands. A golden spider in its golden filigree web, made by the man who collects spiders' webs.

Her throat was throbbing, her knee was on fire, her left ankle had puffed up like an inflated pig's bladder. Heaven knows how she'd find the strength to climb that bank, let alone make it to Fintium.

But, she thought, kilting up the huntsman's tunic, it was definitely the right decision, coming to Sicily.

Hadn't she always said so?

MARILYN TODD

Man Eater

On the eve of the Roman Festivities, the last thing you'd expect Claudia Seferius to be doing is heading in the other direction. However, even beautiful young widows have to put business before pleasure when their vineyards are threatened with arson.

Unfortunately, being run off the road to Etruria by a band of hooligans was not part of Claudia's gameplan. Nor was losing her beloved cat Drusilla. Nor was being forced to seek shelter in the strange home of Sergius Pictor and family – surrounded by the menagerie of wild animals he is training for the Games.

But Claudia is about to become the victim of an even crueller game. For that night a stranger appears at her bedroom door – a knife sticking out of his belly.

And before the first ray of morning sunshine, Claudia is being framed for murder . . .

What follows is a scene from *Man Eater*, the latest Claudia mystery, which is available in hardback from Macmillan (£16.99).

Claudia snapped into wakefulness, instantly aware of the empty space beside her. She cradled the cat's cushion then thumped and punched and rearranged the lumps in her own bolster. What was in here? Firewood? It was good of the Pictors to take her in, she supposed. To patch her wounds, tend the two injured men, to feed, clothe and rest her. But the instant Drusilla turns up, she thought, I am o-f-f, off!

Suddenly there was a blockage in her throat. Oh, she'd find her way here, no question of that. In fact, Claudia had no doubts whatsoever about the intelligence of her sharp, Egyptian cat, only . . .

The trill of a blackbird interrupted her musing. Just one or two notes and faint at that – she could barely make them out between the howls and the growls – but others would follow and the evidence was conclusive.

Juno be praised, the long night was over!

The road accident instantly forgotten, she flung the counterpane round her shoulders and fumbled her way to the window. It was going to be another dank start, she thought, easing open one narrow shutter, but at least the fog lifts quickly as she knew from experience. She unhooked the second leaf. Oh. Her tattered tunic hung limp on the ledge, but of Drusilla there was no sign. And the mist in front of her suddenly seemed denser.

'You don't fool me, you wretched feline.' Claudia's breath was white in the pre-dawn air. 'I know you're out there.'

Just because the bones of your ancestors lie in the tombs of the Pharaohs, don't think you can put on airs and graces with me!

'Sulk all you like, but we both know that one sniff of a sardine and you'll be over this sill like a shot.' Whose was that silly, reedy voice? 'And remember, it's not my fault you used up four of your lives in one go!'

What was that? It sounded like a soft scuffle. There it was again. Claudia's breath came out in a rush. 'Drusilla!'

Tossing the bedspread aside, she picked up her skirts and raced across the room. Although the grey light of dawn was growing paler by the minute, it was nowhere near sufficient and Claudia cursed the up-ended brazier as bronze collided with shinbone. It was only because she was swearing and hobbling and bleeding and hurting all at the same time that she didn't realize, until she reached the door, that whatever talents these clever Egyptian moggies might possess, rattling handles wasn't one of them.

'*What?*' She unlocked the door and flung it open.

The man in the doorway was staring at her. 'I . . . I . . .'

His mouth hung open, and either he had a speech impediment or – as she very much suspected – he was stinking drunk. For good measure he produced another guttural gargle and lurched forward.

'Get away from me, you revolting little dungbeetle!'

346

He really was the most unprepossessing creature she'd ever had the misfortune to lay eyes on.

The dungbeetle's mouth opened and closed. 'I . . .'

Claudia put out her left hand to push him away while the other tried to slam the door in his face, but the dung-beetle was too fast. He dived towards her. Using both hands, Claudia pushed against his chest, but his arms had closed round her shoulders.

'Wrong room, buster.'

She daren't risk connecting her knee with his groin for fear of unbalancing herself – and the prospect of this horny sod on top of her didn't bear thinking about! Along the atrium, still bright with night-torches, a blonde slave emerged from the kitchens with a wide, steaming bowl. Good. Between the two of them, they might be able to prise this animal off! She tried to call out, but the pressure of his body against hers was threatening to squeeze the life right out of her. Mercifully the girl looked up . . . and, incredibly, began to scream.

Silly bitch, Claudia thought, nearly buckling under the weight of the lecherous, gargling dungbeetle, but at least it's brought help. Doors were opening left, right and centre.

Almost rhythmically, Claudia and the drunk danced in the doorway. He pushed, she pushed, he pushed back, but all the time she was growing weaker and weaker. Surely someone had the sense to yank him off?

Inexplicably everyone seemed to be yelling, and it was only when Claudia finally lost the battle with the dung-beetle and they toppled sideways together, she began to understand why.

The dungbeetle wasn't drunk.

The dungbeetle wasn't gargling.
The dungbeetle had a bloody great knife in his belly.

MARILYN TODD

I, Claudia

Pan Books   £4.99

Claudia Seferius has successfully inveigled her way into marriage
with a wealthy Roman wine merchant. But when her secret gambling
debts spiral, she hits on another resourceful way to make money –
offering her 'personal services' to high-ranking Citizens.

Unfortunately her clients are now turning up dead – the victims of
a sadistic serial killer . . .

When Marcus Cornelius Orbilio, the handsome investigating officer,
starts digging deep for clues, Claudia realizes she must track down
the murderer herself – before her husband discovers what she's been
up to.

And before another man meets his grisly end . . .

STEPHEN BOGART

Play It Again

Pan Books   £4.99

Film legend Belle Fontaine found murdered in love nest. Unknown killer still at large.

There was nothing else Manhattan private detective R.J. Brooks needed to know. His movie star mother was dead. And if your mother is murdered you have to do something about it.

He doesn't have a lot to go on, though. Until he sees a face at the funeral that is hauntingly familiar . . .

What R.J. cannot know is that he's just looked into the eyes of a ruthless psychopath who has already selected his next victim – R.J. Brooks.

'The characters feel real, the dialogue is killer bee, and the book smells like New York. *Play It Again* offers the reader what every good mystery novel should.'
Kinky Friedman

'Recalls the glory days of *Black Mask* magazine. Smart hijacking of the Bogart screen persona.'
Philip Oakes, *Literary Review*

STEPHEN BOGART

As Time Goes By

Pan Books   £4.99

When New York private eye R.J. Brooks heard the news it was like
a slug in his guts. Andromeda Studios were about to make a cheap
sequel to the classic black and white movie that had made his parents
big stars.

R.J. quickly makes his objections known, very strongly and very
loudly. So when the movie's lawyer is found dead soon afterwards,
the police believe R.J. had the motive and the opportunity.

But it's not just enemies on the police force with whom R.J. has to
contend. For it soon becomes clear that the killer is about to strike
again . . .

'An enjoyable thriller, in the tradition of Raymond Chandler
and Dashiell Hammett, made more enjoyable as one tries to spot
the biographical parallels.'
Sunday Times

'Though the action is set in the 1990s, it evokes the *film noir*
of the 1940s . . . good fun.'
Charles Spencer, *Sunday Telegraph*

SIMON BRETT

Mrs Pargeter's Plot

Pan Books   £5.99

'I'm afraid, Mrs Pargeter, it does look as if my client has been – as he himself might put it – very thoroughly stitched up.'
  But Mrs Pargeter was not so easily daunted. 'Well then,' she said with a sweet smile, 'it's up to us to unpick the stitches, isn't it?'

The indomitable Melita Pargeter has decided to build her dream house on the plot of land left to her by her husband, the much-loved, much-missed 'business man' Mr Pargeter. And there is only one person she could possibly trust to make this dream come true – her talented builder Concrete Jacket.

Scuppering her plans, however, are the dead body lying in her new wine cellar – and Concrete's arrest for murder . . .

SIMON BRETT

Mrs Pargeter's Package

Pan Books £5.99

'It was remarkable, Mrs Pargeter reflected, what one would do in the cause of friendship . . .'

Mrs Pargeter had not reached the indomitable age of sixty-something (and a little bit more) by neglecting her friends. Even if two weeks in Corfu – self-catering – was probably just about as far as she was prepared to go.

Joyce Dover had recently lost her husband. She needed the company. Yet the hot sunshine soon revealed an unsuspected dark side to the widow.

For Joyce Dover came to Agios Nikitas to die. But, wondered Mrs Pargeter, was it really suicide? Or murder . . .?

SIMON BRETT

Mrs Pargeter's Pound of Flesh

Pan Books £5.99

Although she's never felt the need to change her own ample form, Mrs Pargeter could see nothing wrong with joining her weight-conscious friend at Brotherton Hall Spa.

While Kim strained to lose her excess inches, Mrs P would enjoy a luxurious rest in the health farm's mud-baths. A pleasure entirely spoilt when, in the dead of night, she watches the body of a young girl being mysteriously wheeled away.

The death sets Mrs Pargeter off on a furious trail of detection. Because although slimming might be murder, *covering up the evidence demands a suitable revenge . . .*

SIMON BRETT

A Nice Class of Corpse

Pan Books   £5.99

Mrs Pargeter's arrival at the Devereux does not exemplify the decorum which the hotel's genteel owner, Miss Naismith, had come to expect from her guests. But was that any reason to blame her for the untoward incidents which followed?

Namely, the discovery of one frail resident's body at the foot of the stairs, closely shadowed by the appearance of a second corpse.

Unfortunate accidents, claimed the upstanding proprietor of ancient nobilities. *Murder, said the altogether more practical Mrs Pargeter . . .*